ELK RIVER

Also by Gregory C. Randall

NON-FICTION
America's Original GI Town, Park Forest, Illinois

FICTION
THE SHARON O'MARA CHRONICLES
Land Swap 4 Death
Containers 4 Death

ELK RIVER
A NOVEL

GREGORY C. RANDALL

WINDSOR HILL PUBLISHING
WALNUT CREEK,
CALIFORNIA

Windsor Hill Publishing

Warning to Readers and Travelers

This is a work of fiction. All the characters and events portrayed in this novel are either the products of the author's imagination or are used fictitiously.

While the geography of Michigan in this tale is not entirely imaginary - many of the landmarks and communities in this book can be visited, roads followed, and similar villages found. I have taken liberties, but not as many as you might imagine, but liberties nonetheless.

I have obscured the location of several of the places in this book: the village of Elk River, for example, and the Smith farm. You may look for them if you wish. You might even find them.

FIRST EDITION

DESIGNED BY GREGORY C. RANDALL

TITLE FONTS: BONNIE
TEXT FONT: CONSTANTIA

Copyright 2011 by Gregory C. Randall.
All rights reserved. Printed in the United States of America. For information, address:
Windsor Hill Publishing,
119 Poppy Court, Walnut Creek, California, 94596

www.gregorycrandall.com

Randall, Gregory C. 1949-
Elk river / Gregory C. Randall. - 1st ed.
p. cm.
ISBN: 978-9828376-7-2

For my family,
grandparents, uncles, aunts, cousins and
parents; living and passed.
All with roots deep in Michigan soil.

ACKNOWLEDGEMENTS

While this book is a work of fiction, it is also an account of the region around Traverse City, Michigan in the mid-1950s. Many have asked if this book is autobiographical; it is only to the extent of location and family anecdotes. I would like to thank many for this finished product, Dennis DeRose my editor, the historical society in Elk Rapids, Michigan (a similar village), and my father John, for his memories. And, for their patience through many versions of this story, thanks to Gail Kilby and Laurie Stroud for their insightful comments and multiple readings.

A thank you and hug to my patient wife Bonnie for the hours spent listening to my ramblings about the story and her thoughts on the characters. Her family also has its roots in farming.

I also wish to thank my art teachers and instructors for their lessons, I did pay attention. All the illustrations are mine.

And a sincere thank you to the people of this northern region of Michigan. They live here because of family, their love of the land and its dramatic seasons, and Lake Michigan.

Summer, 2011

JUNE

PROLOGUE

Formed from small corals and animals a half billion years ago; compressed and metamorphosed to inflexible stone; its patterns of life held in eternal suspension; crushed by roiling seas and countless glaciers; foundered in the sand on a sallow beach; to be rescued by an old woman, given to a fledgling at the start of a fleeting summer when green cherries turned red, boys became men, lost souls died, and for a very, very brief second of the primordial stone's life, the leaden, time encapsulating Petoskey stone conned its holder into believing it held miracles in its hard heart.

Boys to men, stones to gravel, life to death, it was the time when waves of change pushed a simple family forward, to hold each one for a moment, then release them to the next swell. What to hold on to, what raft, what drifting piece of debris keeps them afloat? They flounder, but never climb on each other's shoulders to gasp, one last time. They release themselves to time and the seasons. These govern all: time holds the parts of their lives together; the seasons are the whip-masters of their art.

A boy, a summer, lives gained and lost. All governed by tart red rubies and uncontrollable electric storms. The struggle between the real and the loved is contested; change, as all changes are, is fought, there is no winner. Yet again, time drags them to its bosom, and they're left to breathe heavily of its promise. There is a difference between the civil and the wild; one tries to own time. The other – with arms thrown high – gives of itself lovingly.

CHAPTER ONE

Eve Titus screamed, "You look at me one more time, you bastard, and I'll grab you by that deformed arm of yours and throw you across the grass!" She threw her highball glass, half full of bourbon, at the boy. "I don't want to see your face, or even think that you're anywhere near me, you cripple."

He ducked; it was easy to duck her throw. It hit the base of the tree. Howie knew this was coming, it had happened before, and it would happen again.

"Howie, what's going on?"

"Nothing Grams, Aunt Eve and I were just having a conversation," Howie Smith said, as he turned toward the screen door where his grandmother stood. "Aunt Eve seems to have spilled her drink again."

"You little son-of-a-bitch," was all Howie heard over his shoulder.

"Eve, you quiet down now. Howie, pick up that glass, someone might step on it, and your mother needs your help unpacking. She's upstairs."

"You leave that glass right there, boy."

Howie glared at his aunt and turned toward the screen door.

"Yes Ma'am," Howie squeezed past his grandmother and disappeared into the kitchen.

"My Lord, Eve, why do-ya' do that?"

"Do what?"

"Go after that boy, don't you think he has enough to deal with without your badgering?"

"He's a bastard and he's disrespectful. No one tells me when I've had enough to drink. I know my limits and I'm not even half way there yet. But I know when I'm not welcome no more. I'll leave, but you'll just have to wait 'till the old man comes back. I'm here and this is where I'll drink." Eve picked up the glass, tipped it to the sky and caught the last drops on her tongue. She took the flask out from her black patent leather purse and poured another two fingers of bourbon. She looked to the screen door, lifted the glass, smiled and emptied it in one gulp.

"That boy's a son-of-a-bitch and so's his sneaky little brother, they're both bastards." Eve poured the last of the bourbon into her glass, slumped back on the slider and, within a minute, was passed out.

For the next hour, the family acted as though Eve Titus was not even there, and for all intent, she wasn't. A slight, but nasty bit of drool coursed from the corners of her well decorated lips to her less than well powdered chin. When she was finally taken home, the young boy with the withered arm could breathe freely again.

Howie Smith squatted on the edge of the creek, his toes hidden in the warm sandy mud; the hot Michigan sun baked his back and darkened his already deep brown hide. He paid no mind to the wet sticky air and sat, quiet and still, watching the red tannin tinged creek drain from the larch forest deep within the swamp; his eyes, wide, watched the miracle continue.

Twice the muskrat swam up the creek and twice the muskrat floated upside down, paws to the sky, rubbing its belly, rubbing its face, and once, Howie was real sure, its crotch. If the muskrat had thoughts about him, Howie didn't care; it was a miracle, just a great fucking miracle, that he was damn sure of. Again the muskrat swam up the creek and, for a moment just before flipping over, looked straight into the right eye of the boy, and seemed to wink. Of course muskrats don't wink, but sure as Howie sat there he was sure it winked. Both were caught in the same closed world: the boy felt the water flowing over his muskrat fur, his heart swelling with joy, and the warmth of the sun on his upturned belly.

He left the farmhouse early that morning, just after a breakfast of toasted homemade bread, peanut butter and apple butter. He loved the farm and its foreignness. The rest of the year his world was: trains, Catholic school, his sometime friends, his family, nuclear war and hiding under desks, his room; the busy-busy, the crazy-crazy. The woods, beaches and orchards were his world even if for only two months every hot and sticky summer, and far from one Russian target, Chicago. The family came during the hardness of winter, but it was the rounder, edgeless summer that shaped the boy.

He pushed his way through the low branches of the sour cherries heavy with green fruit and morning dew; in no particular direction, just through, then down below. The orderly rows surrounded him, throwing out a deep green tunnel ahead and behind. The morning sun flashed through them and pushed the humidity up as it pulled the dew from the trees. The branches hung just low enough to allow the hard clusters of fruit to be touched. The green marbles sparkled like emeralds against the dark saw-toothed leaves and peeling red and black bark. They dreamed of becoming rubies.

The edge of the orchard, where the last row of trees stood on the old lake bluff, delimited the edge of the real world. The orchard's orderly world clashed and stood in mortal conflict with the Michigan woods spread below. One would win in the end. The boy understood the battle: the orchard is man's world; the forest is owned by no one, a wilderness.

He called it "below the hill," below civilization, below the safe, the known, the comfortable. The path from the crest of the bluff to the woods below carved a hallway from one life to another, from one place that held his family to another that held him. It was a place to learn, to poke and prod, to watch and wonder, and, to see miracles.

The creek flowed from high in the hills above the farms and orchards, down an old valley cut by glacial run-off, through the dense larch and tamarack swamp to emerge and carve its way across the beach into Lake Michigan. The boy counted three hundred and twenty two paces, out loud, from the point where the dark water of the creek washed into the lake. Between the lake and the swamp stood a sand dune covered in scrub pine and juniper. In the spring, the creek would cut a sharp V shaped notch through the dune and force itself to the lake with a reddish riffle not more than a foot deep. Here the sand fines washed into the lake leaving a gravelly bottom armored with flat hard gray stones excellent for skipping.

Every few winters the creek changed, wandered, left home to find a new address somewhere up or down the beach. Last year it was up a hundred yards or so, the old abandoned channel could barely be seen. Howie knew that the great plates of thick ice, pushed up on the beach by the winter winds, had cut this new channel and plowed away last year's. Every year things were different, changed, but he really only remembered the last three years. That summer, three years back, the beach was twice as wide as it is now. A dry winter lowered the lake, the bottom was exposed. He could easily climb the newly emerged logs and boards still stuck in the sand from the lumber days. Small pools between the snags held clams, minnows and finger long muskies. But now those worlds were covered by fifteen feet of water; it looked normal, the way God wanted it; Gramps said it's the way it is supposed to be. Howie liked it more when the water was low.

He watched the muskrat flip over one more time and then he backed up the bank slowly into the shade of an over-reaching white pine and pulled out the packet of Pall Malls (liberated from the carton in the kitchen); his second fag of the morning. He smelled the earthiness of the short unfiltered cigarette and how it was full of the aromas of the damp litter of the woods. The farm and the forest were different worlds grinding into and abusing each other; for the moment the farm seemed to be winning. He held the matches in his right hand's twisted fingers, struck the match across the box, and, as he took his first drag, imagined he was in a kingdom where he could make his own rules. Change washed over him; his crotch now growing hairy; his face seemed rougher, the longer down, scratchy. His own internal worlds grated; some days he was happy, and others, his family really pissed him off. But he welcomed the physical turmoil and mixed-up emotions. His left arm felt stronger, a tight bicep showed; his right was only a minor annoyance, something that made him unique, in school he had developed an act that used it as a prop to the delight of his friends and the shock of his too sensible teachers. No one pitied him.

He dug his toes into the cool sand under the pine needles. The cigarette burned to the end and he crushed the butt and rolled his fingers through the ash and paper, making sure it was out, dead out. He had been caught once and his mother said, after she said she was disappointed (mothers always say that), "Make sure the damn thing is out. I don't want you burning down the woods by your stupid smoking."

He did it because she said not to and because of the charge he got when he took the first drag. He liked the smoke and the smell; it made him feel older, but he had to hide the pack, especially from his brother, who would tell even though he was sure he never had. His nosey and sometimes annoying little brother: always there, always around, always yacking.

The beach was empty. The summer cottages, half consumed by the pine and hemlock fringe, were still closed up; it was too early. Someone might be in the Gardener place; he wasn't sure, but maybe. So for now the beach and the woods were his. He headed up the narrow trail to the top of the dune and then cut into the woods toward the farm. The jack pine needles cracked under his feet even in the shade. The air hummed with the background static of cicadas and the staccato clacking of a woodpecker digging into the bark of an overhead tree looking for grubs. Usually the heat started when the cherries were red or even later when the apples started to take color, but this early heat, this furnace, had come in June, not August.

The half-mile trail back to the farm was pure sand, a buff to pinkish yellow color, and edged by ferns, bracken and maples which grew thick in the foreground of the deep woods of pine and hemlock. Staghorn sumac stood proud on the higher places; ancient dunes which, a hundred generations ago, were the lake's shore.

He had tied his shoes together and hung them over his shoulder. His toes dug into the sand; the grit felt hot in the sunny spots and cool in the shade. Along the bluff, the dark tops of the cherries squatted like soldiers, waiting for the signal to attack. The large clearing, at the base of the bluff, held one sentinel pine and the ragged stumps of its brothers, all that was left after it was cleared fifty years ago. Gramps told him that the stumps were the remnants of the lumbering and clearing of the forest, stumps from the pine and hemlock that built Chicago, Milwaukee and Detroit. *"It would have been a wonder to see this forest then,"* thought the boy. Now, except for the woodland's insect life, it sat quiet and, as hard as Howie tried, he could not hear the echoes of the axes and saws.

He reached the crest and the road that ran along the edge of the orchard; on one side stood the unremitting neatness and order of the orchard, to the other, a ramble of blackberries, like green barbwire, buffered the forest from the regiment of cherries. At the end of the rows stood the wine-saps; great tall apple trees twice as high as the cherries. They reminded the boy of sentries at attention, guarding the orchard. The barn stood proud above the trees and hid the farmhouse.

"Is that you Howie, been down below?" a voice called out from within the orchard.

"Down on the beach, Roger. Watching muskrats and hawks–they're pretty neat."

Roger Barton walked out from among the trees carrying a long pole with a wicked saw bolted to one end.

"Cutting out dead limbs?" Howie said.

"Yeah, winter kill was not as bad this year, just a few limbs here and there. Mostly shaping, looking for weak structures where the branches are loaded with fruit. Damn, it's hot," Roger said. "You and your folks come up yesterday?"

"Yeah, yesterday. Real hot all the way. Chicago's been hot for a week, not much better up here. But it's good there are less dead branches, less to clean up. Saw that big pile in that canker clearing;

we gonna burn it?"

"Yes sir, but not when it's this dry; supposed to rain tomorrow, maybe then."

Burning the winter pruning meant something very different from the usual Chicago day to day stuff. How often could you set fire to a pile of wood as big as your house in the South Side suburbs? Roger usually fired off the pile before the spring rains but it had been too wet for too long to get a good burn this year, so he waited. Now it would be something, even if later, but it had to be done.

"Can't wait," Howie said.

The trimmings lay in piles under the rows of cherries. Some rows were clear, others were full. Roger started to load the cut limbs onto the trailer hitched to the tractor.

"Are you going to stand there like a toad or are you going to help?"

"Sorry, where do I start?"

"Anywhere, boy." Roger pointed in the general direction of everywhere, swinging his arm in a half circle.

They drove through the orchard loading the trailer. The orchard opened into a clearing, the result of an apple canker that struck down thirty-six trees a few years back, and left a third of an acre hole in the orchard's rigid fabric. Tomorrow, Howie hoped, Roger would douse the pile with kerosene and set it afire. The night would then become as grand as the fireworks on the Fourth of July.

Howie jumped from the trailer, as they neared the barn, and walked between it and the large galvanized tanks of water used to fill the sprayer. A breeze, kicked up by the heat, lifted the sulfur dust covering the ground; the acrid smell was another foreign odor wedded to this place. The orchard had already been sprayed twice to keep down the mildew, but, in this heat, the fungus would be held in check for only a few days. The rain would be a mixed blessing. He would watch the great bonfire and then, the next day, help his uncle dust.

He sat next to the taller tank and laced up his tennis shoes. It would take a week to get his feet used to the sand, but around the farm: "You'll wear shoes everywhere around the barn and farm, no buts, no excuses," his grandmother ordered. "There are no exceptions; I don't want cut or infected feet around here."

Deep in the cool barn, he slowly opened the shop door and peeked in to see if it was empty. Safe, empty, Howie took his pack of cigarettes and gently slid it up onto his secret ledge under the tool bench. Earlier in the morning, he had run his hand along this same ledge and found nothing. Mice or something had gotten the pack during the winter and it was well shredded, colored bits of paper lay about the floor. Now there was a lot for them to eat so he had no worries about his new pack. He laid the match box next to the cigarettes, and strolled back into the sun, whistling.

The farmhouse stood low and long against a back hedgerow of jack pines and sugar maples; a few pear and apple trees filled the lawn, and bright beds of roses and irises ran at angles to the house. This time of year these beds were his grandmother's favorites, at least until the hydrangeas bloomed. For now, it was the cool reds and purples of late spring and early summer; later, in the full heat of summer, the hot yellows and oranges would dominate these beds with gaillardias, cone flowers, and sunflowers. When these bloomed, he knew his summer was almost over.

"Where you been, Howie?" A voice called out from deep within the flowers.

"Down by the swamp, Grams," he answered as he walked to the beds. "Saw the strangest thing, a muskrat swimming up the creek and then floating down on his back. Never seen anything like it; it was a wonder."

"I should say so, muskrats all over that swamp. You know your dad used to hunt and trap them when he was your age."

Liz Smith stood up amongst the roses and ran her hands down her hips and against the saffron yellow apron she always wore in the garden.

"Yes Howie, he would trap them, clean and skin them; he would get twenty-five cents a skin in those days. Some guy in town would sell them down in Detroit, for Lord knows what. Never could find out and probably didn't want to know anyway. That boy read about a recipe for muskrat stew in *Boy's Life* or something and cooked it right up on the stove in the kitchen, took one taste, picked up the pot, carried it outside and dumped it over the fence. Never said a word to your grandfather or me; never said anything. Two things for sure though, we never had muskrat stew again and he stopped hunting the things." She smiled and winked at Howie.

"Don't think I could ever kill one for either its skin or for stew. They're just too much fun to watch. He acted like he didn't have a care in the world. Just swam and looked at me like I was his personal audience, it was something."

"Fresh lemonade in the Frigidaire, if you want it." She always called it "The Frigidaire," pronouncing every syllable. In this part of Michigan, the newer models were still rare and only successful farms had one as big as hers. They bought it in Detroit the previous fall, after the picking. Her other pride and joy was the huge white enameled box freezer that she kept near the breakfast table. Howie was sure she could have kept a whole steer in it if she had to, but Elizabeth Smith kept mostly fruits and vegetables–and most especially, frozen pies in its cavernous interior.

She was tall and a bit thin with a casual grace and elegance, her simple dress hung on her as if she were a high fashion model. Howie remembered that she said she was once a dancer in New York, Howie was certain she had been a great dancer. Now, silvery hair matured from blond framed her face; blue eyes, the color of a clear Michigan sky, sparkled from behind wire glasses, and her firm lips always held a smile.

Howie hitched himself up onto the slider that was out under the apple tree just outside the kitchen door and looked up into the vast tangle of branches, leaves, and quarter-sized fruit, becoming instantly lost, his eyes chasing a nuthatch. The screen door screeched opened, slammed, and his grandmother handed him a tall glass. A quick swallow puckered his cheeks and then he relaxed when he tasted the sugar. *"God, she makes good lemonade,"* he thought to himself.

"Your mom went to town to see Eve. She called and said she wasn't feeling well. Anne said she would see if she was alright, took Bill with her."

"She should be drunk right about now," Howie said. "Just like yesterday."

"That's not a Christian thing to say about your aunt. You know she's got it tough these days," Liz said.

"That's for sure, especially when you're drunk so much you can't remember what day it is. And she has a foul mouth."

"Howard, that's enough. At least your mother went to see how she's doing. She said she'd be back by four." Liz sat down next to the boy and pushed the slider into motion. Just enough of a breeze cooled his cheeks and added to the acid sweetness of his next sip.

"Gramps around?" he asked.

"No, went to town to check with the canners; trying to get an idea of the going price and the size of the crop this year. With this heat, we should be picking in four to six weeks. Looks like a good crop, so far."

Liz and Charlie Smith had been through too many of these late warm springs to get their hopes up too high. High winds, a sudden freeze, even in early June, or rain at the wrong time could bruise and ruin even a good year. She never said anything about the weather; she firmly believed it would hex the whole crop, and when someone else started to talk about it, she but put her hand up, like a traffic cop, and stopped them. And she never talked about the money they hoped to make; God would punish her if she did. But every night she prayed silently for good weather and a profitable crop.

He finished the lemonade and walked back through the barn into the open yard behind the big double sliding doors. The old chicken coop, now the picker's quarters, stood at ninety degrees to the barn. The sound of the tractor grew louder and Howie watched Roger drive through the cherry trees and roll onto the packed sand and gravel.

"Can I drive?" Howie asked.

"Not today, tomorrow maybe. Let's get this unloaded and get all this gear put away. I have to get home by six. Lisa expects me to pick her up at the hospital, then head for home; besides, I'm beat."

Roger and Lisa Barton had been married less than a year, and, according to Howie, still acted silly. He liked Lisa a lot, she was a bit taller than Roger, "She's pretty sharp and looks real good in tight sweaters." Howie, now fourteen, was becoming more and more interested in her when she was around.

"Your dad driving up tomorrow?"

"Supposed to, Roger. We came up on the train; Gramps picked us up at Traverse. Dad'll follow tomorrow with the rest of our stuff."

"Your dad and your Uncle Jim loved to set off those bonfires when we were kids, of course he and Jim were much older than me, but it was always fun. We'd stand out there for hours watching the sparks rise to the sky, crackling and popping and hot enough to burn your face. God we loved it. First time I met your mom was when Doug brought her here on a date. We all stood around and watched the sparks turn into stars. Doug and Anne and Jim and me, that was quite a night."

Howie never knew his Uncle James. He was killed in France when Howie was just a few months old. They always kept a place for James at the Christmas and Thanksgiving tables'. It wasn't a morbid thing, just out of respect. Liz still missed her oldest but twelve years had helped to lessen the ache and the pain. Gramps was stoic; his grandfather never talked about it.

Howie helped his uncle finish stowing the gear, then wandered back toward the house by way of the backside of the picker's quarters. The gooseberries and red currents were blooming along the edge of the vegetable garden. Rows and rows of crisp young greens, carrot tops and early celery were mixed between expectant mounds of potatoes. The mustard-colored Ford station wagon was now parked under the pear tree; his mother and brother were back.

"Hope to hell they didn't bring Eve," Howie said to no one.

He always tried to avoid his father's sister or half-sister; he still wasn't sure which it was. His run in with Eve the day before only reinforced it. He could never get a straight answer, only different versions, so he tried to put his own ideas together to make up his own story. He did know that she was divorced and her two kids lived with her ex-husband. He saw his cousins once or twice a year, if that. They lived a couple of hours away and mom would never drive there.

His brother, Bill, sat on the slider holding a glass of lemonade, swinging his legs and banging his heals against the metal in an agitated and impatient manner. Howie sat next to him. The boy looked at him and smiled. Bill always amazed his older brother. He seldom spoke long sentences, and, unless he was very excited, the conversations were only one sentence at a time. But, when he got started, he talked like he would never stop and you never knew where the train was headed. Howie and Bill got along just fine, for brothers.

"She was so drunk I don't know why I bother or give a damn, Liz. She was foul and looked like hell and damnation," the boys heard their mother through the screen door.

"She's had it tough, Anne," Liz answered.

"Yes, so tough. So tough she forgot she had a husband and two kids and then she walked out. Hell Liz, when you walk out you go somewhere, even if to run away. She went nowhere. Now she lives off the monthly check from her ex and the few bucks you and Charlie give her. There's nothing in her future; I'm glad I only have to see her a few times a year. You should get her back to the hospital before she hurts herself again, or, God forbid, she hurts someone else while she's having one of her fits," Anne said, breathless from her venting.

"Yes, I know," answered Liz. "She's a burden, believe me I know. We do all we can, but she has to want to help herself and she doesn't."

"Seen Howie?" Anne asked, changing direction.

"He was working with Roger in the barn about an hour ago. Should be back by now, Roger has to pick up Lisa at the hospital."

Howie and Bill watched their mother push open the screen door; still a young woman, but, by the boys' standards, ageless. Howie didn't make comparisons with other moms, didn't realize the freedoms she gave him because they were always there. The limits were few, he knew his manners, was always prompt, didn't lie (or at least get caught) and was respectful to adults, even his Aunt Eve, though in her case he tried hard to be elsewhere when she came to the farm.

Anne's brunette hair stuck to her damp forehead, but clear green eyes took in everyone on the porch, strong boned and a full woman, Anne Smith's German heritage was tough to conceal, if she cared to try to hide it at all. She didn't.

"There you are boy, what were you doing with Roger?" she asked.

"Picking up trimmings and stacking them on the bonfire. Roger thinks maybe we can burn it tomorrow if it rains a little. If not, we'll have to wait, because of the heat," Howie said.

"That's for sure. Dad should be here tomorrow night, ought to be a big fire." Anne sank into the large wicker chair, took a deep breath and slowly exhaled; eyes fixed, her stare went out past the garden and into the orchard.

"Damn that woman," she said softly under her breath.

"Why is Aunt Eve the way she is, always drunk and always swearing?" Howie asked.

"Boy, sometimes people are just that way, a bit off in the head, and sometimes confused. They feel imaginary pain, but it's real to them," Anne said. "Drinking makes her forget the pain, but it also makes her crazy and then mad. I just don't know why; just wish to God that it wasn't her."

"Saw the darnedest thing this morning in the swamp; you know, where the creek flows out. I saw a muskrat swim up the creek and float down on his back three or four times. It was something, Mom, really something; looked right at me and just continued to do it."

"Nature is a strange thing, boys. You stay in the woods long enough and you'll see things no scientist would ever believe. The things my Uncle Bob told me when I was your age seemed like stories; he was always telling tall tales. Yet, he swears they were true," she answered.

"Like what?" asked Bill, enthralled.

"Well, let me think." She stopped for a moment and then asked, "What happens when you take a fish out of the water?"

"It dies," Bill answered quickly.

"So true, Bill. But Uncle Bob said he caught this strange fish out in the lake years ago, fins all the way down its back, almost scaleless. Never saw one before, he said, and took it to the Fish and Game to find out what it was. Didn't have a bucket or anything so he threw it in a gunnysack, took it home and called the Fish and Game warden. They said bring it down. Uncle Bob took it to the warden's house and dumped it out of the bag, and darned if that fish wasn't still alive. This was an hour or two after he'd caught it. They threw it in a bucket and it started to swim around. Damnedest thing, he said, and just before they threw it in the bucket, it was opening and closing its mouth like it was breathing air."

"What was it?" Howie asked.

"Bowfin, the warden said. Real rare and real tough, no good to eat, though."

"What did Uncle Bob do?" Bill asked.

"Didn't have the heart to kill it, so he drove back down to the lake and gently put it back into the water; swam away like nothing ever happened."

"Bet that fish could tell a tale," Howie said.

"I ask you boy, if you were a fish, another bowfin, and this other bowfin swims up to you and told you a story about being pulled out your cozy rocky world, wrapped in a rough bag, forced to almost suffocate because you couldn't breathe and then these huge things carried you and poked you, then dumped you into a tiny version of your world where you could breathe again, and finally dumped you back into your home, would you believe him?"

"Probably not, too strange," Howie said. "Maybe that's how Aunt Eve feels sometimes."

Anne stopped and gazed out into the orchard. "Howie, sometimes you're too damn smart." She ran her hand through his blond hair.

"Hi, Anne," a voiced called out behind them.

"Good evening, Roger. Cherries okay?" Anne asked.

"They look great right now, if the weather holds and no great surprises; should be a fine crop," Roger said.

"Hope it's better than last year's, with the late frost and then the rain. What a mess."

"Yes, thirty percent of normal, barely enough to make it worth the pickers' efforts. Didn't make a penny. But with God's watchful eye, and some good luck, we should do okay."

"Is Lisa doing alright? Just a couple of months left, right?" Anne asked with a smile.

"Yes, three months, tough parts over, now she wants to eat everything in sight. She craves her mother's sweet pickles, now Edna has to ration them or there won't be any of last year's pickles left. Lisa swears her mother is continuing with the rationing, like the war was still on," Roger laughed. "Gotta go. See you tomorrow, maybe we can fire off the pile." Roger turned to go and then asked, "Doug in tomorrow?"

"Yes, if he can get away. It's a long drive but he should be here by 6:00 p.m.." Anne answered.

"Thanks Anne. See you fellows tomorrow."

Howie waved with a quick flip of his good wrist as Roger turned toward the barn.

The crunching of tires on gravel announced the large black Buick before it pulled into the open spot next to the farm's station wagon. A man, tall, erect, with steel gray hair, slowly unfolded from the front seat and stood, with regal bearing, beside the Buick's huge door; he had a crisp checked shirt on, dark slacks, polished shoes. His clothing and demeanor set him apart; too distinguished to be a farmer. He and his father had planted this orchard almost forty years before. They cleared the land soon after the loggers left. Now the farm was into its second generation of cherries, the original apples and pears were fully matured. To Charles Smith, there was no better world.

He pulled a pack of Pall Malls out of his shirt pocket and lit a cigarette as he strolled up to his family gathered under the pear. Liz pushed the screen door open and watched her husband cross the lawn.

"Saw Roger as he went down the drive. Said he cleared out the rest of the trimmings, that right boy?" he asked looking at Howie. He was the first to call him boy, now most of the family did.

"That's right, Gramps. Roger said we can burn it tomorrow."

"We'll see; need a bit more rain to dampen things first." He took a long drag and blew the smoke overhead into the tree.

"Price looks good right now according to Ernie at the cannery. Way down on supply, the storage counts are low and the crops down south are starting to come up short. We may be alright this year."

"That's what I wanted to hear," Liz said. "You get the mail?"

"Damn, left it in the car. Howie can you run and get it for me? And get other bag on the front seat, too."

"You bet." Howie took off toward the Buick.

Charlie watched the young man run across the lawn. "Wish I

could wire that boy into the house, would power it for a week. Makes me tired just watching him."

"Can I get you a drink, old man?" asked Liz.

"Old, I'm not an old man, can still do one armed push-ups," he answered.

"Yes you can, but that boy can out run you to the barn and back, so be careful. Still love you," Liz answered and pulled the handle of the screen door. "Want something to drink Anne?"

"Manhattan would be nice," Anne said.

"Three Manhattans coming up," Liz said and went inside; the screen door slammed behind her.

"Did you see Eve?" Charlie asked Anne.

"Yes Charlie, and she was drunk at two o'clock in the afternoon. Damn it Charlie, she's forty-two years old. She has real, very real problems, and she's dangerous. She gets mad; she lashes out; she's willful and what's worse is that she doesn't care. All of these things make her dangerous to herself and others." Anne sat looking at her father-in-law wishing she could make him understand.

"I'll talk to Father O'Brian about her, maybe he'll know what to do."

"Yes Charlie and this time tell the priest the whole story," Anne said.

Charlie protected his daughter and tried to help her the best way he could but this usually led to increasing dependence, and eventual drunken rejection. Father O'Brian placed her in a Catholic charity hospital for six months; she improved or at least dried out, but the demons returned quickly and now, two years later, she was worse.

Howie held the mail in his good hand the bag was snuggly couched under his bad arm; a small box sat on top of the letters and two newspapers. He handed the mail and bag to Charlie as Liz walked out of the kitchen, caught the door with her hip, allowed it to shut softly and handed the drinks to Anne and Charlie. She sat across from her husband.

"Howie, still some lemonade if you want it," Liz said.

"That's okay, I'll get some later." It was the box that held his attention.

"What interests you, boy?" asked Charlie. The box sat next to him on a wicker table, he looked through the mail and handed two letters to Liz, and one to Anne.

"Nothing," Howie lied.

"Here then, open this." Charlie pitched the box to Howie.

Howie caught it in mid-flight and looked it over. He took out his pocketknife, a four-inch long bone handled clasp knife his grandfather had given him last Christmas, held it with his withered hand, opened the blade, slid it along the box's edge and opened it. Nestled inside was a smaller box cushioned with excelsior, the blade cut the securing tape and he slowly opened the flaps. With two fingers he extracted a small metal part with a spring attached to one side and a flat piece of steel which opened and closed over a round hole on the other. He looked at his grandfather, questions written all over his face.

Charlie just laughed.

"Sometimes boy there isn't always magic in a box. It's just the new carburetor for the spray pump engine. The old one is about to go and this is not the time to lose the pump." Charlie took a sip of his Manhattan, smiled, lit another cigarette, and opened the paper.

After five minutes all he could offer was, "Seems like the end of the world is writ all over these pages, Khrushchev is spouting off, Egypt is going crazy, who knows what the Jews in Israel will do to protect themselves, and this hillbilly kid, Elvis Presley, makes the news, the front page no less. Good lord, what are we coming to? What's the matter Bill?" Charlie said.

"They made us hide under our desks the last day of school, when the siren blew. We gonna get blown up, Grandpa?" Bill asked, a slight tremor in his voice.

"Don't nearly think so Bill, lots of huffing and puffing, Eisenhower can handle that commie Khrushchev; I wouldn't think too much more about it," Charlie said, flipping to the next page.

Liz knew he was not as sure as he sounded, about both the Near East and the bomb.

Howie's look of disappointment over the package faded quickly. He knew that it meant the engine would be dismantled; parts everywhere, the new part installed and then put back together. It was almost as exciting as anything else he could do around the farm.

Bill sat quietly through the rest of the conversation and the expectation of the box and its contents. Taking a sharp deep breath, he turned to his brother and gently shoved his elbow into his side.

"Can we go below the hill tomorrow, Howie?" he asked. "The pond' gotta be full of big tadpoles about now, need some for my aquarium."

Howie shared his forest with his younger brother but always kept certain parts of it to himself. In his world he owned the creek; but the frog pond was everyone's, neutral ground. Howie, years ago, continuing a long Smith tradition, started collecting tadpoles early in their summer, put them in an aquarium, and then watched them grow into frogs. Usually, by the time they went home, the tadpoles had all their legs and a short tail. Then he returned them to the pond. It was Bill's fourth year to collect, the second going with his brother and he was ready.

"Sure, gotta be up early though. Suppose to rain tomorrow. We need to get back by noon," Howie said.

"Neato, I'll get the big jar and the cheesecloth," Bill answered.

"Great, we'll leave right after breakfast."

"What you two jabbering about?" Liz asked. "What plans are you hatching?"

"Nothing, Grams, me and Howie are going to the frog pond tomorrow," Bill said.

"Howie and I are going to the frog pond tomorrow," she corrected him.

"Sorry Grams," Bill said.

He repeated her phrasing correctly and then sat back with a smile.

"After breakfast, Howie," Anne said.

"Yes, Ma'am."

"Bill, that pond's been there since your dad was a boy," Charlie said. "He and Jim brought up tadpoles and all sorts of other bugs and larvae. Hellgrammites were his specialty; used them to catch smallmouth bass down at the power plant on Elk River. Never failed, he loved the woods as much as you two do."

Why they never cleared the woods and planted more cherries down below puzzled Howie. He would take long walks down the beach and see other orchards close to the lake, still on the bluff, but still much closer. When he asked his father, the answer was something about frost and how it settled in the lower spots in late spring and could knock off the flower buds and the young fruit. Maybe, but he was sure glad they hadn't cleared the woods.

The woods provided a lot for them: Christmas trees in winter, big morel mushrooms in late spring, frogs and snakes in the summer, and big buck deer in the fall. It was a magic land to a boy from Chicago.

"Seen Frank, Liz?" Charlie asked, finishing his drink. "Cal, at the drug store, said he stopped by earlier today for his medicine, told him it wasn't ready; asked me to give it to him."

"No, haven't seen his car," she said.

Franklin Rex, Liz's older brother by four years, was eccentric by everyone's definition; he painted in oil, had a beard, and spent every winter in southern Spain. He painted portraits, landscapes and religious art and lived in a small studio in the back of the orchard with windows that overlooked the pines and the lake. His dark sunken eyes sat over a hard nose and crisply trimmed salt and pepper beard that topped an athletic body. Frank Rex also had a cancer in his gut that was eating him alive.

"He may have slipped in just before Anne returned," Liz said.

"Howie, could you walk back to the studio and give Uncle Frank his medicine," Charlie said handing the bag to Howie.

"Sure Gramps, wan'na come, Bill?" Howie asked.

Bill shook his head and looked down. "No, too scary out there. All those big paintings and besides Uncle Frank is strange; I'll only go when I have class."

"Yes, he is that Bill," laughed Charlie.

"He is not, Charles," Liz corrected him. "Maybe eccentric, but he's not strange." The smile on her face portrayed her real belief.

The gravel and sand road, split down the center by a strip of wiry grass left there because tires and time had not worn it away, led to the Rex studio. A double colonnade of old apple trees provided shade and the gravel crunched under Howie's feet and the buzz of bees teased the sticky air.

A sharp left, before it slid down the slope, turned him toward the studio, a simple one-story building built by his uncle twenty years before Howie was born. Its simple shape, built from concrete blocks (their color pulled out of the buff sand), supported a shingled roof and windows with dark green trim. A rich and colorful, but unkempt, garden surrounded the studio; roses, peonies, Russian olives, small apple and peach trees lined the fence. A dried-out pond with a concrete bottom sat filled with orange and yellow nasturtiums.

The door was red, not just a Christmas red but an Andalusian red that Frank Rex had found under the hot sun of southern Spain. This color, Howie was sure, could not be found anywhere in Michigan. It only existed here and when he knocked on the door he felt as though he had knocked on a portal to a foreign land. He waited and then knocked again.

"Who, the fuck is out there? Speak up, you thoughtless son-of-a-bitch, and don't bang on that door again; I heard you the first time."

"It's Howie, Uncle Frank."

"Just a moment boy," Frank yelled loudly from behind the door. There was a crash of glass and then an almost perceptible two-count beat before the door jerked open.

The smell of turpentine washed out of the studio and engulfed the lanky man standing in the doorway. He was dressed in a long muslin smock covered in splashes and dabs of a hundred colors of paint from his chest to its edges near his knees. From there, his hairy legs extended to sandals, both his legs and the sandals were colored with paint.

"Good evening boy, come in, come in. I broke a fucking jar of turpentine just as you knocked. Wasn't paying attention. Damn, had that jar for years; got it in Toledo just after the war. That's Toledo fucking fascist Spain, Howie, not Ohio. Got careless, happens more and more these days, don't know whether it's the drugs or the fucking cancer. What's in the bag?" Frank Rex looked at the bag Howie was unconsciously clutching tight to his chest with his deformed arm.

"Gramps said he got your medicine from the drug store," Howie said.

"Excellent, need it to help cut the pain a little. My fucking side hurts like hell today. But the paint's flowing and I feel real good about that. It seems I can't get one without the other." Frank took the sharp edge of Howie's shoulder and gently pulled him into the studio. "Yes, it seems like I need pain to be able to paint these days. It really fucking stinks, to get the pleasure of the paint I get the pain of the gut."

Howie was sure he was about the only one who could put up with the semi-recluse. Frank Gilbert Rex made everyone uncomfortable. He challenged just about everything that everyone, up in this part of the world, believed in. So they avoided him when they could, said things about him he didn't care about and, in general, thought he was insane or at least nuts. He would spend the summers in Elk River and the winters in a small village near Barcelona where he had a studio like this one. Not one person in Michigan had seen it.

Howie considered him exotic, Rex swore so well that he tried hard to remember the words so he could use them later. He practiced so he could casually throw off a "What the fuck?" yet somehow it never had the polish like his uncle's, but he believed that someday practice would make perfect.

The studio was cramped and disorderly, even by the standards of a fourteen-year-old. Stacks of canvases lined the walls and leaned against everything. A hundred eyes stared at him. The pungent mixture of linseed oil, turpentine, and Turkish pipe tobacco filled his nostrils, smells that only existed here in this house, his uncle's world. A tall canvas stood on a large easel; a table, next to it, held a large sheet of glass covered in small and large globs of oil paints in hundreds of colors.

The rough bloody cross extended from the top of the painting to the bottom, the crossbeam almost touched both sides. The three people, at the bottom of the canvas, created a triangle of anguish. Christ's bloody head sat on the shoulder of the younger women, His naked body extended across her lap. His bloody feet sat nestled in the fold of her brilliant white robe. The other woman, on the right, was older, her hand extended to touch the long gash on the Savior's breast. The triangle they formed placed Christ's head in the center and at the base of the cross; a golden ring enclosed his thorn crowned head and enclosed the wood of the cross, the carnage was intense. Howie stood transfixed, mostly because the younger woman looked like his mother, the older woman his grandmother and the bearded face of Christ, resembled Frank. It mesmerized him and scared the hell out of him at the same time.

"Upset you boy?" Frank asked. "I can see it in your face; that's good. If it scares an innocent boy like you, it will certainly scare old Father O'Brien. He wants to hang this in the sanctuary of the church, on the left side. Need's a bit more work though, maybe a week or two. I've painted a dozen or more crucifixions, and I'm still not sure this is the one, still not satisfied. Want a coke?"

Frank always had a cold Coca-Cola in his refrigerator for Howie. Howie believed they were just for him since no one else ever came here, or at least he thought so until he saw the likenesses in the paintings.

"Thanks, Uncle Frank. Someday I'll paint like you," he said.

"God, hope to hell not Howie, you should be better, much better. I started too late to really learn and now I am trying to make up for it in quantity; but I lose out to the fucking quality. Now with this cancer eating me up, I'll never live to be good."

"Stop saying that, Uncle Frank," Howie said.

"We all die boy, some die sooner than we want, some, not soon enough. Me? God plans and I just do what he wants. But it still pisses me off that he didn't ask my opinion."

Howie walked around the studio while Frank dabbed at the painting. The turpentine lay on the concrete floor; glass bits lay about in the liquid mess.

"Should I clean this up?" Howie asked.

"Suit yourself boy. I'll do it later." Frank stood back from the crucifixion for a moment and then slid his frame into the sheet-draped chair in front of the painting.

Howie cleaned up the turpentine and the glass, and threw the rags into the metal can outside the rear door. The can was half full of paint-covered rags.

He came back into the studio and found his uncle asleep in the chair, his legs extended straight out, heels resting on the floor. The sheet was curiously free of paint. Frank still held a paintbrush tipped in the color of the blood on the chest of Christ but it was also like the color of the Spanish door. Howie saw that Frank Rex's sleeping body was extended out and twisted like the angle of the Son of God lying in his mother's lap, just like in the painting.

The dense shadows from the apples were long as Howie headed back to the farmhouse.

CHAPTER TWO

The boys, both up and dressed as the first light brightened the window of their upstairs room, quietly climbed down the stairs and made their way into the dark kitchen. Bill clicked on the light switch; Howie opened the cabinet doors and pulled out the peanut butter and jam. Bill opened the breadbox and retrieved a loaf of homemade bread still wrapped in wax paper; so fresh it almost felt warm.

Howie cut four thick slices of the butter yellow bread and laid them out on the counter; troweled on a thick layer of peanut butter and then added a thicker layer of strawberry jam. He placed the dry slice on top of the filling and pressed the two together until the jam began to ooze out of the gap. He wrapped the two sandwiches in wax paper and stretched a rubber band around each of the small bundles. Bill took the pitcher of lemonade from the Frigidaire and filled a large mouth Mason jar he had retrieved from the pantry and, after twisting on the cap, set it next to the sandwiches.

Next Bill retrieved, from the mud-room, the dark Army surplus rucksack that Howie always carried on their long hikes. He also took down another large Mason jar that they would put the tadpoles in. The boys were too intent in their activities to notice Charlie standing in the doorway of the kitchen; the smell from his cigarette caught their attention. They stopped, looked and smiled.

"You want to come along, Gramps?" asked Howie.

"No boys; love to though," Charlie said. "Have to go into Traverse City later today, have some papers to sign and need to check-in with the county ag agent. There's been some trouble a few miles north of here with blight or something similar to it. He wants me to take a look. I'll be back before lunch, maybe to have one of those sandwiches you just made. They look mighty good!"

"We're going to the frog pond and then to the beach. Mom knows," Bill added.

"Have a great time boys," Charlie said. "Be back by two o'clock though, Roger may need your help. If it starts to rain, better head back, don't want you gettin' too wet."

Charlie took another short puff on his cigarette. "That pond's been there as long as I can remember, even before all the white pine was cut. Pretty little glen back then, someday it will be pretty again when the pines grow back."

Charlie turned and walked back toward the front room. Bill and Howie placed the sandwiches and jars in the sack. Bill pointed to a large piece of cherry pie on the counter left over from dinner. Howie wrapped the slice in wax paper and placed it on top of the jars.

"No need to get the pie smashed; right Bill?" Howie said.

"Righty-O, gets too gooey."

Howie cut two more slices of the bread and gave them to Bill. He hitched the rucksack to his shoulders and secured the straps; the bag settled just right on his young angular frame. Bill handed one of the slices to Howie; they both took a big bite. Bill slowly pulled opened the door, pushed the screen door open, and, after Howie passed, caught it before it slammed shut.

The early blue-grey light threw shadows across the damp lawn leaving it like an early shower had quickly passed. Howie's cheek felt a puff of warm air wash over them as they headed toward the barn, and, looking furtively over his shoulder, slipped through the partially opened double doors, felt under the bench, pulled out his cigarettes, stuck them into his breast pocket and shoved the matches in the left pocket of his shorts. They passed the picker's quarters where, to the right of each open door frame, a square dark window sat in the red trim, a thin curtain hung behind the glass. The farm sat quiet, expectant, yawning; the only sounds were the crisp chirping of birds and the irritating incessant calls of the ravens. In another week or so this would all change when the pickers from Texas arrived. But, for now, the rows of windows and doors of the Depression era chicken coop were open to the air; soon there would be the thick odor of kerosene stoves, lard, corn tortillas and Spanish filling the morning air.

The boys reached the fork in the road at the bluff; one path led to Uncle Frank's, the other, down the hill, to the forest.

"Bill, let's wake up Uncle Frank," Howie said egging on his brother.

"No way, he'd only yell and besides he's weird," answered Bill.

"Is not. Mom says he's eccentric which just means he's different."

"Probably also means weird," Bill said. "Let's go."

Howie adjusted the bag on his shoulders and followed Bill. The trail cut a ramp into the hillside wide enough for a single tractor to pass through, not an inch more. The dark canopy of the maples added to the brightening early morning gloom of the trail. Below them, and, out onto the bracken covered sand, the first rays of the sun rippled over the brilliant green carpet of ferns. A soft breeze disturbed the tops like a large golden hand slowly moving across a green lake. Pushing further down the trail, they entered the maple grove that, fifty years ago, the loggers left alone; they were after pine, not hardwoods. Since then, the sugar maples spread into the clearing, pushing out pines and hemlock. It would be a hundred more years at least before the pines would again dominate this edge of Lake Michigan.

Reaching the foot of the trail, where it leveled out before entering the clearing, the wood suddenly quieted, like something important was about to happen, like the silence after an introduction and before the performer steps onto the stage. Howie paused, looked at Bill, and put his finger to his lips. A crack of bracken, a rustling, and a short snort caught Howie's ear. He gently grabbed Bill's shoulder and softly said, "Hold here a second, wait."

A soft morning breeze, a bit damp, blew into their faces carrying the musky scent; Howie smelt him before he saw him.

Again the bracken cracked and into the sun-lit opening, straddling the trail, stepped a white-tailed buck; taller than the boys at its shoulder; the deer's antlers spanned three feet and supported more spikes than the boys could count.

"Jesus. He's beautiful, Howie," Bill said. "Never seen one that big, not even in the zoo. He's huge, look at the antlers."

The buck pranced two steps; a shaft of sunlight cut through the tree branches and lit his antlers all draped in ragged skin shed from the bone of the rack. The velvet was both white and bloody where the buck had scraped and rubbed away the annoying peeling cover, the rack looked like it was on fire. He stood proud, regal, like a landholder. He slowly turned his massive head to survey his forest. The stag knew he owned this part of Antrim County and the boys understood that.

They stood quietly and watched until, with a start, the grand buck saw them. A second passed and, with a noticeable shiver, his withers twitched; with one great leap he crashed into the bracken and scrub.

"God, he's beautiful," Bill repeated.

"Sure is, Bill, never seen anything like it down here. Sometimes a doe or a fawn, but never a big stag buck. He's gone so let's get to the pond."

After a brief stop to look at the deep cloven impressions of the hooves, they were almost the length of Bill's shoe, they broke into the full sunlight of the clearing. The heat warmed their faces. More bracken lined the trail but it was shorter and rougher. The sun reached here and the ferns had hardened to the light. In the middle of the clearing stood a sentinel white pine.

"Howie, it's gotta be a hundred times taller than me, and don't it look like a big Christmas tree, all pointy like. Someday I'm gonna climb to the very top. Bet I can see Chicago from up there."

"No way, but it would be neat to climb." Howie's eyes coursed the tree from base to tip and down again.

The bracken abruptly stopped with a sharp edge of bending fronds against the bright yellow of the sand. The squat scrub growth and blueberries began here. These gray-green shrubs sprawled, not more than a foot high; their berries, bright green the size of BBs, promised great treats later in the summer when they would turn a rich blue with a dusting of white. The family would pick handfuls and fill boxes, eat them with fresh cream, turn them into pies and jam, and would be reminded about them for weeks by their blue stained fingertips even after returning to Chicago. Howie pointed out the staghorn sumac with its red jagged shafts of rough flowers, the jays flitting about in the maples.

The frog pond sat in the bottom of a shallow depression, the sand scraped out eons ago by something mysterious. Gramps said it was from a huge chunk of ice left as the glaciers retreated; Dad said ice too; the pond being dug much later by a huge wedge of winter ice which shoveled its way into the shore. This was once beach; the lake reached this far inland. Mystery surrounded this place, like sacred grounds guarded by seers and priests. Why was there standing water here? The sand had to be ten to twenty feet deep, yet water pooled here, it never dried. Maybe from a spring which started high up on the hill; maybe from a buried creek on top of the limestone underlying everything? What the boys did know was that there were always bugs and frogs in its water. Tall cattails fringed the pond and one lone water lily had somehow found its home among the reeds. Arrow shaped deer prints stippled the steep narrow beach and raccoon and possum prints mingled with the deer prints. It looked like an unimaginable all night dance had just finished.

"It looks bigger this year, much bigger," Howie said.

"Why?"

"Probably from all the snow; the lakes way up too. Just means more tadpoles and frogs."

"Neato."

"Needs to warm-up more to get 'em to the shallows before we can catch 'em. Wanna split a sandwich?"

"Okay!"

Howie opened the bag, pulled out one of the wax paper bundles and handed half of a sandwich to Bill; he retrieved the Mason jar, held the jar against his chest with his right arm and twisted off the cap with his left. He took a short swig of the sweetly bitter juice. The sun stood halfway up the tall Christmasy white pine, the temperature rose as the sun climbed higher. Humidity added to the warmth, their tee shirts stuck to their young frames as they sat quietly watching the pond, eating, and waiting.

Howie laid back and stared into the blue sky only slightly blemished by a thin band of clouds sliding from north to south; a pair of seagulls crisscrossed the sky, marking an X. Only the grating buzz of a cicada stirred the quiet.

"Howie, does it hurt?"

"What hurt?"

"Your arm, never asked before. But I wondered; does it hurt?"

"I don't pay it no mind, Bill. Never knew anything different, just is. No, it doesn't, but it hurts when it gets pricked or cut. Mom says it was just something that happened before I was born. Kinda pisses me off a bit when I see other fellows playing sports and stuff, hard to catch and throw a ball one handed, or hold a bat. But I can out-run 'em all. So I guess God gave me speed instead of a good arm. Still sucks though, but it don't hurt."

Bill thought for a long moment, "Good," he said, and then asked, "Howie, are the pickers coming this year?"

"Believe so, maybe in a week or two. Why?"

"Because they're different and they talk funny. They smell different and talk gibberish."

"They speak Spanish."

"Yeah, I know. But they're Mexican, why don't they speak Mexican?"

"They ain't Mexican, and they do, kind of. It's like us. We're not English but we speak English. Spain used to run Mexico long ago and that's why they speak Spanish."

"They should speak English, not right they don't talk like us. They need to talk the same way we do."

"They speak English but Spanish is easier. That's why they speak Spanish to each other, it's easier."

"Yeah, but nobody can understand 'em. So they should talk so we can understand 'em." Bill would not let go of the idea.

"Bill, you say things all the time that I don't understand and you speak English. Just don't worry about them. They talk the way they talk. That's it. No more, no less. Roger speaks Spanish and so does Gramps, and everything is A-OK, right?" Howie looked at his younger brother and wondered what was going on inside his head. "And besides, they're from Texas, not Mexico, they're as American as you and I."

"Are not! They speak Mexican so they ain't Americans. Need to speak American to be American, till they speak American they can never be Americans."

Bill took another bite, swallowed, and watched two enormous golden yellow dragonflies, almost as large as his hand, fly schizophrenically about the pond. He stood and picked up three small stones. Spotting one of the dragonflies as it landed on the bent edge of a cattail leaf, he took good aim and pitched one of the stones at the bug. He missed by a foot; the stone disappeared into the cattails.

"Damn it, missed."

"Don't swear; God will mark it down, Bill."

Howie didn't know if God marked it down or even cared, but he had been raised as a good Catholic all his young life and it was just one of those things you believed in.

Howie quickly joined his brother, flinging rocks at the buzzing insects. There were big yellow ones, middle-sized red and orange ones and even smaller blue ones. They never hit any, never had and never would. Howie was sure that, if those dragonflies could avoid birds, they could easily dodge their mean stones.

After a dozen throws, the boys slid on their butts down the slope to the flat damp ground surrounding the edge of the pool. The steep sides hid them from the rest of the clearing and their world shrank to just this pond. Cattails, dragonflies, sand, and green water was their magical kingdom, a complete universe, whole.

Howie grabbed a handful of damp sand and dumped in on Bill's head.

"Why did you go and do that, boy?" Bill asked.

"Don't call me boy."

"Gramps does."

"And so does Mom and Dad and now Roger. But Gramps was the first to call me boy. Someday he will call me by my name, till then boy is just fine. But you can't."

Howie sat with his knees together, his arms wrapped around his legs, and became an idle spectator as the assorted dragonflies flew back and forth within their shared kingdom and settled into their timeless pattern of being busy.

"Howie, what makes Aunt Eve so mean and why does she always get drunk?"

"Don't know outright, Bill. Dad said her mother, Gramps' first wife, was an opium user, that's a really bad drug that makes you crazy, so crazy you don't care about anything or anyone else. So she didn't care about Gramps or Aunt Eve. Aunt Eve grew up somewhere else after Gramps and her mother split-up. Aunt Eve's mother died a long time ago, and Eve came back from somewhere in Ohio to stay with Gramps. Grandpa and Grandma were married sometime around then; then Uncle Jim was born, then Dad. Dad and Eve are half-brother and sister, I think. That's why Aunt Eve is so much older than Dad. Mom said she disappeared again during World War Two, about the same time I was born." Howie stopped to think about what he said.

"World War Two?"

"Yes. About the time Dad left to fight the Nazis, she left; at least that's what Mom says. Then she showed up here at the farm just before Dad came home at the end of the war. She had Harold and Jane with her, I kind of remember a bit; Mom and me was living up here then and it was before you were born. You remember Uncle Ralph?"

"Yes, he's the big man with one arm and metal pincers where is other arm was."

"That's to help him grab things. His arm got blown off in the war in France."

"Probably hurt a lot," Bill said, continuing to flick stones into the water, just missing the dragonflies as they buzzed about in their kingdom.

"Sure, hurt a hell of a lot, million times more than when you cut yourself or get stuck by a hawthorn or get stung by a bee. Well Uncle Ralph and Aunt Eve lived in Elk River till a few years ago. Mom says Uncle Ralph left with the kids and went to Cadillac to get a job. Eve stayed here, drank all the time and stunk like cigarettes, and every time she came over here she bossed everyone around. When I could, I just stayed outside. She seems even worse now."

"She's mean, Howie. She told Mom I was a bastard and a son-of-a-bitch. If I could have, I'd of punched her for saying that to Mom."

"That's the liquor talking. Pay it no mind, ignore it or try to. You're not a bastard and Mom and Dad love us; just ignore her. She's mean and likes to hurt people; that's why she's alone." Howie pitched a rock at a small leopard frog which had crawled up a stalk of cattail.

"I'm not going there again, Mom can't make me. Next time Mom wants me to go, can you come?"

"Yeah, I'll go. We can walk around town and maybe go over to the power plant to fish."

"That'd be neat."

The boys fell back onto the sandy slope and again stared up into the sky. Their kingdom was peaceful and warm, no famine, no pestilence, not a Hun to be seen.

"It's time," Howie said. "Tadpoles, get the rucksack."

Bill dragged the green canvas bag down to Howie, the oldest pulled out the jar and the cheesecloth net. They would unroll the cheesecloth and, stretching it out between them, wade in and drag the net through the warm emerald green water, snagging their prizes.

After removing shoes and socks, Howie waded out into the deeper part of the pond, holding one end of the cheesecloth, Bill held on to his end and waded in to his knees.

"Far enough," Howie said. "You dip your end in and I'll pull my end tight, then walk around you to the bank."

Bent over, with the warm water running up his arms, Howie slowly dragged the net in an arc through the water. Bill held his end tight. Howie, intent on his work, only caught a quick glimpse of the long shape as it slid out of the cattails and wiggled between his legs.

But the glimpse was more than enough to startle the boy beyond a chance to recover his balance.

"Snake!" screamed Howie.

By the time Howie hit the water, the gray-green snake, with its long dark stripes, quickly disappeared after its sneak attack. Arms and swearwords flew across the surface of the pond, white gauze waved through the air like a rain soaked banner signaling a surrender that the kingdom had never seen. The vanquished sat on the bottom of the pond, the water crested in waves at his chin.

Bill laughed hard as he looked at his sodden brother: head just above the water, encased in cheesecloth; two large tadpoles wiggled between the layers of the cloth and his face.

"Fucking water moccasin," yelled the defeated as he pulled and yanked the cloth from his face. The tadpoles fell into the pond.

"Was not. Was a garter snake, a big one, but not a water moccasin."

"Easy for you to say, you wasn't looking at it face to face like I was."

Howie stood up, looked about, and began to laugh, water dripped into the pond, his wet hair hung in rings on his forehead.

"Back to work."

He straightened out the cheesecloth and pitched one end to his brother. Again Howie made a sweep and after filling the jar with thirty-three tadpoles, five hellgrammites, a dozen or so caddis flies still in their sand castles (minor fiefdoms in their own kingdoms), and maybe a few may fly larvae, they sat down to admire their booty.

Bill held the jar to the sunlight and watched the small world they had just created. All was chaos. The bugs darted about; the tadpoles banged their noses against the glass, their short tails waved about in the green water. The largest one had small legs hanging loosely near its tail.

"That one's got legs."

"Great, maybe he'll grow up in the aquarium?"

"I'll bet that snake remembers you from last year when you caught him and kept him in that box for a week."

"Snakes don't remember."

"They do too, and I'll bet he was trying to teach you a lesson. I think he did."

The boys settled into the warm sand, Howie pulled out the other sandwich and began to twist off the lid of the jar. The sun stood high overhead, the mid-day heat was rising.

The second sound the boys heard was the pounding of sharp hooves on dry sand; the first was the crack of a rifle. The ground shook, ripples slid across the glassy surface of the pond. Howie saw the buck in the mirror of the water just before he put his hand to his brow and looked up to see the buck's huge head and antlers eclipse the sun, throwing a dark shadow across the boys on the margin of the green water. Great sprays of blood from the dying stag's muzzle misted the air. Rearing on its hind legs, trying with all its might to fly across the pond, to escape the pain and the fear, it snorted a death rattle then tumbled, crown over hindquarters, down the slope into the pond, half in-half out. The green water turned to red from the blood pumping from the crisp hole in its side. The blood stopped when his heart stopped.

"Grab your gear," Howie yelled at his brother. "Now!"

They stuffed their Mason jars full of tadpoles and what was left of their lunch back into the rucksack. They climbed the sandy slope to the top of the bowl; Howie took one last look at the ravaged kingdom and the dead stag, quickly turned, and searched the maple and scrub pine.

"Nobody yet, but he'll be here soon. Fucking poacher," Howie said softly to his brother.

"Where?"

"Into the woods, there," Howie pointed. "Then the trail up to the farm. Have to tell Gramps."

They dove headlong into the bracken, kept low and ran as quickly as possible toward the trail.

"This ain't hunting season," Bill said while gulping air.

"No it's not, must be a poacher," Howie answered. "He's not supposed to hunt till winter. This is not good."

The boys kept wide of the trail till it ramped up toward the orchard, then after joining the trail, they ran through the orchard, to the barn, and then to the farmhouse. Liz was on the porch with Anne.

"Slow down boys, what's the hurry?" Liz grabbed Bill by the arm.

"Hunter in the woods, shot the big stag, almost fell on us," Bill blurted out almost in tears now. "Fell into the pond, we got out fast."

"Charlie," Liz yelled. "Get out here quick."

Anne had both boys under her arms. Charlie almost ran through the screen door; after years of living together he knew the signs. Liz never yelled unless there was a problem, a serious problem.

"We have a poacher below, killed that big buck, almost hurt the boys. Get Roger and take a look, probably long gone, but see if you can find out who it was," Liz said.

Charlie walked back into the house and shortly returned; his 30-30 under one arm and his holster and pistol cinched around his waist. Liz looked at him and didn't say a word. Anne pulled the boys closer, Bill was crying.

"Can I go Gramps?" asked Howie, mustering up courage.

"Not this time, boy. Roger and I will go take a look and be back in an hour or so. Liz, call Tom Eller at Fish and Game and let him know what happened."

Charlie headed out toward the barn just as Roger opened the big doors and walked outside. They talked; Roger went back into the barn, then came back out, a holster cinched about his waist. He took the rifle from Charlie as two men rounded the corner of the barn and disappeared.

Liz went inside to make the call.

"You boys' alright?" Anne asked.

"Yes ma'am, we're okay but it scared us," said Bill in all earnest, between sobs.

Anne looked the boys over, especially Howie. "What happened to you? You look soaked."

"Not too bad, Mom," Howie answered.

"He fell into the pond when a giant snake attacked him, just before the big deer fell into the pond," Bill said, filling in the details, calming a bit seeing that he had a chance to make fun of his older brother.

"Snake?" Anne asked.

"Yes ma'am, huge water moccasin," Howie said.

"I doubt that, boy, none around here. Maybe it was that ten foot long anaconda that's been seen around these parts," Liz said. She'd been standing behind the screen and just had to add the part about the anaconda. She was still rattled but the diversion was also working its magic.

"Where Grandma, what anaconda?" asked Bill.

"Just kidding Bill, nothing that big around here except old garter snakes. Howie go hose yourself down and strip off your wet clothes. Go change and we'll see about getting that jar full of bugs into the aquarium. Bill, while Howie's cleaning up, we'll go find that aquarium." Liz led Bill, holding the jar, into the house.

Anne watched her oldest walk to the hose and take off his shirt, and, as she watched him hose himself down, she could see that her boy was turning into a young man. The muscles in his back were beginning to show and there was the faintest, yet true, sign of the boy coming of age. The sun glistened off his shoulders and back, his blond hair, even with the summer sun, had started to turn dark underneath. When he turned and his arm was hidden, he looked whole, perfect, magnificent, a young Adonis. He stripped to his skivvies, and, for the first time, turned to his mother. She felt embarrassed by his near nakedness.

"Mom, for God's sake, turn around, I'm not a kid anymore." Howie's shoulders blushed.

"Yes, dear. I'll go get you a towel and some shorts. I'll be right back." She laughed to herself, *"Yes, he's becoming a man."*

Anne returned and pitched the towel and shorts to Howie. After a quick rub down, he slid on the shorts over his wet underpants.

"You going to change those aren't you, Howard?" Anne said.

"Yes ma'am, later. I am getting used to wet underwear." Howie cracked a smile and toweled out his shaggy head of blond hair.

"Are you okay? Did you see anything else after the buck tumbled into the pond?" She took the towel from the boy and handed him the tee shirt.

"No, mother, I grabbed our gear and then took Bill by the arm and we climbed up and out of the pond. It was awful. Why would someone kill that buck? We saw him earlier in the morning and he looked so grand. Why kill him?" Howie was almost in tears as the morning replayed itself in his mind.

"You did good getting your brother out of there; you did a good thing. The buck was shot for food maybe, maybe for his rack. I saw him last year and it would be worth a lot to a collector, but it's still wrong. That's why there's a hunting season and why Fish and Game controls these things. But you two are safe and my bet is that the fellow saw you two leap out of the hole and it scared him as well. He won't be back around here for a long time. I'm glad you two are safe." Anne pulled her oldest to her breast and held him tight. What she told him was a half-truth, she was afraid that he would be back; they would keep their eyes and ears open for a few days, but she hoped that what she told Howie was true. He wouldn't be back.

"Grandma and Bill say you got some good tadpoles, that's great," she said changing the subject. "Bill is still laughing at the snake in the pond; he keeps telling Grandma that it was a ten foot long water moccasin. There are no water moccasins up here, not one foot long or ten feet long, and you know that."

"Yes ma'am, I know," Howie said. "But it did scare me; and I lost my balance and fell in up to my neck. Just after I waded out, we heard the gunshot and then the deer fell into the pond. I pulled Bill out as fast as I could and we got out of there. Poor buck, he was so beautiful and then to see him die like that was just wrong."

"Yes Howie, it was very wrong," Anne said. "Fish and Game said someone would be out in an hour or so. Hopefully Charlie and Roger will be back by then."

Howie stood up from the chair and headed toward the screen door. Bill burst out as he reached for the handle.

"They are all alive, even the bugs," Bill said. "Come and take a look. You have to look now."

"Okay, I'm coming," Howie answered.

Howie followed Bill; the door slammed behind them. Anne watched him disappear. *"God damned poacher,"* she thought to herself. He had no right to even be on this farm, let alone kill its animals;

that bullet could have hurt one of her boys. She stood and turned toward the orchard, shaking with fear and anger. She knew her fears were, for the most part, unfounded. There were always poachers around and until the canneries got into full production, there were enough gun toting unemployed in the area to form a small army. They stayed to themselves but they occasionally did something stupid, like this, to remind everyone they were still out there.

She gathered up Howie's wet clothes and felt a damp bundle in his shirt pocket. She knew they were cigarettes, probably one of the missing packs Charlie mentioned. She smiled but also promised herself she would talk to Howie about it and make sure he paid for them. She dumped the pile of clothes on the chair next to the screen door, took out the pack, squeezed out some water and tossed the pack into the small trash bin near the door. Then she sat back in one of the chairs, took one of Charlie's cigarettes, lit it and inhaled. She seldom smoked but smoked often enough to enjoy the sudden shot of nicotine. Smoking relaxed her; she took another long pull and then crushed the cigarette into the ashtray. The door screeched open and Liz stepped out.

"The boys are fine, Anne. No harm but it's scary," Liz said. "The aquarium is full of big tadpoles, hellgrammites, and may fly larvae. They will be there for an hour setting it up just right."

"Thanks Liz. Yes, I know they'll be fine and the son-of-a-bitch is gone but it really pisses me off. Who the hell does he think he is?"

"Maybe a man with a family, maybe a man who hasn't had a meal for a week," Liz said.

"Maybe a bounty hunter who doesn't care what could happen to a couple of kids," Anne argued.

Anne and Liz sat on the porch for an hour, only a few words were exchanged. Both watched the corner of the barn, hoping to be the first to see the men return. They saw Roger first, then Charlie. There was purpose to their gait as they waved to the women.

A green pickup truck with an emblem painted on its door pulled in behind the two men as they walked up to the women. A tall young man, dressed in a dark green uniform, placed a broad brimmed campaign style hat on his close-cropped hair, and joined the group.

"Hi Tom," Charlie said. "Thanks for coming out so quickly. Anne, this is Tom Eller, the county's only fish and game warden."

"Glad to see you again, "Anne said. "Thanks for coming so soon. Doug and I met Tom a few years ago at the church hall." She smiled; he tipped his hat to her and Liz.

Eller had taken Liz's call and was able to get over to their side of the county in less than an hour.

"Liz said there might be a poacher down along the lake. What did you find?" Tom said after seeing that men were armed.

"Definitely a poacher's kill, meat my guess," Charlie said. "There's a small pond below the bluff, half-way to the lake; natural watering hole. My two grandsons were playing there when the stag, a big ten to twelve pointer, headed toward the pond to drink, tracks were easy to follow. When he reached the edge he was shot, and, from the looks of it, fell into the pond and scared the boys half to death. They got the hell out of there and hightailed it back here. Maybe the poacher saw them climb out, I don't know," Charlie said as he lit a cigarette.

"The feller climbed down to the pond, left huge footprints, and, from the amount of blood, cut the stag's throat," Charlie said. "The buck may have been alive, couldn't tell, at least he didn't try to gut it before it was dead. Knew what he was doing; dragged that buck up out of the pond and field dressed it quickly. The offal was left in a pile. He carried it down to the old cabin road near the lake, very efficient, very clean, no amateur. Plus, he was a big boy, Roger wears an eleven and this guy's boots were easily fourteens or fifteens. No tire marks but we followed his tracks to the road. Son-of-a-bitch carried that buck out, deer must have weighed at least two-hundred pounds. Whoever he was, he was a very big man. Only one set of tracks."

"Same damn thing happened about two months ago near Torch Lake. No kids involved except for one very surprised school teacher on an early morning walk," Eller said.

"Tom, why don't you follow me out, we'll drive the cabin road, and I'll show you the spot," Roger said.

"Thanks," answered Eller.

As Roger and Tom Eller turned toward the trucks, a redressed Howie opened the door.

"Is this one of the boys?" asked Eller.

"Yes Tom, my eldest," answered Anne. "Howard, this is Mr. Eller, he's the game warden with the Fish and Game Department."

"Good afternoon, sir," Howie said. The uniform dazzled and impressed him. "You gonna arrest the guy who killed the buck, sir?"

"Hope to, Howard, I really hope to. If not today, soon," Eller said.

"Good. He's one no good son-of-a-bitch," Howie said.

"Howard Smith, you watch your mouth," Anne said.

"Sorry Mom, but it was so wrong and I am so mad. I'm sorry. Please catch him, sir." Howie looked at Eller, tears filled his eyes.

"We will son, we will. You ready, Roger?" Eller asked.

Roger headed toward the barn; Tom tipped his hat to the ladies, shook the men's hands, walked over to his truck and waited until Roger rounded the barn. He followed him down the road to the state highway.

It was quiet for a few minutes, and then Howie asked, "Bonfire tonight, Grandpa?"

"Probably not," Charlie said. "But after this cold front passes, maybe tomorrow. Then your dad will be here, he's going to be too tired tonight after the drive up anyway. Some clouds building up, good bet that fronts on its way. I'm going to put the carburetor on the pump. Do you want to come along?" Charlie asked.

"Yes sir," Howie answered, his disappointment dampened.

"Liz, would you call Gus in Traverse and tell him I'll make it later in the week, too late to go into town now," Charlie said.

She said she would immediately and the two women watched them leave.

"Anne, Tom's a good warden, caught that sturgeon poacher last winter and has been a friend of Roger's since they were kids. Doug also went to school with Tom's older brother; he's maybe seven or eight years younger than Douglas," Liz said.

"Liz, it's a small world up here, isn't it?" Anne said. "Strangers stand out; he'll find the guy."

"Good chance, but not certain. Could be from over toward Gaylord or Grayling; probably used a spotlight during the last few nights to shine 'em; then tracked him this morning. Too bad the boys were there. Anne, it's a part of life up here but I still don't like it. Some families think it's like it was twenty-five years ago. Then they hunted to fill their bellies. You were too young, but everyone was touched by the bad times. For some, they were too proud to ask for help, others were too ignorant. My guess is this guy was from the ignorant group. There're still places inland that don't have electricity. Tough living, but they don't know anything different."

"Yes, I know. I have a cousin somewhere out in the plains area. They say he has some kids and an Indian wife. His family hasn't seen him in ten years. It's just the way it is up here. It's not just two hundred and fifty miles from Chicago; it's a hundred years as well."

Charlie asked for the small screwdriver sitting on the end of the bench. Nervous, Howie's cigarette stash was not more than five inches from Charlie's tough hands which were adjusting the carburetor. Howie suddenly remembered the pack in his shirt; *"I need get it before Mom does,"* he thought.

"There, that should do it. Howie get me that gas can." Charlie pointed to the red can with the bent spout.

He slowly filled the tank mounted on the frame of the trailer. "Still low, but enough to see how it works."

Charlie pulled the starter cord. On the third pull, the engine popped and a white puff of smoke shot from the muffler. Charlie adjusted the choke and pulled again. The engine roared. He adjusted the throttle cable and the needle valve. The engine quieted to a full-throated rumble; Charlie threaded on the black rubber hose to the hose bib on the tank.

"Howie, I rinsed the tank this morning, just water in it. Want to give it a try?"

"Sure Gramps."

Howie climbed up on the tractor and Charlie slid into the single seat. The tractor shook to life and Charlie backed the tractor and sprayer out into the yard. He engaged the sprayer; the arms at the rear began rocking back and forth and up and down. He pointed to the lever mounted on the tank and Howie pulled it toward high. Instantly a fine mist exploded from the nozzles mounted on the ends of the arms. Charlie climbed down and stood behind the rig, a watery mist covered everything.

"Push in the lever, boy," Charlie yelled.

Howie pushed and the water stopped.

"Disengage the sprayer," he yelled again.

Howie pulled the lever on the tractor and the flailing arms stopped. Charlie climbed off the rig and adjusted three of the nozzles.

"Engage 'em, boy."

Howie pushed the first lever and then pulled the second. A fine mist engulfed the rear of the sprayer.

"Great, turn everything off."

Again Howie pushed and pulled; the sprayer stopped.

"Cut the tractor," Charlie said walking up to the side of one of the five-foot high tires. Howie pushed the starter in, the engine stopped.

"Runs great, I'll pull her in and disconnect the sprayer. It's all ready for Roger."

Charlie and Howie pushed the two large doors together after they pulled the tractor out of the barn.

"What the fuck was all the commotion, Charlie? I saw you and Roger come up from down below, toting pistols and a rifle." Frank Rex's voice carried over the sudden silence.

"Poacher below; killed that big stud stag. Almost fell on the two boys, they were in the pond," Charlie said.

"Fucking asshole," Frank said. "Thought I heard a rifle shot early this morning; hear them all the time, but this time sounded close. You okay, boy?"

"Yes sir, but it was a son-of-a-bitch."

Charlie lightly cuffed Howie on the back of the head. "That was from your mother." Charlie smiled at Howie.

Howie looked up and returned the smile.

"Watched that fellow for over ten years; he was one wily son-of-a-bitch. Caught off guard or getting old. Who knows? Probably every doe and young buck around here is his. Damn, he was a handsome animal," Frank said.

"I was standing in the water netting tadpoles, and the deer fell down the slope almost on top of me; got out of there fast. Grandpa and Roger went down to find him, but he was gone," Howie said.

"Bill alright?"

"Yes sir and we saved all the tadpoles too." Howie smiled at his small victory.

"Good boy,"

The three walked back to the house. Frank seemed in a better mood than yesterday, his step lighter.

After a late lunch Howie took a long nap along with his brother. The heat was building; Liz put a small fan in their bedroom to cool them. He woke long enough to hear Tom Eller's voice in the downstairs foyer. He drifted off and dreamed of the buck in the clearing and the bright sun in his eyes.

Bill and Howie were lying on the lawn when the Ford sedan pulled in next to the station wagon. An angular yet large chested man, medium height, with hair the color of beach sand, stood next to the car. His dark horn-rimmed sunglasses shrouded his eyes; he gave a noticeable sigh and straightened his back, fists to hips. He scanned the farm and orchard to see if all was in place and looked right.

"Dad," they both yelled, and ran to their father. Bill grabbed his waist and Howie slipped his deformed arm through his strong, sunburnt, left arm. Doug Smith rubbed each blond head, hard.

"Anything exciting happened up here since I saw you last?" Howie put his finger to his lips and looked at Bill. Bill smiled back and nodded.

"What's the secret?" asked Doug.

"Nothing much, get Dad's bag."

"No, you get it," Bill answered.

"Bill," Howie said, trying to reestablish Bill's place.

"O....kay," Bill released his arm and walked back to the car.

They waited as Bill pulled the small leather valise from the rear seat.

"Hot trip boys, good to be here. Cooler up here; Chicago is a scorcher. Had all the windows open for the whole trip. I can stay till

Monday and then back to work. Where's your mother?"

"Inside with Grams," answered Howie.

The boys sat expectantly on the porch; the only words they heard were a loud "God damn son-of-a-bitch," which flew out the window and disappeared into the pines behind the house.

Doug sat down between the two boys and pulled them close.

"You two all right?" he asked, looking them each in the eye. "You act like it."

"Yes sir, we're tough, like Gramps," offered Bill. His tone was as defiant as only a nine-year old's could be.

"Good stock," Doug said.

Anne stood in the doorway; the screen softened her shape. Doug smiled.

"While you fellows were taking a nap, your grandmother tells me that the Fish and Game warden stopped by to tell her they think they caught the fellow," Doug said, seeing his mother standing next to Anne. "Seems a fellow was driving a little too fast on the road between Williamsburg and Kalkaska. When the state troopers pulled him over they found the buck in the back of his truck. Everything points to him being the poacher, a big guy, really big. Lives out in the pine barrens, has a wife and a couple of kids, needed the buck for food was all he said. Said the rack might bring him thirty bucks from some trophy shop. Desperate man and his family, lot of that going around up here, right Mom?"

"Yes son, too much of it; too much desperation, too much ignorance, too much fear."

The afternoon heat pushed the youngest two out of the house, off the porch and into the pear tree's shade. Bill and Howie hung close to their father. Their parents talked about the farm, the cherries, Eve, and the poacher. After a while, Liz and Charlie joined them.

"How's Frank doing?" Doug asked.

"Better, the medicine seems to help knock down the pain," answered Anne.

"Yes, but he complains it hurts his painting. The Spaniard says the pain forces him to concentrate on the painting, pushes him. He's doing more religious work now." Liz said. She had called him the

Spaniard since they were children.

Liz and Frank were raised in Elk River during the summer and in Chicago and Paris and New York and Madrid and a hundred other places around the world during the rest of the year. Their father, Jamison William Rex, built the largest distribution system for freight and grain in the Midwest and then opened auto and truck dealerships in Chicago and Gary, Indiana. In 1907, he built a vacation home in Elk River where Elizabeth Ann Rex and Franklin Adam Rex grew up when not traveling or in private school.

Jamison Rex was an attentive father, far better than what was fashionable of men with money. Julie Elizabeth Randolf Rex, their aloof cold mother, was the product of more Chicago money, slaughterhouse cattle. During her young life, before Jamison Rex and a comfortably arranged and socially correct marriage, the only real cow she had ever seen was at the end of a silver dinner fork.

Franklin loved Spain and worked hard on his craft in the dry hills above Madrid; he also realized his talent fell short of his desire, but he could paint well enough to live by selling his paintings to churches; he also sold an occasional portrait to anyone who was so inclined. He demanded little of the world, but he was a son-of-a-bitch when he was drunk or after the bull fights in Barcelona. Thirty years earlier, he got drunk with a raw, but talented, writer in a small cantina in the shadow of the Plaza de las Arenas bullring. There they fought off the local guardia with fists and chairs till they were clubbed senseless. Frank still carried a small scar on his forehead as a reminder and he still saw the writer when he came to the family properties in Northern Michigan, and, once in a while in Spain, but the man was spending most of his time in the west these days. His ocean of friends was larger and deeper than the small and introverted pond of Franklin Rex.

Elizabeth spent her teenage years in the St. Agnes School for Girls on the west side of Chicago; a very elite austere boarding school for rich Catholic young ladies; a place where, if God had a conscience, he would have assigned every nun to the lowest ring of hell. Education by writ was paramount; every infraction resulted in a sharp crack to the palms, shoulders, or feet. No blemish to the visible portions was acceptable, especially by the parents who, at times, seemed in abject collusion. She maintained a proper demeanor and avoided much of the discipline. Others, especially those of less means or influence, were not so fortunate.

The six years she spent at St. Agnes were tempered by the summers in Paris and Vienna with her brother. She still could not look at a nun, even today after forty-three years, without catching a chill or flinching. She also danced, small school revues and summer theater. Her long legs, bright skin and talent quickly led to New York and a fling with the Ziegfeld Follies, where, after a year, she had had enough. She spent more and more time at the home in Elk River and married the divorced Charles Owens Smith, a church annulment made it acceptable. After the marriage, they stayed on the farm and raised their boys. Europe was now just a dream, two wars had destroyed much of the wonder that the old country held for her.

Frank went back to Spain and Barcelona every October. First he took a long train ride to New York and then a steamer to Spain. He seldom went to France or Italy, except to visit friends. He painted every day in the warm sun and cold rain. He drank Oloroso sherry, ate seafood and lived an intense and creative life with friends visiting from Paris and Madrid. They were friends that no one in Michigan was even aware of, companions and partners that never came to Michigan. He explained his habits as personally calmative and he justified everything to himself and his confessor, a wizened old priest of the small roughhewn church he attended. The priest told him to say a rosary and pray for his own salvation. God's salvation would be the cancer growing in his gut.

Bill and Howie slid off the slider and headed toward the barn. Liz and Anne had left the porch a few minutes earlier and headed for the kitchen to start dinner. Doug sat next to Charlie, sipped his scotch and then lit another cigarette.

"Dad, what the hell happened down below? The boys could've been shot."

"Not likely," Charlie said. "The fellow was a good shot and probably knew the boys were there; he'd been stalking that buck all morning. He knew what he was doing and was efficient too. Takes me an hour to dress out a deer and he was done in twenty minutes. Damn good. Then he hauled that buck out on his back. Son-of-a-bitch was big, shoes were at least size fourteens or so, bigger than Roger's by an inch. I don't like some fool coming in here and shooting up my farm, especially during summer, too many people about, too damn dangerous. Eller said the fellow's method was similar to a couple of others north of here. Glad they caught the poor son-of-a-bitch, still a damn shame to lose that stag."

Doug took a deep drag. "Boys are okay, that's good," he said. "But they certainly saw something they wouldn't see in Chicago. Not too often a big buck falls dead in your lap in Park Forest."

Doug grew up on the farm and had the reasoning and rationality of a farmer and a woodsman. Well educated and well read, Liz made sure his studies included the hundreds of books lining the walls of the living room, from Hemingway to Omar Kayam, from Dylan Thomas to Fitzgerald. He also fought his way across Europe to finish the war in the woods a hundred miles from Berlin. But his soul was split between the world and the farm. His family had to eat.

He earned his journalism degree from Michigan State College on the GI Bill and found a decent job at the Chicago *Tribune* as a junior copy editor and now, six years later, was a feature editor. The only injuries he received during the war was a nick and a foot infection, while his older brother and ten of his friends lay buried in cemeteries in France, Belgium and Germany. Outside in public's eye, he seemed immune to the effects of the war, solid and implacable. Yet, some nights, Anne would wake him when his screams got too loud.

"The boys'll be alright," Charlie said. "They'll take it in stride and, with everything happening in the world today, they're going to have to learn to deal with change. Who knows what America will look like in ten years?"

Jamison Rex died in 1934, from a fast spreading cancer that took the man in less than six weeks. He survived the bank collapses and economic upheavals of the early thirties, but he couldn't survive the cancer that ate him alive. During the decade before he died, he put money away for his two children who were well on their own with careers and children. He didn't trust banks; he put what monies he could scrape together into property and hard assets. He bought half the buildings on River Street in Elk River, beachfront lots on Torch Lake and Lake Michigan and saw the future in canning in this part of northern Michigan. He leased the land which the current factory sat on to the cannery, but he would not sell those properties while he was still alive; he saved them for his children. But everything else that brought him his wealth withered away; the banks that he hated—killed him.

After his death, the income from the properties dribbled in, at least when the tenants had money to pay the rent. It allowed Charlie and Liz to weather the vagaries of the cherries and allowed Frank the time to paint. The rental income and the meager farm receipts paid for Jim and Doug's education and Eve's medical bills, she was Charlie's responsibility. The poor crop of two years ago and Frank's cancer forced them to sell a few of the Torch Lake lots. Other properties would also be sold, if buyers could be found. The cannery properties were sold during the war.

"Good days down south," offered Doug. "Businesses are expanding, families everywhere, kids everywhere; can't seem to build enough schools. The paper's ad revenues are just rolling in the dough. It's amazing that it hasn't worked its way north. But I'm frazzled most of the time, and, with traveling to and from downtown, I don't see the boys as much as I want. But the craziness now with Eisenhower being sick, the Russians beating their chests, and the English and French running in circles trying to save what's left of their empires, everyone in Chicago is on edge."

"Maybe crazy down there, but still tough on those who work up here," Charlie said. "Those with jobs down south in Detroit and Chicago, they do okay, they send money up, but when winter comes and its only us locals, it's tough, real tough. They found old Mrs. Tyson, you know she lives out on Ford Road, found her frozen to death. No one saw her for two weeks, her son in L.A. called Eller and asked him to stop and take a look; you know she still hadn't put a phone in; Eller found her asleep in bed, only she was dead. Froze, according to the coroner in Traverse, she had no heat, no coal, nothing, was too proud to ask."

"I remember her from when I was a kid. Her boy was older, I think, went to Los Angeles before the war; a real piece of work. Never came back home?"

"Don't know. If he did, never saw him. Eller said she looked peaceful, but still a harsh lonely way to die; alone, in the cold."

The damp heat pushed the men deeper into the shade of the pear. The ice in their glasses had melted away an hour before. Cigarette butts were crushed into the ashtray, three a piece.

"What's the paper think about Eisenhower; is he sick or did he have another heart attack?" Charlie asked Doug.

"The fellows in the newsroom say it's something in his gut, obstruction or something, not another heart attack. He's getting better but it's slow, but that man pushed us across Europe, he's one helluva soldier. It's Egypt, the Suez Canal, the Russians and Israel that have got them all in a frazzle. Not seen such tension since the end of the war and the creation of Israel; some of the more pessimistic writers think this could lead to another world war. Don't know if we can handle another war, Dad; not the kind this would be."

"The world's tired of war. The war that might come next is too horrific to think about," Charlie said. "It would be a war with no refugees, Hiroshima showed the world that. We're safe up here, who the hell would bomb this part of America, but the cities, there's where the fear is."

"And it's a great fear, a deep in the heart fear; it's the kind you can't run away from. We can only trust in Eisenhower, and pray for his health.

"Go get the boys, dinners almost ready," a soft voice called out from behind the screen.

"Yes, Mom." Douglas William Smith stood and headed to the barn to find out what the boys were up to.

CHAPTER THREE

Howie woke with a start. Another flash lit the room like an exploding flash bulb. He counted the seconds, one-thousand one, one-thousand two, one-thousand three and then the concussion of the lightning bolt shattered the air and thunder shook the house.

"Damn, that was close," he said to himself.

Another flash, a two second wait, then another full-throated deep in the pines report shook the bed that he and his brother shared, and the attack began. Howie loved these storms; it seemed like the lightening at the farm sparked more brilliantly and brighter and the thunder seemed bigger and deeper than that of the Chicago storms that blew in from the Midwestern plains. Something about the lake and the radical changes in temperatures from water to land pushed the storms higher and bolder than in Chicago.

Another explosion, then another, and another, all rolling into the first; the detonations bursting almost instantaneously, shook the farm again. Bill sat up, hidden in the intermittent blackness, but with each flash, he sat frozen, outlined, and defined in lingering time on a canvas in Howie's mind, where Bill's eyes, wide, unblinking, stared at him.

"Howie, that one was real fucking close." Bill reached out and took his older brother's hand.

"Don't talk like that; if grandma were to hear you she would give you a *klip-she-klop-sha*." Liz had threatened this ancestral punishment for as long as Howie could remember, but he had never received the dreaded blow. So it had grown into this omnipresent punishment for every infraction of the rules and bylaws of the farm. He hoped he would never find out what the extent of this punishment really was.

"She wouldn't do that," pleaded Bill. "She might whack me on the head but not a *klip-she-klop-sha*."

The room lit up like morning brightness and Howie could see the punishment caused no real fear in his brother who sat grinning in the dark.

"Damn straight she would," the rest was drowned out by the roar of thunder which shook the glass in the windows.

A fresh cool breeze, sharp with electricity, flooded the room through the open window. Another burst, its sound a ten second beat by Bill's count, announced the storm had moved east. The next flash, like a light in a far-away room being clicked on and off, caused no sound to count and left only the ghostly image of splattered rain on glass. Through the open door, a moving bright beam of light flicked off the walls of the staircase and poked its head into the room. Bill and Howie slid down into the bed and watched their grandfather walk into the room carrying a flashlight.

"I know you boys are either awake or dead, no in between. That one strike must have hit the old silo. I'm going to shut the windows, you fellows go back to sleep. If it rains enough maybe we can have that bonfire tomorrow."

"Great," answered Howie from beneath the sheet.

"Neat-o," Bill added.

"Good, you aren't dead, go back to sleep." Charlie shut the windows; the distant thunder muffled by the slashing rain against the window panes and the shingled roof. The boys laid in the dark and even the anticipation and excitement of the next day could not keep them awake.

Howie swung his legs out onto the wooden floor and saw that Bill was missing. He dressed quickly and softly climbed down the stairs to the hallway outside the kitchen and heard and smelled the familiar crackle of bacon, the aromas of coffee and early tobacco. Pushing the swinging door open, a shaft of sunlight lit him up like an actor on a dark stage. He squinted and the shape of his father, grandfather, and brother formed out of the glare.

"Good morning, boy," Charlie said. "Coffee?"

"No sir, never touch the stuff," Howie answered.

Howie answered this same question, the same way, for years. One day, he would answer, "Yes sir, black, no sugar." But that would be a few years from now, he was sure of it, till then, it would be orange juice and milk.

Bill sat on the stool at the end of the table, Doug stood behind him.

"Quite a storm," Doug said.

"Yes sir, bolted right up when that big one hit," answered Howie.

"Hit the silo like I said," Charlie said. "Believe it or not, it knocked a few concrete blocks out of the top. The lightening rod did the best it could though."

"Let's go take a look," said Howie.

Bill slid off his seat and the two headed out into the damp morning. Just as Charlie said, five large chunks of concrete block sat next to the base of the silo. Heavy black soot covered one side where the paint had been burned by the lightening.

"Can you believe this?" Howie asked, as he took his finger and dragged it across the carbonized paint, then took the tip of his finger and slid it down the length of Bill's nose. Bill dragged his fingers across the carbon and drew horizontal lines under both of Howie's eyes.

"You look like an Indian," Bill said.

"How, paleface." Howie held up his hand, palm out, in salute.

Bill put two stripes on each cheek and a long stripe from his forehead to the spot Howie put on his nose.

"Call me Chief Thunderbolt," Bill announced, arms crossed.

"Yes Chief. Big chief want-um breakfast," asked Howie.

Ugh, Chief want-um big breakfast," answered Bill. The two turned back to the house, and, in their best Indian ceremonial toe tapping and bouncing, marched back to the kitchen.

They wore their war paint the rest of the morning and added a few more markings to their chests and arms, no shirts would be worn by these two braves. Anne said that any use of house towels as loincloths was forbidden, but shorts were once worn by a tribe near Mesick so that was their native garb till noon when Tom Eller arrived.

Tom said the man had been released, paid a fine, but it took all his money. The judge understood, but the meat went to the state hospital. Others in the area went over to help the family; fellow hadn't worked since winter when he was hired by the county to clear the roads. His kids hadn't been to school for years.

"Too much of this going on," Eller said. "I see it everywhere outside of Traverse, hasn't changed in some of these backwoods for fifty years. I'm afraid it's going to become a real problem in a few years, the unemployment, the ignorance, and the attitudes. And with the pickers coming, it could be a problem. There's been a few fights over in Saginaw this year, one migrant was killed."

"That's going to be a problem for a lot of us. Thanks," Charlie said.

The boys asked if the woods were safe and Tom said yes, this fellow would not be back. Anne told them to stay close to the farm for a few days, stay near their father. They reluctantly agreed, but brightened when she suggested they go into town that afternoon, when he went in to see his sister. They could go to the power plant to fish while he and Charlie were at her place.

The morning dragged on for the boys, chores were limited. They spent some time in the picker's quarters clearing out old junk and waste paper. They pulled the old smelly mattresses out onto the gravel to air out.

"Who would sleep on these?" Bill asked. "They stink awful."

"They are not that bad," Howie answered, wincing at the smell. "Gramps says the worst ones will get thrown on the bonfire. Said new ones were coming this week."

The small rooms, cut from a long chicken coup used during the war for eggs, were dark and stank of kerosene. The old bedding smelled of piss and mildew. Mice lived in one of the mattresses. Bill showed Howie the hole chewed in the side.

Each room had a bed or two twin cots. Some had four mattresses with two on the floor. A low table with a two-burner kerosene stove sat on one side. Dark oily stains, like flames, ran up the wall by the stove. Sometimes a chair or two filled out the room. The curtains were old and stained. The floor was smooth but cracked concrete. A single light hung from a cord plugged into a two-plug outlet on the wall, from there the cord ran up the wall to a hook, then it traveled in an arc to a short link chain which hung from the rafter where it turned straight down from another hook at the end of a chain; the light turned on and off with a cotton cord attached to a beaded metal chain that draped over the incandescent bulb, so it wouldn't burn; it was screwed into the socket at the end of the cord.

The walls were gray in some rooms and green in the others. Newspapers were strewn about, all in Spanish. Some were stuffed into small holes that were chewed by mice in the walls or from knotholes in the panels. No bathrooms inside. The pickers used a pair of communal outhouses which sat at the end of the row of doors. One said Señor and the other, Señora.

Howie liked to poke about the rooms. To him they were exotic and strange. The smells were so different than anything he would find at home. He never associated the rooms with the people who would live here a few months while they picked cherries.

Last year, after the pickers left, Howie found a girly magazine under one of the beds. The girls on the glossy pages had dark eyes and long black hair, black bras and underwear. He didn't understand the stories, everything was in Spanish. Howie stashed the magazine under the workbench near his cigarettes; it was gone in the spring. He still wondered where it went. Nothing was said by his grandfather or **Roger**.

The boys swept out two of the rooms before their father stuck his head around the corner of the doorway.

"Great job, men," Doug said. "Looks as good as can be expected.

The Martinez family will thank you for doing this, even though Mrs. Martinez will give the place a good cleaning when they arrive. The apple pickers really left it a mess. Mrs. Martinez will not be happy."

"Bonfire?" Bill asked.

"Your grandfather thinks it is exactly what we need," Doug said. "Roger and Lisa will be here and I think Uncle Frank is feeling better today so I expect he'll also be coming. The Claytons from across the road said they can make it too. It'll certainly be fun and we can all use that."

They ate lunch outside on the big farm table: fried chicken, succotash from the big freezer, potato salad and fresh dandelion greens, eight strong, three and four to each side with Charlie at the head. The talk was of cherries, green apples, the weather and the poacher.

"You boys go and get your gear, we're leaving in fifteen minutes," Doug announced after lunch. Howie and Bill raced to the small storeroom which sat at the back of the kitchen; it had its own outside door. They collected their rods and the one shared tackle box, an old dark green army surplus ammo box Charlie had given them. They loaded the gear in the back of the station wagon. Doug and Charlie stepped out of the kitchen; Charlie carried a small wooden box well known to the boys.

"Got these worms from the kitchen bed. Big ones, should do well this afternoon," Charlie said.

Howie lifted the lid, and, in amongst the damp peat moss, finger-sized red worms, hundreds it looked like, squirmed in a wriggling mass. Howie beamed.

"We're gonna knock 'em dead," Howie said.

"Lem'me see," Bill said.

Howie watched his brother push his finger into the red ball of moving string.

"Great," Bill added, passing the final verdict.

The drive took ten minutes but the clock turned back twenty years. It may have been 1956 at the farm but Elk River looked the same as it did before the war; old pre-1940 Fords and Dodges parked along the street completed the time shift. New homes had been built around the town but nothing had changed the look of River Street. A collection of turn-of-the-century wood and concrete buildings lined each side for three blocks, some with colorful awnings, some with balconies, and some with bright neon signs; concrete sidewalks were the only change, before the war they were wooden planks.

Three hairdressers, one barber, one hardware store, one pharmacy and soda shop, one grocer, and one mercantile store stood on one side of River Street and four bars, two attorney's offices, and one bank stood on the other. Eve lived above the bar next to the bank, the normal compliment of layabouts sat in chairs under the bar window. A single set of stairs climbed from a small parking lot behind the bar to a lone east-facing door.

The two men climbed the stairs, the boys followed. Their lack of interest was obvious. The door opened before they reached the landing.

Eve Titus stood in the open doorway; half-in and half-out, a faded flower dress hung from her shoulders and added nothing to her slight frame. Her eyes and face were vacant. Doug shuddered; he had seen this look in the faces of men in the war, a look which said, "I give up. I don't give a fuck and I don't care."

"Well if it's not Daddy and little baby brother, Dougie," Eve said. She looked down the stairway. "They," she pointed, "are not coming in, are they?"

"Calm down, Eve," Charlie said softly. "The boys are going fishing. You two can go now after you say hello."

"Good afternoon Aunt Eve," they said in unison.

"Fuck you," she said. "Get the hell out of here."

"That's enough, Eve," Charlie cut her off.

The boys turned and bolted down the stairs to the station wagon, pulled out their gear, ran around the corner of the building, stopped, and grabbed a breath of air; then broke into laughter. Puffing themselves up they walked across River Street, down Falls Street to the dark red brick building which blocked the end of the street. Falls Street, fifty years earlier, dead-ended at a small but spectacular series of waterfalls where the powerhouse now stood. No one wanted to change the name of the street to Powerhouse Street or Avenue or Alley, so Falls Street no longer led to the waterfalls.

The powerhouse straddled the town's namesake river. The water was twelve feet lower on the Lake Michigan side. The lake, created by the power plant, flooded over two thousand acres of stumps and debris left over from the pine logging of fifty years ago.

The town sat on a slight bluff above the power plant. Remnants of sand dunes separated the town from the river; most were covered with a particularly tough grass that waved in the breezes that blew in from the lake. The cascades forced the trappers and hunters to portage their gear to the higher lake. A pine cabin had sat here, guarding the portage, for over one-hundred years. The cabin became a bar, then a store, then a fire took them both just after the Civil War, but by then the disparate town of Elk River began to spread up the dunes.

A lumber mill once stood just upstream from the cascade and the mill owners built a dam to store the water to power the mill. The dam destroyed the cascade; the lumber helped to build Chicago. Tens of millions of board feet of pine and hemlock started their journey south at the flume into the mill. Using great rafts, the boards were towed south to build the cities of the Great Lakes.

The powerhouse, with its single turbine generator, followed the lumber mill and electrified the power hungry cannery and provided electricity to a region starving for progress. After that, the lights burned into the night and the winters seemed not as bleak.

The auburn red brick building grabbed both sides of the river and dug its roots into the dunes. Tall glass and metal windows filled the upper story of the building and provided light into the generator room. Below these windows, a concrete catwalk hung on the building's brick facing, and connected the dunes. When the plant was in full operation and there was too much water, torrents of foamy water from the generators shot out into the river from the vents under the catwalk. Today all the vents were open and the roar made conversation difficult for the phalanx of fisherman who had staked out their two feet of railing along the catwalk.

Big fish stayed in the fast current below this man-made cascade. They hung in the relative calm behind boulders and other debris that littered the river's bottom, ready to slash out at baitfish and insects stunned in their travels through the vents and the generator. Small mouth bass, rainbow trout, steelhead and even muskellunge and pike took their turns at the banquet table set by the dam. This was a place of predators and victims; lives ended in these waters.

The fishermen, young and old, and women included, arrived early to claim their spots. Some held their rods; others laid them against the rusted railing. They played out taut lines weighted with tire lead and old spark plugs, hoping to keep the bait on the bottom of the maelstrom. Red worms, night crawlers, cured roe and even swimming lures dangled and surged at the ends of their lines. The anglers stood together, disarranged like a mixed stringer of fish, their backs to the brick wall.

Bill and Howie worked their way among the fishermen to get to the far side of the river.

"This'll work. Rest your gear in among the big boulders. I'll set up the rods," Howie said.

"You want the worms?" Bill asked.

"Not yet, need to tie two hooks on this leader, you got the sparkplugs?"

"Yeah, right here." Bill handed Howie the black steel and white porcelain plugs.

Bill pulled a handful of worms from the box, selected four excellent victims and handed them to Howie. Both boys cast their baited poles, under-hand, into the current and watched the lines race out into the river before stopping and holding on the bottom. The black lines cut through the islands of grey foam churned by the generator; bigger and successively grander rafts of foam swallowed these severed chunks before they floated, like great heads of man-of-war jellyfish, out onto the glass smooth surface of Lake Michigan.

"Feel for the bottom, watch for snags," Howie said.

"Got it, I feel it bouncing. Now it's stopped, should be okay there."

Howie tightened his line and lay the rod butt down against a log lodged between two boulders and watched the tip of the rod slowly heave in and out as if transferring the river's breathing through the rod. The boys settled back into the glare of the early afternoon sunlight and felt the heat return, and, with it, the humidity.

Howie studied the fishermen along the catwalk and the far shore, most of the men wore tee shirts, some had short sleeves, others the strappy kind. The two women wore faded cotton dresses. Most wore sunglasses and a hat of some kind: felt fedoras, cotton ball caps, ragged straw hats. They stood fixated on their rods and the river and then slowly raised their eyes out to the lake, then back to their gear, again to the lake and again back to the river. No wind, not a breeze. Along the catwalk, a haze of tobacco smoke drifted about like fog, before it too, floated out toward the lake.

Fishing is the most boring way to spend your time, but that's not the point. Endless hours and dollars are spent chasing a simple Godly animal: for food, for sport, and for bragging rights. Calm and boring, then chaos, anglers always remembered the chaos. They never brag of the boredom, only the fight. Howie felt the guttural rumbling of the power plant in his belly; the catwalk fishermen felt it through their shoes. That rumbling and the incessant caw-screech of a pair of jays in the pines were the only sounds they could hear: pre-chaos time.

"Fish on," a deep raspy voice from the catwalk yelled, startling the boys. They watched as the right side of the gang, all men, spread back from a white tee shirt and a bobbing red cap.

Each picked up their rod and began to reel in their gear, clearing the river. The red-cap's rod bent into a soft arc, the tip pointed to the river, the line cleaved foam islands. The man moved down the catwalk sliding his hard belly against the steel railing to its end, then, his eyes never leaving the river, rod high, he moved onto the sandy path that paralleled the far side all the way to the lake.

"Musky," Howie said, guessing from the bend of the rod and the speed of the fish.

"Neat-o," Bill replied.

"Brown trout and steelhead would've jumped by now, maybe even a big bass. But a big snake musky will use the river and the boulders to break free. He'll pull that man downstream to the lake and the deep water. If that fellow can't stop him by the time he reaches the point, that fish will keep taking line out until there's none and then he'll be gone."

The man ran along the path to where it split; one trail went up the old dune to town, the other continued along the river. He followed the river, knowing, like Howie, that if the fish was not stopped, it would be gone.

Bill glanced back to the power plant. The company on the catwalk had reformed like the foam islands; one new face added itself to the end, as if nothing had changed. Fishing rods pointed to the sky, fishing lines, black and taught, cut into the water. Only one or two were interested in the man's battle, which, in a moment, would be out of their sight.

Red-cap waded into the river to his knees and slowly pumped the rod, reeling in as he bowed to the spot in the river that hid the fish. Waist deep, he kept gaining line. His stained shirt, now wet from the river, clung to his lean body. Howie guessed that the thin woman in the flower dress standing up the dune face was his woman. Lift, soft slow pull upward, lift again, reel fast; Howie watched his hands move quickly as he gained line before he pumped again. Even from fifty yards, Howie could see the sweat on the man's face; then he saw nothing.

Where the man and his rod once stood, now there was only a hole in the foam. Nothing, he was gone. Howie heard someone yell and three men broke free from the catwalk and began running down the trail, jumping and dodging boulders and other fishermen. Howie looked back at the hole in the foam, it had drifted fifty feet, but no one had emerged. The woman was shrieking, hands over her mouth. One man reached the spot and dove into the river. His strong strokes pulled him toward the spot where the red-cap had disappeared. A leg kick and his feet were high, then, he too disappeared. Two holes in the foam drifted toward the lake now. The other men ran down the shore hoping to catch up with both men.

A minute passed, then another as the confused boys stood and watched. The crowd on the catwalk began to break up, some running down the far side of the river, others running behind Howie and Bill to race down their side. The woman continued to wail. A head popped up in the river; it was the swimmer. The head disappeared **again.**

Howie heard a short but emphatic "Fish" and watched as Bill grabbed his rod. He had a fish on. Howie returned his eyes to the river; a group had waded out from the point and was standing in a line, almost arm to arm, where the river shoaled up. Howie thought they might be able to catch or snag the men if they were pushed into them.

"Jesus, he's huge." Bill pulled hard on his rod. It was a fish, a strong fish. A perceptible movement to the line cut through the foam. Howie stood behind his brother hoping to see what would happen to both Bill and the drama. Bill pulled again and the line seemed to lift. He pulled again and reeled, less resistance. The rod dipped with each surge of the river. He kept reeling.

"Slowly, Bill. Slowly," Howie softly said.

Across the river a group of men converged on a spot thirty feet from the shore. Two men helped a man in a blue tee shirt out of the water; the swimmer. The woman was on her knees. The line of men, which now stretched into the river, seemed to fold on itself and grab something that tumbled up to them, a body. They dragged Red-cap to the shore, two knots of men, forty yards apart, surrounded the two bodies. The swimmer's group opened and Howie could see the blue shirt sit up and push people away. He tried to stand, then settled to one knee.

Bill pulled and pulled, reeled, then pulled again, long, arm-aching, pulls. Raising the rod, he reeled as he pulled the tip back from the river; again, and again, and again he pulled.

The second group did not breakup. It held its shape centered on Red-cap. Two men broke away and ran up the dune toward town. Some from the swimmer's group moved down the river to join Red-cap's group. His gal slowly walked toward the knot of men.

Bill's fish was almost to shore. Howie noted this fish did not move to open water, just kept coming in, a few feet at a time.

"Slowly, easy, easy."

The remaining crowd stood upright as one. Two lit cigarettes; the woman walked to the river, her face in one hand, cupping her mouth, another clasped across her breasts to her shoulder. Others stood in pairs, talking. At the top of the dune, the two men reappeared with two others, a policeman and another in a white shirt and tie. Even from his side of the river, Howie could see it was Doctor Abrams.

"Almost here," Bill said.

Howie watched the knot of the leader break the surface at the same time that a chunk of cloth surfaced, red cloth. Bill pulled again and the red hat rolled and caught a piece of foam. The second hook on the leader was snagged on the top eyelet of another fishing rod.

"Careful, real careful like."

Howie waded into the shallow water and grabbed the hooked hat and the rod and reel snagged to Bill's gear, with his good hand. Bill saw the hat and sat down hard on the beach. Howie lifted the new rod, hooked it under his deformity, and felt a surge, he pulled and another surge, and he knew he held Red-hat's rod and his fish. The dead man's fish still lived. Howie pulled again, the fish slowly came to him. Again and again he pulled. The fight ebbed quickly from the exhausted fish, Howie could feel it surrender. Howie lifted the rod again and a dark green V-shaped head broke the water, and, like an island rising from the sea, the largest muskellunge the two brothers had ever seen, or ever heard of, emerged. Howie reeled a final turn and the fish's head sat beached on the sand. The fish, as long as Bill stood tall, the broad spread of its head was easily two hands wide, thumb-to-thumb; it stared at the boys with its cold eyes; only the river pushing against the giant tail of the green and gray striped fish caused movement.

"Let the fish go boys. He killed one man. He deserves his freedom." A deep sonorous voice echoed the *basso profundo* pumping of the power plant. Howie looked up to a giant of a man, full-bearded, eyes as grey as a winter's afternoon, huge boots, stained rough twill pants, open shirt and thick black hair streaked in gray.

"Push him back into the river; let him go. He won his battle. Take the hat and rod over to that girl, she was his woman, and tell her what happened. Nothing in life is really fair. Sometime you think you are winning and then you fuck up. Today he fucked up and the fish won." The man turned and disappeared over the dune.

Howie turned back to the river, Bill's eyes never turned from the fish. Red-cap's group moved up the dune toward town, three stayed

behind. The woman, who stood facing the river, now turned and looked up the hill, her arm outstretched. She stood frozen, then dropped to her knees, again.

Bill looked at the fish; now showing signs of recovery, he stroked its head. He reached along the jaw and caught the shank of the hook and twisted. The fish seemed to open its mouth in acceptance. Howie watched as Bill removed the hook, turned the fish upstream and held the great muskie between his two small hands as the river flowed through the great fish's mouth and over its gills. The plates open and closed with the rhythm of the river; Howie felt the heat on his back, the air was still. The muskie slowly moved ahead, caught the current and turned away into the depths and gradually sank out of sight. Bill waded back to shore and started to cry.

"It's okay," Howie said, consoling his brother.

"It's not okay; a man drowned trying to catch that fish. What for? There's no reason to it; it's just a fucking fish, makes no sense, none!"

"Don't know, Bill. Sometimes it's just shitty what happens; no reason, no rhyme. Get your gear together. Let's see if we can return these things to that woman and then go find dad and gramps." Howie, still stunned by the appearance and disappearance of the giant, wondered who he was; Bill didn't say anything.

The boys crossed the vacant catwalk, dodging abandoned rods and tackle boxes, and climbed the trail toward town. Doug and Charlie met them at the top of the dune.

"You boys alright? We heard someone had fallen into the river and then the police car raced down River Street, then we saw Doc Abrams. You two alright?" Doug's tried to hold back the panic in his voice.

Bill and Howie told the story to the stunned pair of hardened men.

"We're fine Dad, but we have to return these things," Howie said, pointing.

The four walked up the hill to River Street, then walked the block to city hall and the police station. A small crowd had gathered on the steps. The woman Howie saw at the river stood staring into a black station wagon. Howie could see her face reflected in the dark glass as she sobbed, great shoulder racking sobs and heaves, her hands stuck to the hot roof.

"No, no, god-damn-it, no. You can't be dead," she said to everyone and to no one.

Howie and Bill walked up to the policeman. Doug and Charlie stood behind them.

"Jimmy," Charlie said. "These two boys have a story to tell you and something to return to that young woman."

"Afternoon, Charlie," Chief James Dugan said as he turned to the boys. "What's this story boys?"

They slowly told the story again, left nothing out. When they came to the hat and rod and reel they pointed to the young woman. Bill described the great fish and its release, and said it talked to them, said to let him go, he killed enough. Howie interrupted and said that it was a man, a big man that did the talking. Bill said there was no big man there; it was the fish. Howie tried to correct him; Bill got angry.

"You always have to say I'm wrong, well it was the fish that said to let his self go, not some stupid giant. It was the fish. That's why I did, 'cause he said to let him go, that's why."

Howie said okay and walked away.

"Jesus, Mary and Joseph," Dugan said. "Never heard anything like it! Couple of others have drowned down there, but it's been a while, right Charlie?"

"Been maybe three years, but that last one may have been a suicide," Charlie said.

Dugan finally acknowledged Doug. "Afternoon Doug, you here for the week?"

"No, till Monday, Jimmy," Doug said. "You know that big fellow that Howie talked about?"

"It was the fish, Dad, really, it was the fish," Bill said adamantly.

"No, he doesn't ring a bell, and I know most everyone who lives here or spends a lot of time around here. But I'll ask about," Dugan added.

"Thanks Jimmy," Doug added.

Jimmy Dugan led the boys to the young woman. He introduced

them and they repeated the story. Bill passed the hat to the woman and then the rod and reel. She stood stunned and stared at the tangible remains of her man, which were the last things he had touched. She took the hat and snuggly pulled it down to her ears. Her long brown hair hung out from the edge of the cap, a short shadow hid her eyes. She firmly grasped the rod and threw it into the street, a Chevy braked hard, but too slow to miss the rod, crushing it under its tires, the pieces seemed to explode across River Street. She turned to the coroner's wagon, kissed her hand, and placed it against the hot glass. A smear of red lipstick and her tears stayed. She turned and walked toward another group well away from the knot near the wagon and the steps to the police station.

"She and her husband come up here every June for two weeks," Dugan said. "Been coming here for years, staying over at Green Lake at the Welsh's cabins. Doug, you know the place, don't you?"

"Sure do," answered Doug. "We spent our honeymoon there, nice place and quiet."

"Never any trouble there," Dugan said. "They're good people, live near Detroit. He worked for GM on the line; she works in an office or something. They both loved it here, the openness, the clean air, the fishing. Damn sad thing. Howie and Bill, thanks for returning the hat to her, she's too numb to feel anything right now. The group over there comes up with them; she'll be alright, but still a damn shame."

The three men and two boys walked to the station wagon. Nothing was said until they were almost home.

"Dad, that was the biggest fish I ever saw," Howie said. "It was as big as Bill but it looked tired and sad. Looked like it just wanted to die; it laid there, not fighting, not doing nothing, waiting to die."

"Tired and exhausted from fighting for his life," Charlie said. "He could've been a hundred years old if he was that big, who knows; seen a lot and maybe this was enough. But you gave him his life back; most others would have killed him. You boys gave him his release and that's a good thing."

The Ford climbed the gravel drive to the farm. Bill and Howie took the worms to the kitchen garden, released the survivors, and put away their gear.

CHAPTER FOUR

Summer darkness comes late this far north and after two hours of the boys' impatient fretting, Liz threw up her hands and ordered everyone together, "To the bonfire!" The boys led with the starting flares waved high, Charlie and Liz followed, with Roger and Lisa mixed in with the Claytons; Doug and Anne walked with Frank Rex (he held Anne's arm like they were going to a recital). Flashlight beams bounced off the bright berries and rough bark as they wound their way through the orchard, the boys were told twice to stay with the parade. At the bonfire, they found a great pile of cherry limbs and apple branches, and, within the tangle, a half-dozen rotten mattresses from the picker's quarters, scrap lumber from the barn, and household burnable garbage. No one noticed the junk; they only saw the great jumble.

Roger drenched the lower limbs with kerosene along with one of the mattresses that extended deep into the pile. Doug asked Bill for a flare, pulled its cap, and struck its top. The flare sputtered, then burst into orange fire; he handed it back to Bill and repeated the ceremony with Howie's stick. He took it with his good left hand.

"Hold them high boys, way out, arm's length," Doug said over the spitting and crackling of the flares. "Okay, on three toss those flares onto the mattresses."

He turned to his small audience and raised his hands, "On my count, one, two," he looked at his sons, lit orange by the fire in their hands, "three."

Bill and Howie tossed the flares in high arcs to their targets, the flares landed with a bounce; they lay there, impotent, just sputtering and hissing. A one count, a two count passed, and, on a silent three, a small explosion and roar of angry flames blasted upward through the skeleton of dark limbs toward the black sky.

The flames hypnotized Howie, his eyes widened from the ardent heat and ferocity of it all. He felt himself losing weight, floating, as if when the flames rose they carried him, up, along with their haste, to heaven. The fire inhaled the cool air from the woods as it rushed between his legs to give life-giving oxygen to the inferno. He watched one of the Ancient's three elements, air, as it magically changed to another, fire. Transfixed, he stood, split vertically in two front to back, hot on his chest and cold on his back, his feet in the earth.

One great limb burned from its farthest tip to its deepest root, wedged deep, in the pile. Howie traced the branch into the core of the tangle where it was lost behind one of the burning mattresses. One corner unburned but ripped open, exposed stuffing. A furtive movement caught Howie's eye and he spied a sharp pointed head, its nose stuck out into the heat, and then retreated back into the mattress. Twice more it appeared then disappeared.

Transfixed, Howie watched silently as the mice ran from their burning burrow and ignited like small fiery toys, too confused to know a way out, vanishing into the pyre's fiery heart. He turned to his family, they were laughing and pointing at the flames and the rising sparks. Bill threw another branch on the blaze. Howie looked back, wanting to tell them, to show them, but couldn't; he felt frozen within the inferno.

Howie took three steps back and looked up at the width and breadth of the bonfire, a burning pyramid, an almost perfect four-sided Giza. The black of the ground against the red and orange of

the two sides, bent in on themselves to a fiery zenith that, like a hand, pointed upward. The sparks flew higher, twisting and twirling about in the seamless black sky, eternal patterned with unmoving stars; stars that reached across the Ancient's tortoise shell roof of the Earth. Those stars captured busy sparks, to hold them forever. The bonfire sounds Howie heard were like the crackling of stars, only it was the spitting of sparks, and, as he watched, the stars quietly absorbed the twirling and dancing sparks like darkness taking light. A magic time, another miracle, he thought, heat pushed in on his face, his hair was hot, his eyes singed. He spun and the heat would be gone instantly, then he would spin back around and his face felt the heat again, around and around he went. The others stood near the fire talking; his laughing brother moved to stand next to him, throwing small branches on the pile. Howie spun around again, the heat flashed away from his face, his back now hot. He watched the tall pines that ran along the ridge at the top of the hill, they formed a black wall. The projected ghostly patterns of his family danced on this black screen; great shadow puppets against the pines. The heat now warmed his back, piercing the sweater his grandmother made for him.

A giant face flickered on the dark green panel of pines. A strange face, a bearded face, a twisted face, floated on the blackness of the pines, so puzzling that it made Howie squint. The pyre burst brighter and Howie saw the huge rack of antlers growing out of the forehead of the face, boldly etched in red flames and hanging skin. He followed the antlers up into the sky, where the shadows and the tumble of branches obscured the tips.

Howie's heart froze; the face stared directly at him and no one else. The fire painted the antlers red, as red as the cherries the burning limbs once held. Then the face dissolved, only the antlers remained, disconnected, bloody, and pointy; then the rack slowly melted back into the pines. He turned to his father, who, at that same instant, looked and saw the horror on his son's face. Doug Smith turned quickly toward the woods, and, seeing nothing, lunged toward his son and caught him before he collapsed onto the scorched sand of the orchard.

Howie woke with a start and a short but effective scream. Anne's arms were wrapped about him. His face could still feel the warmth of the fire; he looked into her eyes and then the eyes of his family standing above them. Bill started to cry; he also held Howie's disfigured right hand.

"You okay?" Anne asked.

"I think so," Howie answered. "Did you see him, at the edge of the woods, a giant, with antlers on his head, against the pines? Did you see him?"

"You're okay, I can see that," Liz said. "At least the heat didn't affect your imagination."

"He was there, honest." Howie tried to get up but Anne held him close. "He was there," he pointed to the edge of the pines. "Standing right there, against the pines, all red with fire, and real."

"We'll check it out," Doug said. "Grandpa and I will take a look in the morning, besides, it's time for you boys to go in. We'll stay for a while to watch the fire; let it burn down before we come in. Mom, you and Anne take the boys in, okay?"

Howie stood, dusted the sand from his hands and knees. Frank leaned over to his left ear, "I believe you boy, I believe."

Howie turned to his uncle with a look of forlorn hopelessness.

"Yes, Howard, I believe you; now to home and to bed."

The fire burned hard and hot and the pile stood only a fraction of its original height. Anne took Bill's hand; Liz, Lisa, and Linda Clayton joined her, and the five walked toward the barn light that showed through the trees. The men gathered together. Howie turned his back to the fire; the men's shadows merged into one long dark path that ended at the top of the hill. Howie shivered from the cold and followed the women.

CHAPTER FIVE

Sunday meant church. Up early, then into town. Even after the events of Saturday, this Sunday morning would be no different. The family gathered in the kitchen, not much was said. Howie and Bill were dressed smartly, but not as formally as Mass at home in Illinois. Like his fashion, Charlie wore a tie; Doug wore an open shirt, and Liz and Anne wore light, gaily patterned summer dresses. They took two cars.

The boys hadn't eaten since before the bonfire and now their young active bodies needed food, but breakfast would have to wait. They were both told they could take communion even though they hadn't been to confession in almost a month; Howie, for one, did not like to tell his sins to a stranger. He decided to tell God somewhere between the *Kyrie Eleison* and the Gospel that he was sorry for smoking and swearing, two of the worst sins a boy his age had any familiarity with. He often wondered when he would have to confess something really awful, or, really fun.

Frank Rex didn't join them. Charlie had walked out earlier to the studio and found Frank awake but too tired to go with them. He said he would paint and pray alone.

Frank Rex had a strange relationship with the Roman Catholic Church and few asked him about the specifics; they just accepted it. Frank, for his part, wanted to believe and for a few years held, within his heart, the desire to join a monastery to pray and paint; giving his life and soul to God, but Spain interfered and object lessons were taught. There he saw how the village priests, in black, did their best to cope with the poverty and legacy of the court in Madrid where the bishops, in red, strangled the villages for money. But it was what he saw in the 1930s, before the German part of war, that scarred him. He knew Franco and what he did; he knew the Church and what it did not do. He knew the communists, some were even his friends, and he saw their brutal reactions and deadly retaliations, and, like Picasso, he saw the executions and war's destruction. These brutal demonstrations, abject lessons, were more than his faith could endure, but it was the men in the colored vestments he objected to the most. But then, he had always liked the men on the Ford assembly line more than the executives, even though those managers paid him commissions to paint portraits of their wives and daughters.

Sacred Heart Church, attended by the family, stood on a slight rise overlooking the town of Elk River and the lake formed behind the power plant. It was the church that Charlie and Liz, as well as Doug and Anne, were married in. Built at the end of the last century, it was a classic example of American vernacular religious design; hip roofed with a tall louvered steeple whose apex supported a golden cross visible for miles, a line of tall arched stained glass windows flanked both sides, and two stained glass windows guarded the double doors at the top of the broad concrete steps. A gravel parking lot lay to one side, a broad lawn to the other. Two buildings stood adjacent, the church hall, the nearest, with its one story whitewashed cinderblock walls and asphalt shingle roof that Charlie helped to build during the war; and the rectory, the farthest, a strange mixture of Queen Anne, Victorian and Michigan architecture, white like the other two was almost sixty years old. The original owner of the house built the first sawmill in town. Massive dark green junipers and yews planted about its foundation were beginning to devour the building; only the upper windows survived, the lower portions were gone. One concession to color, within this black, white and green landscape, was the bright red brick walk that connected the rectory to the side door of the church. This door led directly into the sacristy and allowed Pastor O'Brien to keep his feet dry.

An outpost of the Grand Rapids Diocese, this small church, with its two hundred and fifty members, formed one of the three sides of the religious trilogy that held the town in thrall. The others were Presbyterian and Lutheran.

The Presbyterian Church was more of a colony or summer school of Detroit WASPS from the executive wings of Ford and General Motors, who summered among the northern lakes near Elk River. The Lutheran church was a leftover from the logging days when many of the Scandinavian lumberjacks and mill operators stayed and made their homes in Antrim County.

The Catholic Church, started by a group of Northern Irish Catholics, which also named the county a hundred years earlier, was also the summer home to a social group that was unacceptable to all the social and racial castes of Detroit and Chicago. Spanish speaking, poor and itinerant, they came from south Texas and northern Mexico to pick fruit in mid-summer. The church provided early Sunday services for these families, sometimes the Diocese of Grand Rapids provided a priest to say Mass in Spanish or, often as not, Mass was held in one of the barns on one of the farms. The Diocese assigned no one this summer.

Father O'Brian, the pastor and janitor at Sacred Heart, admired Frank Rex's paintings and was the reason for the large oils, which were in Goya-like style, displaying the Stations of the Cross along the walls of the small church. The painting Howie saw in the studio was destined to hang on the left side of the sacristy.

Howie and Bill walked down the aisle to their usual pew. Howie sat and examined, maybe for the hundredth time, the paintings by his uncle; each reflected what the pained man could conceive and make real with oil paint and brush. The women, tall, and straight, stared, with deep longing, out of the paintings directly at the viewers.

The men, except for Jesus, were all bent over or their backs were to the viewers, none looked outward, but just down or to their hands. Only the women stood above the dark and bloody tangle of cloaks, arms, thorns, and spears; it was as if they could carry the Son of God and no one else could bear the weight. Howie looked to the left side of the altar where, in a tall and narrow painting, a man held a boy in his arms. The child's small right hand pointed to the heart in his breast, his left arm, small and plump, pointed to the heavens contained in the upper half of the painting. The Christ child's eyes, and those of St. Joseph, focused directly on Howie. This painting hung over the tabernacle that a local cabinetmaker had given to the Church soon after the war, as a memorial to his only son who died in France. The cabinetmaker labored for a year, and, when the tabernacle was placed on the altar, Frank Rex gave that painting to the cabinetmaker, who then hung it above the shrine. Father O'Brien blessed it. Howie had watched this pair watch him for as long as he could remember. Some nights, in his Chicago bed, the vision of this painting would come to him in dreams and he would step into the painting, turn, and look out on the congregation. He could never remember what he saw. This was a memorial to a great love, a greater loss and a profound faith. A small bent man, gray-haired, sat next to a tall, thin woman with a blue embroidered shawl in the first pew. Howie watched the cabinetmaker gaze up at the portrait and cross himself.

Mass seemed shorter than usual. Maybe time had sped up, Howie couldn't tell. The sermon mentioned the death of the fisherman, nothing else. Howie apologized to God for smoking and blamed himself for his brother's swearing incidents and said ten Hail Mary's; he took Communion with a clear conscience. They filed out of the church and into the church hall that stood apart, yet was connected by a corridor. Doug and Anne walked among the other families, shaking hands and giving short cheek kisses. Most had a cup of coffee in one hand and a donut or a piece of cake in the other.

Howie sat on one of the folding chairs against the wall, next to his brother, a donut in one hand and a glass of cold milk in the other, and watched the town's people meet and move about. A few times, after Doug and Anne greeted someone, they would turn to the boys, point and smile. The boys were hoping the conversations and the pointing were about their better features, not their bad ones.

A boy Bill's age separated himself from the crowd and walked up to them.

"I'm John Walsh," he announced proudly. "I'm your second or third cousin, according to my mother." He pointed to a large woman in a bright dress standing off in a corner. "Did you really see a man get drowned?"

The question caught the boys up short for an answer, but Bill piped up, "Sure did, watched him fight a big fish and then watched as the fish pulled him under." Howie elbowed his brother, Bill, unaffected, continued. "Pulled him under and drowned him. Then I caught the fella's red cap and rod and reeled them in. Then Howie took the man's reel and reeled in the big fish, the one that killed the man. We let him go though." Bill stopped, and, with his finger wiggling, beckoned his new found cousin to come closer. "We let him go 'cause the fish told us to, honest to God, the fish told us to let him go."

"Honest to God?" answered John.

"Honest. The fish said, 'I killed one man, now let me go, or I'll kill you.'"

Howie was stunned by what his brother had said. Then he remembered Bill was so close to the fish that he may not have seen the bearded giant. Bill thought the fish spoke to them and begged to be let go. Bill recalled a different story than his. Howie said nothing, but let Bill continue to the end.

John asked Bill to meet his sisters and tell them the story, hoping to scare them. Bill answered, "neat-o," and ran across the hall to his expanding list of cousins.

Howie sat quietly watching, always curious, always looking at the way people stood and scratched and preened and fidgeted. He could spot the shy people, the arrogant men, and the pushy women. He sensed fear in some and comfort from those that could console, or, at least, he thought he did.

Standing at the edge of a small group of young girls, which encircled Bill and his story telling, a young graceful woman, taller than the others, turned to look at Howie. He could tell she was intrigued by Bill's tale. She smiled at Howie and glided over to him, spun smoothly, ran her hands down her young hips in a somewhat grand manner, pulled her full skirt tight to the back of her bottom, and sat down royally. She turned her face to Howie and smiled, displaying the prettiest teeth and softest lips, painted with the slightest touch of artificial red or rose, that Howie had ever seen.

"Good morning, I am Margaret Welsh, Johnny's sister. That's quite a story your brother's telling."

"Good morning, Maggie, been a few years since I saw you here," he answered.

"I call myself Margaret now, Howard," she answered, correcting him.

"I call myself Howie now, Margaret now. I like Maggie better, and, for the most part, it is true, except for the fish talking part."

"Did the man drown?" she asked, passing over his smart-alecky remark.

"Yes. A very, very sad thing it was. No damn reason for it; it was just a fish. Nothing more, but as Father O'Brien said this morning, we never know the reasons for God's work. Kind of a load of crap, if you ask me. The man made a mistake and it cost him his life; small mistake or big mistake same difference, just a stupid mistake. He could catch a hundred more and never get wet, but yesterday was different. Don't know why, but it was him, not God's plan, who made the stupid mistake."

Margaret, for some reason that only she knew, leaned over and kissed him on the cheek, stood up and walked back to the crowd. Howie's heart leapt, a bit of crimson flushed his face. He quickly scanned the room, thank God no one had seen them; that is, until he saw his mother. Her eyes quickly left his, but the soft smile remained, as she turned back to Doug and Father O'Brien.

"You have a scratch on your cheek," Anne said, straightening a drift of hair that hung on Howie's forehead, as they reached the station wagon. "Did Maggie kiss it to make it feel better?"

"Oh, Mom! No, absolutely not!" he answered. "Must have been when I fell."

"Probably, you okay?" she smiled and adjusted his hair a bit more.

"Just fine, but I felt a bit weird," Howie answered. "Margaret's growing up, Mom."

"She certainly is. She's growing into a very pretty young lady. I haven't seen her much this year though."

"Dad says she's at a school in Detroit, or something. Why would Uncle Dick send her to school away from home?"

"I don't know, but it's a good school for girls and God knows Dick has the money. But it's a bit sad. Lord knows I couldn't be apart from all the men in my life. So, until you're much older, I will be looking over your shoulder and straightening your hair." She winked; Howie took another look at his cousin crossing the parking lot. *"Damn she's cute,"* he said to himself, *"damn cute."* She looked back and smiled.

The tradition of Sunday breakfast at the farm after Mass extended back as far as the family's memories went. Doug and Charlie left the warm kitchen early, before the house was awake, before church; first to check on Uncle Frank and repeat something they had done for thirty years. Back then there were three, two boys and a man, then three men, then two; war changed the trio to a duet. When does a tradition start or end? Most are recurring events and actions quietly celebrated, year after year, until they become a part of the soul of the person or peoples involved. The holidays are easy with their fireworks and ornaments, special parties and finery, and most especially, food and drink.

The Smith tradition centered on nature's rudest of fungi, morels; tall, hooded, dark chestnut colored, sponge shaped mushrooms that appear among the toes of the maple trees that sprouted after the pines had been logged. The pair searched the ground and leaf litter for the four inch to even six inch tall brown castles that grew among the trees; they were like Michigan truffles. Charlie knew the best spots but every year they moved within the groves, maybe a few feet, maybe a few yards, never the same. Often a few years would pass before a patch would show its treasures again; some years they would remain asleep in the sandy soil, hidden. The men collected dozens but always left a few to spore out for the next season.

The boys gathered in the kitchen as Charlie placed the basket, full to the top, on the table. The morel aroma, a perfumed mixture of leaf mold, old crumbly wood and forest floor, filled the kitchen. Anne rinsed the mushrooms clean of sand and shook them dry, taking care not to bruise them. Charlie then took a broad bladed knife and a plank of maple, only used for morels, and laid them out like fallen soldiers on the kitchen table. Then gently, with almost sacrificial care, he took one morel and began to slice it, in thin fillets, from cap to base. The largest, the center cuts, with their full shaft and crown, were cream colored with an almost chocolate colored edge, the shape undeniable. Howie was finally old enough to understand the innuendo's thrown about for years. He blushed a bit when Anne made a passing remark about a man's strength and the largest morels. She caught herself; a slight crimson washed her cheek when she realized her son finally understood the comment. To Bill they looked like brown Christmas trees. Anne quickly answered, "Yes Bill, eating one is just like Christmas." Her comment, "It must be the mushrooms;" began to make sense to Howie.

Charlie, with cupped hands full, dropped the sliced fungi into a broad iron skillet, almost smoking with melted butter. The aroma, rising with the steam, filled Charlie's eyes and tears formed at their corners. Howie's first lungful twitched something inside, something very different, and for a moment he thought of Margaret in the church hall.

Liz poured a mixture of whipped eggs and cream over the sizzling morels, and, for a moment, all was quite. Charlie ground black pepper over the yellow slush, threw in a handful of chopped parsley and three pinches of salt. The edges of the eggs and mushrooms began to bubble. Then, using a large wooden spatula, he turned the mixture back onto itself, great chunks of mushrooms rolled among the eggs, again and again, and, as more steam rose to the ceiling, the mixture stiffened. Another hot skillet, sitting to the back of the stove, held a rich pile of crisp potatoes cooked in bacon fat. The pan's previous occupants, rashers of bacon, were stacked next to the stove on a red striped towel. A six-inch stack of toast, watched the theater. The aromas settled deep inside Howie's brain; he would carry them for the rest of his life.

The boys set the table, under the pear, with silverware and orange juice. Liz dealt out, on the kitchen table, an orderly row of old red patterned China plates; Charlie followed with great spoonful's of eggs and morels, potatoes and three strips of bacon each. Under the light shade of pear and the midmorning sunshine, breakfast began. Charlie raised his coffee cup to the group, "To us this fine morning, to my family."

"Salute," answered Frank, and, with a mouthful of egg and forest, looked brighter and younger.

Howie and Bill ate with gusto; no one could eat fast enough or chew slow enough. Coffee and orange juice washed down the eggs and freshly sliced toast. A small bit, left in the pan, was offered to the boys as a reward for the excitement they had brought during the last few days, it disappeared in a second.

"Martinez's should arrive this week, Dad," Doug said after the family moved from the kitchen to the porch.

"Should happen," Charlie answered. "They're usually prompt and, by now, tired of weeding sugar beets. Barbara Martinez will want to get things cleaned up, new mattresses are coming soon."

"A good family," added Anne, "but a hard way to live."

Anne Smith married into the Smith family a year before the war in Europe became an American war. Doug and Anne met at a summer dance while she was a senior in high school. One of two surviving children, after their parents were killed in a car crash, they were raised by their maternal grandmother. Doug, a recent graduate from Elk River High School, worked hard to gain her affection and acknowledgement, both proved difficult. She, reticent and with hopes of seeing the world, dated Doug on and off for a year after graduation, inevitably time and the unspeakable changes to the world pushed them together. In an era of June weddings, Anne added their names to the book at Sacred Heart for later that month. Cherries would be ready to pick two weeks after they returned from their honeymoon. A mild summer, a profitable crop, and anxious war worries, helped knit their affection into a strong bond.

The attack on Pearl Harbor changed their lives as much as it changed the world. Living on the farm, Doug studied mail-order journalism and made a few dollars repairing farm equipment; he hoped to follow in his father's footsteps and enter Michigan State College in the spring. The war had other ideas and demands.

After three bitterly cold months of bad news from the Pacific and Europe, Doug and James sat with Anne and Liz and told them they would be joining the army. They talked of honor and duty, no mention of fear and dying was made. Only Anne and Liz thought about the possibility of death.

Charlie, proud and hopeful, understood the reasons why his two sons had to go; twenty-two years earlier, he had the same conversation with his parents, but he also wished there was some other way they could stay and still serve. Hard pressed to give up his two sons to a government that was seldom there to help him and his neighbors, Charlie knew that political forces, like the weather, were uncontrollable. Since the times when white Europeans cut the pelts from beavers, cut down the pines, and stuck trees in the ground, these old dunes of northern Michigan were another American back-water, much like Appalachia and the Blue Ridge mountains, where time and folk stood frozen, marking time, not in minutes, days, or weeks, but in seasons and generations. Ten hard years of Depression were less difficult here than in Chicago and Detroit. Yet hard times they were, and, even now, a dollar was stretched to the length of a week. If this war could clear Hitler and Tojo from this world, it was a good reason to support it with his sons, but it split his soul to think of them killing others, even for peace. For a moment, he leaned back in his chair, closed his eyes, and dreamed of his sons liberating his beloved Paris.

Frank Rex hated war with every fiber, muscle and sinew of his body. He survived in Barcelona during the Spanish Revolution and watched fascism murder whole towns. Rabidly non-political, he saw the war's excesses rip apart the country he loved. He hated the men, the leaders, the thinkers who used war as a way to further their own insatiable need for power. He tried to sympathize with the communists, yet painted a canvas where two wolves turned on a third, ready to tear it apart. When he was asked what it meant, he simply said,

"They are all wolves, which of them deserves the most hatred?"

Anne didn't realize she was pregnant when Doug and Jim left for Chicago and boot camp. Writing a long letter to Doug in mid-April, she talked about the farm and spring, and, in the last line, told him to be careful because their son will need a father to show him the best morel spots. She was sure it would be a boy; Howie was born that November.

Doug and Jim were separated after basic training. Jim, a natural leader, left for officer's training school in New Jersey. Doug's affinity for writing took second place to his ability to shoot a carbine. His brigade was sent to Fort Bragg, North Carolina.

Doug's war consisted of training and waiting, more training, then more waiting; beach landings followed by more beach landing; men died during training, men died in stupid accidents, and some days he thought the war itself couldn't be worse. Doug's division was held back from Africa. They were sure they would go to Italy. Again they remained state side. Jim survived Africa and was promoted to lieutenant colonel; he was reassigned to England to assist in preparing for the invasion. Doug and his division were finally sent to England, for more training, in the late fall of 1943.

Anne spent those years with her new family and she and Liz formed bonds like a mother and a daughter would. For her, the winters were unbearably cold and only Howie helped to make time fly. The warmth of her precious child comforted her, he seldom cried and then, only for a good reason.

Anne and Doug's letters were about day-to-day things, each living the other's life, four weeks later. The routine of three weekly letters carried them through the winter into the spring and then Doug's letters stopped abruptly. Charlie told her to keep on writing.

"They're being blocked and held because of the invasion, it'll be soon, maybe late spring or early summer. Wars are fought best in summer, like farming," Charlie said.

The coldest word she heard from people's lips that spring was 'invasion'. It was hard for her, very hard.

The morning of Tuesday, June 6, was clear with a slippery touch of moisture in the air, the orchard rich with green fruit. The news broke about the invasion; everyone listened to the radio, spelled each other during the long nights and the following days. The advances were reported but nothing of losses or the dead. The terror in the women's hearts was great. They spent an hour every evening at Sacred Heart with a hundred other wives and mothers.

A week into the invasion, a dark green sedan pulled up the gravel drive to the farm and a young officer emerged. He walked to the door of the house solemnly; Charlie stood tall and straight when he took the telegram from the soldier, the son of a close friend from town. Charlie read that his eldest was dead; "Killed in action in Northern France on the eighth of June," nothing more.

Liz, screamed "No, no, no!" and collapsed. Anne helped carry her to her bedroom. Gloom spread through the house; no other information came. On June twenty-eighth, the first of what seemed like a hundred letters arrived from Doug. Almost as many came from Jim to Liz and Charlie. They read the last first.

Dear Dad and Mom and my beloved Anne and Howie,

You have probably been told by now that Jim is dead. If not, he died two days after we landed. I have seen so much death in the last week that my brother's seems lost in the carnage; he's just a number, something that happened to someone else. He was in the first wave to hit the beach and survived to move inland. God, the beach was so wide and the dunes stood as tall as those at Sleeping Bear. I came in that afternoon when things were a bit quieter; but my buddy from Cadillac, Jimmy Ried, was killed by a sniper as we walked down a narrow path along the top of the dune. No place was safe.

I found out on the tenth that he was killed the day after I saw him at the aid station. We caught up with his company and I found his company commander during a brief lull (too brief). He said Jim was leading a forward group into a village called St. Lo. They took shelling and rifle fire and he pushed his men into the center of the town and secured it. While he sat on the church steps, with his men smoking and taking a break, a sniper killed him. They buried him in the small churchyard. I found his grave and prayed for his soul and for the life he lost. I miss him so much.

I am fine, no wounds, only scratches and a nick. We are moving out tonight, my heart aches from missing you and will write more when things are a bit safer.

Love you all so much,
Doug

Another letter from Doug told them he had just left Jim. They met at an aid station where Jim had gone to have his ears checked; an explosion almost on top of his position had stunned him and caused him to become deaf in his left ear. Doug said his hearing was getting better but he was also going back to the front lines, not more than a half mile away. Doug said he was there at the aid station, no more than a torn tent with cots, to have his leg looked at. A piece of shrapnel nicked his calf just before it killed the fellow next to him. He was fine but the chaos was evident. It was sheer coincidence that the two met. Doug and Jim talked for more than an hour; both would write to see whose letter arrived first.

Anne looked at Liz and could tell she would wait in pain for Jim's letter and wondered if it was in the pile sitting on the table. Anne knew Liz loved both her boys more than the farm, more than Charlie, more than her own life. Anne could see she was cut in two by fear and agony. The tears would not stop. She stood in her kitchen with a towel to her face, twisting it between bouts of crying, each memory exploding in tears. Charlie held her close, but her private pain was beyond anything Anne and Charlie could do. Doug finished his letters asking for their prayers, Liz asked Charlie to take her to Sacred Heart.

After Charlie and Liz left, Anne went into Howie's room and picked up the one and half year old, held him close and talked softly to him about his father and his uncle and their love for him. She saw in his blond hair, Doug's hair, in his eyes, Doug's eyes, but the tears on his cheek were her tears. She didn't let Howie out of her sight for the next two weeks.

Jim's last letter finally arrived along with a letter telling about the day of the invasion. Liz carried Jim's letter and would open it, read for a moment, then sigh.

Anne's dearest moment arrived on a warm late July afternoon. Liz was hoeing in her garden; the rows of deep blue delphiniums and yellow coreopsis were at their peak, mixed red lettuce and young cabbages danced among the flowers. The russet and orange gaillardias pushed their heads through the spikes of blue salvias. It was her hot colored garden, Liz's favorite, a rich change after the cool colors of her spring beds. Tall and straight hollyhocks, like colorful soldiers, marched across the back of the garden. Broad gray green leaves climbed the stalks and blossomed into flowers as big as her hand. Pink, lavender, yellow, and white flowers formed a fence that separated the bed from the garage. Hollyhocks were Anne's favorite; singly, they looked like a preacher giving a sermon to his flowered congregation; as a group they looked like a choir. They would bloom past the first frosts.

Anne watched Liz stand straight amongst the flowers and open the letter again; she read it slowly, and then looked deep into the orchard and in an arc across the farm, to the barn, to the house, and, lastly, through the garden; a dappled shaft of sunlight lit her hair. Liz turned to the hollyhocks and walked among the roses that sat snug below them; their thorns snagged her apron like a small child would grab the hem of their mother's dress. Anne remembered that these hollyhocks were from seeds collected from plants growing along a lane that led to a delightful garden north of Paris. Liz had plucked the tight coils of seeds from those dried shafts of flowers almost thirty years earlier; she would say of her garden, "God makes these flowers, I provide the opportunities." Standing near a deep pink, almost magenta, shaft of flowers, Liz reached to the topmost flower, easily six inches across, and with a deft twist, took the flower, gently pulled off one of the petals, folded it into the letter, and placed the letter in her apron pocket. Anne never saw her read the letter again in public.

The summer was difficult; the cherry crop was good and would make many pies for canteens, mess tents and galleys. Anne thought of Doug eating a slice of cherry pie and would smile; maybe one berry would be from his own orchard. Charlie said there were many ways to fight this war, but his boys would travel on their stomachs full of cherry pie and applesauce.

Doug, wounded again near Bastogne, felt lucky compared to the many frozen bodies filling the woods around him and his platoon as the Bulge pushed west. Right place-wrong time; he had jeeped back from the front to collect supplies, and, after fighting his way back in the early morning, found half his men gone and could only help the remaining soldiers by suggesting a full retreat. The winter, as cold as anything ever in Michigan, became their enemy, along with the Nazis. Anne stood in the cold snow and biting wind on Christmas day, holding Howie, and thought of nothing but Doug and his Christmas; Charlie took her arm and tried to pull her back into the house.

Anne resisted, "I need to feel the cold that Doug is feeling; Howie needs to feel it on his face."

"No, you don't, you need to keep the boy warm and you'll keep Doug warm," Charlie admonished.

Doug's letters continued to arrive, each a verification of life; their letters continued to leave for Europe, each a statement of hope. No more green sedans pulled up their driveway, but fifteen other families in town were visited during the war.

A fine spring day with daffodils, hellebores, and crocus heralded the news of Germany's surrender. The intense cold of the winter forced the plants and trees to present a show beyond the usual spring in northern Michigan. Anne walked through the woods below the hill; white trilliums covered the ground and fiddleheads began to unroll through the litter, life began to rise from the frozen earth. Chartreuse buds and leaves covered the branches of the sugar maples. She knew the morels would be following in a month or two. "Maybe Doug will be here to pick them," she said aloud. Doug returned when the apples were ripe.

Anne never left his side; he was jubilant at times, then manic, his moods swung from day to day. Sad, almost despondent, Doug sat for hours still, silent, and quiet, watching Liz's garden, cigarette after cigarette filling the ashtray. By late fall, the hard frosts and early snows had knocked many of the plants to the ground, brown branches and dead leaves covered the buried hearts of the plants; hearts that waited, pensive, almost unbeating, for spring when they would pump life up into the plant, push it out of the ground, and into the warmth of the air. He would brighten when Roger dropped by and he became almost joyous when Frank Rex would share a cigarette and they could talk about Paris. Doug spent part of the fall, after the liberation, in a small hotel near the Pont Neuf. Frank wanted to know everything that had happened to the city.

"Frank," Doug said, "Paris is everything it was ten years earlier, bright, exciting, glorious. The museums and cafés were reopening, a few at first; they were cautious and uncertain, but the sidewalks overflowed with people from all over the world. But it is also a town of sad tales and death. Fear walked the streets, retributions and politics of the darkest kind. Many want to make up for lost time as well as get even, Communists, Bolsheviks, a new French form of fascism, and de Gaulle. I fear for their future, but they have been through occupations, revolutions and conquests before. They will recover from this."

Frank's eyes would tear-up when he asked about the Louvre and other small galleries and museums that he knew. Doug told him about a gallery he visited, owned by a Spaniard from Barcelona, a Señor Sandeval, who knew Frank's work and wanted to see him again very much.

"He's a scoundrel, a devious peddler of art, but I would drink for hours with him. I remember that he can't return to Spain because of Franco. So he survived the war, well it just goes to show you that you never know," Frank said.

By spring, Doug was sleeping through the night, deeply involved with the affairs of the farm and beginning to write for the small weekly paper, *The Coronet*, in Elk River. The short articles concerned local happenings and, at times, a little gossip and rumor; small towns hold secrets but they are secrets that everyone knows.

Anne announced one August morning that there would be one more at the table in May or June, and, soon after, Doug announced he would be going to Michigan State in the fall, and the family would be going with him. The double shock of happiness and loss confused Liz but she and Charlie resigned themselves to the coming changes.

Jim had always been the son meant for the farm and Doug for the world. Even with Jim gone, this couldn't change.

Four years later, the four Smiths moved to Chicago where Doug had been offered a job with the *Tribune*. It didn't pay well but they had managed with so little for so many years that the money coming in was more than enough for their family and the few things needed for a better life. Six years later, life was as good as it could be, on one hundred and eight dollars a week.

CHAPTER SIX

The phone in the hall rang three times before Liz could reach it from the kitchen. Supper was over, Doug and the boys were out in the orchard and Charlie and the girls were sitting around the kitchen table drinking coffee and smoking.

"Good evening, Liz Smith here."

"Good evening Liz, is Charlie there?"

"Hi Jimmy, yes he's finishing his coffee, anything I can do?"

"No Liz, I just need to talk to Charlie." Jimmy Dugan would talk to Liz for an hour if it was a social call; this was not a social call.

"Good evening Jimmy, what's up?" Charlie said.

"It's Eve. I need your help and didn't want to make a big scene. I have her in the cruiser and she's not happy about it. Had to take her out of the Suds; she'd been there since mid-afternoon, now she's drunk and was beginning to fool with the boys and pick fights with the women. I'd have brought her out to the farm but I am short-handed tonight and need to stay in town. Can you come and get her?"

"Certainly, be there in ten minutes. Where are you?"

"River Street across from the hardware; see you in ten."

Charlie set the phone down slowly and stood for a moment, looking out the window into the fading light washing over the garden. He remembered Eve walking through this garden as a teenager, touching the flower tops and spinning about with her yellow dress filling with air as she spun. He watched her stop and, in a casual jaunty manner, skip over to the tallest of the roses, place her hand about the largest bloom and crush it, the yellow petals bleeding red from the gash the thorn had torn in her palm.

"I have to go to town and get Eve; she's drunk and she's with Jimmy. Caused some problems at the Suds and I'll need to patch that up. Be back before eleven."

"Want me to go with you Dad?" Anne asked.

"Might help if I need to get her to bed; I know it's a thankless task but I appreciate the help."

Charlie and Anne sat quietly as they drove into town, each remembering similar trips made and each hoping this would be the last. Eve never made it easy for those who tried to love her. Her half-brothers, her father, her husband, her sister-in-law and especially Liz, all suffered her dark days and often her good days. She could be as high and as bright as the moon on a summer evening and then, in minutes, as dark and cold as only the winters could be in this part of the world.

Charlie pulled up behind Dugan and his cruiser. Jimmy stood leaning against the door smoking a cigarette; two crushed butts lay near his polished right boot. Eve was kneeling on the back seat staring out the rear window, lit by Charlie's headlights, just like the best director in Hollywood would have used in a Bette Davis movie.

"Get me da'fuck out of here, Charlie," she yelled through the half opened window. "He's got no right to keep me here away from my friends."

"It was her friends who called me," Dugan said. "They could see what was coming and the fun was disappearing fast. She already threw two shot glasses against a wall and slapped one of the women who said she was trying to jump her man. Charlie, she's getting worse and this can't go on. You take her home; give her what you can to calm her down. We'll talk tomorrow. We've been friends a long time and I've known this girl since she was fifteen. She needs to go back to the state hospital, and, hopefully, they can help her. If not, something bad's going to happen and it's my job to make sure it doesn't happen to anyone in this town. Sorry, Charlie."

"I understand, and I'm sorry this was put on you. Let her out and Anne and I will walk her home. Anne has some medicine that should help; we'll stay with her until she's asleep. I'll stop by tomorrow and talk to Bob about the shot glasses and anything else. He's a good man and it's not fair to him either. You are probably right; she needs to get back to the hospital. It's just so damn difficult and hard."

"Dad," Anne said, "sometimes we get along when she's in a good mood and sober. Jimmy, we'll try to work something out next week; I'll call and find out if they have room at the hospital. She's been there twice and she did a good job convincing them she was better when she wasn't. She has always been good at acting; maybe now they'll understand she needs to be there longer."

Eve almost tumbled out of the car; she steadied herself on the edge of the open door and smiled at everyone.

"And how the hell are all you sons-of-bitches? Nice of you to come down to see little ol' me. Charlie, that asshole," she pointed at Dugan, "pulled me away from my friends and then locked me up in his fucking police car. That's kidnapping; he's no good and I really think he just wants to get in my pants." She turned to Jimmy Dugan and gave him a seductive look, which, even to Anne, seemed hilarious. Jimmy scrunched his face and tilted his head a bit; the shrug of his shoulders said it all.

"Let's go, Eve. Officer Dugan is tired of you and your antics and so am I," Charlie said, taking her by the arm. To his surprise, she softened instantly, the tenseness in her shoulders and arms dropped away. She wheeled around under his power. They started to walk across the dark street, their shadows pointed back to Dugan.

"That man tried to fuck me, Charlie," Eve said in an offhand manner. "That son-of-a-bitch tried to pull off my dress and screw me. You need to punish him."

"Eve, he did not try anything, so stop your lying," Charlie told her.

"Honest to God, Charlie, you saw how he looked at me. Annie dear," she turned to her sister-in-law, "if that's not a 'I wan'na fuck you' look, I never seen one and I seen a lot of them, yes I have. You got'ta watched that man, he's wanted to get in my pants for years and he was going take his chance tonight. I am glad you came and stopped him. That man is evil, why do you let'em be the police around here? He is just a fucker in a blue uniform."

They stumbled down the alley to the stair that led to Eve's apartment; Charlie tried to hold Eve upright. Anne led the way; the door was unlocked and slightly open. Reaching around the jamb she found the light switch; the room was a shambles. It had not been ransacked or torn apart, this was how Eve lived. Crusty dishes and dirty glasses covered the small kitchen counter, three overflowing bags of garbage stood in one corner, newspapers and fashion magazines littered the sofa and the floor, various bits of clothing and underwear hung on the edges of chairs and in piles. Anne, not shocked by the scene, just shrugged. It had barely improved since her last visit.

Charlie pushed Eve through the door and took her into the small bedroom off to the side, sat her on the bed, and told to her stay there. He rummaged through the medicine cabinet in the bathroom and found her empty prescription for depression, no additional prescription boxes evident. The prescription had lapsed two weeks earlier and the effects were obvious.

Anne began to undress her; Charlie turned away and began to straighten things. He thought it would be easier to throw everything out and start over, she had so little and she treated everyone and everything in her life as if people and things were nothing. She wouldn't miss any of it.

"Do you have the sedative and the antidepressant?"

Charlie reached into his breast pocket and took out two small manila envelopes. Anne took them and found a reasonably clean glass, filled it with water, and went back into the bedroom.

"She's exhausted," Anne said. "She gets so wound up and agitated it just saps everything in her to keep going. The liquor works for a bit then she crashes; she took the pills and I left the rest of the antidepressants on the night stand. I have the sedatives; we'll take them with us." She handed them back to Charlie.

They spent an hour cleaning the apartment. Anne washed some of the dishes; there was no dish soap, so she used a bar of Ivory. Anne checked Eve one last time, she was sprawled across the bed; it saddened Anne to see her. She had plumped out a bit and was too large for her underwear. Her hair was a tangle and what remained of her makeup was smeared. Anne could only guess about the brier tangle of her mind.

They brightened up the drive back to the farm with a stop at the Dairy Cone. Only open during the summer, the gravel parking area looked like a used car lot packed with teenagers and summer tourists. The warm summer air, the humidity low, the moon high, and above the trees the stars twinkled with a background soundtrack of scrunching gravel and squealing tires when they met the asphalt of the state highway.

"She needs to be in the hospital," Anne said, licking her soft ice cream. "You know it and so does Liz. If she stays out here, she'll hurt herself, or, God forbid, someone else. Call Doc Iverson at the hospital in the morning and get the paperwork started."

"Yes I know, and it hurts to see her this way, but in the hospital she becomes a shadow, a wasted version of herself. They keep her drugged and quiet; they don't need the trouble she causes so they keep her docile and tame, like a domesticated wildcat. I hate seeing her that way, it's like she is eighty years old. You're right; she needs to be cared for. Liz can't do it ; she had all she could do two years ago during Eve's last crazy spell and has told me flat out that this is now my problem. She has so much to deal with now with her brother and his cancer. I can't, no, I won't ask her to help anymore."

"Eat your ice cream; it's melting down your hand," Anne said.

Charlie grinned and licked the back of his hand where the ice cream had started to run. Anne smiled at the childish action. She admired the man and what he'd been through most of his life. He was still the rock of the family, its lodestone and sometime anchor. No other life is as hard as farming. Early on, Anne knew that Doug would have to raise their family some other way and their future would be in the city. Torn between the two, split by the farm's needs and the future, she only had to look at her boys to see the truth. Doug told her that if he could make living up here, he would jump at the chance. But now, even with the booming growth in the big cities, life up here on the edge of the civilized world was tough and unforgiving.

A souped-up thirty-two Ford shot more gravel across the lot and took off down the highway. *"Where's Dugan?"* Anne thought, with a smile.

A light blazed in the window of the living room when they pulled into the driveway. Liz sat in the corner reading and smiled as they stepped into the room.

"Is she okay?"

"Yes, she's sleeping; I'll go and see her in the morning," Charlie said. "I'll also make a stop at Doc Iverson's and see if we can get her recommitted. She can't stay out here and she can't take care of herself; there're no other options."

"That's good. She will be safer there," Liz answered.

Charlie poured a small glass of bourbon and lit a cigarette; the flame illuminated the tear coursing down his cheek. It ended up in his sharp, but thin grey, mustache. Eve was from a time of enthusiastic chaos and youthful exuberance.

More than forty years ago, Lucille Sue Ellington, beguiled and bewitched him. Older and exotic in appearance, she was the first to bed him. Somewhat wealthy, reasonably educated, and nineteen when Charles Smith met Lucy, he became addicted to her. They drank and screwed their way through Detroit and Cleveland, she taking the lead. They stayed at fine hotels and ate French food, all paid for by Charlie with money sent from Elk River. Charlie lied to his father to get more money; and would agree later that he was one spoiled son-of-a-bitch and only thought about Lucy-Sue and bourbon. They were married six months after they met. Charlie, as big as he was, lied about his age. Lucy-Sue was six years older; they honeymooned on a train to Niagara Falls. Three months after that, Lucy-Sue was pregnant.

Charlie and Lucy-Sue went back to Elk River and Abraham Smith to beg for forgiveness. Abraham and his mother, Eleanor, welcomed their prodigal son, but were not taken with Lucille. She was aloof as she swelled; seldom helped and would demand much from the two servants.

In late summer, Eve Smith was born. Loud, demanding, and unhappy was all Eleanor could say about the child. Lucy-Sue had a tough pregnancy and a painful childbirth, and took laudanum to ease the pain. After two years, she took the child and left for Detroit to look for real people, she said, in a terse note, who understood her needs. She filed for divorce, saying Charlie was unfaithful. He was confused about why she left, blaming himself; he tried to find her. The police said no one with the name Ellington or Smith showed up in their records. The divorce was finalized with papers sent back and forth to a lawyer's office in Toledo; they would not give out any information about Lucille Sue Smith. The lawyer told Charlie flat out that he would not give any information to a wife beater.

Charlie never saw her again, alive.

Charlie married Elizabeth Ann Rex three weeks before he was to be shipped out to England and the war. The Armistice saved him the trip and probably saved his life.

The police, from a series of small towns in Ohio, called a few times during the next few years when Lucy-Sue got into trouble. He was shocked at first, wondering why she would always give them his name; he wasn't hard to find, there were only a few phones in the town. But Charlie could do little; he sent a few dollars once and he never heard back. Then nothing, he tried to find Lucy-Sue and Eve, but it was as if they had fallen off the face of the Earth.

"Charles Smith here," he said, answering the phone.

"Sorry to disturb you sir, we had a devil of a time finding you, I'm Sergeant Willis, with the Dayton, Ohio police. Lucky one of our deputies knew someone up in your part of Michigan. Do you know a Lucille Smith?"

"Yes sir, she was my wife."

"I am sorry to say this then sir, she was found dead in her apartment. Looks like an overdose of some kind and excessive alcohol use. The apartment was a mess, ransacked, we think, no money was found. We have her identification from some things found near her, her purse, a notebook had your name written in it. There were a number of Smiths listed, many local, we checked them but most gave another name rather than Smith, none said they knew her and they told us not to ever call again. I'm trying to be delicate here, sir," the sergeant offered.

"I understand sergeant; she probably had a lot of male friends. I have not seen her for almost twelve years."

"There's a daughter, says she's fifteen, but acts like she's twenty. Eve was the name she gave, Eve Smith."

Charlie was stunned. Liz watched overwhelming sadness turn his face grey. They had two boys, and now, it seems, a third child was to be added.

Frank drove Charlie to Traverse City and then, after three transfers, Charlie arrived by train in Dayton. He stopped by the police station and the funeral home where Lucy-Sue was being prepared. Eve had been placed in a home for young girls until he arrived to pick her up.

The police believed she probably died from opium poisoning; something, the sergeant said, being spread among the big cities of Toledo and Cleveland.

"It's those god damn negras that bring it down here to corrupt our young folks. We catch two or three of them a month with tins of that brown shit they sell to the local kids. Your ex must have been enticed by that stuff."

"Yes, I am sure that is what happened, Sergeant." For all Charlie knew, she was probably the one bringing it into Dayton. Where else would she have gotten money if it weren't by some other means rather than on her back?

Charlie found Eve on the porch of the Dayton Home for Young Ladies. An older woman was sitting with her.

"Good morning," Charlie said as he climbed the steps. "I'm Charles Smith."

The older of the two stood, "Good morning, Mr. Smith, I'm Mary Willis, my brother is the sergeant you talked to this morning. He said you were on your way over." She turned and, for the first time in twelve years, he saw his daughter. "And this Eve Smith."

She looked up at him and Charlie quietly braced himself against what he saw. Her piercing gaze fired bullets full of hatred. They screamed, "Who the hell are you old man and what do you want from me. Just leave me alone!"

"Eve, this is your father, please stand up and say hello."

Eve instantly jumped up and pushed Mary aside. "And what the hell do you want with me, fahh-ther. Since you were obviously in the area and heard mom was dead, it was convenient to stop by and say hello." The vitriol in Eve's voice and her body's position said that she expected to be hit for the remark.

"No Eve, I only heard about you and your mother two days ago from Mary's brother, Sergeant Willis. I live in Elk River up in Michigan, with my family," Charlie replied softly.

"So what are you gonna do now? Take me back to your house, make me a part of your sweet little family; give me a fucking deb-butant's ball."

"Eve, please watch your language," Mary chided, but obviously this was language she had heard from Eve all too often these last few days.

"Mom was a doper, smoked opium and, when she could get the good stuff, she did heroin," Eve said. "I never touched the junk, made her worthless and I was into having a lot more fun than sitting around doped up all day. I have my friends here and I ain't moving out just to please you and some old family shit." Eve pulled a pack of cigarettes out of her shirt pocket, tamped it on the top, and lit one. She did not offer one to Charlie or Mary.

"Put that out child, I told you not to smoke anywhere on the property."

Eve took another drag and ignored Mary Willis; in fact, she acted as though she was not even on the porch.

"So what are we going to do . . . fahh-ther? I will not leave my friends and go to some god forsaken hole in the middle of fucking nowhere, just so you can feel better about yourself."

Charlie was stunned by what he saw and heard, he saw Lucy-Sue standing defiantly in front of him. Her exotic looks, her auburn hair, her angled poise, and arrogance were all there; Eve was Lucy-Sue at fifteen. *"Would she become like her mother in her twenties, would she soften, would she be the death of his soul, again?"* Charlie thought.

"Yes, you are going home with me, Eve. We'll work this out somehow."

"Like hell I will," she said and turned to the matron. "Well, sweet Mary sunshine, are you going to let this degenerate take me out of here? You know very well the Mann Act is still enforced in this country." She looked straight at Mary Willis like it was the first time she noticed she was there.

"Yes dear," Mary replied. "Mr. Smith, your father, will be taking you from here, hopefully today. He and I have some things to discuss and take care of, you go pack your things and be ready in thirty minutes." Charlie could sense that even thirty minutes was too long for Mary.

Eve turned sharply from the pair, flipped the cigarette onto the lawn, and went inside. The door slammed and Charlie could hear her shoes on the hardwood as she climbed the stairs.

"I don't wish to be too forward Mr. Smith, but she's far too headstrong and rude for a child her age. She should be put in a strict home for young ladies so she'll learn manners, become educated, and be acceptable to society. My sister has such a place . . ."

Charlie cut her off abruptly. "No, she'll leave with me; I have made arrangements for her mother's body to be shipped for burial. Her mother had no one in her life, other than me, who cared for her and I'll continue to care for our daughter. So please, no more advice."

"Yes Mr. Smith," Mary said. "I was only trying to help."

"Yes, I understand, please see that she's ready."

Mary turned and followed Eve up the stairs. Charlie stood at the railing and looked down the elm shrouded street, took a cigarette from his pocket and noticed Eve's discarded butt on the lawn, still smoldering. Stepping down the stairs, he picked up the cigarette and lit his from the ember. He crushed the butt in his fingers, the paper and tobacco fell on the grass.

The trip back to Traverse City became difficult especially with Eve who made it abundantly, and vocally, clear that she would cooperate very little; after two train transfers, the last three hours late, they arrived in Traverse City in the middle of the night. The casket would follow during the next few days.

Charlie called Frank Rex from Grand Rapids and gave him the arrival time. Frank had waited for the train even though it was hours late.

"And who the hell is this bearded freak, fahh-ther?" Eve asked turning to Charlie. "Another one of your hillbilly friends?"

"My god Charles, she is a handful, and has the mouth to go with it. No, my dear, I'm just one fucking lunatic of a painter who will never put up with your bullshit, your mouth, your insolence, or your teenage angst ridden demeanor," answered Frank, staring through her eyes, deep into her dark soul.

Eve stopped and stared into a face that said: "I know who you are and what you are; you have no power here child, so cut the act."

Eve climbed into the back of the car and sat without saying a word during the drive to the farm. It was pitch black, blacker than anywhere Eve had ever been in her life. There were no lights in farm windows, no stores, and no streetlights. Mailboxes were passed, lit for a moment by the car's headlights, then were lost to the blackness. The Depression was consuming not only the energy from the people but the light from their lives.

Eve lasted two years at the farm, her two half-brothers stayed away from her as much as possible, not because they had other things to do, which was true, but mostly because they did not want to be around her. Five years older than Jim and six older than Doug, they were like children to an adult. She found a few friends at school until their parents told Liz they did not want their daughters and sons to see Eve anymore. Liz understood.

She left a curt note blaming them for her sad state; it explained nothing. She added a PS, saying she would send them an address where Charlie could send money when she needed it.

"You okay," Liz asked, standing at the door. "She'll be happy someday."

"I pray to God she will." Charlie took the last sip of his bourbon, stood, walked to the door and gave his wife a kiss. "Good night."

CHAPTER SEVEN

The warm days and warm nights pushed color and sugar into the sour cherries. The sweets were developing even faster. Rows of yellow and red blushed Royal Anns came first, (Doug, in a tender moment, reminded Anne that she was like these jewels, luscious), then the deep red Bings and Black Tartarians, all for fresh eating; the remaining cherries were the tart Montmorency: row after row, twenty two feet on center, ninety trees to the acre, one hundred and sixty acres, fourteen thousand four hundred trees. A deep sulfur smell, mixed with the rising sweetness of the cherries, filled the air as Howie walked the gravel to the studio; the sprayer left the leaves lightly dusted with the yellow sulfur powder along with another chemical that Howie knew had to be toxic because his grandfather always wore a mask when mixing it.

The familiar aromas of paint and linseed oil filled Howie's nose; his eyes watered from the turpentine as he entered the studio. Across the room, lounging on a couch, a strikingly red haired woman quickly pulled a sheet to her chin. She smiled at Howie. He noticed the smile and also saw that it and the sheet were all that she wore.

"Good morning boy," Frank Rex's said. His voice carried over the low wall that partly crossed the room, a large canvas stood high above the partition; in his left hand he held a large oval palette, spotted with colors. In his right hand, he held a long narrow brush covered with white paint; he waved it about, like a conductor of a symphony, as he talked.

"Howard Smith, this is Jennie. She is a professional model and she's working with me on this Madonna."

"Yes sir," Howie said. His eyes jumped back and forth from the painting to the woman, then back to the painting. She smiled again and he smiled back, not sure why, but it seemed appropriate. He was embarrassed but also curious. The painting left little to his youthful imagination. Jennie, on the other hand, also began to leave little to his imagination; the sheet, due to gravity of the best kind, had retreated to reveal most of one breast. Howie turned to the painting, then back again.

"Now calm down boy, you'll hurt your neck. It's rare to see a nude woman in America, especially one as beautiful as Jennie, but I forget myself; Europe is so much more open and understanding."

"Someday you must take me there, Mr. Rex," Jennie said.

Her voice brought Howie back to reality. He smiled even though his embarrassment and excitement were still evident by the flushed color of his face.

"Jennie, we're through for today, thank you," Frank said, wiping the brush with a turpentine rag.

"Next week, Mr. Rex?" Jennie asked.

"Yes, if I am well enough. Please call on Friday. Your envelope is on the table." Frank pointed with his brush to the low mahogany table near the door.

"Thank you," Jennie answered and stood gracefully. She gathered the sheet around her, and, for a moment, stood backlit in front of the window, posing for Howie. Howie swallowed as the most spectacular woman he had ever seen stood, in shadow, behind the shear cloth. He stood transfixed to the floor, his mouth open, eyes wide.

"I would suggest you move boy; if your mother saw you right now she would give both you and me a whack on the back of the head and drive us both to Sacred Heart to confession." The mention of his mother sadly brought him back to the studio.

"Come over here," Frank said and motioned to him.

Jennie walked through the open door of the kitchen, off to one side was the bathroom. Howie slowly worked his way through the canvases and small tables strewn about the room. Paintings, many half-finished portraits, stood against the walls like casual observers of the day-to-day happenings in the studio.

"Painting from life is the best way paint, especially the human form. Sketches and photos help, but the sun on a shoulder, a cheek, or a breast is the best way to express a shape or a color. A woman's skin can be translucent in the sunlight, especially if backlit as Jennie was; and you can see here," he pointed to the left shoulder, "the sun seems to flow through her skin and reflect up onto her face. The hair, especially hers, captures the sun then acts like a filter as it reaches to her breast."

Howie, for a moment, was a student again, interested in what Frank Rex was saying and why he was pointing at the nipple of her right breast, her long red hair encircled the broader oval of deep pink. Then, just as quickly, Howie's mind succumbed to his first view of a naked woman and a breast, her breast, as large as his hand, now not more than two feet away, painted; yes, but it was hers, and he remembered Jennie on the couch, gravity, and the sheet, and all it might have been.

"I see you're still recovering from your fall from the other night," Frank said with a smile. "Go sit and I'll be with you in a moment."

Frank went into the kitchen and Howie sat on the still warm couch where Jennie had posed. Frank returned with Jennie, her arm entwined in his. He said good-by to the now very properly dressed model; she picked up the envelope, blew Frank and Howie each a kiss, and strolled out the door.

"See you next week, Jennie," Frank said.

"Good-by, Mr. Rex, and it's a pleasure to meet you Howard, good-bye." Then to Howie's sad pleasure, she was gone. His eyes followed her out the door.

"God damn it, stop that. Haven't you ever seen a naked woman before? You fourteen or fifteen, and still never seen a naked woman, not even in one of those nature magazines?" Frank looked at Howie and then realized, "I guess you haven't." His last remark offered with a big smile on his face.

"She work for you?"

"Yes she does. Models for me, and keeps me sharp with my figure drawing. A very proper woman, reasonably educated, can draw well herself; that's where I met her, at a class I was teaching on sketching and drawing. I think you're the only one around here who hasn't met her. They all think something else is going on, but sadly, at my age and with all the medication I am taking, it just proves that the mind is willing but the flesh is weak. The old pecker doesn't seem to work like it used to."

Howie smiled at the joke, but also understood the sadness behind his uncle's comment.

"Well, let's talk about painting. Come over here and let's go over the basics again. Did you bring your sketch book?"

Howie's interest in drawing and sketching the scenes about the farm was high at times and low at times. He would draw with his soft pencils for a few days, then, when other things caught his interest, he would completely forget his pencils and sketchbook. He had all the discipline of a fourteen year old, mixed with the need to learn everything.

Frank Rex taught well, but he wanted Howie to learn everything in one summer that a half-century of painting had taught him. This was too much information but he knew that Howie tried. There were moments of comprehension, and then, moments of confusion, far too many of the latter. Why this color over that and not the other way around? Why rough canvas instead of smooth? Why is one white better than another white?

"White paint is white paint, Uncle," Howie said, frustrated.

"Maybe, but each white acts differently with the other paints, their pigments blend with the basic nature of the colors and the oils; it's a chemical reaction for some."

But Frank knew the boy tried and his two small canvases of fruit and crockery were acceptable. Frank knew that the boy worked hard to please him.

The late morning heat started to fill the cinderblock building through the open windows, cicadas buzzed in the trees just outside.

"Smells like a small village in Catalonia," Frank said with a sigh. "A touch of heat on the pines gives off the aroma of turpentine and the woods begin to smell like a fresh painting. A whiff of a breeze off the lake is like a draft of wind from the Riu Cardener and even the birds sound the same. God, Howie, how I miss Spain and Barcelona; I probably won't see them again due to this god damn cancer but I see them every day in my mind and in my sketch books."

Frank walked to a stack of spiral sketchbooks piled on the shelves of a bookcase. Howie could make out the names of the books on the shelves; Hemingway's name, a well-worn encyclopedia, large books with Sargent and Homer on the edges, and a tattered Audubon. He saw books on insects, wildlife, farming, and a collection of volumes with red binders and the name Thomas Aquinas. Howie had heard of Hemingway, but the others were unknown to him.

Frank pulled three of the sketchbooks from the pile, crossed the room and sat next to Howie.

"These are from a small village, near Barcelona, where I spent many winters, mostly before the war."

He opened the first and the sharp lines and boldness of the drawings struck Howie; so different from the work his uncle drew now. Each line placed with purpose and direction, the streets solid bases for the adobe walls and tile roofs. Howie could see the colors in the sketches even though they were charcoal or brown conté crayon. He could feel the warmth of the sun on the dusty street and the cool shade under the awnings and tarps hung over tables overflowing with fruit. He heard the voices in the market, the smell of the animals, and his wet fingers as he dragged them through the water in the public fountain. For the first time in his life, he knew what art could do. It was beyond a pleasant picture, more than a photograph; it was his uncle's senses, drawn by his fingers, bringing to life his uncle's view of the world, a street in Cardona, market day, one late hot Spanish afternoon.

Howie watched Frank turn the pages, the next sketch, an hour later, the same day, a bit different but the same street, same shops. The day was passing. The shadows became shorter, rather then longer. The canvas awnings hung limp, then lifted by an afternoon breeze, then limp again. The last page, almost dark, a negative of the others, lights could be seen in the windows now, glowing, pushing light into the street. And throughout all the drawings, in every hour, one figure, a woman, was constant.

Howie pointed to the figure, Frank smiled.

"She was ninety eight years old in 1932. She would sit there day after day with her tea. Her great-granddaughter would bring her what she needed and then take away her cup and refill it. A remarkable woman, Anna was her name, same as your mother's. I wrote it in the corner." He pointed to her name and a date, November 3, 1932. "She sat in this same spot from morning till night, occasionally shelling beans or fixing some lace, but usually she would just sit and watch. Notice in these sketches, she is a part of the drawing but doesn't dominate the drawing, you have to understand what you are sketching, and here, I'm trying to show her what I was, someone who watches, observes, no judgments. Her name was Anna Teresa d'Berga, Anna from Berga, a small village about twenty miles away."

"Did you talk to her?"

"Often," Frank said, "She had wonderful stories to tell and tales of life and the changes in her small part of the world. She had never seen the sea, even though she lived less than forty miles from the Mediterranean. She had four husbands, all dead. She had seven children, twenty-four grandchildren, and she had lost count at forty of the number of great and great-great grandchildren she had. Most of them she had never seen; they lived in Barcelona, Valencia and Madrid. She felt that her life was as full as it could have been and she would enjoy her old age until she died."

Frank opened a second book and the first piece was a sketch, a fine line drawing of a woman's face, clear eyes, full cheeks, thin eyebrows, lips still full, and everything was supported and held firmly in place by a strong but crisp jaw. Her nose was Roman yet, even at her great age, feminine. Her eyes were blue, or that's what Howie saw in the sepia sketch, blue as the Spanish sky.

"Is this Anna?" Howie asked.

"Yes it is, in the winter of 1938, she is 104." Frank turned away from the book and walked toward the window, he faced the sun, his back to Howie. "In 1939, when the Loyalists had been forced into Barcelona, Franco's men took each small village, one after another. When they took Cardona, Anna was still sitting in her chair. Three women, one was her granddaughter, stood next to her and Anna challenged two of Franco's soldiers and told them to leave, "Go back to your mothers and your wives and children and leave us alone." The soldiers shot each of them in the head and then left."

Howie stared at Anna's face; this book was all that held a memory of a century of a life. He turned to his uncle; a tear rolled down the man's face and was lost in his beard.

"Why did she sit there for so many years, Uncle Frank?"

Frank turned back to the window; a breath of resin-scented air ruffled his steel grey hair. "I asked her once and she smiled and said quietly, *'Estoy viendo la vida,'* I am watching life. La vida, Howard, life."

His mind reeling, all he could see, as he walked back to the farm, were Jennie's breasts and the soft curve of her shoulder. Unconsciously, he rubbed his crotch and a quick wash of soft electricity caused him to shudder. He rubbed again and the mild shock shook him one more time. It felt good.

The warmth of the morning again turned to afternoon heat, a humid heat; now clouds covered the brilliant blue sky of the morning and the humidity, rising from the ground, was tangible, as if moisture was being drawn from every still green leaf and blade of grass. The stifling air was full with tawny dust. Howie turned the corner of the barn and met Charlie and Bill heading toward him.

"There ya'are boy, been looking for you," Charlie said. "Your mother said I should find you and bring you home. Frank okay?"

"Uncle Frank is much better today. He's been painting and showed me sketches of Spain," Howie answered.

"Drawings?" Bill asked.

"Yes they were, wonderful sketches."

"He should draw more; he could make more money from magazines if he drew more," Charlie added.

"Grandpa, I really don't think he cares. To him, his art is his life, his way of seeing. He draws to capture a part of what he is that day, that minute. I really don't think he cares what other people see or think."

"That's for damn sure. I can tell you for the forty odd years I have known the man he has never concerned himself with what others thought or what their opinions were. He has been, and always will be, his own man and counsel; it's also gotten him in trouble over the years."

"What trouble?" Bill asked.

"Never mind, Bill, I'll tell you when you're older," Charlie said and winked at Howie, "Much older. Anyway, your mother wants you home. The radio forecasts a windy rainstorm late this afternoon. It's raining and blowing hard across the lake in Wisconsin and it's coming this way. So she wants you home."

"How about Uncle Frank?" Bill asked.

"He'll be just fine, Bill. That cinderblock building of his has stopped blizzards; a rain storm isn't a big deal."

Anne was waiting on the porch; she and Liz were shucking peas into a bowl, another bowl held the shells. Tall glasses of iced tea sat nearby on the table.

"How's Frank?" Liz asked.

"Howie says he's painting, feels much better," Charlie said.

"I would think so, I saw Jennifer Parsons drive out about an hour ago. She looked quite happy," Liz said.

Anne turned and looked at Liz. Liz shrugged a bit and smiled.

"Did you meet Jennie?" Anne asked.

"Yes ma'am, very pretty for an older woman." Howie was becoming a bit uncomfortable. "Do you know her, Mom?"

"We've met. Yes, she's very pretty and Uncle Frank enjoys her company." With that comment, the conversation about Jennie seemed to end abruptly. It was obvious to Howie that the women did not approve of Jennie and her relationship with Frank Rex. He looked at **Charlie**.

"What are you grinning at old man?" Liz said.

"I'm not that old, as you well know, and I would appreciate a change of subject," Charlie said.

"Boys, with the Fourth of July coming up, your father is supposed to be here for the whole week, so I suggest you put your heads together and see what you can come up with," Anne said.

"Neat-o," Bill answered.

"Something that's beyond fun; something that we will remember the rest of our lives."

"Mom," Bill said, "I'm sure I can come up with something."

JULY

CHAPTER EIGHT

John Adams believed the Fourth of July would be celebrated, *". . . by succeeding generations as the great anniversary festival. It ought to be solemnized with pomp and parade, with shows, games, sports, guns, bells, bonfires and illuminations from one end of this Continent to the other, from this time forward, forever more."* And every effort would be made by the town of Elk River to meet Adams's beliefs and expectations. Since the war, the Fourth of July had grown into a day set aside from the rest of summer. It alone, even in the middle of the week, could shut stores down and quiet the cannery for the afternoon. It also stopped the picking if it had started early, when, after a warm winter and mild spring, cherry picking started early; but the afternoon of the Fourth, cherries or not, was reserved for parades, picnics, long-winded speeches, illuminations and fireworks.

River Street ran north to south: the north end died at a parking lot that overlooked Elk Lake; the south end stopped at the gate to a grand mansion built by Charlie's father sixty years earlier when he owned the sawmill. The home sat on a rock ledge that overlooked the outlet carved by Elk River as it rushed into Lake Michigan. On this Fourth of July, the general manager of the cannery was renting the home; Charlie's father sold the house in the 1920s.

River Street was five blocks long because that was all the length it could find; people sat on curbs waiting for the parade. A small park, with two memorials in the center, created an open space between the clapboard houses and the brick storefronts that faced the street. The first memorial, granite and bronze with crossed flags cut into the hard stone, listed eight men who died in the First World War. The crisply cut names were carved deep into the stone below the flags. The bronze casting of an olive wreath was bolted hard into the granite above the names. The second monument was broader and shorter. It needed its width and mass to hold the bronze plaque listing fifteen men who died in World War II. James Allan Smith, the thirteenth down, had a star and a heart next to his name: the star was for bravery, the heart for a wound, and the name for his death. Two of the squat memorial's sides were plain, like they anticipated holding something, but on the fourth side a bright bronze panel said Korea, three names were cast into its face. On this Fourth of July these men would be honored; no other area of northern Michigan had given so many to war.

Bill and Howie sat in front of the town hall. Margaret and her brothers joined them; she jostled Howie with her hip and, to his astonishment, it didn't annoy him as much as it once did. He also noticed that the bright red pullover, snug over her bathing suit, only accentuated her sylphlike breasts, items Howie, to his wonder, had never noticed before. He felt the warmth of her through her hip as she snuggled close and offered a stick of gum.

"Thanks Maggie," he said.

"You're welcome," Margaret answered, in a tone of voice that Howie had never heard before; and, after he took the gum, she smiled and winked. Then, to Howie's horror and delight, she gave him a kiss on the cheek; he liked her soft lips, but he looked around quickly to see if anyone had noticed them, nobody was looking. When she turned away, he touched his fingers to the spot, as if he could catch the moment.

The parade formed behind the township hall, and, as it strung out along River Street, expanded to the full eight blocks. The twenty-member high school band might, if the cadence was slow enough, play three marches. The mayor and other officials followed the band in surplus jeeps. Small, but disciplined, formations of men marched behind the politicians. The first group, men in their seventies, fought the Germans in World War I; and, even though he hadn't fought in the trenches, Charlie marched with his friends and comrades. The second group, dressed in their navy and army World War II uniforms, were, for the most part, the children of the men in the first group. Doug Smith marched proudly with these men, his uniform a bit worn. The Korean contingent followed.

Each year, the comrades in the first group grew smaller by a man; the second and third groups remained strong even though many would drive up from Detroit for the parade and the holiday.

The town's fire truck lined up in front of a war surplus Willeys jeep that somehow showed up every year, a few straws still stuck to its underside and the tires. Howie remembered that real army reserve half-tracks and howitzers rolled down River Street two years ago. He also remembered staring into the sun as three P-38 Mustangs flew low over the town; someday maybe jets would fly low over the pines. There might be a chance, his grandfather said; the huge orange Coast Guard helicopters might fly over today.

The parade was a success: the band played four tunes; two Souzas, one march that Howie hadn't heard before, and the Michigan fight song. Charlie grumbled because the high school principal went to Michigan and took every opportunity to annoy Michigan State graduates, even though there were few that had gone to any college in this town.

Howie waved to Officer Dugan as he drove by and saluted his grandfather, his father, and Roger as they marched by. He knew Roger had never fought in Korea but spent his time stationed on a supply ship in Hawaii that made monthly runs to Japan. Roger looked different in his seaman's whites, deeply tanned, the uniform almost glowed from the contrast. After the parade, the soldiers stood at attention around the two monuments. Howie watched as Roger saluted the memorial, and, in the bright sunshine, saw a tear sit on the top of his cheek. It never moved; it hung there till the final note of Taps disappeared in the pines, and he quickly brushed it away as he brought down his salute. Two of the fallen on the bronze plate were close friends of Roger's. Howie watched his father and grandfather approach the monument; his father kissed his own hand and placed it on his brother's name; the bronze warmed for a moment, then he slowly withdrew it. Charlie did the same.

The parade started at 2:00, the helicopters flew low and loud at 2:15, and it was over at 2:30. Patriotic and political speeches blustered from the steps of the township hall, the last thanking God for Eisenhower's return to health, another half-hour passed until the speechifying finally stopped, and the picnic started. To Howie, all the activities were appetizers to the fireworks.

To Bill, the speeches were torture; Anne told him to sit still and listen.

"Why do I have to listen to all this yak-yaking, Mom? It's the same thing they said last year," Bill said without the slightest bit of empathy.

"You sit and listen like everyone else. It's the price you have to pay for ice cream," Anne ordered.

Speeches be damned, it was all Bill could do not to get up and run to the long table piled with great tubs of chocolate, strawberry, vanilla and cherry ice cream kept frozen by great wedges of dry ice that misted up a white fog that fell in whirling cascades to the ground.

Six foot long iron grills stood nearby billowing smoke and steam into the air. The racks, almost red over the charcoal, were covered with snapping and sizzling hamburger patties, hot dogs, and sausages. Another wire and steel contraption, higher, and overhanging the meat, held rows of yellow corn singed black. Great stoneware bowls of potato salad, beans, and pickles sat on long tables stretched out from the ends of the grills. Piles of buns, right-sized for each type of meat, were stacked behind bowls of catsup, mustard and chopped relish. Paintbrushes sat in the sauces to make it easier to slather the buns and meat. Meals were eaten at the picnic tables, on blankets, and on the grass covered dunes.

Music blared from the town hall steps. A record player sang into the microphone used by the politicians, and, for the last hour, played Jimmy Dorsey and Benny Goodman for the crowd. Howie was stunned by his parents who waved to all from the middle of the street, just before they started to jitterbug their way along the centerline. Soon others joined in.

"They won championships before the war," Liz said.

"For dancing?"

"Yes, for dancing, they're very good, don't you think?"

"Yeah, I guess so, but they're old. They're not supposed to dance like that!"

"It's in the blood, Howie. I see my blood in your father; he's so full of life when he's up here. The two of them just sort of light up, kind of shows, don't you think?" Liz said, her hips followed the music until Charlie took her hand and then walked her toward the street. Howie saw his grandfather's butt start to bounce back and forth a bit.

Howie felt a tap on his shoulder.

"Hi cous," Margaret said. "This music is so boring. What do you think?"

Howie didn't know how to answer. He just stared at her red hair and her even redder swimsuit, her pullover had disappeared, Howie was glad. "Yeah, it's pretty lame," he said, not knowing why.

"Lame? Howard, it's the worst noise I've ever heard. Wait here and watch."

Before he understood what she said, she quickly bolted through the crowd, bounded up the steps and produced, from under her arm, a flat square colored board. She smiled at Howie, sat next to the record player, and coolly waited until Sinatra's Come Fly with Me finished. Then picking up the record, she gently placed it on the pile next to the player, quickly withdrew a black record from her album, and reverently placed it on the player.

The loud and deep voice of Elvis Presley blasted across the street, through the park and out into Lake Michigan yelling something about staying off his blue shoes and something else Howie couldn't understand. The crowd, en masse, turned toward the steps; most were smiling and a few of the younger teenage girls started to dance. Margaret stood defiantly, next to the record player, willing to defend her music and her idol; Patton would have been proud. A tall red-haired man walked calmly up the steps, stood next to Margaret, waited until Elvis finished singing, then took the record off the player, and slid it in the cardboard cover as Margaret watched, helpless. Then smiling to all, he took his daughter by the waist, picked her up, and carried her down the steps, her red hair bouncing at every step. Laughter, applause and boos were heard from all parts of the crowd. She waved to everyone, said something about the king and quickly ran to Howie after her father sat her down.

"He's the best," Margaret said.

"Your father?" answered Howie.

"No, lame brain, Elvis Presley. He's the greatest thing in rock and roll. I have two of his long play records and a bunch of 45's. Every nickel I can get is spent buying his music. He's great; he's the king of rock and roll."

"I've heard his music. He's okay."

"Okay! He's more than okay. He's dark, he's handsome, and he's so cool. He's a dream. His songs reach into my heart. He was on Milton Berle a few months ago and that's the second time I've seen him on live television. He's so cool."

"You said that," Howie said.

"Well, he is; he's very cool."

Howie wasn't sure about Margaret, Elvis was interesting but he wiggled around too much, kind of silly looking. All the girls at home and in school were crazy over him; he couldn't figure it out.

Howie watched as Margaret walked away swinging her hips to a march. Almost immediately, the crowd formed lines and started dancing down River Street following Margaret. He saw Bill get in line behind their mother and watched him dance along with the rest.

Liz came back to Howie. "Why aren't you dancing, Howard?"

Calling him Howard startled him. "Don't really feel like it, Grams." He continued to stare at Margaret as she disappeared into the crowd.

"She's a very pretty young woman. It's hard to dance and watch her at the same time; when the next song starts, go ask her to dance."

Howie looked at Liz like she'd told him to go and eat worms. "Don't think so, she likes rock and roll and I like baseball. It's hard to dance to baseball."

Liz chuckled. "Yes I do believe you're right, but my guess is that someday she'll want to play baseball and you had better be there to catch."

"What?" Howie asked with a strange look on his face.

"You'll find out someday and from the looks of you, it won't be too long. Want a hotdog?"

"Sure."

Liz and Howie walked over to the grills and pulled two bratwurst off the fire; they slathered them up and sat at the family picnic table under the pines.

"Grams, do you think she's going to get in trouble for putting on that record?"

"Don't think so, lot a people were dancing to the tune, kind of catchy, if you ask me. Her father was only a little annoyed, but he had a big smile on his face and was telling everyone he was a big Bill Haley fan anyway."

"Bill Haley?"

"Get with it boy; seems to have been the guy that coined the term 'rock and roll' or something close to it. In fact, I like the sound of what he plays and the same thing goes for that good-looking guy, Elvis Presley. If I were forty years younger, I would be all dreamy about those guys."

Howie looked at his grandmother and had the most difficult time imagining her falling for somebody as slick as Elvis.

"Did you dance when you were younger?" Howie asked.

"Did I dance? Yes, Howie, I did. I danced professionally for about two years just before I met your grandfather. I went to New York City in 1914 and worked as a floor girl for Florenz Ziegfeld in his Follies. My mother, your great-grandmother, had a fit, but my father knew I had to get it out of my blood. I won a talent contest in Chicago, Flo's hometown, and it included a chance to audition in New York.

So there I was, rooming with two other girls, one from Iowa, I think, and the other one never said where she was from. I worked my feet off for what seemed like twenty-four hours a day, practicing steps and moves so that all of us, must have been fifty girls, could move together as one. I needed to know at least fifty different routines and they really kept at us to keep thin and, since I couldn't sing, I just burned out. But yes, I danced at the Ziegfeld Follies and I wouldn't change a thing."

Howie looked at his grandmother in a new light and now understood the lightness in her step and the graceful way she did things.

"Why did you quit New York and dancing, Grams; you didn't like it?" Howie said.

"I loved it. Howie, it was the most exciting thing I ever did, and I miss it, even today, almost forty some odd years later. I was good, very good, but I wasn't strong enough; you almost have to be an athlete, it just takes too much out of you, so I left," Liz said, sadness in her last words.

The afternoon eased softly into evening; Howie danced twice with his cousin and once with his mother. The ladies formed small groups with their baby carriages, a drink in one hand and a cigarette in the other, many of the men asleep on the grassy dunes.

A woman walked unsteadily across the shuffleboard courts; she wore a bold print dress, it hung tight in the humid air. She turned toward Howie and stared at him, he was stunned; it was his aunt. A shiver coursed through him like cold lightning. She held a drink in one hand and a cigarette in the other. She spotted him and then raised her glass slightly. He was struck by her strange attitude and her look. "God, don't let her walk over here,'" he said to himself. As if that were a cue, she stumbled toward Howie.

"You staring at me, Howard? Why you staring at me, you little one-armed creep?"

"Sorry, Aunt Eve, I wasn't staring at you. I was looking past you down to the river," he answered.

"Looking at fucking what?" she said with a crooked grin, lipstick pushed away from the corner of her mouth.

"Nothing, Aunt Eve. Just the river, wondered when the fireworks was gonna start." Howie looked at his aunt's face, at a loss for words. She drained his mind of everything, just like a syringe had sucked it dry. He tried to build a wall of defense but it was hard, "The fireworks, okay?"

Eve Titus just glowered, waved her cigarette at him, and said, "If I ever catch you staring at me again, I will personally pop you in the eye, you and that son-of-a-bitch brother of yours. And you should hide that thing; no one wants to see it."

"Bill has nothing to do with this, or with whatever your problem is," Howie shot back. "And my arm ain't none of your business."

"Oh, a fucking tough guy, protects his little baby brother. Well that doesn't mean a god damn thing to me, I'll still pop you one."

"That's enough, Eve," Charlie's deep voice came over Eve's shoulder. "Why don't you go home now and rest. Howie wants to go to the fireworks and so do I. You hate them and it would be a good time for you to go home. I'll walk you across the street, ok?"

Eve turned slowly to face her father; Howie couldn't see her face, but her shoulders slumped a bit. She turned her tangled head away from her father and looked into the darkening sky, "There's a storm coming Father, and it will swallow us, whole." She flicked her cigarette to the grass. Howie saw her stiffen as she inhaled quickly, her back swelled across the bold fabric. "Sure, why the fuck stay around here, probably something good on the radio anyway," she said to no one.

Howie watched the two fade into the dusk as they crossed the street heading toward the alley. Her remark stunned him; she always wanted to fight, to complain, and try to be superior. He saw how pathetic she had become, like a lost soul hiding from God and screaming at the world from the shadows.

Bill and Margaret strolled across the grass toward Howie. He watched her approach; he tingled inside. It felt good.

"Howie, Margaret wants to see where the fisherman drowned and wants you to show her; she asked for you special," Bill said, giggling at his remark.

The three of them walked toward the power plant. Even in the deepening light they could see three fishermen on the catwalk. In this part of Michigan, a holiday was not granted to the fish.

"It was there that he slipped," Howie said, indicating the narrow shelf extending out directly below them. "He disappeared about there and, at the point, out there where the river turns flat, is where they pulled him out." Howie then pointed to where they were fishing and where they snagged in the man's fishing gear and his musky.

"I am the guy that did that," Bill said, as he puffed up his chest.

"Nothing to be proud of Bill," Howie said. "A man died who didn't need to. It was a stupid accident, all for a damned fish."

They stood quietly for a moment till Bill said, "Let's go see the fireworks."

"I have to stay with my baby sister," Margaret said. "Mom asked me to baby sit and this is where I'll be, sort of a penalty for playing Elvis Presley. I can see them from here."

"Too bad Margaret," Bill said. "They're really neat when you are right under 'em."

"Sorry you can't go. Would you like me to stay?" Howie asked.

"With my baby sister and a couple of my mom's friends, I hope not. You watch the fireworks. I'll see you later."

Bill grabbed his brother's hand and pulled him away, "Let's go."

"Okay Bill, later Margaret."

"Goodbye, Howard, and please, come by later."

The boys headed down River Street to the small park that overlooked Elk Lake. The street was littered with sparkler wires, black snakes of carbon from ignited pellets, and the debris of noisy firecrackers. The light from handheld sparklers lit the way; the crowd along the lake's edge seemed larger than the group that watched the parade.

Charlie told Howie that fireworks had been shot from the spit of land to the west over Elk Lake for almost fifty years, but this was the first year they were using a raft. When the river was dammed and the lake formed, a small forest of birch and maple trees were drowned. Now these stumps and snags stuck out of the water, like silent sentries across the shallows, waiting, at broken attention. These blackened and broken stumps, brought to life by the eerie light of the rockets, now marched across a mirrored battlefield. Flares of red, bursts of

yellow, and irradiated green showered these wooden soldiers as they waded toward a beachhead they would never reach. Great arcing shafts of sparks and stars exploded in colors over the glass smooth water. The two reflecting images, above and below, reached toward Howie and the shore.

Each explosion showered the crowd with color. Howie turned to watch their faces light up, red, white, blue; his tennis shoes were wet from the lake's shallows. He looked to the lake then back to their faces, then to the whole crowd, and felt lightheaded again, floating, detached, here, but not here. The crowd thinned where the poplars filled in along the shore, their silvery green leaves and almost white bark glowed with each burst. The timing of the shells intensified and Howie could sense the show's conclusion. The concussions and colors came faster and faster until they blended into one giant roar. Howie watched one single rocket veer off to the right, arch over the poplars, and spin itself into the wood. It blasted into a shower of red sparks and white stars. A shadow stood between Howie and the explosion. A giant man, with hands on his hips and legs as large as the trees, faced him. The flares continued behind the man, the wood now burned, great sheets of flames fired high into the blackness. The man stood, unmoving. Howie slowly pulled his right arm upward and extended his tortured hand toward the figure. The man's face briefly flashed in the light from the fire, beard, dark eyes, shaggy head of hair; he then turned and walked into the poplar grove and into the fire.

The rocket fizzled out but the trees still burned; Howie heard fire trucks, their claxons added to the din of the crowd. Men raced by Howie toward the fire. He stood, looking into the darkest part of the grove, the part untouched by the flames. A hand gently took his shoulder.

"You okay boy? Didn't get burned, did you?" Charlie asked.

"No Grandfather, but it sure was spectacular."

He looked up at the man's grey eyes, the color faded from his grandfather's face as the fire quickly died down.

"He was there, Grandfather. There, in the woods. He stood and stared at me just like at the river. He stood looking at me."

"Who stood there, Howie?"

"I don't know, but he was there, a giant, eight feet tall, huge shoulders and a beard. Couldn't see his face tonight, but I did last week when the man drowned. He was right there." Howie pointed, this time with his left arm, at the woods.

"You sure you're okay? Been a rough couple of weeks, maybe you're just a little tired and are seeing things, especially with the fire and all."

"No. I'm fine. There was a man, a big man, there." He pointed again, this time like he was throwing a baseball. "There, damn it, and then he turned away toward the fire and walked into it. Then everyone came and he was gone."

Charlie turned Howie around and led him back to the parking lot. Car lights washed through the crowd sending shafts of light out onto the lake; the wooden soldiers continued to stand, frozen, at attention, lifeless.

Margaret waited for Howie, but he did come back.

CHAPTER NINE

There is nothing as spectacular as a Mid-western weather front surging in from the northwest, driven by a cold front from Montana, mixing violently with a warm tropical low being sucked up the Mississippi Valley into the heartland of America. Anvil storms sixty thousand feet high, lit by the afternoon sun, make photographers weep with joy, and farmers fear for their very lives; but when the warm summer waters of Lake Michigan are added to the stew, frightening things materialize: torrential rain, fist-sized hail, and fearsome windstorms that can shred a crop of corn or an orchard of cherries, in minutes.

Doug Smith pulled into the driveway. Bill ran to the car and grabbed his father's hand to lead him to the porch but turned when he heard the sound of the passenger door slam. Eve Titus, standing next to the car, stared at the young boy. She looked sober in a bright green and blue flowered dress, white shoes and white belt. Her hair, neatly secured with a band that pulled her mousey brunette hair tightly back, emphasized her gaunt, but well made-up, face. Small gold earrings dangled from her ears and a black patent leather purse was wedged tightly under her arm, only the purse seemed wrong: ill chosen, too black, too shiny; it tilted the look.

"Good afternoon, Eve," Anne said. "You look great, and thank you for coming out to dinner."

"Thank you, Anne, I feel much better today. A little rest was all I needed. How are you boys, you look so fine and handsome. Nice tans. Sorry about the other day, I wasn't feeling very well."

Howie shrugged and Bill fidgeted and twisted about. The last thing Bill wanted to do was to be here with his aunt.

"I can't stand her, why does she have to be here and wreck the time we have with dad? She's a witch," Bill said, a whisper in Howie's ear.

"She's not a witch but she's dad's half-sister and our aunt, for better or worse, so you will just have to make the best of it. Besides, after today we may not have to see her for a while, maybe a couple of days. Dad mentioned Sleeping Bear Dunes so maybe a field trip is planned for tomorrow before he goes back to Chicago. What do you think?"

"That would be cool, as long as she doesn't have to go," Bill said.

"You boys can go inside and get ready for supper, and stop your whispering; it's not polite. Stay close by though; this storm will be a big one I think. Has all the signs," Liz said. She looked to the south, above the orchard, tumbles of clouds reached ten times higher than the trees.

"Yes ma'am," Bill answered, and followed his brother into the house.

Eve sat near Anne and ran her hands down the top of her legs, smoothing the colored dress over her thighs. Her hands were steady, yet Anne could see the red nicks, bruises, and scars from wear and tear. Her small watch, with its black strap, had stopped at 8:43 someday in the past; Anne wondered whether it happened in the morning or afternoon.

Charlie came out with a glass of lemonade for Eve. "Thank you, Dad," Eve said. Charlie seemed a bit taken aback by her thank you and smiled at his daughter. Turning toward the orchard, he looked directly to the south, his smile faded, he knitted his brow.

The air stilled and became a thick blanket laid over the farm and the orchard; the sky had turned to a greenish gray and the world seemed to flatten, no shadows; the white barn now glowed a bilious yellow. Olive green washed across the horizon above the trees and a dark musty brown edge now slashed across the onrushing front.

"Liz, get everyone inside, quickly," Charlie said and slowly turned to his family, some seated, some standing; the boys looked through the screen door. "When this thing hits it will be sudden and very wet; everyone in, now!"

Liz and Anne grabbed the cushions and Charlie grabbed the glasses; they went inside. Eve carried nothing; she stood, staring at the clouds. Doug watched her dress ripple from the first breath of the front. In a matter of seconds the tops of the trees twisted about from shearing wind gusts pushed out from the unstoppable wall of brown clouds.

"Come inside, Eve," Doug said. "Come inside, now!"

"God is coming," Eve cried. "God is coming, Douglas. I can see him in the blackness. He's coming to take me away from this world; my ride home is in those clouds." She turned as yellow as the barn; her dress pushed tight against her thin body by the wind. Her breasts and waist and hips were thinly covered; the wind pushed hard against her body and left nothing for the cloth to hide. Doug turned quickly away, embarrassed. His half-sister stood naked but covered in blue and green and yellow; her hair exploded from the restraining hairclip and slapped her face.

"He is coming for me, Douglas," she yelled.

"Don't be foolish, get in the house," Doug said.

"God doesn't fool with anyone," she screamed. "He's in this storm and it's my ride away from this fucking hellhole of a world." The wind roared with an answer that raged through the pines that tried to bulwark the farm, limbs cracked and splintered, cherries flew like bullets; green debris choked the air.

"Get inside now, Eve." Doug grabbed her arm and pulled her toward the door. The screen door slammed wide open and Charlie dashed out to grab both of his children. He grabbed and pulled Doug's free arm and reached for his oldest child.

A crack of lightning struck the tallest pine directly above the house, the explosion deafened everyone. Doug felt a sharp electric tingle and released his grip on Eve's wrist; she twisted away and ran toward the black wall of wind consuming the orchard. The sheeting rain, running ahead of the blackness, shrouded his view of her disappearing into the trees. He turned back to his father for help and saw him sprawled across the ground; raindrops bounced off his aged face and filled the wells of his wide opened eyes. He looked again for Eve; he saw nothing but wind, water, and blackness.

Grabbing his father, hoisting him over his shoulder, he ran into the house. The screen door slammed behind them unheard, the roaring of the storm drowned out the sound of it being sucked open, ripped away from the frame and splintered into a hundred wind scattered pieces. The storm's throat became a profound growl louder than a locomotive. Liz stood near the door to the basement, bracing it open, as Anne rushed past to help her husband carry Charlie's body down the stairway.

"The boys, where are the boys?" Doug screamed.

"In the cellar," Anne yelled back. Doug took the first step down the stair and twisted to clear himself and his father from the door, Charlie's head nicked the frame. Anne held his legs and Liz quickly pulled the heavy storm door shut behind them. Doug stumbled his way down the steps to the earthen floor of the cellar followed by the women. Liz cradled her husband's head in her arms as Doug knelt and set his body down on the floor. Blood began to flow from the cut on Charlie's forehead. She took her skirt hem and pushed hard against his forehead; his eyes never closed or blinked.

"He's alive, he bleeds," Liz said.

The boys ran to their father. Howie stood for a moment and stared at the face of his grandfather, then he placed his twisted hand on his grandfather's face. At the touch, Charlie breathed in suddenly, his chest heaved, he blinked, and the breath slowly left his body. Another short series of staccato breaths were followed by a sigh that seemed audible over of the storm. He looked at his wife and smiled.

The roar outside was the loudest sound Howie had ever heard. They sat two feet apart and he could not hear his mother. Her mouth moved but no sound came out. A bang slammed the house; then the building shuddered like a body blow to a fighter, then another bang, then a cracking that twisted through everyone. Then the popping started, Howie's ears seemed to suck into his head and explode outward, again and again.

Howie watched everything move in slow motion; he looked at Bill sitting on the floor; his small hands covered his ears, his eyes small blue centered circles surrounded by a wide band of white; he didn't blink. His mother moved slowly to her husband's side and pulled herself under his arm. Charlie moved a little, his hand slowly cupped the face of his wife. Howie stood apart and watched his family through the din and thunder of the storm; he felt like he was drifting above them.

Another crash hammered the house and it pulled Howie back to reality; he heard sounds again. He looked up the stairway, toward the small window that filled the stair with a yellow-green light and watched a tree limb as it pierced the glass and drove itself into the wall and exploded into a thousand pieces of wood and glass, all in slow motion. Sparkling glass covered the stairway; the branch prevented their escape. Howie moved to his parents and Doug placed his other arm around Howie.

The storm continued to pummel the house, Howie's ears popped again and again. Then the roar diminished and stopped suddenly as if a roaring electric fan had been turned off. No noise, no sound, nothing.

The group sat huddled together on the floor, waiting. Charlie's breathing had returned to normal. Doug moved to his side.

"You okay, Dad?" Doug asked.

"Thought I was dead did you? I was awake but couldn't move. Paralyzed or something. Until you banged me into the door, I thought I was dead myself, but damn that hurt so much I knew if I were dead I shouldn't feel it. Anyway, whatever that spark from Howie's finger was, it kind of shocked me back."

Howie remembered touching his grandfather and the feel of

static electricity but it was lost amongst the confusion of the last half-hour.

"Where's Eve, Doug?" Charlie asked; Liz looked up at her son.

"She twisted away from me after the lightning strike," Doug said and looked at his mother. "Dad and I tried to pull her into the house but she broke away and ran into the orchard. I couldn't hold her; she was screaming "God is coming." Then the lightning struck and I had to get you inside. We need to get upstairs and find her."

Doug climbed the stair and tried to push the tree branch back out the window. It wouldn't move, wedged in too hard. He managed to crawl under the trunk and to the stair door; it opened easily. To his amazement, not a thing was disturbed in the kitchen, the dishes and glasses still sat on the counter and all the windows were intact, the door was wide open. Doug went back to the stair and helped Liz and Anne.

"I'll stay with grandpa, Dad," Howie said from the darkness of the basement.

"Good boy," Doug answered. Bill peeked out from under the tree branch. "It's okay, Bill, you can come up." Bill scrambled up the stair and then all four looked through the window into the yard.

A rustling noise came up the stairway, then a familiar, "God damn it". They watched Charlie climb through the door; a small branch of pine needles stuck behind his ear.

"I told him to stay in the basement, Dad, but there was no way I could stop him from climbing up here."

"Don't worry, Howie. You okay, Dad?"

"Yes, just fine, now let's go find Eve," Charlie said.

"First I'll put a bandage on that cut old man, then you, Doug, and Howie can go look for her. Damn, it's bleeding again." Liz directed Charlie to the bathroom; they stopped to look through the living room doors. The bookcases were gone or a least most of them. The great crash they heard was the huge pear tree and at the end of the house being driven through the last ten feet of the room. Papers and book pages littered the room; Liz steadied herself on a chair and took a deep breath.

"What a mess, but not as bad as it could have been; must have been a tornado. Only that kind of storm could have been so selective in its damage."

"I think you are right, Mother. Get that bandage on me so I can get the hell out of here; we'll clean this mess up later."

Five minutes later Charlie walked into the kitchen; Anne looked at the white gauze bandanna wrapping Charlie's head.

"Where's Doug?" he asked.

"Already left to look for Eve, took Howie with him. He told me to go with you as soon as you were fixed up. Couldn't keep him here and two looking for Eve was a good start."

"Good, you ready? Liz, please stay here with Bill in case she comes back; we will be back as soon as we can. I'll check out the studio in case she ended up there."

The four left the house and walked toward the spot in the orchard where Eve had entered it.

"Never been hit by lightning ladies, now I know what it's like and I do not want to do it again. My God, would you look at that." Charlie pointed to the house.

To the left, the house looked as if nothing more than a touch of rain had fallen, to the right was destruction. The uprooted pear and its crown rested on the corner of the living room, a huge branch had cleaved through the roof. Two tall white pines behind the house were cracked and broken off about ten feet from the ground. One car was engulfed in pine branches. Even from here, when they turned away from the house, they could see the canyon carved through the orchard. The rift began in the yard and continued down the hill, across the highway and into the Clayton's orchard. The storm had schizophrenically worked its way through the orchards and left a scar, three to five rows wide, of broken, ripped and stripped cherry trees. The canyon aimed directly at the farmhouse, then turned away at the driveway after knocking down the pear. Then it seemed to leap over the fence and disappear to the north.

Charlie placed his arm around Liz. "We were lucky," Liz said.

"I love you," Charlie said. Liz smiled and touched his cheek.

"Mom, Dad's coming," Bill pointed to the tangle of trees in the scar caused by the tornado.

Doug and Howie slowly walked through the last orchard row of debris and broken trees, Howie held something black. Behind them walked Frank Rex; in his arms he held Eve swaddled in her blue and green dress.

Charlie stood stoically between the women and waited for the men to reach him. His eyes never left his daughter.

"I'm sorry Dad, Eve is dead," Doug said.

Frank looked into the eyes of his brother-in-law. "Charles, I found her tangled in a tree. The storm broke her body and killed her."

Charlie ran his fingers across the cheek of his only girl; a wave of profound sadness rocked him. Howie touched his grandfather's hand.

"She looks happy Grandpa, happier than I ever remember."

"Yes Howie, she does look happy. She said God was in the storm and she had to go; I think she was right." Charlie again stroked her cheek. "I hope that He can take better care of this child than I ever could."

Liz hooked her arm under Charlie's arm and together they followed Frank toward the house. Red-green cherry marbles littered the ground.

Later in the evening, after Jimmy Dugan left, the coroner stopped at the farm briefly to issue the necessary papers. He told Doug and Anne that the tornado moved north, crossed the lake, and slammed into a small campground, injuring two men; it moved further north and destroyed a barn and took the roof off a farmhouse. Luckily, no one else was injured.

Gideon Walker rolled out of bed, sweaty and physically exhausted. The storm, fresh from its lake crossing, rolled over his small rental cabin like the hand on God; the noise, as it ripped through the pines, could not be diminished with hands held over his ears, the flashes of lightning and gut wrenching thunder drove him to his bed; where he wrapped himself in a quilt and tried to hide, and yet, could not stop what he saw.

The frigid night exploded in blood and phosphorus; the concussions threw frozen debris over him as he inched through the snow.

His nose, covered with dirt from being so close to the ground, bled from the left nostril. Ahead of him, another explosion blew off the top of a tree; it twisted through the air like a macabre tumbler, just missing him as it impaled itself in the ground. He still crawled forward.

"Got to get to the tent," he said aloud to no one, "the tent."

The canvas tent provided no more safety against the exploding shells than gauze to a grenade, but the real reasons were the men inside: forty men, men with holes in their bodies and holes in their souls. Walker crawled toward the odd dark shape that kept appearing after every whistle and every explosion. Tree bursts, high in the pines, threw shrapnel and splinters at the men as they dug into holes in the ground. The results lay in the tent: his maimed and shattered men.

They called him "Conchie" for conscientious objector. He, this man from Grosse Pointe, Michigan, had followed a difficult road to this small frozen clearing in the Belgium woods. He wore the title well and he would say, when listened to, "Yes, the war is necessary, but I cannot kill another man." It wasn't his religious beliefs, that would have been the easy way out; but, as much as he believed in a God, it was his belief deep in his soul that killing was an act far beyond his comprehension and his strength. He could defend his belief but couldn't put form to it. This belief went beyond his father, who owned one of the many small companies that supplied parts for the growing auto builders in the Detroit area and now parts for the war. It was beyond his philosophy professors at Michigan who would teach and lecture about Plato and Socrates and the dignity of man, then say this war in Europe must be fought with blood to stop Hitler. He argued for two years, while completing his masters; there had to be another way to stop this man, but it fell on attentive but deaf ears. Some days these learned men lecture this war would stop Hitler, stop his hatred and stop him from saying the things he said; other days they rationalized the opposite, that Germany had been treated unfairly, wrongly, punitively. Walker read Hitler's book, such as it was. More of a tirade than a philosophical discussion, it sent fearful shudders through him: a rant by a disillusioned man, a treatise of fear, a listing of retributions. Now, as a treatise by the leader of one of the most powerful countries in the world, it became the blueprint for his meat-grinder, his Blitzkrieg. Wars raged around the world; America stood safe, a world apart, uninvolved.

"Let the bastards kill themselves," he heard people say. "We have no place in their fights ... they've been doing it for a thousand years... that's why my grandfather left," they said. "My family wanted to be free of their wars and petty fights, they left them there. We are not involved, we will not be involved."

Gideon Walker chose to be a conscientious objector. It wasn't because he was afraid to die, he knew that would happen someday; it wasn't because he needed to make a political statement, he had no agenda. It wasn't even because he thought killing of any kind was wrong, he hunted as a youngster, with his father and uncle, for deer and other game. It came from his sense of the dignity of man, regardless of who they were or had become; this respect for the humanity in people forced him into his only choice.

That choice led him to a trail of ridicule, damnation, segregation and outright hatred. At first, he tried to believe they just didn't understand; they were acting out of anger, a lack of understanding: if he wasn't going to kill the enemy to protect America and freedom then he must be on the other side. He was slugged a couple of times and, after one altercation, spent a few nights in jail as the sheriff said, "for his own good;" the other guy went home that night even though he started it. Walker took it in stride, part of his burden; "It's the weight I must carry for my beliefs". But after a year of unrelenting death and war, he knew he had to do something, so he enlisted and joined as a CO and a medic.

Gideon Walker landed in France two days after D-Day and, for the next six months, followed the front. Now lying as flat as he could on the frozen mud in Belgium, he crawled toward the tent.

Walker worked his way through the snow and slime (from the exploded latrine where he had sat only ten seconds before the first shells hit), to the edge of the tent and his men. Another explosion and he saw the gaping hole in the side of the tent and a body lying between the cots. With his flashlight he saw the face of his lieutenant, a large slice of his face gone.

"Shit," Gideon said.

The shelling stopped. He heard moans and screams from the cots and knew some men were still alive. He worked his way down one row of cots, then the other; the lucky ones were still drugged unconscious. A couple of fellows had arms broken from a truck accident.

"Damn, you go four thousand miles around the world to fight the Nazis and the second day at the front you run into another truck at the only fucking four way intersection in all of Belgium," one of the men said, after he spit out a tooth. "It's just not right, goddamnit, just not right."

Two were dead, probably killed by the same shell as the lieutenant. He tried to calm one man who was screaming from the noise; and he eventually quieted him enough to give him a shot of morphine.

Walker crawled to end of the tent and righted the overturned medical box, and, with his flashlight, located some of the gauze and tape that had rolled under the nearest cot. He also spotted the M-1 under the bed of the last heavily bandaged soldier in the row.

"He'll be lucky if he can ever use that rifle again, assuming he even lives," Walker said, "poor bastard."

The thunder of the shelling had moved west of the hollow. Only occasional bursts came from the nearby woods, and, for the most part, silence invaded the forest; the hold your breath, wait for it, pray it doesn't end kind of silence. No lights - it would call attention to his location - the doctor and the two nurses had gone back to the base aid station to get supplies hours before the attack, said they would be back in the morning. Now, he was not sure when he would see them again.

For the rest of the night, he tried his best to help the men, talked softly to some, calmed them as best he could, and kept the IV's and drugs flowing. Finally the dark gray light slowly pushed its way through the cold fog that hung deep in the woods. He could see his hands; he could see the faces of the men, and their fear.

At first light, he pulled the lieutenant outside and laid a dark green blanket over him. Walker said a few words and went back into the tent to set up what meager defense he could against the impending Germans. Walker sat on the floor at the end tent, pulled his six foot eight inch body into as small a ball as possible and waited.

The frigid leaden morning also brought the Germans. First, he heard the roaring of the Panzers, then the distinct chatter of the soldiers as they moved up toward the aid station. No firing, he hoped the big red-cross on the tent's roof would afford him and the men some protection but it was only paint.

A sharply dressed German cut through the side of the canvas, orders bellowed and, even though Walker had some limited understanding of German, he knew in his gut that this was not the Wehrmacht, he waited. At the far end of the tent, three soldiers pushed their way through the flaps and joined the officer. They quickly surveyed the cots and the officer, his uniform black with crisp SS insignia on his collar, visible even in the gloom, he pulled out his luger, the others followed his lead. The Nazi took aim at the first cot and fired, another aimed at the body on the second cot; the man put his hands up in an effort to stop the bullet.

Gideon Walker slowly moved behind the last cot when the Germans entered, still too dark to see clearly, especially to the opposite end of the tent, only shapes and uniforms were visible. He knew what was happening, he felt for the rifle and pulled it toward him. He wasn't sure what he would do, but for some reason the rifle gave him comfort. He watched the first Nazi fire; the muzzle flash lit the far end of the tent.

"No," Gideon Walker screamed. "No fucking way."

The four SS soldiers, taken by surprise, quickly recovered, but not as fast as Walker; he pushed the rifle to his shoulder, fired four quick rounds, one at each man; each fell with a bullet in their face.

Walker stood waiting, waiting for machine gun fire to rake the tent, waiting for a grenade, waiting for anything that would put him out of his misery. Nothing happened.

"Murder, I'm no better than they are," he thought aloud. *"Murderer."*

No gunfire came, no welcoming death. The aid station sat in the silence of the hollow, only the far off rumbles of war echoed through the frozen woods. Walker dragged the Nazis out into the wooded tangle behind the tent, threw snow and branches over the bodies, hiding them to make sure that, if more civilized Germans arrived, they would not be found. He went back to his men; the man in the first cot was dead with a gunshot to his head. Walker felt sorry for the man but also, in strange way, happy for him: both the dead soldier's legs were gone, blown off by a mine, an arm gone, severely burned and blind.

"Still no good reason to be killed," Walker said to the soldier as he pulled his body out of the tent and laid him next to the lieutenant.

The others, still conscious, knew what had happened to the Nazis and were proud of the best soldier they knew, even if he was a conchie. One joked that he had never seen a coward shoot as straight and as well as Gideon. He smiled, but his heart felt ripped apart. He thought of the four men, their lives, their families and what he had done to them. What would their mothers say when they heard they were dead? What would their children be told? He internalized each man, and, even though the next three days were difficult, he could only think about the men he killed, not about the men he saved. He avoided going near the frozen bodies.

The German front moved over them and passed them on both sides, for some unexplainable reason, the SS were the only Germans Walker saw. Then a wave of shells came over the tent from the west and he knew the Americans had countered. He waited for the Germans to be pushed back through his hollow, waited to deal with whatever they would offer as reprisals for him killing Nazis. They never came.

On the fourth day, three jeeps pulled up, a captain with eight soldiers climbed out, along with the doctor and the nurses.

He never told the army what had happened, even denied it when one of the soldiers from the tent told his commanding officer about the Nazis, saying that Walker deserved a medal. He denied that anyone was shot; said the men were crazy from the shelling; the dead lieutenant and the soldier were transported back to the rear on the jeeps. Walker and the medical team moved forward chasing war and death. The four Waffen SS, left under the snow and debris, were not found until the warmth of spring thawed their bodies and some other "conchies," working the burial details, found their remains. No one, except Gideon Walker, knew what happened exactly. Their ID's found their way through channels to villages in Germany where four mothers and wives and children learned their sons and husbands had died in the war. None would ever know their men were killers and executioners.

Walker spent the next two years working with a group of reconstruction specialists helping to rebuild schools and a small college outside of Cologne. Many in his group were also conscientious objectors. The soldiers fought and then went home; he and many other CO's stayed and helped rebuild Germany. He finally went back to Grosse Point on a tramp tanker by way of Hamburg and Houston, paying his own way; then took a train to Michigan and spent the next two years near his parents until his father died, worn out by the Depression, the war and the recovery his company missed. His mother left the area to go and live with a sister. The money that was left to him allowed him to return to Germany where he worked in a small hospital. He began to write and spend winters in Barcelona with a close friend. He lived a quiet life, but some nights nightmares washed over him and he would see the four men as they stood at the end of his bed, all pointing lugers toward the men in their cots.

CHAPTER TEN

The storm's effects were more personal than physical, after tending to the injured and clearing the debris, much of the town of Elk River surprisingly stood undamaged. The campers left for home with their injured and Eve rested in a funeral home. Doug received a call from Chicago and had to return for a few days, his editor understood his tragedy, but his skills were needed to set up the weekend editions. Anne and Charlie said that they would take of everything. He left late in the morning the day after the storm, and would return for the funeral. He had all he could do to keep from damning the son-of-a-bitch he worked for.

Three days after the storm, the small funeral home, one block from her apartment, hosted the wake for Eve Titus. For all of the difficulties she caused Father O'Brien, he understood the Church's part in transitioning Eve's mortal body from life to the cemetery. The funeral director prepared the body for the ground; Father O'Brien prepared her soul for heaven.

"What's this about a man watching you at the fireworks?" Anne asked at breakfast, Howie turned to his grandfather with a questioning glance.

"Yes, your grandfather told me. Why didn't you?"

"Was no big deal, Mom. And I wasn't even sure I really saw him. It was dark and I never saw his face."

"He says you said it was the same man at the power plant."

"Yes ma'am. But he only talked to me at the plant, told me to let the fish go."

"And why would he tell you that?"

"I didn't see him, Mom," Bill added. "I didn't see him anywhere around the power plant."

"Thank you, Bill," Anne said. "Tell me more about this man, Howie."

"He's huge, with a black beard and checkered shirt. No hat."

"Finish your breakfast, your cousins will be here in a few hours, and then we have to go to town to see Eve," Anne said.

The boys finished and then headed out to the barn. Anne stood on the porch talking with Charlie; she turned and watched the boys as they disappeared through the double door.

"I need a smoke," Howie said to his brother.

The kitchen door slammed and the boys heard Charlie's voice from the porch. "Don't go too far boys," he yelled.

"Ok Grandpa," Bill answered. "You shouldn't smoke Howie; you know how mom hates it, 'specially near the house."

"Yes, Bill, but sometimes it's something you have to do; it actually feels good. Sets your mind right a bit. Strange though, one drag and you light up inside, then after a couple more it goes away."

Howie retrieved his cigarettes and the two boys walked deep into the rows of cherries. Red had started to rise in the green berries. Some hanging in the top branches were almost all red; they were the earliest to flower and set, the rest were green and hard.

"Three more weeks Bill; and it also looks like the wind didn't do too much damage," Howie said.

"How do you know?" his brother asked.

"The berries always ripen in the middle of July, almost the same time every year. The sweets are a few weeks earlier; you saw the Royal Anns near Uncle Frank's; they may be ready in a couple of weeks. The

Martinez's will be picking those in two weeks, then the sours sometime after the Cherry Parade in Traverse."

The air hung heavy between the trees, not a breeze stirred the leaves. The rain and the storm had washed away the dust and sulfur. Short clumps of grass grew in the shade, the aisles were open and showed tractor treads in the sand. On one particular tree a great branch angled out, almost parallel to the ground. Howie sat in the hollow of the branch and trunk, his brother sat a foot or two further out on the limb. Howie lightly pounded a cigarette out from the pack and into his hand, lit it and inhaled. He reacted with a short cough but Howie was getting used to smoking; the nicotine surged through his body and he took a deep breath.

"Was there a giant?" Bill asked.

"Don't know. I know I saw him, but now I'm not sure. No one else saw him or even his tracks but I am pretty sure I saw him; huge fellow, beard and all, spooky."

"You seeing things?"

"Maybe, don't know."

"It wasn't the fish talking, was it?"

"Fish don't talk, you know that. Still not sure if there was a giant, just don't know."

Howie leaned back onto the trunk of the tree and took another drag. The cicadas buzzed in the thick air. *Gramps said this was an off year for the locust cycles*. When it was right, they filled the air from all directions with their constant hum; their drone became the real sound of summer. Three years earlier, he remembered, the drone was deafening; millions of seventeen year locusts were everywhere. Howie took one last drag and crushed the cigarette out on the trunk. He caught his brother as he climbed down.

They walked through the dark rows to the edge of the bluff and stared into the woods below. Deep green bracken covered the sandy ground and then flowed like a coarse verdant carpet into the maples and pines. A couple of sand dunes poked through the fern cover and looked like small buff colored islands in a green sea. They could see a line had formed along the top of the hill separating the order of the cherries and the ramble of the wilds below. Frank Rex's studio straddled this line, now all too visible. The building blocked their path, but for twenty years tractors had cut a road on the orchard side. They stood by the gate to Frank's garden, Howie lit another cigarette.

"Uncle Frank went to town," Bill said. "Saw him drive out before breakfast; probably going to the doctor." He paused for a moment, "Is Uncle Frank dying?"

"Yes, or I think so. Cancer is a disease eating him from the inside out. Dad says nothing can be done."

"That's sad. Seems like a lot of death this year: the big buck, the man at the power plant, Aunt Eve, Uncle Frank."

"He's not dead yet."

"I know, but it seems like death's always around. We celebrate the Fourth of July and all anyone talked about was the dead men who grew up here, the men who died in the wars. Sister Mary, at school, says we never die; we just change and go to heaven."

"She could be right."

"She also says, if there's any life in outer space it had to come from Earth where God created it," Bill said.

Howie looked at his little brother, amazed at his disconnected way of thinking, or at least disconnected in Howie's mind. "You believe that?"

"Believe what? That there's life in outer space or it came from Earth."

"The second."

"Don't know, but that's what she said. And besides, she's from New York City and says the Yankees can always beat the White Sox."

"All that proves is that she really doesn't know anything."

The boys passed the trail leading to the woods and headed back to the farm. They heard Frank Rex's car before they could see it. Howie buried his cigarette in the sand.

"You boys coming up from the lake?" Frank asked, after stopping the car next to them.

"No Uncle Frank, just a walk in the orchard," Howie said.

"Watch where you smoke out here, don't want any grass fires." He winked as he looked at Howie. "Can smell it in the air and there's no one out here but you guys. See you later at the funeral home." Frank drove on to his studio.

"Howie, I didn't see the man you talked about with Mom and Grandpa when I caught that fish."

"I know I saw him. He was there, but not there. Never spoke to me any other time sep't at the river. He seemed strange but somehow not dangerous or at least then. But nobody else saw him, only me."

"That's weird," Bill said.

The two hurried home when the large bell near the kitchen door rang. The bell signaled the workers in the orchard; it signaled lunch and sometimes dinner. It could be heard as far as the lake.

The two boys sat on the porch picking through their fishing tackle when Eve's husband, Ralph Titus, arrived with their two children, Harold and Jane. Ralph never divorced Eve and the pain of his loss was evident. Over coffee, with Anne and Liz, he talked about how he tried to tell the children about their mother; how much he loved her, but her mood swings and drinking continually drove him away. He feared for the kids. She couldn't take care of herself, let alone a family. The kids were old enough to understand but he couldn't answer all their questions: Why did she have to die? Why didn't she live with us?

Howie had known Harold and Jane his whole life, but they never spent the summer at the farm. He only knew them from the short visits they took when Charlie, Liz and Anne would drive down to see them in Cadillac. They acted like city kids, Howie remembered. Cadillac was not a big city but it did have its own TV station. They had television; one station came in clear, the other was too fuzzy. Eve's kids stayed close to the house when they visited, were quiet most of the time, and seldom spoke unless spoken to. While pleasant, Howie thought they were strange.

Ralph managed a hardware store, the biggest in Cadillac, and puffed up when asked about it. The store was his first job after coming back from the war, and, even with his metal arm, he seemed to be doing okay. But his boss was strict.

"Will work there until I'm dead," he said.

Eve left him because he worked in a hardware store, because they had two children, and because he had a metal arm. She left because of the house he bought, the car he bought, and the lack of excitement that seemed to own him. She craved stimulation, demanded attention, and then begged for comfort when she got crazy. Ralph would take the kids and leave when it got too bad.

"Wake is tonight from five to eight, the funeral is tomorrow at 2:00," Anne said.

"Thanks for putting up with us and taking care of Eve. I know she loved you." Ralph said this sincerely and probably believed it.

Anne touched the back of his hand, and smiled. "She was difficult, we all knew it, yet, at times, she could be sweet and tender. I think, after all she'd been through, this was what she wanted. Tough as it is to say, she wanted to die." Anne turned to Liz, who was leaning against the doorframe with a cup of coffee in her hand. She nodded when Anne finished.

Howie and Bill's cousins sat on the long bench on the porch. Jane fidgeted with her hair and pushed her hands down her dress, continually; her older brother, by a year, looked bored. He wore an open checkered shirt and a ball cap. Howie sat next to him.

"It's tough I guess," Howie said.

"Yeah, real tough," answered Harold. "She's gone for months at a time and now she's gone for good."

Howie, taken aback by Harold's attitude, tried to understand; he'd just lost his mother but there didn't seem to be much caring in his words.

"We had to come over here for the funeral; Pa wouldn't let me stay in Cadillac. I'm gonna miss two ballgames, and all because of her. Last time I saw her, she whacked me across the face, said I was an insolent bastard. Well, she should know."

"Just shut up, Harold," Jane said. "She was nice often enough."

"Like when? When she was sober or drunk? When she was yelling at Pa or when she was yelling at you, or me? Sure, I'll miss her sometimes, but not today."

Harold stood up and looked at Howie, "Let's go to the barn." He launched himself off the porch.

Howie hurried to catch up.

"I need a cigarette. You still have them in the barn, under the bench?" Harold asked.

"How the hell you know about those?"

"Been sneaking a smoke now and then when we was visiting, found them last summer, assumed they was yours. Actually, smoked a whole pack after you left last year, stole a pack from Gramps to replace it. Didn't want you suspecting someone else knew about your stash." A big smile crossed his face, "Let's go have a smoke."

Howie retrieved the pack and passed a cigarette to Harold, who pulled a lighter from his pocket and lit it; Howie didn't light up. "Cool lighter," Howie offered.

"A Zippo with Detroit Tigers on it," Harold said, showing Howie the face of the lighter with its logo and lettering. "Real neat, won it playing cards from a kid at home. Poker, real poker it was, I'm pretty good at it too. And, by the way, I stole your Mexican girly mag, made a hit at school when I passed it around."

Howie walked out the back of the barn toward the picker's quarters. He had never played poker. Now his cousin seemed years older than he remembered, but now he was also a thief.

"Yeah, Pa's not around much, the store takes up most of his time, so me and Jane had some spare time this summer. She went to stay with our aunt in Grayling for a few weeks; I hung around, mowed a few lawns for quarters and caddied down at the club. One time I had fifty bucks in my pocket, thought about going to Detroit on the bus to see the Tigers, never did though, but I would have, damn straight, I would of."

"Sure Harold, I know you would've," Howie said, kicking the sandy dirt. "Aunt Eve was acting real strange the last few weeks, had something against me, I guess, don't know why the hell she did. She never said a decent thing to me when I saw her."

"Seldom had a decent word for anyone, I guess. Probably made fun of your arm, hated Pa's pinchers," Harold said. "Pa said some guy drowned at the power plant, said you saw it."

"Yeah, Bill and I were there, fishing for smallmouths; real damn shame, stupid accident in fact." Howie told the story to Harold, but left out the part about the giant man.

"Fuck, real stupid shame. Now this storm killed Mom; all of

it's stupid." Harold looked through the windows into the quarters, "Hellava place to live ain't it? Still stinks like kerosene. What a fucking way to live, but they don't know no better, dumb Mexicans, should stay there in Mexico."

"They're from Texas, not Mexico, and if they stayed there, who would pick the cherries, you?" Howie did little to hide his dislike for the comment and the cousin who stole his cigarettes and his magazine.

"There's always trash from Detroit and the south who'd pick for a few pennies a lug. Don't need no Mexicans."

"Hey you two, come up to the house and clean up; we're leaving for the funeral home in ten minutes. And you Harold; put that cigarette out. You know what I said about smoking around the barn," Charlie said, standing in the barn door looking at the boys. "Your brother is ready to go and Jane is still sitting where you left her, so get up there."

Howie took another look at his cousin and turned back to the barn. He stayed three steps ahead all the way to the house.

The cousins spent the afternoon waiting outside the funeral home. Ralph and Charlie went in first, then Anne and Liz followed. The four kids stayed in the shade of the building, walked to River Street for a coke, then back to the funeral parlor.

"You can come in now," Anne said, after she opened the back door of the parlor. "There is a small washroom just as you come in, so wash up and wait in the hallway."

"Yes ma'am," Howie answered.

They stood quietly in the hall until Anne came to get them.

"I want you all to stand against the wall; you two boys stand near your grandmother, Harold and Jane, you stand next to your father. He's okay now, but Harold, you need to help him if he asks."

"Yes, Aunt Anne," answered Harold.

Howie had never seen Harold so quiet; he almost seemed scared.

They filed into the viewing room; the adults stood near the casket, talking. Eve, laid out in a print dress, had that the same peaceful face she had when Frank carried her out of the orchard.

"Mamma," Harold screamed, as he placed his hands on the edge of the coffin; he began to heave in and out with great sighs, tears coursed down his face. "Mamma, Mamma."

Jane walked slowly to Harold's side and took his hand. Harold turned to her, "I can't see her, can you help?" Harold looked at his sister, and then, after another deep breath, picked her up. Jane looked at her mother for a long time and then put her small hand on Eve's face and lips. Finally she said, "You can let me down now."

They took their place by their father's side. Roger stood near Anne and the boys, all remained to one side, except for Charlie, who stood behind his daughter.

During the next three hours, thirty people came through the funeral parlor. Some came only for a moment and then left, others spent a few minutes with Charlie or Ralph, then left. Few stayed more than five minutes.

Shortly after eight o'clock, the director took Ralph and Charlie to one side; they talked for a few minutes.

"The funeral is at 2:00 tomorrow. That should give Doug enough time to get here by late morning. He'll be tired but the service won't be long," Charlie said to Anne and Liz.

"Ralph," Anna said, "Doug wanted to be here but he needed to get back to the paper, even if for only two days."

"I understand; he was there for her when the storm hit," Ralph said to everyone.

Doug Smith arrived at noon, hot and exhausted. The drive from Chicago took eight hours on the narrow roads; he had made the trip so many times that he paid little attention to the time anymore. On other trips, he would have stopped for a break at his cousins' in Grand Rapids or even Manistee, but not today.

"Need a quick bath and I'll be ready to go," he said to Anne as he pulled his briefcase from the back seat. "Roads weren't too bad coming up, just the usual stuff around Gary and Benton Harbor. Muggy all the way, had the windows open, stopped at that diner outside of Muskegon, had to or I would have fallen asleep."

Anne gave her husband a kiss on the cheek. The newly mounted screen door squeaked, and Charlie walked over to his son and gave him a hug.

"Sorry I couldn't stay the last few days, Dad," Doug said.

"More than enough people here to take care of things; fact is there really wasn't much to do after we moved Eve to the funeral home. Father O'Brien helped a lot; I think he'll miss her, even as challenging as she was. Ralph arrived yesterday with the kids; they are staying in town, in her place. Get cleaned up, we'll leave about 1:30."

The family took separate cars. The church lot had only six cars in it when they pulled in; one was Father O'Brien's. A Cadillac hearse parked near the back door of the church, the funeral director, a thin man in a shiny black suit, stood nearby.

A young woman, also dressed in black, walked down the steps to meet Charlie and the family. "We have placed your daughter inside, Mr. Smith. Everything is as we talked about. Father O'Brien is in the sacristy, he would like to talk to you before the service."

"Thank you, Gloria," Charlie said, as he turned to Liz. "I'll be right back."

Charlie headed toward the rear of the church; the rest of the family took their places in the front pews. Eve's casket had been placed in front of the Communion rail. The casket was open.

"She looks asleep," Howie thought. The calm on Eve's face masked the past turmoil within. He remembered, when she fell asleep or passed out in grandma's living room, she looked like she was in pain, always in pain and always angry.

Charlie walked out of the sacristy and up to his daughter. He placed his hand on her face and looked toward Frank's painting. A sigh and a slight shudder shook his body, tears hung on his tensed cheek. For a long moment, he stood tall and straight, then he walked to Liz and kissed her on the cheek. She took his hand as he sat.

Only a dozen or so joined the service, a few people Howie recognized from town and others he remembered from brief introductions from his dad. Roger and Lisa and the Claytons sat behind Charlie and Liz, Jimmy Dugan sat to the rear, in uniform. Howie looked around and wondered how many would show up if he died, his mind wandered and he began to count those he hoped would show up.

The service was brief, no Mass. Charlie said Eve had a problem with the Church and the Church had a problem with her. Father O'Brien wanted to extend the full rights of the Church but Charlie said a short service would be enough for his daughter. Father O'Brien had come out to the farm an hour or so after the storm and gave Eve her Last Rights, Charlie was grateful for that and that was enough.

The ride to the cemetery was quiet, Howie and Bill just stared out the open window; the wind tussled their hair. The heat had returned and the car's exterior became too hot to touch, Howie sat quietly and watched the other cars pass by.

The Smith family had an area in the cemetery where they had buried their dead for over fifty years. Charlie's father and mother were off to one side under a broad-headed sugar maple. Charlie said he planted that tree when his father died to shade him forever, now his mother also lay in the shade. Twenty-six years earlier, Charlie buried Lucille Susan Smith about ten paces from Abraham Smith's grave.

Abraham Smith came to Antrim County in 1889 after losing much of the small wealth he had earned in the lakes area of New York State. He invested in bank securities and then lost most of it during the crash of 1888. He was a lumberman and a sawmill owner and the timber he cut in New York helped to build Syracuse and Rochester. He moved west with the growth of the United States and borrowed enough money to start a small mill on Elk River; it stood where the power plant stood now. The river provided the power and the Irish and Swedish immigrants provided the backs and arms to cut white pine and cedar for the insatiable need for timber in Detroit, Milwaukee and Chicago. The wood he cut floated on large rafts to Chicago to help build the Columbian Exposition in 1893.

The mill was where Charles Smith grew up. He could walk the logs in the pond as nimble as the best and could guess how many board feet a log would yield just from pacing its length. There was even a story floating about that, when he was six, he danced with hob-nailed boots on the bars on River Street for pennies from the lumberjacks. He also said he knew where a couple of men were buried along the tracks outside of town after serious arguments ended with knives and stabbings. But he also said he would never tell, "Leave the dead to their rest," he would say. "They were nobodies in life and now they're nobodies in death. What would the difference be?"

Abraham Smith died from a stroke in 1919; his wife Eleanor died two years later. Charlie believed it was from a broken heart. The two married late in life, and Charlie was born to an older mother in 1896. Abraham Smith was buried in the large plot he bought for the family. Never a showy man, his headstone, while tall, was simple and direct, just his name and birth date, Eleanor's was added when she was buried next to him. Now there were others laid out below Abraham Smith's marker, a family he never knew.

Father O'Brien led the family to the grave that was nine paces from Abraham Smith's marker; it was cut next to Lucy-Sue's headstone. The casket lay atop three timbers that spanned the hole. The Titus' stood quietly as a group to one side. Ralph stared at the coffin, Jane fidgeted and Harold seemed detached. The Smiths' aligned on the opposite side, the boys to the front, Doug and Charlie stood at each end, Liz and Anne directly behind the boys. Frank stood back from the family. A few from town were standing outside the circle formed by the family; some were there out of curiosity and some out of some form of bizarre respect. The bar owner came because Eve still owed him fifty dollars in rent and he was hoping to catch Charlie in a weak moment.

After the usual words from Father O'Brien, written for such occasions by the Catholic Church, a church Eve fought more than she fought with anything or anybody, the families turned from the grave of Eve Smith Titus and walked the few paces to the relatively cooler shade of the maples.

"I am heading back to Cadillac with the kids, Charlie," Ralph Titus said. "Not much else here needs doing and my boss only gave me today off."

"Nice guy," Anne said under her breath.

"We've got big days coming up with the picking season and all; so I need to be at the store to watch over things."

"Sure Ralph, I understand. If there's anything else that needs to be done, I'll call you or send a letter. I assume after you went through the apartment you got everything you wanted."

"Yeah, not much there. A few pictures the kids wanted, some jewelry, and, for some reason, she had the Titus family Bible. Couldn't figure that out, wrote her name and the kid's dates inside, after my moms. Did you put the date she died in it?"

"What? No, none of us did, in fact only Anne and I went back to the apartment to find her a dress and some jewelry. Why?" Charlie asked.

"Someone wrote the date of her death in the book, that's all. You think maybe she did it?"

"That's crazy talk, Ralph, someone else had to, just leave it at that," Anne said.

Ralph looked at the family and shrugged, "Anyway, after Liz looks at the jewelry to see if there's anything of your family's in the box, she's going to send the rest to Jane."

Ralph stuck his hand out to Charlie; they shook. Then he went to each of the men and the boys, then to Liz and Anne. Liz gave him a quick kiss on the cheek that surprised Ralph. He gathered the two kids and walked to the car.

"I am not sure if that man is happy, sad, relieved, confused or just stupid," Anne said. "He was part of her problem; might not have caused it, but he was damned required to help her, not run from her."

"The children," Liz said, "they needed to be protected from her rages and her anger and that's what he did."

"Maybe, Liz. But Jane's so withdrawn that she could be heading down the same path her mother and grandmother walked, and Harold will be very difficult, so head strong and arrogant for someone only fifteen. The army would be a good place for him."

"We can't solve their problems, Anne," Doug said, putting his arm around her waist. "They'll do what they have to do, we have our own problems to deal with and we have 200 acres of cherries to pick in the next month."

"And we have the Cherry Festival in three days," Bill chimed in.

"Yes Bill, we do," Charlie answered, "and we have lots of work to do before we can go to Traverse."

The family walked back up the hill to the cars; Howie turned toward Eve's grave and watched as the three men and Father O'Brien lowered Eve into the ground. The straps were let out inch by inch until they stopped and then they stood upright. The priest paused for a moment then bent and picked up a handful of sandy dirt, up-righted himself again, and tossed the dirt into the hole. Howie heard a stone hit the casket. The priest turned away and, almost on cue, the men picked up their shovels and began to fill the grave. Howie turned and followed his family up the hill from the cemetery, wondering if Eve really did fill in the Bible with the date of her death.

INTERMEZZO

Twisted now by time and wind, a boy turns to changes that boil his soul, fleshy vestiges take hold and gut storms rage. Blood surges with a mind of its own, pushing forward, it demands respect, and gives none in return. Excuses will be made, but there are none to hand out forgiveness; a penitent soul hopes for release and, finding none, makes bold excuses and rationalizes. But sweetness lingers, its dew is the dew of life.

Choices are made and tolerated, the ocean swells carry the simple family from crest to hollow to crest again. What choices do families have? Few are masters; even more suffer their fortune, providence is cast by others. The need for a dollar forces a choice, the bonds of family tie all to fate, a destiny driven across miles of hard country and past intolerant eyes.

Each holds within the heart a wildness; a rebellion is fought, flags of victory are flown, treaties signed and broken. A heart is rent, never to be whole. But time will never be tamed; its unruliness pushes away bold hands and slaps the cheek of the believer. It pushes everything; all is trundled in a barrow from a place of quiet solitude to a place of war. What can transcend this inexorable beast? Linen, linseed, and lustral love.

CHAPTER ELEVEN

Charlie and Doug spent most of their free time clearing the living room and securing the tarps and canvases needed to protect the undamaged portions of the house. They agreed to leave much of the heavy work, like removing the tree, for the Martinez men when they arrived. Doug Smith left for Chicago early Sunday morning.

Howie stayed close to home and didn't go below the hill; he helped his grandfather and Roger with chores, read a little and wondered about the giant. Anne studied her oldest; he was growing up, becoming a man, yet, still a tussle-haired boy. *Had he really seen this man, this giant; did the stag's death trigger weird imaginings; or did all the recent deaths just rile up his imagination?*

Anne shook Howie gently, the early light sneaking around the curtain.

"Breakfast, boys."

The two dressed and climbed down the stairs to the kitchen. The dining room table was piled high with clothing, sheets, socks, and blankets. The boys noticed some of their clothes within the piles.

"They're for the Martinez children," Anne said. "Every year we collect our old clothes and give them to Barbara Martinez. She needs all she can get. It's a hard road and a hard life they travel. They move five or six times a summer before heading back down south."

"They drive all the way up here?" Bill asked.

"Yes Bill, but in short trips; they may drive two to four hundred miles at a time. They stop in Arkansas and Missouri, then Illinois and Indiana to plant tomatoes, then to southern Michigan to pick strawberries, then to Saginaw to hoe sugar beets, then here, then back south to pick tomatoes and then home. They live just outside of El Paso, Texas," Liz said.

"They're Americans, aren't they?" Howie asked.

"Damn straight boy," Liz said, "been there since before the Alamo. Texas kind of formed around them. Most of us up here treat them like they were Mexicans, but they're not. It's a hard life, but an honorable one, unlike some of the white trash I have to hire to help pick. God help us, some of those men are just plain evil." She stopped and looked at each of the boys. "When those fellows show up, you stay away from them, especially you, Bill. Don't talk to them, and for heaven's sake don't listen to what they have to say. For the most part they're worthless and they'll only waste your time. Hopefully, they won't be here when the Martinez's are out back; I don't need fights between them."

"Yes'em," they both answered, but Howie knew that if one fellow showed up, he would be a bit happier. Howie called him Al, but everyone else called him Albert, Albert Beck.

Howie met him two summers back. Albert was older than his father and had war and travel stories to tell. Howie would listen to him talk about the world. He would write down the names of places Beck described and then look them up in the living room library, exotic places in Asia and Africa. Last year, Beck was late; he walked up the gravel driveway on the last day of picking. He had his arm in a sling and a bandage over his eye. Liz told him she had no work for him; he was too late. He could spend a few days but would have to move on. Al told Howie he fell off the back of a flatbed truck outside of Detroit. Said he helped to load it in exchange for a ride and took a tumble when it hit a bump. Howie noticed his knuckles were still raw and beginning to scab. He also noticed that the swelling below his eye had definite bruise marks that matched the pattern of three knuckles thrown with a right hand.

"Why can't he work, grandma?" Howie asked.

"He has one good arm and you need two to pick; besides, he's been fighting and I don't want that here. Detroit, that's a story. Don't believe him."

Howie spent part of two afternoons with Al before he left on the back of a truck heading further north. He told Howie he spent the winter in Florida picking oranges and grapefruit. He talked about the big swamps and alligators and six-foot long rattlesnakes. Howie imagined picking oranges while stepping over giant rattlers; Al was one brave man. Howie hoped Al would show up this year.

After breakfast, Charlie and Anne headed into Elk River and passed Roger and his truck piled with mattresses. Roger parked in front of the quarters and Howie helped him unload the bedding. He grabbed a mattress around the middle and carried it through the door, pitched it on the metal springs and webbing of the old war surplus bed frame, three beds to a room, one mattress went on the concrete floor. Howie thought of the bonfire and the mice; he wondered which room they came from. After a general straightening up and a quick sweep out, they were out of there; even with the new mattresses, the rooms still stunk of kerosene.

"Señora Martinez will make them a lot nicer," Roger said, talking to Howie. "Somehow she always makes this place better than it is."

"Can these rooms be any better, Roger?" Bill asked. He had been watching the unloading and helped with the sweeping.

"Tough question, Bill, costs a lot of money to make these rooms better and it's just not there. Crop looks good this year, but if it is, then the prices will be down, more cherries yield less money. Strange way to make a living; you try to get the best crop you can and the result is more fruit at a lower price. Same with everyone, so you keep your costs down, watch your budget, watch how much you pay out and pray for good weather, always pray for good weather. Maybe, in the end, you'll have enough money to live on, to get you through one more year. Then you get to do it all over him again."

A claxon sounded through the open door of the barn as two trucks pulled onto the gravel next to Roger's car. A full-bodied man climbed down from the cab of the first truck; he was barrel-chested, deeply tanned, with black hair neatly combed straight back, a full black mustache matched his heavy eyebrows. He was dressed simply in a white short-sleeved cotton shirt, black pants and, centered on his flat belly, sat a silver buckle the size of Bill's hand. He held a buff cowboy hat in his hand, the band matched his mustache.

"Good morning, Señor Roger."

"Buenos dias, Señor Martinez," Roger answered.

Roger walked briskly between the boys and clasped the callused hand of Ernesto Martinez.

"Good morning boys. Como estas?" Ernesto said

"Good morning, Mr. Martinez. We're both fine," answered Howie.

Ernesto reached over and shook Howie's hand, then Bill's. "Madre Dios, you have both grown six inches." He stood tall over both boys, a good foot taller than Howie. "Good Texas handshakes, especially yours Bill. See Bill, you grab a man's hand with a strong grip and look him straight in the eye. Bueno, Señor Bill, bueno."

The back gate of each truck slammed loud against the chassis and people began to tumble out, or at least the first three tumbled out, then they helped the others out.

A petite woman in a bright skirt and full white blouse climbed down from the cab of Ernesto's truck, a small child held on close to her leg.

"Good morning, Señora Martinez."

"Good morning, Señor Roger," Barbara Martinez answered.

"This isn't the baby?" Roger asked.

"Si, Señor Roger, this is my Bonita and she is as much a handful as she was a year ago." Barbara stroked her black hair, pulling strands away from the child's eyes. The three year old hid in the folds of her mother's dress. "She looks innocent but the devils are in her, but we love her just the same."

The kitchen door slammed and Liz crossed the lawn heading toward the crowd, drying her hands in a towel. Another truck pulled in behind the first two, then two sedans pulled up, all worn and dusty. Sixteen people in all exited the vehicles, eleven adults and five children.

"Madre Dios," Ernesto said, as he looked across the yard at the destruction from the tornado. "We heard about the storm but did not know you got hit."

Roger turned and looked at the house and the tarps that covered the crushed living room, tree branches still held up parts of the tarp, the upended roots still had dirt clinging to them.

"It also killed Eve, Señor Smith's daughter," Liz said.

Ernesto and Barbara and most of the workers crossed themselves and Howie saw their lips move in a silent prayer. Ernesto turned to Liz.

"And Señor Smith?" Ernesto asked, as if he didn't want to hear the answer.

"He's well. He and Anne are in town taking care of some legal things. They will be back later; he'll be so glad to see you and your family. Doug is in Chicago and will be back before we start picking."

"Yes and we will be glad to see him, out back as usual. Señor Roger?" Ernesto asked.

"Yes, Ernesto," Roger answered. "Same as last year, new mattresses and we tried to straighten them up a bit."

"Señor Roger, you say that every year but I still have to make it right," Barbara Martinez said with a laugh. "We know what to expect, we look forward to the cherries and the beach and the money. A dry room is more than we get at most places, so thank you. We still have to dry out the tents from Saginaw."

"And, after we settle in," Ernesto said turning to Liz, "we will help clear that tree and get the house back in order, ok. Also, looks like some clearing work needs to be done in the orchard, ok Roger?"

"Yes Ernesto, muy bueno. We will get the house back in order and get the trees cut and cleared."

Howie watched a couple of the younger men climb into the trucks and drive them toward the picker's quarters. *"How could people live like this?"* he thought. They moved from place to place for a day's wage. Howie called them gypsies but he remembered his Uncle Frank chastising him for using that word. "You don't know what you're talking about. They are not Gypsies, no more than you're a pygmy because you're small. It's a dishonor to call them gypsies; in Europe gypsies are thieves and pickpockets. They have no honor and would steal a watch just to tell you the time. No, Howie, the Martinez's and the other pickers work hard for their few bucks and are honorable people. Someday they will run Texas and California because us Anglos don't work hard enough; they do, and their children will reap the benefits. That's also why they're hated up here; they work too hard."

Howie always remembered what Uncle Frank said but it was tough to understand their lives; most of the time, he knew they were happy and enjoyed being here.

"Good morning, Señora Martinez. Was the trip from Saginaw an easy one?" Liz asked.

"Yes, the trip was easy, Señora Smith, but tough on my back. After having all these kids, that old truck just hits you wrong. But I will be fine. Did you see my Bonita?" The child peeked out from behind her dress.

"My lord, she's grown and is very pretty but I see a touch of the fire of her mother in her eyes," Liz answered.

"I tell everyone it's my grandmother's blood in her, God rest her soul, but my husband says she's more my blood. So, either way, she's a Martinez woman. Isn't that right, Bonita?" The girl suddenly brightened at the sound of her name, smiled, and then looked piercingly at her mother.

"Si, Mamma," Bonita Martinez answered. "Si."

For the rest of the day the Martinez's and their extended family disappeared into the picker's quarters. Howie watched from inside the dark barn as boxes and cardboard suitcases were moved from the trucks to various rooms, grocery bags of food were moved in, along with stacks of blankets, and an assortment of boxes with dishes and pots and pans following. They sang songs he didn't understand and he saw the drab row of windows transformed with new curtains and, just outside each door, colorful blankets hung over chairs to air out. The men set up canvas tents on the gravel to air out and dry.

After the men emptied the trucks and moved their families into quarters, they marched up the road to the farmhouse. Roger had saws and axes waiting, two of the pickers carried their own.

"Buenas tardes, Señor Martinez," Charlie bellowed from inside the screen door, as he pushed it open. He gave Ernesto a big handshake and then he did something he seldom did, gave him a big bear hug. Ernesto seemed surprised but proud to be taken into such company.

"Señor Smith, my family and I," as he waved his arms about toward all the men, "are very sorry to hear about your daughter, may she be with God."

"Yes, Ernesto, she is with God and is now a much happier soul. I think she would have been happy to see you and your family this year."

"Yes Señor, I think she would have."

These were formalities and social niceties said to ease the tension that would have normally been present if Eve were alive and standing among these men. She, by now, would have insulted many of the men, mostly Ernesto. Charlie always made sure that Eve was not at the farm when the pickers arrived; it was better for Charlie and Liz and almost always better for the Martinez's.

"Well Señor Smith, we have work to do, let's get that tree out of the house before it decides to grow there forever," Ernesto said with a laugh.

"Si Ernesto, trabajar," Roger said.

Clearing the tree would have been three hard days' work for Charlie and Roger; three days that were needed to tend the orchard and the cherries. The twelve men and boys took the tree down in hours; the branches and limbs were neatly stacked behind the house to be moved later. The stump of the old pear was cut to within a foot of the crown and was left as is. The trunk sections were stacked to be split after the picking was done. Another hour and the tarps were secured to the house and much of the interior was swept and straightened out.

"It was crushed," Liz said to Charlie, standing in the broken end of the living room, "but only a few of the books were destroyed; my old copy of The Thousand and One Nights was the most precious, but you can get me a new copy for Christmas, in French, if you do not mind."

Charlie gave Liz a quick kiss, "Yes dear."

Howie and Bill walked across the gravel, attracted by the bouquet of sharp cilantro, pork fat and Spanish songs carried on the air from the open doors of the quarters. The Martinez children sat against the wall of the old chicken coup, each with a rolled piece of tortilla in their hand. Howie remembered the pork burritos from last year, their exotic taste and rich smell. They headed to the bench where three of the boys sat.

"I'm Bill Smith," Bill announced in an arrogant tone.

"And I am Ricardo Alfonso Romero Martinez and I remember you from last year when you bit into a chili pepper and damn near exploded. You ran crying to your mama, I think."

"Yes, that was me, but I am much wiser now. I don't eat red chili peppers and I don't run to my mother anymore, so there. And besides, I am here on vacation; I don't have to work, not like you. So there, again."

"That's enough, Bill," Howie said. "They work hard because they work to help their families and you know you're gonna work right next to them. So remember that when you're sweating and carrying lugs of cherries." Howie chided his brother to help him understand that arrogance is not the proper way to start and stay in a conversation. "Besides, you can barely speak English while each of these fellows can speak Spanish and English; so mind your manners."

Bill turned to his brother and said, "I'm sorry."

Ricardo said something in Spanish to the other boys, and they laughed a bit. Then he added something and Howie heard the word *"muerte;"* the boys crossed themselves. Gonzalo, Ricardo's younger brother, sat quietly just outside the group and looked at Bill with a sad smile.

"Señor Howie," Ricardo said, "we are very sorry to hear about your, how you say, tia. Aunt is the right word, yes?"

"Yes, Ricardo," said Howie. "Thank you. Maybe later in the week, before the work starts, we can go down to the beach. The lake is warm and clear; it's early."

"Si Señor Howie, it is a good idea. Did you not have a dog last year? What was it, a wiener dog?"

"Yes," answered Howie.

"Where is he, you never went anywhere without him?"

"Dead."

The boys looked at Howie.

"Got run over. Hot day and the maid from next door backed over him. He was asleep under her car." Howie turned away from the boys and walked back into the barn. Bill turned and followed him.

He did not dwell on his Aunt Eve or even his dog, much as a storm that hits and then passes; you don't remember the wind and the rain, you only remember the damage that's left behind.

CHAPTER TWELVE

Doug arrived the next Friday afternoon; he sped up the driveway and sprayed gravel across the lawn when he braked. Adjusting his straw hat, he slid out of the sticky seat of the sedan, stood, slammed the car door and took a long look around the farm. Anne walked out the kitchen door, holding it so it would not slam.

"What're you looking so happy about?" Anne asked as they met halfway across the lawn; he swept her up in his arms and, after a more than perfunctory kiss, said, "We're all going to the movies tonight, haven't been all summer and tonight will be perfect."

"What gave you that idea?" Anne asked.

"Jimmy, in the design studio, saw Gregory Peck in *Moby Dick* last week in Chicago and said it was the greatest movie he had seen in years; said we just had to see it. And as I was driving through Acme, I saw the big billboard at the drive-in announcing in three-foot high letters, *Moby Dick* starring Gregory Peck and Orson Wells. Well there you are and that's where we'll all be tonight."

"You know your dad and mom won't be interested. Your mother

will say 'since a decent movie has never been made from a book, there is no reason to support their foolishness by buying tickets.'"

"Yes, I know, but we need a chance to get out and the boys will really like the story, maybe they'll even read the book. I know mom has it somewhere in the library, or at least she did until the tornado hit."

They strolled arm in arm into the kitchen. The boys were doing some of their summer study work under the sharp eye of Liz. Both jumped when Doug walked through the door, Liz had kept their eyes glued to their papers even when they first heard Doug's car in the driveway.

"Everything okay at home?" Howie asked.

"Good, but the planting beds' need weeding and the lawn just can't seem to get mowed often enough. Other than that, everything is in good shape. Even your fish are still alive, every last one of them." Doug turned to Anne. "The Burke's put their home up for sale; he was transferred to Minneapolis. In fact, he's there now, will be back in two weeks, then they'll pack up to get there in time for school."

"Bobby's leaving?" Bill asked.

"Sorry champ. Yes, she's leaving in a few weeks and I don't think you'll have a chance to say good-by," Doug said. "You should write her a letter and have her send you their Minnesota address."

"That's the third family in the last year to come and go on the street. It's certainly an *Organization Man* village; everybody coming and going, never staying long, getting promoted, then on to another new city. It is tough on the kids and even tougher on the women, glad you don't have to do that." Anne sat on a kitchen chair and swirled the ice tea she'd been nursing most of the afternoon.

"It's good to have that job, but it's getting to be pain to keep driving back and forth. For what, I ask myself, for what?"

"For a job and an income," Anne said with a smile.

"It's difficult these days. You have to move to move-up, continually uprooting, changing schools, churches, and friends," Doug said. "Like gypsies."

"I saw gypsies once, somewhere near Vienna when I was girl. Seemed like a romantic way to live," Liz added.

"They're thieves and opportunists," Doug said. "Couldn't be

trusted, yet they seemed to survive; during the war, they tried to stay out the way of the Germans. If the Germans found them, especially the Nazis SS, they'd just disappear."

"Why would they disappear?" Howie asked.

"To the Nazis and Hitler, they were not fit to live so he had them killed when he could find them. To him they were like the Jews, unfit. But this conversation is all wrong; I said they were like gypsies because they seldom stayed in one place long. After that there are no similarities," Doug said, "Sorry I made the comparison."

"Are you taking the family to the festival tomorrow?" Charlie asked, changing the subject.

"Probably, Dad, it's been a few years since I was there, the last two or three times I was down in Chicago. We'll take the boys into town. Anne wants to see her cousin and then we can grab a spot in the shade for the parade. After that, to the fair for pies and a ride or two on the Ferris wheel and we can watch the boys get sick on cotton candy and popcorn. On second thought, maybe I'll stay home. Why don't you take them, Dad?"

"Oh you'll go; you might even see that Olson girl," Charlie said, whispering in his ear.

"Thanks Dad, for the memory," Doug said with a glare and a grin. He looked at his wife. "If Anne heard what you just said, I wouldn't have a moments rest for a week. You know she's married and has three kids and lives somewhere out near Buckley. Besides, that was almost twenty years ago, so just let it lie, and you know damn well she liked James a lot more than me; when he didn't return, I think it broke her heart. I hope she's doing well."

"What are you too conspiring about?" Anne asked, looking at the men. "Did I hear the word, Olson?"

"Nothing, it is nothing," Doug answered a bit flustered.

"Anyway, the good news is we're going to the movies tonight in Acme."

"Not me!" chimed Liz.

"Yes Mother, I know, just Anne and the boys and I for a ride on a whale's back"

"*Moby Dick*, neat-o," added Howie. Bill's eyes were as wide as possible.

"How did you know that?" Doug asked.

"Saw the ad in the paper and it's the only movie in Acme, so it just had to be the one."

"Good deduction. We'll head out of here about seven-thirty, try to get toward the front. Movie starts fifteen minutes after sunset."

"Popcorn and soda pop, maybe some of that cotton candy, some hot dogs, cool," Bill said. "Have to get in practice for the fair."

"All I see is a potentially sick young man," Anne said.

"Not me, I have a stomach made of iron," Bill answered.

"We'll see," Anne said. "We'll see."

They spent the rest of the afternoon keeping busy about the house and helping to clean-up and begin repairs to the living room. Charlie and two of the Martinez men started on the walls and the roof. The windows would take a week to assemble, till then canvas and boards held back the weather. The rest of the Martinez men helped Roger begin to clear the storm damage from the orchard.

Liz salvaged her books and stored them in boxes out of harm's way. She also started to think about the new bookcases.

"Charlie, do you still have those cherry planks in the loft of the barn? They would make great bookshelves."

"Yes, dear," Charlie answered. "There's about ten or twelve and they'd make great shelves. When we get this mess cleaned up I'll pull them down, plane them, and build you the best cases you can imagine. Wasn't saving them for much anyway, probably been up there for fifteen years."

After dinner, the four Chicago Smiths piled into the Ford and headed out to Acme; the night was warm and for once, clear. The line into the drive-in extended out to the highway. Like a college homecoming, the Cherry Festival brought people back to reassert their roots. Whether they owned cherries or picked them, managed a cannery or worked in one, or just liked the idea of a summer party, the license plates in the queue were from all over the Midwest.

They found a stall in the third row and clamped the heavy metal speaker onto the window. The smell of bug spray hung in the air and the haze from the mosquito smoke pots gave an ethereal feel to the parking lot. People sat on the hoods of their cars and some even brought aluminum lawn chairs. The snack shop glowed like an out-of-this-world operating room; its fluorescent lights and neon beckoned everyone to popcorn and ice cream.

Howie had never seen the ocean, deep black waves and huge whales filled his head; the movie took over his senses. Anne looked at her boy and saw him transfixed, an almost hypnotic state brought on by the sound and the pictures. Captain Ahab, lashed to the white whale repeatedly driving his harpoon home, neither man nor beast able to free themselves from their fate; only a kick from his fast asleep brother brought him back to the world of northern Michigan. She smiled, *"he's alright,"* she thought, *"he's alright."*

There was little conversation during the drive back to the farm, Doug held Anne's hand, Bill continued to sleep, and Howie watched the lights fly by, his mind raced. He looked at the dark ceiling of his bedroom for an hour before falling asleep.

Bill pulled on his brother to get him out of bed. "Up lazy, we're going to the festival in one hour and you need to get dressed and eat, so hurry."

"Leave me alone; I'll get up when I'm ready." Pulling the branches from the house and moving hundreds of lugs into the orchard had exhausted even his young body. He had the nicks and cuts on his legs and his left hand to prove it.

"No you won't. You need to get up now so we can get there early. Dad and mom are already up and finished with breakfast. Get up, now!"

Howie swung his legs out to the wood floor and stretched as only a fourteen year old can stretch, sinew and muscle pulling out toward the ceiling, legs taught, back twisting back-and-forth, his right arced up, not nearly as high as his left, but he had been privately trying to make it stronger. He pulled on his shorts and the striped tee shirt his mother laid over the end of the bed, tennis shoes and no socks. A quick stop to brush his teeth, wash up and comb out his blond hair and he was ready for Traverse City.

"Good morning, boy, glad to see you could join us," Charlie said from behind a newspaper and smoke. "You're going into town?"

"You know we are gramps," Howie answered. "The parade is today and the carnie fair tonight; it'll be great."

"I am gonna eat ten hot dogs and six ice cream cones," Bill offered.

"You will be as sick as a pig," Howie said.

"Won't, been practicing, right Grams?"

"Well let me think, Bill, you did have a hot dog or two at the 4th of July and maybe an ice cream in town, but that sure is a long way from practicing. How'd he do last night, Howie?" Liz said.

"One hot dog, some popcorn, a little pop and then he fell asleep, not sure that counts."

"Why're you going to eat that much? Like your brother said, it'll make you sick," Liz said.

"I am a growing boy, I need my hot dogs, the ice cream will make 'em go down easier, kind of like grease, and then it'll fill in the spaces not filled with more hot dogs."

Everyone around the table thought, amused at the image Bill put in their heads. They all shook their heads at the same time.

"You say the damnedest things, William Smith," Charlie said. "Some of the damn strangest things ever uttered."

"What?" Bill asked.

After breakfast, Doug and Charlie walked through the part of the orchard ripped apart by the tornado, almost twelve twisted and torn acres, by Charlie's estimation. Over eight hundred trees were destroyed or damaged, many pulled from the ground, some shredded and whole limbs sheared off; most were stripped of leaves and fruit.

"It's just amazing Dad that along the edge there, the trees still have their fruit, simply amazing," Doug said, pointing to the dark green wall of survivors.

"That twister must've been very tight not to strip those trees. You're right, it's amazing. I think we can wait until winter to finish clearing this mess up. The Martinez boys did a good job clearing the lanes but it's going to take a lot of work and tractor time, probably have to pull them and drag them to the center and fire them off. Damn, I remember when I planted this part of the orchard; you were just a lad about Howie's age. You and Jim would come out here with your mother and give us a hand after school. We looked at those sticks and wondered about the future. Was about the same time Eve came, twenty-five or so years ago. Even then she was a storm to deal with," Charlie said, looking across the wreckage.

"The rest of the crop doesn't look too bad, great color, bit late but the Martinez's should be able to start next week," Doug said. "Figure we will start picking back by Frank's studio, the Royal Anns, and work this way. Maybe less than a week to finish, then we can get to the sours."

"That'll work fine. Roger stacked the lugs; it is good to be back to work after all the sadness of the past few weeks. Your boy okay?" Charlie asked.

"Howie will be fine. Anne and I aren't sure if he's seeing things or there really is this giant wandering about," Doug answered.

"Talking to the boy at the powerhouse and staring at the young man during fireworks is hardly wandering about. Keep an eye out."

"Yes Dad, we will. But I'll not keep the boys in their room; they have strong people about to protect them. That man, whatever he is, will stay away."

"Did not say they should be kept in their room, just watched over."

"I'll be going back to Chicago on Sunday, need to be at my desk on Monday. With all the turmoil about the Suez Canal and the Russians, things are hectic. It's good that the president's better, been overwhelming, especially with the paper and its Republican politics. Anything you need from Chicago when I come back?"

"A dozen of those Polish sausages from that butcher under the EL, you know the one," Charlie answered.

"Sure do, two dozen it is, just to make sure," Doug said.

The men walked back to the farm, Howie and Bill met them on the porch.

"Good breakfast boys?' Charlie asked.

"Real good," Bill said. "Hot oatmeal with frozen cherries and milk, cherries softened and cooled the oatmeal, wonderful. Grandma said she needed to clean out the last of the frozen berries to make room for this year. So it's cherries in the oatmeal."

"It was pretty good," Howie added.

"We'll be leaving in an hour, your mother has some errands to do and I have to get some film at the camera store. Should be some great photos to take during the parade and out at the fairgrounds," Doug said.

"The weather had been cooler and dryer since the tornado; but there's rain coming, at least the days are comfortable, not hot and muggy. Anything is better than a tornado," Anne said.

They took two cars. Charlie and Liz were going back to the farm after the parade. They had been to enough fairs, "too crowded and too many tourists," Liz said. She remembered all the times she went to the fair when they were with the boys and she'd tear up remembering the time Jim introduced her to one of the prettiest young ladies in town. They were standing under the Ferris wheel, the big circle of lights going around and around and Jim, puffed up and proud, with his arm around the young lady. Then, from high above, a deluge of Coca-Cola fell out of the sky and drenched him, and, by some miracle, missed the girl. Liz looked up and saw three big fellows, all Jim's friends, laughing.

"Great shot," one yelled. The others were slapping him on the back.

Jim slowly turned, coke running down his face, and looked up at the three; they were at the top of the wheel. He said, "excuse me," to his date, walked over to the base of the Ferris wheel, and waited patiently for their cab to reach his level.

"You had better never get off this wheel," Jim said, "because if I see any of you on the ground, I will take each of you apart, starting with you, Mikey, and then the rest of you. You got that."

The three just looked at Jim and then at each other and, as the cab rose again, another cupful of coke arched through the air and landed with a slushy crash on Jim's head. He just stood there staring at them. Then he started to laugh and walked back to his date.

"I'll wait until the right time and then I'll get them, each of them," Jim said to his mother as he changed out of his sticky clothes when he got home. "They'll wonder when it will come. That'll get 'em in a knot."

Liz never heard about any retribution, but she knew that fellow Mikey was with Jim in basic training a few years later at the start of the war and Jim saved his life in a training accident. Jim saved him for the war; Mikey died in France, blown to pieces by a shell that landed in his foxhole.

The younger Smith's followed Charlie and Liz into Traverse City. Howie stared out the car window as they passed open fields and small woods on some of the steeper land, orchard after orchard were passed on both sides of the two-lane road. The land the Scotts sold was now a motor court for tourists. "Lost the best orchard on the road," Charlie said about the sale, "damn shame they don't know what they lost."

All this ground was an edge of Lake Michigan at one time. The lake moved inland for a time, then out; and for thousands of years, it lay crushed under a mile of ice, then, following the melting, new banks would be cut and the shore would resume its seasonal breathing, moving in and out. New ridges would be laid, and shallow valleys cut, finally forests of hemlock and pine would grow to cover the scraped land. Eventually maple and birch would fill in the gaps. Then, in another ten or fifteen thousand years, it will happen again. The orchards looked permanent to Howie, neat and orderly, perfect. He could not believe that, at some time in the future, this would all be scraped away and be replaced with something new and different—like a motor court.

Traverse City sits in the bottom a large glacial bay left in the east side of Lake Michigan. It is split by a thin sliver of land extending out, needle-like, at its tip stands a monument that announces you are half-way between the equator and the north pole. It was a transfer point of the traverse made by the trappers of the seventeenth and eighteenth centuries between the inland fur grounds and the Great Lakes. They would load their pelts of beaver, fox and wolverine here to be paddled or shipped to St. Louis and eventually to New Orleans. Inland, numerous streams and rivers joined together, flowed west through the pine barrens, and here, opened their mouths into the lake. In time, a squalid strip of buildings paralleled the river near its mouth, with a short shingle of beach to pull up canoes. Later, a town grew here that provided trade goods to the inland reaches of the rivers and creeks. When it was found that cherry trees, Royal Ann, Bing, Black Tartarian and sour cherries called Montmorency and others would grow well in the sandy soil, a new industry took root and grew. It wasn't the warmth of the lake that made a difference—it was the cold water. The cold temperatures of the lake held back the false spring and the bud killing frosts along this narrow shore of the lake. More often than not, from year to year, the cold edge of the lake held back the budding until true and permanent spring began. There were still some late frosts but not as many here, along this strand. There were more frosts five miles inland.

Orchards need farm equipment and farm equipment suppliers; cherries brought canneries and jobs, and the canneries followed the timber industry that had brought the railroad. Now the country opened up to the summer tourists escaping the summer heat of Detroit, Chicago, Gary, and Toledo. Other than cherries, there was little else here except for the miles of pure sand ringing Lake Michigan. Some of the best beaches in America, especially in the late summer when the lake could be bath water warm, were found in this part of Michigan.

The Smiths' pulled into the temporary parking provided on the high school softball field, one quarter for the whole day (money for the baseball team), a couple of young men in baseball uniforms directed cars to facilitate orderly parking. They walked the few blocks to Front Street where hundreds strolled along the sidewalks and boardwalks that paralleled the parade route. Shops' doors stood open and within minutes Bill held his first ice cream cone. Being a summer resident, Howie didn't know any of the boys running about in packs, pushing and shoving each other up and down the street. Howie didn't see any of the thousands of pickers that were on the farms; they weren't welcome there.

"Mom and Dad, I'm going down to the bridge to look for fish. I'll catch up with you in an hour or so," Howie said.

"See you in an hour near the soda shop," Doug answered.

"Hi cousin," a lilting voice said from behind as Howie walked toward the Boardman River.

Howie turned, "Hi Maggie."

"Are you with anyone?"

"No, Bill and the folks are walking toward the far end and he seems to be more interested in ice cream and the fact that Mom has money to get the ice cream."

"I ditched my brother, so I am fancy-free to be your date and your guide."

"Date?" Howie answered with more surprise than a question. "I don't think I need a date or a guide."

"Of course you do, we'll walk down toward where the parade starts and walk between the floats, look at the bands, and even some of the cars, the new Studebakers are there and they're so dreamy, even the new Cadillac convertibles, you know the dealer is a friend of my dad's so we may be able to sit in one, the red one he says is for the Cherry Queen - red for cherries he said, but I did see he had the signs for his dealership taped to the doors, "Cherry Queen cars provided by Boardman Chevrolet and Cadillac," it said; I saw it this morning."

Howie was amazed, not because of the information, but because she said it all in one breath. Too numb and surprised to argue he said, "Sure."

Margaret tried to take Howie's hand but he held it back.

"We can be together but I am not your date; let's leave it at that, Margaret."

The two pushed their way through the crowds to where Front Street turned to the left; Howie wanted to head toward the bridge, his original destination, but Margaret steered them to the twenty floats, on large flatbed trailers, all hooked up to John Deere tractors stretched out down the street. Signs were draped over the engines of the tractors announcing two dealerships: one in Traverse City, the other in Cadillac. Margaret said the same guy owned them, also a friend of her father's. She also added that the theme for this year's parade was the sea, so some floats had sea monsters and octopuses draped over huge pirate chests full of papier-mâché cherries and cherry trees; one had a boat with a sign that said "George Washington Crossing the Delaware."

"As if that's never been done before, the Daughters of the Revolution have used George Washington as their theme almost every year; they really should be more creative," Margaret said. "Besides, just because they are using a boat doesn't mean that they meet the theme of the sea."

To Howie the best float had the Great White Whale from *Moby Dick* stretched down its length. A hole cut in its side would be for one of the townsfolk playing Ahab, it would look like he was strapped to the giant's side by lengths of rope. Baskets of cherry candy were set about; a couple of young men in sailor's outfits were standing around with harpoons; he assumed they would be on the float for the action scenes. He was still recovering from the movie and, while the float was a poor imitation, it excited him.

"You ever read *Moby Dick*, Howie?" Margaret asked.

"No not yet, but Dad took us to see the movie last night in Acme, was really exciting. I want to see it again."

"Maybe we can go on a date, just you and me."

Howie looked at her again, she continually surprised him, and not in a good way. "And how'll we get there?"

"I'll have my Dad drive us," she answered. "What do you think?"

Howie tried to ignore her pushiness but it was hard, real hard.

"They all died, Ahab and his whole crew, except for Ishmael. "Call me Ishmael, it starts," Margaret added. "It's a story about one man's blind ambition, my teacher said hubris, and nothing but his own need for vengeance and he takes all those with him to the bottom of the ocean."

"My teacher," she continued, "said it was also about those demons that are hidden in our heads, where we hide our nightmares and see things that may not be there. She used the word paranoia."

Howie continued to just stare at her.

"Paranoia, believing something is after you that's not really there, but to Ahab and his shipmates it became real, he made them believe it was real. So are you paranoid if there really is something after you?" she asked, not really looking at Howie now, just waving her hands about and pointing at the float.

Howie looked at Margaret and wondered what the hell she was

talking about. He looked up at the whale and antlers appeared to be growing out of its head, great grey and white antlers with shaggy strips of skin, red antlers. He took a sharp deep breath and shuddered.

"You okay, you look white," Margaret said.

Howie steadied himself and looked back to his cousin, then back to the whale but, instead of antlers, he only saw dead branches on the tree behind the whale. They looked like antlers, but a second ago they were very real and very bloody.

"It's nothing, Margaret. Nothing."

The two caught up with his parents and his brother.

"We have been looking for you but I see you have found a date," Anne said. "Good morning, Margaret."

"Good morning, Aunt Anne and Uncle Doug, I found this lonely boy lost and wandering in the crowd so I saved him from the mob, toured the floats, killed a whale and then brought him home to you."

"You are an amazing young lady," Anne said. "You did all that and not one scratch."

"We are in your debt for saving this rascal," Doug said. "What can we do to repay this?"

"Ice cream," Bill yelled. "Ice cream, she must have ice cream."

"Yes, I think that's a fair payment for such a debt," Doug agreed.

Howie stood back and just smiled at all the silliness going on at his expense. "She's not my date," he said to no one. "She's not." The bleeding antlers still stuck in his head, paranoia, seeing things. *"Great, now I'm going crazy."*

The parade started at 12:00 sharp and chugged and snorted the fifteen blocks through the center of town. The last vehicles in the parade were, of course, the red convertibles; three of them, the Mayor first, then the Grand Marshall (who just happened to own the John Deere dealerships), and, in the last car, the Cherry Queen.

"I fell in love with you when you were in the back seat of that red Packard sixteen years ago, Anne Smith," Doug whispered in his wife's ear. "I fought through twenty guys to get to you at the end of the parade, just to say . . ."

"Every year you repeat the same old guff, Mr. Smith. And, I told you then, and now, there was no fight. You won me weeks before the parade."

"Yeah, but I like saying it."

Bill, his pockets full of candy, managed to get one of the free balloons being passed out, Margaret left to find her family. The four Smiths joined the two older Smiths for a late lunch at the Lion's barbeque. An hour later, Charlie and Liz headed back to the farm; Doug, Anne, and the boys went on to the fair grounds.

The Cherry Festival was the biggest fair in the northern part of the state, even bigger than the county fair in September. A few miles north of town, it had plenty of parking and enough ice cream even for Bill, but Anne could see that even he was beginning to drag.

They left the boys near the Ferris wheel, put three dollars each in their hands and told them to be back at the same place as soon as the fireworks were over.

"Yes ma'am," Bill said. "Let's go, Howie."

"Slow down Bill, slow down," Howie answered.

They made the circuit of the games and ring tosses and stumbled through the haunted house."

"That was stupid," Bill said when they exited. "After what we've seen the last few weeks, that's nothing, especially the fake hair."

Howie had to agree. "It's almost 9:00, fireworks?"

They found a spot near the fence along the rail of the racetrack and sat on the ground. The fireworks exploded almost directly overhead; Howie missed seeing their reflections off the water like the Fourth, but they were still great. Howie watched the crowd in the stands; each explosion lit their faces in green and red then blue. He scanned the crowd; saw Margaret with her family; a few other relatives he knew also flashed by in yellow and white. He watched a couple kissing to each explosion until his eyes caught the only face not looking at the fireworks.

Dark eyes stared only at him, the face constantly changed color, except for the black hair and beard. The finale pulled him back to the sky and the cascade of fire and sparks and noise; when he looked back at the crowd, the eyes and the face were gone.

Howie pulled is brother to his feet and they quickly beat a retreat, through the crowd, to the Ferris wheel. They had a few minutes to spare and Bill demanded they use his last quarter to ride the wheel before their folks arrived. They got in line and waited as one cab after another was loaded; being last, they had the longest ride on the wheel. Finally it began to turn, up to the top and then over, again, and again. Bill looked around and wondered out loud if they could see the lights from the farm, then lights from Traverse, and then he pointed to all the lights from the carnival. Howie sat, wondering about the face at the top of the bleachers, was it real? Did he see it?

The wheel slowed to a stop and began to unload. Bill was excited because, for some reason, the kid running the wheel missed them, must have thought they were the last car filled.

"We get one more turn, Howie, one more turn, neat-o."

"Great," Howie answered, not sure why. "Just great."

At the top, Bill pointed to the ground and waved, "Look, there's Mom and Dad."

Howie peered over the edge, Bill and Anne waved back. His eyes caught a peculiar movement along the edge between the light and dark sandy ground under the wheel, a black head of hair rotated up to catch his gaze. Howie froze. The same face, no exploding colors, just the black stare of his eyes; Howie instantly became lost in the eyes.

Anne saw her son's gaze and it froze her heart, Doug looked at her perplexed, then back up at Howie, and then toward where his son was looking. The crowd, thick and pushy, filled the area under the Ferris wheel. Doug could see nothing peculiar or out of the ordinary, only the flashing lights of the carnival and the chaotic ringing of bells from every stand. He flashed back at Howie, then back to the crowd. Nothing there. The Ferris wheel jerked one more time and came to rest at the bottom; Anne, already at the railing, stood ready to grab both the boys as soon as they came down the steps.

"Whatever it was, it's gone," Doug said to Anne over her shoulder. "It's gone."

Anne grabbed the boys, "You two alright?"

"Great Mom, very cool, can almost see Elk River from up there,"

Bill offered excitedly, pointing to the top of the wheel.

"And you?" she said turning to Howie.

"I'm fine," Howie answered in a distracted manner. "Fine, and yes, it was very cool."

As they walked to the car, Doug and Howie hung back a bit behind Anne and Bill.

"What was it, what did you see?" Doug asked.

"See what?"

"You looked like you saw something, from the top of the wheel."

"See what?" he repeated. "I didn't see a giant," Howie said. "There was no giant, no bearded man, nobody, just nobody, Dad. Just nobody."

Doug slowed a bit and watched his eldest catch up with his mother and take her hand. *"What giant, what bearded man,"* he said to himself.

CHAPTER THIRTEEN

Sunday morning, after church and breakfast, Doug put his small suitcase in the backseat of the station wagon, got down on one knee and hugged his youngest son, stood and shook Howie's hand, kissed his wife, gave both his parents a hug and left.

All five turned back to the house. Faint music and the crisp voices of the children from the picker's quarters drifted through the barn. The warmth of the day began to rise and pull the moisture of the past week's storms from the ground.

"Mom, I'm going down to the beach," Howie said.

Anne turned and looked at Howie. "Why? You may be needed up here today and, with your father gone, Roger may need you. Besides with what happened at the festival . . ." Her voice tailed off.

"Just for a bit, back in a couple of hours," Howie said, not allowing his mother to finish. "And Gramps said he was going into town and taking Bill. So I have a couple of hours to myself, and the festival, it was nothing."

Whatever happened at the festival was twenty miles away and, since the boy was almost fifteen, some room had to be given.

"Be back by 1:00, no later."

"Thanks."

Howie pulled on his shorts, striped tee shirt, tennis shoes and stuffed his knife into his pocket and hung a small canteen on his belt. Bill didn't say anything; he and Charlie were going to town to do some shopping for the house, stop at the hardware store, and finish clearing out what was left in Eve's apartment, more than enough excitement for Bill.

"Put your hat on," Liz said. "Going to be hot and I don't want to deal with sunstroke." She smiled at Howie.

Not wanting to run into any of the pickers, Howie cut into the orchard after stopping in the barn to get his cigarettes. He pushed his way through the dark green leaves and red fruit, cutting an arc among the trees, until he came to the top of the bluff that overlooked the pines below. This time, instead of turning and walking past Frank's studio, Howie cut a new path down the slope into the woods. Not straight down, he angled a bit to give his tennis shoes better traction; it was like walking sidesaddle through the sandy soil. At the bottom, he cut directly through the bracken and sumac, across the meadow created after the logging, past the pond and then back into the woods. His shirt already stuck to his back.

Sitting at the base of a large pine, he lit a cigarette and took a short tug from his canteen. Outside of the occasional squawk from the ravens or the background grind of the insects, quiet invaded the woods. The smoke settled in a small cloud around his head in the still air. Howie's eyes followed the path of an ant as it quickly crossed the sand, dodging small twigs and bits of leaves, until it came to the top of a cone shaped depression pushed into the sand. It stood on its six legs, then raised the front two, almost like sniffing the air, then the edge collapsed and the ant slid down the face of the cone toward its bottom, legs struggling the whole way. At the bottom, with a sudden movement the ant was caught in two sharp pincers that appeared as if from nowhere. The ant struggled for a moment, was drawn into the sand and disappeared.

"Lion ant," Howie exhaled. "Poor son-of-a-bitch didn't need to go that way."

Howie picked up a thin piece of grass straw and noodled the bottom of the cone, a bit of a tug and he slowly pulled up a half inch long grayish brown bug with two huge pincers holding tight to the straw. It let go, then dropped down back into the cone. The ant came roaring out of the sandy pit, but, in an instant, was snagged and drawn back under the sand again.

"It's a bitch, ain't it?"

Howie crushed his cigarette and looked through the trees toward the lake just visible beyond the last row of hemlock and pine. He walked toward the thin foamy edge between the lake and the sand, no waves or even riffles on the glassy surface, only a gentle swelling and receding, again and then again slower. Sitting on a low dune, he tapped another cigarette from the pack of Pall Malls, lit and touched the match to the tip and inhaled. He watched the water, thoughts irreverently bounced about in his head, until the cigarette burned to his fingers. He crushed the butt into the sand and then walked along the crest of the dune to where the larch swamp cut its exiting creek through the dune and into Lake Michigan. The storms had raised the creek and it ran turbid and rusty with the tannins from the swamp. It swirled about when it mixed with the clear lake water; the patterns twisted and eddied, then faded into the blue of the lake. Along this churning edge, a large fish broke the surface and jumped, small minnows flew in all directions. Another jump and more minnows cut loose, one did not make it.

"Nice snag," Howie said out loud. "Good catch."

Howie learned from his grandfather that it was here, along the edges between twisting currents and sharp drop offs, that predators stalked. The big fish, like the one at the powerhouse, waited to catch bait swept into predictable paths; they pushed away the smaller contenders until they controlled the whole flow.

Another bass jumped, another minnow was lost.

Pulling his shoes off, he tied the laces together and hung them over his shoulder. His bare feet cut into the damp sand along the creek, hot then cool, as his feet pushed deeper. He climbed part way up another dune and sat on the pine straw near the place where he saw the muskrat almost a month earlier and he lit another cigarette.

"Must have washed out by the rain," Howie said, noticing a butt lying on the ground. He picked up the old butt and would have put it in his pocket but noticed the paper did not have the familiar Pall Mall logo on it, this one was different, very different and not like anything he had ever seen. He studied the paper, finally shredding it in small pieces; the cigarette and the heat started to make him light-headed.

The creek below carried bits of sedge and leaves. A light breeze blew across the swamp; the tops of the grasses and cattails slightly bowed, then rose back, even the swamp breathed.

He crushed the cigarette and started back up the creek. Two ravens flew over, their shadows crossed his path; their cawing broke the silence. Another step and a third raven flew up, Howie threw his hands up to protect his face and fell back stunned, his hat fell off the back of his head. The raven flew upwards, screaming the whole time; when he pulled his hands away, a stench, carried by the moist air, washed over him. At his feet, caught in a steel trap, lay the muskrat. The ravens had plucked out its eyes and had started on its soft belly. Dead, its past agony was displayed by the mess that was its leg.

"Son-of-a-bitch," Howie said. "God damn it."

He stood for a long time watching the carcass; the ravens had settled in the pine over his head and continued to scream at him. Flies started to take their turn, a few bottleflies buzzed about the head and one walked along the length of the tail. The muskrat bore a grimace that, with the vacant sockets of its eyes, looked like the face on the outside of the horror house.

"You poor bastard, you do what you do, nothing more is asked other than to be a muskrat and then you get your leg caught in a damn trap, try to gnaw your fucking leg off to get free, mercifully die and then have these assholes pluck your eyes out. Shit. Well, you're not gonna stay here so some asshole will cut off your hide."

Howie found the chain strung to the trap and ran his fingers back to the stake. It easily came free from the damp sand. He held the trap and the muskrat at arm's length.

"You poor son-of-a-bitch."

He climbed the dune and found a good view across the pond to the wood on the other side. With his left hand and a short pine branch, he dug a two-foot deep hole in the sand. Pulling the jaws apart, he gently dropped the muskrat into the grave and adjusted the carcass so it looked like the rodent was sleeping. He pushed sand over the body and then, with a branch from the pine, swept the ground to remove his tracks. He threw pine straw over the area and, as he backed down the slope, brushed away his tracks.

"I'll not allow your body to be dug up by that fucking trapper," Howie said. "And you, you noisy bastards, can go and find another place to eat. Too fucking bad."

The birds stopped their clacking and cawing after he yelled. All three took off silently and flew across the swamp. He watched them go; then, swinging the trap over his head by its chain, he let it fly deep into the swamp. "Go find that, you asshole."

Howie followed the creek to the lake, then walked along the shore back toward the cabins. The sun was high, almost noon, time to start heading back. He skipped a few stones across the water; counted to eight, one time. He turned away from the lake to head back up the dunes to the farm.

He heard the giggle before he saw the top of the painting. He stopped and slowly lowered himself to the sand. Another giggle, then soft words floated through the stiff grass along the top of the dune.

"Move your leg a little to the left and raise your bottom off the blanket a bit. Good," the man said.

"Yes, Mr. Rex."

Howie slid down the dune a bit and smiled, *"What the hell, Uncle Frank here, but with who?"*

He inched his way back up the dune to a point where it dipped and he could see through the grass. To his right sat Frank Rex, his back to Howie. A large wooden palette in one hand, covered in paint, and a canvas trapped on an easel, stood in front of him. Howie looked to the left and on a red blanket lay Jennie, naked, across from the canvas. One leg raised and bent, turned with her shoulder and face toward Frank, both arms raised over her head, her fingers locked together.

"Excellent, we're making good progress today Jennie, my love," Frank said. "Wonderful, you're not getting too much sun?"

Howie turned back to look at Jennie, she shook her head. "I'm fine. I love the sun on my body; it feels so warm and almost sinful."

"Probably is, especially if that priest was to see you this way, but with this light you look almost glowing. Turn your head a bit more so I can get the color just right."

Jennie moved her head slowly and her eyes scanned the dune behind Frank Rex; she squinted. Her eyes caught Howie's and a slight, but very seductive, smile passed her lips.

"That's a good look, Jennie, hold that for a moment."

Jennie held the smile and continued to look at Howie.

"Move your hips a bit to the left," Frank directed.

Jennie did, but her eyes never left Howie; Howie followed her legs up to her hips and confirmed that she was all redhead, and this time, her breasts were not covered with a thin sheet. Howie felt his dick start to stiffen and throb, he was getting uncomfortable but in a way that seemed exciting. He pushed down on his crotch to ease the pressure, a shot of electricity surged through him.

"Move your leg down a bit," Frank said.

She did as Frank requested and Howie pushed harder. Jennie continued to stare and smile at Howie. Oil flew across the canvas; Frank started to work the area under her breast with a brush. Howie looked at the canvas, then the spot on Jennie's breast, a small bit of sweat rolled down its curve and held for a moment before falling to the blanket.

Howie pushed harder and harder. Jennie asked Frank, "May I wipe some of this sweat away?"

"Yes my dear, please do. And move your legs apart just a bit; the light is changing."

Jennie moved her hand slowly across her chest to both breasts, wiping away the sweat, seen as a caress to Howie, as his caress; he pushed harder and faster. The surges continued in short waves, the harder he pushed, the better if felt. Jennie continued to smile at Howie. She adjusted her legs like Frank asked; Howie could see all of her.

He pushed harder, his crotch starting to jerk by itself. He looked at her and he pushed and he rubbed and the jerking continued.

Slowly it subsided and Jennie continued to smile at him, Howie saw the smile broaden a bit, she ran her tongue along her lips and then, a wink. Howie rolled on his back, his hand still on his crotch.

"You okay, Jennie? You look very happy for some reason just now, what are you thinking, you wench you?" Frank asked. "Let me see if I can capture that."

"Oh, Mr. Rex, I'm very happy right now, more pleased than I've been in a long time."

Howie pulled his hand away from his crotch, stickiness and wetness spread across his shorts. He lay back for a moment in the warm sand and took a deep breath, he rubbed his crotch again and short jolts of electricity shot through him, but not with nearly the same intensity as a moment ago. He turned back to Jennie, who no longer looked at him; Frank continued to push oil across the canvas as the two talked quietly. Howie inched his way down the dune toward its base and then walked out toward the lake. He rubbed his dick again but all the electricity was gone, just the dampness remained. He walked to the beach and looked across the water to the hills on the other side, everything seemed crystal clear and in total focus. A small sailboat sat motionless in the still air, it appeared as if two boats were stacked one on top of the other, only one was upside down. Howie walked into the lake until the water was chest high and then lowered himself slowly until completely immersed, his hat floated over him. He looked through the clear water and all his senses felt electric. The water washed him; he rubbed himself all over, cleaned his shorts, and then stood up. The sun started to dry his blond hair immediately.

He circled Jennie and Frank's hollow in the dune and pushed his way through the scrub junipers and into the cool shade of the hemlocks and maples. The heat dried his shirt and shorts as he strutted back through the woods to the place where the path ramped up the slope to the farm.

Howie put his hand in his back pocket. "Fuck, cigs are soaked, again." He dug a hole in the sand with his heel and buried the pack. He then rubbed his crotch again, this time with his bad hand.

"Is this what sex is like? The thrill, the electric surge, the push and release; pretty damn fucking exciting. Am I grown now? Am I a man now? Will it be obvious to everyone that I jacked-off? Shit, will I have to tell the priest that I jacked-off? How do you say that, what do I tell him?

Bless me Father for I have sinned, I jacked-off. Or, on the other hand, bless me Father for I have sinned, I watched a naked woman lying on a red blanket in the sand and got a hard-on and it was—great. But I am sorry, now. Hell, that's a bigger lie. Or maybe, not tell him at all but say something like, bless me Father for I have sinned, Sunday after church I had impure thoughts and I am very sorry. Yeah, that'll do it, use the impure thoughts line, the one from religion class, seems to be the coverall for all actions, impure thoughts. That'll work, it's got to! Don't want to go to hell over jacking-off."

Howie smiled and stopped. He could see the top of the frog pond where the stag was killed and beyond it to the lone sentinel pine in the clearing.

Addressing the tree, Howie said, "You've certainly seen a lot in your life. Seen a lot but never said a damn thing."

Pushing through the bracken, he reached the pond, the tops of the cattails waved in the warm breeze. He slid down the face of the slope. Looking around, he could just barely make out the soft depressions that were his footprints from a month ago. Dragonflies still buzzed about in their purpose-driven chaotic flight. Here, go there, stop, go, then gone, then back again. Two eyes broke the surface and sat motionless, staring at him, a big leopard frog, its arched back drifted in the sun's warmth directly behind the eyes. He leaned back against the sand, closed his eyes, and looked toward the sun. Specs danced on the inside of his eyelids, bright yellow, bits of dust, and he heard the buzzing of the pond. A raven cawed.

Howie ran his good hand down his pants and his shirt. *"Getting dry, can't have Mom wondering how'd I got wet,"* he thought. *"No, not sure she'd understand, probably even less than Father O'Brien."*

The black bird's cawing increased. The calls bounced from one horizon to the other.

"Not much has changed," Howie said looking about. "The rain washed the footprints and blood away. Just a few new hoofprints and raccoon prints, like nothing ever happened."

The cawing and the cackling increased in volume and frequency.

"What has them all riled up?"

A shadow flew over the green water and a raven's reflection bounced off the mirror-like surface.

"Now what?" he said looking up. A towering shape blocked the sun and cast its shadow across the sand and water to engulf Howie. He squinted.

A man formed in the glare, a giant of a man with a black beard and broad shoulders. Howie stood, the man's face brightened after he turned a bit toward the sun. A face emerged from the shade; grey eyes looked down at the boy.

"Why you following me?" Howie demanded. "Why? You're everywhere."

"I'm not following you, you just happen to be where I am."

"Don't believe you. I saw you yesterday at the fair."

"Yes, I was there, kind of fun, why do you keep showing up? "

"What? You're following me."

"Only in your dreams. Anyway, wrong foot to start all of this back and forth," the man, replied. "Definitely the wrong way to start this conversation." He dropped his great frame to the sand and sat at the top of the slope. "Introductions?"

Howie took a defensive stance, "Why? Why should I introduce myself?"

"Because that's what civilized men do, young man, they state their name. Simple."

Howie thought for moment, "You're trespassing. This is my grandfather's land; you need to leave."

"Well, I'll start. I am Gideon Walker and I live in a small cabin on the beach, there." He pointed toward the lake. "I am spending the summer, renting. I live in Germany, but was from Detroit when I was a kid your age. Used to summer here thirty years ago, a chance to relive my youth. I write a little and stay to myself, now you."

Again Howie paused. "Well okay, I am Howard Franklin Smith, and this is my grandfather's land."

"Yes, I know and you are quite insistent on my knowing that; your grandfather seems to be a good man, his orchard is well kept and well managed. The painter, is he your uncle or something?" Walker asked.

"Yes, he's my Uncle Frank. How do you know about him?"

"I may know him, even if I don't formally introduce myself to the family; been meaning to do that for some time."

"I saw you at the powerhouse and at the fireworks, I knew it was you."

"Likely, I was there both times, but the only time we talked was when you pulled that huge fish up on the beach. I was the fellow who told you to let him go. You remember that, I'm sure."

Howie stared at the man. "You!"

"Me, guilty as charged. Was at the fireworks, stood watching them until the woods caught fire, went to get help, but someone beat me to it, so I left. Did see you and your brother at the fair, but you kept staring at me with a weird look, so I left."

"You're weird, a giant," Howie said.

"Not at all, just tall," Walker answered as he stood. "Someday I'll tell you a story about all this, but for today, it's a pleasure to meet you."

"Howie," another voice, loud and clear, carried out of the woods and over the pond. "Howie!"

Howie turned to the sound and then back to Walker, he was gone.

Climbing to the top of the pond, he heard Roger call out again, "Howie."

"Roger."

Howie watched Roger push his way through the ferns.

"Roger," Howie yelled. "Here."

Roger stumbled over a stump but caught his balance. "Howard Smith, I've been looking for you for an hour. Your mom is worried. Told you to be back at 1:00, it's almost 2:30."

"No watch Roger, time just got away. Did you see him?"

"Who?"

"The giant, he was here 'til you yelled. Sitting right there."

Roger reached around behind his back and pulled out a revolver.

Howie stared at him. He held the gun to his side.

"Here?"

"Yeah, sat there," Howie pointed again.

The sand was still discolored from the boots, and the footprints, The spot where the man had pushed off was evident.

"What did he want?"

"To know my name, not much else, introduced himself. Disappeared when he heard you yell, didn't see him go."

Roger scanned out across the woods and looked deep into the trees, a few boot prints in the sand but they quickly disappeared in the bracken.

"Must move quick and silent-like," Roger said. "Never saw him. Lets get back up the hill; your mother was vexed an hour ago, she's probably got the sheriff looking by now."

"She wouldn't do that, I'm sure."

"Yeah, you're probably right but no need to keep her worrying."

They climbed back up the hill, past Frank's studio. Howie took a look down the path, hoping to catch sight of Jennie, but no one was about. They passed the pickers' quarters and the barn. Ricardo called out and Howie waved to him, but he continued on with Roger through the barn.

Anne sat outside on the porch and watched her son walk across the yard.

"You are very late," Anne said with a stern and direct tone. "Very late, I told you 1:00."

"Found him down at the frog pond," Roger said. He looked at Anne with a concerned set to his jaw, and pursed his lips a bit, nodded toward Howie.

"You go in now; I'll come and talk to you in a minute."

Howie went through the screen door; he let it go slowly so it wouldn't slam. He looked back at his mother through the mesh and then went to wash up.

Roger told Anne what Howie had said.

"You believe him?"

"Maybe. But there is no way a man that big can disappear that quickly; too open and nowhere to hide. Unless that fellow can move faster than a cloud's shadow, I just don't know. Sure, some sands been kicked about but nothing else tells me a giant was there. That boy's been seeing things, hearing things and getting ideas in his head. Best you keep him up here; the woods just get his imagination running."

Anne thought about Roger's comments; Howie never acted this way before. Why now? Was he seeing things? Was there a man? If there is, then why was he after her son? And, if there was no man, then what was Howie seeing and why?

He is getting older and will be gone soon; she only had a few years left with her oldest, then the world would take him. She closed her eyes for a moment, sighed, and looked at the screen door. Howie stood in the doorway, the shade of the dark house hid most of him; she watched him smile at her. He opened the door, walked over and gave her a kiss on the cheek, and then went back inside.

CHAPTER FOURTEEN

After what happened at the pond, Roger never let Howie stray too far from the farm. He had him do chores and odd jobs and even let him run the tractor out into the orchard. Howie carried sacks of sulfur and pesticides to the prep tanks for the sprayer. Charlie wouldn't let Howie spray; he and Roger would do that. Anne watched and spent quiet afternoons with Liz talking about Howie. Bill watched the bugs grow in the aquarium; the tadpoles were almost frogs now, one inch long and developing a greenish glaze to their skin.

"What's with that boy?" Anne said.

"Howie seems good to me," Liz answered. "In fact, the last few days, he seems to be almost strutting about. I swear that boy is seriously becoming a man. I've watched two strong boys grow to be the best men I've ever known. I watched them learn to walk and run and then bring families to this farm. I also waited for one to come home and he never did. They're a part of your body and a part of your soul, but they're men; they have to stand on their own. Howie's like that, a lot like James with his creative hands, but also like his father, introspective. He lives in two worlds, ours and his."

"I can't keep him locked up," Anne said. "But I am afraid to let him out of my sight."

"I understand and if he was younger I'd tie him to this porch with a tether ten feet long. He'd never leave my sight, but he's not and you can't and I wouldn't."

"Yes I know, but . . ."

"No buts, it is what it is. It is a fearful thing growing up, fearful for us because we can only watch and guide them and hope to keep them from hurting themselves. We teach them, but it's their world and they have to grow up alone, each day is easy or hard, confusing and simple. You've seen those sketch books on the shelves of the living room. They aren't Frank's, their James'."

"I thought they were Frank's, the nudes and the figure studies. They're good, very good."

"No, they're James'. He was fourteen when I found them; he had hidden them in his closet behind some boxes. I was looking for some old toys to give away when I found them. I was stunned; I knew they weren't Frank's. They were amateurish and naïve but well drafted, in fact, strongly drawn. I sat for an hour looking at them. I cried. Not because my son was drawing naked women but because he understood what he was drawing and why."

"Did you talk to James?"

"In a manner, I took James out to the studio; Frank had just finished building it. He would have women over to model for him. I was sure there was more going on; he was a handsome devil in those days. It was a warm afternoon and James had just come in from school, June I think, last days of the school year. Yes, that's it. I was sitting at this table when he walked in, his sketchpads all laid out in front of me. He saw them and turned the most delightful crimson. That blond hair and his red face, he was a sight. He started to say something but I stopped him, put the books in his arms and marched him down the path to Frank's and banged on that red door of his. Frank pulled the door open, ready to scream, and before he could say anything I simply said, 'Spaniard, if you're going to allow this boy to study figures and models of the human form, then he should use the real thing, not copy from your sketch books; he's old enough, and you're good enough to teach him.' I could see a very full-bodied brunette over his shoulder on the small stage in the middle of the room; the aromas almost knocked me down."

"He was fourteen and you let him look at naked women?"

"Anne, these are the fifties, somehow we don't do those things now, but it really doesn't make a difference when it was. These boys grow into men, we can guide them and point them and even push them, but my father told me: 'You can do everything you can, but eventually they do what they want; they'll live their own lives. The more room you give them, the bigger their lives will be.' Didn't understand it for the longest time, but that day at Frank's studio I did. And because of that, Doug also became a better man and you were lucky to get him," Liz winked at Anne. She blushed.

"Did Doug sketch naked women when he was fourteen?"

"No, Doug had other interests. Though I am sure James let Doug look at the books, he never had his brother's artistic soul. He was a bookworm; I believe he read everything in my library by the time he was fifteen, so he was well informed, you might say." She smiled and winked again. "They also knew respect and propriety and I was sure they weren't going to get that from Frank. I never knew if James showed his books to anyone; he always left them in Frank's studio. It set him up well when he decided he wanted to become an architect; I have wondered since his death what he would be doing now if he were alive. With all this growth and great things happening in the cities, I believe, in my soul, he would have been a great builder and designer." Liz turned her gaze to the orchard and sighed.

"Damn it, why is he back?" Liz said, looking past the garage to the road. A colored fellow in a denim shirt and a narrow brimmed hat turned the corner and strolled toward the porch. A strap crossed his chest, a leather bag hung on its end.

"Good morning, Mrs. Smith, and good morning to you, Mrs. Smith," the black man said. "Glorious morning this is, really glorious." The man took off his hat, waved it through the air and bowed.

"And good morning to you, Mr. Beck," Liz said with little warmth. "What brings you here, as if I didn't know?"

"The miracle of nature's bounty brought to bear under the watchful eyes and hands of man. Cherries, Mrs. Smith, cherries; that and the need for a few dollars to tide me over until I can get back to my wonderful home in Jackson, Mississippi."

"You haven't been back to your wonderful home in twenty years, have you?" Liz asked, looking directly down at the man.

"Well, no ma'am, it's a circuitous trip I have laid before me, a trip with a long list of places to see and to be seen. My list, mind you, my list is paramount."

"And why is Elk River on your list? I don't think it's on anyone's list."

"A way station: a momentary delay, a watering stop, if you will. Yes, a watering stop to replenish my boiler. After this, I am on to Canada, then to Siam. Yes, they're on my list, my list."

"Well, Mister Albert Beck, I am not sure I have work for you this year. The Martinez's have a full load of workers and I'm not sure we can use you."

"Excellent family, those Martinez's, very excellent. Señora Barbara Martinez is an excellent woman, excellent. I'll work under her management and not be a bother to anyone, anyone. Follow her every order," Albert Beck replied earnestly.

The screen door slammed and all three turned toward the door. Howie stood staring at Beck.

"Good God almighty, is that Master Howard Smith?" Beck said. "I think you were only this high, this high, when I saw you last." He waved his arm around at about mid chest, "This high."

"Good morning, Mr. Beck. Are you here to work or just to tell stories?" Howie asked.

"Work young man, work, but only if your excellent grandmother will allow me to. I will be no bother and, as you can see from my frame, I don't eat much either. I'll put a few dollars in my pocket then move on, get back to my list. And yes, my boy, I have a few new stories to tell; yes, wonderful and frightening new stories to tell."

Howie turned to his mother and grandmother, he did not ask, they understood.

"Yes, Mr. Beck, you can stay until the cherries are done. There's a cot in the loft in the barn, the usual. I want no trouble from you this year; I want no fights or you're out. I want no arguments with the pickers and you'll follow Ernesto and Barbara's directions without fail. Do you understand me, Mr. Albert Beck? Do I have your bond?" Liz looked directly at Beck during this instruction; he stood straight, hat in hands.

"Yes, Mrs. Smith. I will do exactly as you require, exactly."

Howie was thrilled to see Albert Beck; Beck's stories of his travels grew more exciting and adventurous every year, even more than his uncle's, stories of Mexico, deep in the mountains Mexico, South America, Peru, Chile, and the Orient, Japan, the Philippines and even Hong Kong. All the places he wanted to see and were all on his list.

"Howie, show him to the loft in case he doesn't remember where it is and get him some extra bedding. Mr. Beck, your meals are your responsibility and I want no fires in the barn, understand? And no smoking!"

"I understand, understand completely. Señora Martinez has always been kind enough to sell me a dinner or a breakfast, so I'll work something out with her. Excellent woman, excellent."

Howie put his hand out. Beck shook it like it was a dinner bell, loud and full of anticipation. He looked directly at Beck.

"Let's get to the barn and you can tell me where you've been and where you think you're going."

"Master Smith, I have been everywhere and I'll know exactly where I am going as soon as I get there," Beck said with a grin.

Beck looked around the interior of the barn, "Hasn't changed much, not much, Howard," and started up the ladder to the loft. Howie watched his weathered and wiry hands grab each rung like a practiced sailor. In the corner of the loft, a dusty cot stood propped against the wooden wall, dust hung in the air and each step kicked up another cloud. An orchard barn is different than a cattle or a horse barn. No hay or straw, just bags of chemicals, old pruning saws, hooks, broken ladders needing repair, buckets everywhere, and an old sofa from some past tenant, it looked more like a rummage sale than a working barn.

"Howie, this is excellent," Beck announced. "Quarters fit for a king."

"Please, Mr. Beck, even the pickers won't sleep up here."

"On the contrary, my boy, on the contrary, if you had seen the places I have slept, or tried to sleep, you would understand the pleasure of this palace, yes, I said palace."

They dusted off the cot. Beck hung the small leather satchel he always carried on a hook; he noticed Howie looking at it.

"This bag, my boy, is my whole world. Everything a traveler needs, I have in there. The list is so long it would take an hour to explain."

Howie looked at the bag and wondered how all the things he could imagine would be in that pouch.

"You don't believe me, do you?" Beck asked. He lifted the worn flap and pulled out a large eight inch clasp knife and a small metal knife-like contraption. "I traded for this knife in Spain and I got this here contraption from a German soldier just after the war. Our company, all black fellows like me, had guard duty over the captured soldiers. Learned a lot about Germany and the people, even picked up a fair bit of their jabber, I seem to be able to pick up a language fast, needing to eat does that, I guess. Look closely, two knife blades, a corkscrew, very handy some days, two screw driver tips, a scissors, a reamer, great for my pipe, even a saw, tweezers, and a spot for a toothpick, lost that years ago, years ago."

Beck passed the contraption to Howie. He turned it over in his hand, touched the worn red surface, opened and closed the blades, even extracted the tweezers; *"a most wondrous knife,"* he thought, *"wondrous."*

"You see with a knife like this, and few other things in this bag, I can go anywhere and do anything. Only need to wash my clothes and myself every so often and I'm set. Howard, the world is a big and magical place if you walk proud, care about those you are with, treat people with respect and deference, and, most especially, say thank you and mean it, really mean it."

"Grandma says you get into fights."

"Ah, yes my boy, I do, yes, sadly and unfortunately I do, but some people need to be treated with the utmost respect and an occasional punch in the eye is a good way to teach them," Beck looked at Howie and smiled. "Yes, an occasional thrashing is always a good way, a very good way to teach respect."

"Howie," Roger's voice carried through the barn.

"Yes sir, up in the loft."

"Need you down here as soon as you're done."

"Right away."

"I'm sure your mother has told Mr. Barton I'm here, so I'll hole up for a while until he gets used to the idea of me being around again, I'll catch up with you later. Yes, later."

Howie met Roger just outside the barn.

"That lay-about up in the loft?" Roger asked.

"Yes."

"Wants to work or whatever he calls it. Well after Ernesto gets going on him he'll be working," Roger said with a snort.

Beck climbed down from the loft and ambled back to the picker's quarters. Barbara Martinez sat with Bonita stripping husks from ears of corn.

"First of the season," Beck said. "They look very good, very good."

"Señor Beck, buenos dios," Barbara answered with a sharp edge to the 'e' in his name. "Yes, it's early, but the color is good. The warm days and nights have helped. My cousin brought them up from Indiana. He's at the Miller's."

"Good yellow color, yes, good color. I would like to make an arrangement with you for a meal a day and maybe a beer. Do you think that's possible?"

"It's possible; I can always use a dollar or two. How about one dollar for the meal and twenty-five cents for the beer, if we have any? That fair?"

Beck stood around for a moment and thought about the conditions of this transaction. More than excellent, he knew that, but still a bargain must be reached.

"If I throw in an extra twenty cents, can I purchase a couple of those excellent tortillas you make for lunch as well? They're very tasty; as good as anything I ever had in Matamoros."

"Mine are far better than anything from that miserable border town. So be careful, twenty cents more, excelente," Barbara said with emphasis.

"Yes excellent, excellent."

Beck did odd jobs around the farm and helped Roger get the ladders repaired and repainted. This helped to clear some of the debris out of his bedroom. He and Howie also started to repaint the buckets stacked about the loft in a deep red cherry color; the painted buckets sat, with bottoms up, near the barn to dry in the sun.

"Mr. Beck, you said you were in Germany at the end of the war, did you ever meet my uncle?" Howie asked Beck as they put the last of the buckets outside .

"No Howard, I did not. Sadly, I never met him. Been only the last four or five years that I have been traveling through this part of Michigan. Your uncle, if I remember, has been gone since you were a little boy. France somewhere if I recall, left a lot of friends of mine in parts of Europe as well. They didn't return home either."

"How did you get there?"

"On a boat, same as everyone, on a boat. Only, I been to lots of places before I enlisted, needed a job so to speak then, so the army became my employer. They probably would never have drafted me since they had no idea where I was since I didn't have a permanent place of residence. So I saved them the trouble. I also figured, if I didn't get myself killed, I would be somewhere in Europe on another fellow's ticket, and that's how it worked out; I had places on my list I needed to see. I was thirty miles outside Frankfort at the end of the war. I was an MP then, a colored cop. So, instead of being shipped home, I got hired by one of the local civilian American administrators as his personal guard, lived well and saw a lot of Germany and France. Came back in 1949, stayed a few months, then went back."

"I was seven then," Howie volunteered. "What is Germany like?"

"It is a country of beautiful mountains and elegant farmlands where the war was not fought and utter mindless destruction where it was fought. Whole cities leveled, mountains of debris and churned farmlands, some still with bombs sticking up in the air like they was planted nose down. Sometimes they exploded when no one was around, mind you this was months after the war was over, and sometimes they exploded when there was people standing around, not good, not good and very messy."

"You were a guard? A cop?"

"Yes I was, and, because I could read and write reasonably well, they put me in charge of a company of colored soldiers, most from the south, some from my hometown of Jackson, Mississippi. We were responsible for keeping guard over Germans who had been captured or had just given up. Even at the war's end, there needed to be some kind of management of the people, couldn't have them wandering about the countryside causing mischief, so we took care of them and, as time went on, they were released and most returned to their homes, I heard many of them walked hundreds of miles. Hans was the fellow I traded a good army watch with in exchange for his Swiss knife, the contraption I showed you. Said he had another at home and that was where he was going. Somewhere near Kassel, he said. A few months later, I was in Kassel to see if I could find him, found his house or what was left of it, a woman was outside with a young boy, summer almost gone. I asked, in the best German I could muster, it wasn't too bad then, if Hans was around. She simply said he was dead. I made out from her that he had walked home after he was released and it was late in the evening so he took a short-cut across the field behind the house, must have tripped over one of the duds, only it wasn't a dud and blew the poor fellow to Valhalla. He could see his house after being gone for four years, then he was no more. So this knife will never leave me. I saw that look you had when I pulled it out, so remember that story. It's these little things that keep us moving forward, and even though a man like me only has few things to carry, just a few things, but they are excellent things, excellent."

Bill dragged a few buckets around the corner of the barn, Beck and Howie stared at the boy.

"Where are you going with those buckets? I am not painting any more of those; you want them red, then you paint them," Beck said with a grin.

"I intend to paint these buckets myself," Bill replied. "All by myself, yes, myself."

CHAPTER FIFTEEN

Not a leaf moved in the orchard; the morning lay still, holding its breath. Howie and Bill felt the stickiness of the humid air as they stepped off the porch, "It's gonna be real hot, Bill. Real hot! So stay in the shade and drink lots of water."

"Yes, Howie, Grams told me at breakfast. Maybe when the first day's picking is over, we can go down to the beach."

"Good idea," answered Howie. "Nut'ten better than a swim to wash off the sweat and cherry juice."

Ernesto approached the house, his large straw hat in his hands. Charlie walked out the door behind the boys.

"Buenos dias, Señor Smith. We pick today?" Ernesto asked.

"Buenos dias to you too Ernesto, yes, today we begin. Let's start with the Royal Anns out by Señor Rex's studio, then keep picking the sweets north down to the road. Should be through in two or three days if the weather holds, sour's are getting ready sooner than I expected, we may end up picking them at the same time. We'll go through them as fast as we can. Roger stacked lugs out back and, as they are filled with cherries, we'll move them up front to the truck.

Got a call last night that a fresh fruit buyer is looking for sweets for Grand Rapids and Detroit, so the sooner I call him, the quicker they can get moved out."

"Bueno, Señor Smith. The ladders, they are already on the trailer so Roger or the boy there," pointing at Howie, "can haul them out with the lugs. Everyone has their buckets and straps; they'll take them out. It's good to be back to work," Ernesto said.

"Good, how many you got this year, Ernesto?" Charlie asked.

"Diez, Señor Smith. That's how many adults came over with us from Saginaw. There are a few others, and the two young boys can help a little, and my cousin says three others from the Miller place can work this week since they have more than enough pickers there. They're good boys but this is the first year they pick. So it may take a few days to learn how. They'll stay at the Miller's if it's okay. Will that hombre, Beck, also pick?"

"Good, Ernesto, good crew. Yes, Mr. Beck will be picking near you, but if I know him he will be off to himself," Charlie said. "What do you think of him?"

"Trouble follows him," Señor Smith. "He goes to trouble like a moth to a flame, but if I was in trouble, I would want him on my side. One seriously tough colored fellow and he will not back down, very smart, but stupid too. He'll be dead in an alley someday, but it will be a very nice alley."

"I am afraid you may be right, Ernesto," Charlie answered with a laugh.

Howie listened to the comments, his heart quickened. "He's a good man; he'll stay out of trouble, grandpa. I know he will."

"I sure hope to hell he does, I don't need the kind of trouble that man can bring."

"How much per lug this year, Señor Smith?" Ernesto asked.

The two men had had this same conversation for more than ten years. Ernesto Martinez knew exactly how much every other farm paid per lug; he also knew that every grower knew that price as well. A lug was a wooden box about one foot wide, two feet long and about six inches high. Grooves were cut into end panels to make it easier to pick up. Each about a cubic foot, it took six to ten buckets to fill each lug and about ten minutes of very fast picking to fill each bucket. Each lug, fully loaded, weighed about forty pounds. The cherries must be clean and free of leaves and twigs and not include any bad, black or bird damaged berries. Pickers were paid by the lug, not by the hour. Summer hours could be from sunrise to sunset as long as there were berries and good weather. Time off was Saturday afternoon and Sunday, sometimes. If there was rain or the heat was too much, they picked as fast as they could to get all the berries in before they split or became overripe; that meant picking Saturdays and Sundays.

Picking as a family meant that they dumped all their buckets into their own lugs. Each family kept their lugs separate. They were stacked in the shade and marked with paper tags. Each family, or individual if picking alone, kept track of their lug count. When Roger came through to collect the boxes, he had a ring of cards he hand punched with the count. The picker had his own card punched as a record. This was the only way to match up the picker's count of lugs with the grower. Any discrepancy went to the grower. Only when it became frantic did conflicts arise between picker's stacks of lugs or someone forgetting to punch cards.

"Ernesto, we're paying one dollar and two cents per lug for the sweets and ninety-eight cents for the sours," Charlie said.

"Señor, you have always been fair, but we were hoping for about one dollar and five cents and one dollar and a penny. Gas is up and the niños need new clothes," Ernesto had a large smile when he said this; his children always needed new clothes and he always felt it would be worth a couple of cents more.

"I'll give you one dollar and four cents and one dollar for the sours, if the weather holds and if we get everything picked by the first of August, we can discuss a bonus. But the lugs must be clean and no rejects from the cannery, I'll have none of that crap from the new boys. They all work, understood?"

"Si, Señor Smith. They are good boys but I will watch them; if they get out of line or slow down, Barbara will kick their asses," Ernesto said with a laugh.

"Ernesto, if there's one thing for sure it is that Señora Barbara Marie Martinez will kick their asses back to Texas if they don't work as hard as she wants them to." Ernesto's wife had a reputation as a no-nonsense field boss and usually it meant everything was picked as clean and as fast as possible.

Howie and Bill listened to this conversation between the two men. Howie knew how much work was involved filling the lugs and he was amazed at how fast they were filled by the Martinez family. He tried to pick as fast as they could to earn a little money, but it was tough, and using a tall ladder was forbidden by his mother, it was harder to hold onto. When he finally filled one lug, which took him over an hour, the Martinez stack stood at four and one half. At the end of a long and very hot day, his arms were sore and scratched; his shirt was soaked with sticky dried cherry juice and he had only filled four lugs. The Martinez family had stacked thirty-two boxes.

"Yeah, but they had four people picking," he said to Bill that night, calculating that they still picked twice the amount he did in the same time. "Maybe they each had four hands, versus my one good arm."

This year he would work with Roger. He would drive the tractor while Roger loaded the boxes on the back of the trailer, and unloaded them at the farm. He would get fifty cents an hour knowing it would be easier than picking.

"That's a lot of money they make if they pick a lot," Bill said. "They can make hundreds of dollars every day, wow."

"No one can pick that fast, besides, when the picking is done, it's done," Howie answered. "Whether they pick the orchard in two weeks or one day, it does not make a difference. They'll make the same. Hopefully, the weather holds and they can get it done in time. But this heat may cause some problems, the cherries will get too ripe and start to mold; it might rain, then the cherries will soak up the water and split open and then we have to sort through the cherries to find only good ones. The price may go down if there are too many cherries from all the other farms and then Gramps has to renegotiate the price with Mr. Martinez. Hope for cool temperatures, no wind, no storms, and no surprises."

Mexican music drifted from one of the small windows, and a woman's voice, with a soft lilt, kept up with the music. The men stacked red buckets and ladders in the center of the yard. There were two different sized buckets: the small one was about ten inches high, the larger was almost twice as big, rings hung on each side, no handles. Web belts and shoulder straps allowed the buckets to hang at waist level, making it easier to pull the berries directly into the bucket. There were two types of ladders. The shorter ladders had three legs and ten steps, the taller ladders stood almost twice as high, these were for the treetops. The sides of the lower portion of the taller ladders swept out from the lowest steps to provide a wide base, the other leg, nothing more than one long straight two by four, provided the third leg of the tripod. Stable in the soft sand, they had to be set up carefully; a fall from twenty feet onto the sand could be as painful as any fall from that height.

Bill saw Ricardo Martinez stacking buckets. "Ricky, do you want to play catch?"

"No, can't. Momma says now we work, so we work, Pappa says we load the buckets, so we load." Ricardo was Bill's age but had grown up all over the United States. Born in Texas, and, like his older brother and younger sister, he knew that summers meant work and sitting in the back of a truck for hours at a time. Too young to climb ladders, he carried things to and from the fields with his older brother, brought water to his parents and his uncles and, occasionally, did some hoeing and weeding. Legally, he was not allowed to work, but a busy boy always needed something to keep busy. He went to school near their house in Texas during the winter but only for a few months before they headed north again. He could read and write a little but his education was incomplete. He seldom went to school during the family's travels up from Texas even though, one time in Indiana, a church group offered classes to the children, classes in reading and religion. Ernesto removed his children quietly when he found out that they were more interested in teaching their brand of religion then helping the children learn. The Martinez family and all the cousins and uncles and aunts were Catholic; Ernesto would have nothing to do with their fire and brimstone preaching.

"That's okay. Can I help?" A minute later they were both adding red buckets to the pile.

"He is beginning to grow up," Howie thought, watching his broth-

er leave. A tug on his shirt brought him back, "Buenos dias, Gonzalo. How are you today?" Howie asked.

"I am very good, Señor Howie. So we begin to pick, si?"

"Yes, si. We pick," Howie answered slowly.

Gonzalo Martinez, the oldest (and the youngest) of the Martinez children was a pretty boy of ten, black hair cut straight across his forehead, dark almost black eyes and a very soft and rich melodious voice; but he was, as his mother said, slow. He fumbled with words in both Spanish and English. He seemed bright about some things but could not recite more than three sentences together without either losing his train of thought or becoming distracted. He had a faraway look at times that would cause even his elders to be uneasy, as if he saw things that only he could see, and, occasionally, would say things that would dumfound and confuse the adults; a simple child that smiled and always did as he was told. The littlest, Bonita, seemed to understand him and, even at three years old, take Gonzalo's hand and lead him about, always jabbering about things and pointing out things in the compound and the orchard. They had a strong bond between them, even though the boy was seven years older. Ricardo was industrious and would be like his father; Bonita, a beautiful child, would be like her mother. But when Howie looked at Gonzalo, the first thought that came to his mind was his Uncle Frank, Howie didn't know why, but they seemed to fit.

"Are you going to help pick?" Howie asked.

"Yes, Señor Howie, I will pick and I will help. Bonita told me if I helped she would sing to me every night." Gonzalo stopped and looked to the sky; a raven flew over, cawing incessantly, and hid itself in the first row of trees. It continued to caw at the group like a woman scolding her children. Gonzalo turned his dark eyes to Howie. "More," he said, pointing to the roof of the quarters, the sky was empty. After two heart beats, five more rose over the metal roof and followed the first one into the orchard. "They're here to steal cherries and tortillas," Gonzalo said. "They are," he paused, trying to think of a word, "banditos. I do not like them." Again he paused and stared into the dark trees laden with red cherries. "Bonita says they are evil souls and we should cross ourselves when we see them." Gonzalo crossed himself then spit on the ground.

Howie, astonished by what had just happened, seldom paid any attention the noisy birds in the woods, where he usually saw them. He remembered the morning he saw the muskrat and ravens in the pines; they were seldom in the orchard unless there was food available or something to steal. In the woods, they made a racket that would precede him, spooking everything is his path. They acted like sentries, squawking to the world that someone was trespassing, that someone was coming. Here, in the orchard, they seemed to watch and to wait. Last year, he remembered two particular ravens landing among the worker's things stacked under the trees; they picked though the pile of belongings until they found lunch bags and then pulled out the tortillas and flew off with their booty. A raucous fight ensued until one beat the other. It was Bonita's job to keep the birds away from the food. It worked well for a day or two, but then the birds started to stalk the goods and, with one eye on Bonita, make quick forays into the pile. Gonzalo helped his sister but they were persistent and eventually the ravens gained small victories.

"Howie, they are evil," Gonzalo repeated slowly. "Evil follows them. That's what Bonita says."

"Gonzalo, Bonita is just a baby; she doesn't say those things," Howie said.

"Bonita is small but she is not a baby. She knows these things," Gonzalo said; he continued to stare into the orchard and slowly put his hands over his ears to muffle the cawing coming from the trees.

Bonita, dressed in a brilliant white dress embroidered with flowers and edges of yellows and reds, stood near her mother. She took short, but almost adult-like, steps across the compound to her brother, reached up and slowly pulled his right arm down away from his ears, gently kissed the back of his hand, smiled at Howie, and then led her brother back to their mother. Barbara ran her fingers through Gonzalo's hair and watched Bonita take him through the dark door of their quarters. Bonita briefly turned to Howie and, as only a child would, waved at him by wiggling her fingers.

Barbara Maria Martinez continued to stack bags and boxes that would be hauled out into the orchard; she smiled at Howie with an aristocratic expression. Bonita returned to her side with a glass of water, Barbara touched her cheek. For a moment, in the heat of the early morning, he felt a bit lightheaded. Then unexpectedly he remembered his uncle's sketches: the drawings of the old woman in Spain, the royalty and the pain of the woman and her daughter. The ravens flew out of the orchard and over the quarters raucously; when their sharp shadows crossed over mother and daughter, only Bonita looked up. Howie, for some reason he didn't understand, crossed himself.

As if the ravens had cued the action, the door to the barn swung open and the first cough of the tractor changed from a series of hacks and gurgles to a deep metallic rattle that smoothed out as the nose of the tractor left the barn and rolled into the courtyard. Roger sat high in the seat, a broad straw hat shading his face in the morning sunshine. The hat, like Roger, had worked many cherry seasons. He waved at the boys and swung the tractor around the group and the pile of belongings and cherry picking gear. Two of the Martinez men and Gonzalo climbed aboard to stack the ladders neatly. The buckets were nestled among the rungs of the ladders. They left a foot-wide shelf along the edge of the pile for the pickers, legs dangled over the edge.

"Ernesto, es que todos aqui?" Roger asked.

"Si, vamanos," Ernesto said, and smiled. His English was a lot better than Roger's Spanish.

The caravan, with a few walking behind, dove into the green wall of the orchard and headed to the southern corner of the sweets. They would work from the farthest point to the nearest, the sweet cherries would be picked first. Charlie said they had an order for two hundred lugs of Royal Anns and Bings for a buyer in Grand Rapids; the truck would pick up the fruit at 6:00. Cash money, on delivery; Charlie knew this would help get the season moving. After that he hoped that the other arrangements he had made would come through and the packed lugs would find their way to Detroit and Lansing. The next two weeks would be crazy. Charlie wished Doug could be here.

Two thousand lugs were stacked along the driveway and next to the orchard; it seemed like a lot, but they would not last a week if the pick-ups didn't return the lugs after they were emptied. Each of the lugs had been branded with canning company names and ownerships. The big farms had their names printed on the ends, By the end of the season, the boxes were so mixed up that ending up with more than a hundred of any one specific name was unusual and, at season's end, getting the right lugs back to their original owners was impossible.

Most mornings, the Martinez family walked out to the trees. Howie and Roger loaded the trailer with empty boxes and unloaded them in neat and orderly stacks about a row or two ahead of the picking. They would then swing by the pickers and start loading the full lugs. Howie drove when they picked up the full lugs; they were too heavy for a one armed boy. Empty lugs he could manage. Roger stacked them. Twice, sometimes three times a day, they would make this circuit. The full lugs would be unloaded in the shade of the large maples that flanked the garage; this became the defacto processing, inspecting, and shipping area. Liz, Charlie, and Anne would go through each lug, cleaning out debris, leaves, damaged berries and other junk. Early in the season, this went quickly, the berries were fresh and some were even a tad unripe; they would be ripe by the time they were eaten. But as the season wore on, if it rained, if the heat rose too high, if, for some reason unknown but to God, a problem developed, the berries would need to be inspected carefully. Then each lug would be sorted and cleared of decayed fruit, berries gouged by birds, and even cherries that had started to dry out. Then the work went well into the night with conveyors belts pushing the fruit past the inspectors, forty hands sorting out the good from the bad. Then each lug would lose half its fruit. At the end of the season, the pickers would be paid for their lugs but would not get paid for helping with the sorting. It was also the time when the canneries were the most picky; they would reject a whole truckload if the berries weren't perfect. But those problems were three short weeks away; today the picking was easy.

The men worked the top of the trees, fifteen to twenty feet in the air, standing on the three-legged ladders. The tripod setup was the most flexible and most stable. The climbers developed a keen sense of balance and accidents were few. The older children and the women used the short ladders; the children picked from the underside of the canopy. The majority of the berries were toward the top where pollination and sunshine produced more fruit. They pulled the fruit, one after another, until they held a handful, then, in one motion, dumped them into the bucket, trying not to crush the fruit underneath. Sweet cherries required the stems remain attached; sour cherries needed only the berry, so the stem stayed with the tree. Reach in and pull as many as you can as fast as you can, pull the berries, drop them, then pull more. Arms were continually held over the head and, within a day or two, hands and shoulders ached with a deep muscle soreness. Add to these pains, the sugary cherry juice that ran down arms, the fruit flies that gathered about the face and, on muggy days, the mosquitoes; the excitement of picking soon led to a monotonous routine that all had to endure.

"At least it's shady," Juan Martinez said to his older brother. "It's not like hoeing sugar beets or picking tomatoes. There, my God, the sun cooks your back, the only drinking water is hot, and the wages stink."

"Si," Ernesto answered. "Two more months and we'll be home in Texas."

Bill let Roger and Howie know that he was old enough to help with the loading and unloading but Rodger said no.

"I won't stay with the children," Bill said. "I am old enough to do a man's work. I will not run around shooing away blackbirds."

"No, Bill, there's too much going on and I need to know where everyone is at all times, don't want to run over you. Okay?"

"But I can help,"

"No, go help your mother and your grandmother,"

Bill turned, huffing his way back to the farm, "I'll go and help Gramps." He brought water and cold drinks to the sorters in the garage and helped the three men finish the repairs to the living room.

Howie did not see his brother some days until dinner. Bone tired, he usually fell asleep by eight o'clock. The next day would be like the previous, but only more hectic. As each day of the season passed, it developed into a race against an unseen opponent. When would he show up? Would he show up? What would he do?

He showed up on the sixth day. The intense heat of the morning and the stifling humidity quietly announced its pending arrival. For five days, the picking had been excellent: the sweets were down to the last row of trees; ten loads had left for Detroit and Grand Rapids, and Ernesto and three of the men had started on the first sours. They would be the first to the cannery, good berries, solid, bright red and so translucent that, when the early sun showed through them, they hung like rubies to be snatched.

Charlie watched the skies and listened to the radio like it was World War II all over again. He would listen into the night on the powerful box, for the weather in Chicago, Milwaukee, and Green Bay, and, if he could on some nights, St. Paul, Minnesota. He was as interested in the weather as the things brewing in Europe and the Near East. The summer weather moved west to east with surges from the southwest. A storm could start as a low-pressure area over Milwaukee and, in six hours, race across the lake sucking up water, gaining power from the lake's heat, and, like the early July storm, hit with a ferocity that could push over trees and strip the fruit from the branches. If it rained, the water sucked up by the thirsty trees would push into the fruit and the berries would split wide open, like small balloons that could not stretch fast enough, and explode.

The radio station in Madison reported a damp windy front moving through southern Wisconsin. Not a lot of rain but winds to thirty miles an hour, on the backside, the temperature ten degrees cooler. As weather goes, not too dramatic, but, to a cherry grower, ominous.

"We have until about three o'clock, then this thing will hit," Charlie said to Roger over a breakfast of coffee and cherry pie. "Don't know what it will be like but watch for the signs; get the people in if the rain picks up, there're tarps in the barn, take them out this morning to cover the boxes. Ernesto knows what to do. But get them to the quarters if the wind starts to blow. I don't want anyone in the trees when it hits. May last an hour but it could be a strong one."

Albert Beck had picked over one hundred lugs during the past week. His arms were beyond sore but payday would be one of his best for this summer. He took a short tortilla break with Howie.

"Did you hear the news last night about that ship getting rammed in the Atlantic, somewhere off Nantucket?" Beck asked Howie. "They think she may sink, damn shame."

"Yeah, Grams said something about it this morning. Why? Do you know something about that boat?"

"Ship, boy. Ship," Beck corrected. "She's more than a ship; she's a floating castle, a castle. At least I hope she still is; hate to think of her as some pile of steel on the bottom of the sea. And yes, Howard, I do know something about that boat, I crossed the Atlantic on her three times. Sometimes being a black fellow works to my advantage, yes my advantage. After the war, I wandered around Europe and ended up in northern Italy, beautiful town called Genoa. Worked some odd jobs, even then, eight years after the war, things were still tough in Italy. Finally hooked a job in a small restaurant on the waterfront and worked as a bartender. The owner was okay and I faked an accent with the tourists, so I came off as some kind of North African fellow. The owner loved it but a couple of fellows in another joint didn't or they didn't like the owner, still not sure. So after a couple of loud discussions, nobody can argue like an Italian, I decided to leave. And the next boat out was the Doria, the Andrea Doria."

Howie sat enraptured, even Roger climbed down from the tractor and sat on the edge of the trailer.

"You buy a ticket?" Howie asked.

"Ticket? Don't think I have ever bought a ticket for anything in my life, no. I walked down to the ship's office along the quay, saw a guy who loved to drink my Cuba Libres, that's another story, told him I was the best bartender in Italy and wanted to be the best bartender on the Atlantic. He said okay, he was in a bind; one of his bartenders was in jail. I had ten hours to get my gear and my bag together and get onboard. That was three years ago, late spring. Made three trips, got bored and jumped ship in New York. I think I left some pay somewhere."

The trees began to rustle a bit with the coming storm.

"She's a great ship my boy, a great ship. The most beautiful interior, art work on the walls, real Italian marble statues and crystal glassware to drink only the best liquor in. I shared a cabin with three other fellows, all black Africans, who worked somewhere in the engine room; thank God I didn't have to be there all the time. Good Lord, did they stink; stank to high heaven. And the room wasn't bigger than this trailer. Sad to think she might sink and be gone, man can make some beautiful things if he wants to and sometimes he can be a real beast; four years in Germany proved that to me."

"Roger, let's get these lugs covered; the storm is rushing in fast across the lake," Charlie said hiking in from the sorting and pushing his way through the cherries. "Green Bay got hit hard with wind and it's cool behind the front. Let's get everybody down and inside now. If she blows through fast, we may be able to get back out here while there's still some light. If it's fast we may not get a lot of rain."

"Wrap it up. Storm, *lo evuelvo*," Roger yelled out into the trees.

For the next hour, they loaded up the trailer and the pickers kept pulling cherries. Howie and Roger took one load to the garage and quickly unloaded. They were back and reloading when the first strong winds began to rustle the trees. Within minutes the tops began to bend and churn in the wind.

"Ernesto, get those boys out of the trees, too damn much wind," Roger called out. He turned back, heard a crack and watched a man fall and hit the ground. The man laid still, his arm with a very unnatural bend to it. Barbara reached him first.

"Bad break; looks like he's unconscious," Roger said leaning over the fellow. "Ernesto, he's one of your boys from over at Miller's?"

"Si Señor, Julio."

The man's eyes opened slowly, then the pain hit. His face contorted, twisted by the agony from his arm and the small sharp edge of white bone that pierced through the skin, with only a little bleeding.

"You be still, Julio, you fell and broke your arm; we'll get you to the hospital," Ernesto said.

"Si. It hurts like hell."

"Si, I know. But you're a big boy and very strong. And besides, you don't want to cry in front of momma do you?"

Julio looked up at Barbara and choked back a smile; tears welled in his eyes.

Charlie bent down to Barbara, "Tell Julio we're going to lift him and put him on the trailer and then take him to the hospital.

"Si, Señor Smith."

There was a crack from behind the group and they looked back to see Beck jumping on a lug, busting it to pieces. He split one side into three long pieces.

"Splints, Roger, splints."

They lifted Julio off the ground and onto the trailer; Barbara had already ripped some rags into strips. Sitting on the trailer, she held Julio's head while Beck secured the splints to the arm with the rags. *"The pain must be unbearable,"* Howie thought and looked at his crooked fingers, but the man laid there quietly, his eyes focused on Barbara. Ernesto started to climb on the trailer, next to Charlie.

"No, Ernesto, you stay here and get these people inside," Barbara ordered. She turned to Howie. "You help get the children together, comprendes?"

"Si Señora," she smiled at his Spanish.

The trailer pushed into the trees, Roger driving. They could hear the tractor for a few minutes, then only the wind. Raindrops started to bounce off the tops of the overturned cherry buckets. They threw the tarps over the stacks of lugs, bags and other personal equipment.

By the time they had reached the picker's quarters, they were drenched.

Howie pulled the tractor into the barn and dried off with towels hung on racks near the door, Roger followed through the door. Beck climbed up the ladder to his loft. Anne walked through the door wearing a yellow oilcloth slicker.

"You two look like drowned rats," was all she could say with a laugh. "Charlie and Barbara took the poor fellow to the hospital in Traverse. Nasty break, all we had was aspirin so he had to bear the pain. Went into shock a bit, started to get a bit groggy."

"He'll be fine, but won't be pick'n anymore this year," a voice said from above. "Tough kid, tough kid. Seen boys with less of a break scream their heads off, I have."

"I'm sure you have, Mr. Beck," Anne answered. "He's young and strong and I think nobody wants to show her their pain when they are around Barbara; she just brings out the strength in her people."

"She is one tough, beautiful woman," Beck said.

"Do not let Ernesto hear that or you'll be in one of those fights you are famous for."

All they heard was a short laugh.

They waited for two hours for the rain to lighten up; it rained more than they expected. Charlie, Barbara and Julio drove up to the house just as the front passed and the clouds started to break up.

"Those bastards at the hospital wouldn't take care of the fellow," Charlie said, still in a foul mood. "They said there was a clinic or something for the migrants. I looked at the nurse and said, 'You take care of this fellow or I'll have Dr. Andrew's kick your fat ass down the hallway and out the door. I don't play golf with that son-of-bitch so I can have my people not taken care.' She pointed to a bench and we would probably still be sitting there if I hadn't walked to the desk, took the phone, called Andrews and stuck the phone in that nurse's ear. She said yes maybe ten times, then hung-up. She looked at me, spun on her heels, told an orderly to get a nurse's aide and a doctor. 'We'll have him taken care of immediately sir, but you can't stay here tonight.' I was still pissed but I told her it was fine and that we would have better care provided at home. Seems like they have some policy about non-residents and their hospital, just a load of crap if you ask me. If a tourist walked in with a broken arm or a splinter, they would be all over him to help out. Pays to be white and have money, damn bastards, I can tell you that. These pickers can make money for these people but they can't use their services. She demanded that I pay in cash."

Ernesto stood in the barn waiting for his wife; they walked the man back to the picker's quarters, his arm bandaged.

"Let him rest overnight, then we can take him to the clinic," Charlie said. "They said the swelling had to go down; they gave him morphine or something along with some other pills. They reset the bone and stitched up the break in the skin. Doctor apologized but his hands were tied, young guy, nice guy; he also volunteers at the clinic. Said to take him in tomorrow morning and he'll finish the job, needs a cast."

"I'll drive him in Dad," Anne offered. "I know where it is, actually closer than the hospital; Barbara can come along to translate and hold his hand. Bill, you want to go?"

"Cool," the youngster answered. "Finally, something exciting to do around here."

"Thanks," Charlie answered and turned to Roger. "Let's take a walk and see what we have here after this rain. Still have maybe three hours of light left, it's only six."

"I'll make you fellows a sandwich," Liz offered.

"Make me one too Grams, I'm with them," Howie said.

The three walked into the orchard, the rain gone from the surface of the sandy soil, the ground almost dry, the trees still dripping. The air, ten degrees cooler than at noon and, even after the rain, the humidity, lower.

"Not good, looks like at least an inch, maybe a little more. Let's get Ernesto's people out here. We will need to push them for the next three days while this rain settles in," Charlie said to Howie, standing under the trees. "Not much time, but we need every minute to finish these sweets. The sours may be able to take a little water, but the faster we can get picking them the better."

They worked fifteen hours a day for the next three days, finished all the sweets and were well into the sours. Some of the older berries began to split; they sorted them out in the garage under the overhead lights. They finished the last lugs for the day at one o'clock in the morning. Then they were up at five to start over. Every load made it out to Detroit on time, none missed, none rejected.

CHAPTER SIXTEEN

Sunday, after mass and breakfast, Liz and Anne announced that the whole family would be going to the beach after picking. Doug arrived late Saturday afternoon and said he would stay till Monday night, then head back to Chicago. It seems a couple of the people on the Andrea Doria were from Elmhurst and were arriving on Tuesday; his editor told him to put together a human interest story. Saturday night he went into great detail about the collision and the rescue; only about fifty people were missing but over fifteen hundred were saved. Could have been a disaster similar to that of the Titanic but because of radios and the *SS Ile de France's* return to take all the people on board and back to New York, there was significantly fewer lives lost than might have been.

"Albert Beck said he worked on board as a bartender on three trips across the Atlantic," Howie offered.

Doug turned to Anne, "He's here?"

"Yes, arrived a couple of weeks ago, been working hard."

"Any trouble?"

"No, has kept to himself and actually picked well, made some good money."

"I also took that boat two years ago, got off at Gibraltar and took the train to Barcelona. Wonderful boat," Frank Rex said, "very beautiful and elegant. I had the opportunity to study some great art she had aboard, most is sadly at the bottom of the Atlantic."

"Ship, Mr. Beck says that it is called a ship," Howie corrected.

"Boy, when you cross the Atlantic as many times as I have, you can call it a boat, a ship, a ferry, a steamer, a tug, a tub, a liner, or in the case of a couple of crossings, a God damn scow."

"How many?" Bill asked.

"I believe that it's twenty round trips," Frank said after a few moments of thought.

"Did you include the four times when we were kids?" Liz asked.

"No, I didn't, so that's twenty-four. Sometimes the Atlantic was rough, sometimes she lay down and it was like sailing on glass. All my trips were interesting and each one allowed me five days to read and do very little. They are a delight. I'm on the *SS United States* next month to Le Harve, then to Paris, then by train to Barcelona."

Charlie took Liz's hand in his and squeezed a bit.

"And this will be my last crossing, getting too old and too tired to do all this," Frank laughed. "Yes, it'll be my last." He inhaled on his pipe and then seated himself at the table.

"Why your last Uncle Frank?" Bill said, looking at his uncle quizzically.

Frank looked to Anne, not happy where this conversation was going.

"Uncle Frank is moving to Spain for a while, someday maybe you can visit him," Anne said.

"Cool, do they speak Spanish in Spain or Mexican?" Bill asked.

A laugh rolled across the table.

"You do say the damnedest things, William Smith, you really do," Frank said, then looked at Anne and smiled.

"What I'd say?"

"We will be heading down about 4:00, so there's a lot to do before then," Liz directed.

Charlie, Doug and Roger had already walked the orchard before breakfast. The Martinez's had already been picking for two hours, they would work until 4:00, then take the rest of the day off. The rain had thrown everyone off schedule. Roger told Bill and Howie that they had the morning off and he would see them before they left for the beach.

The two boys kicked sandy dust on each other as they went back to the studio with Frank Rex.

"You feeling okay, Uncle Frank?" Howie asked.

"Not bad today, pain's a little less, the bowels still function, and I can still piss in a straight line and not get much on my shoes. Ah yes boys, life is good. If only I wasn't so fucked up, I'd be having a great time."

"Mom says it's not nice to swear," Bill said.

"Young man, remember this for your whole life, your dear beautiful mother is absolutely correct. And there will come a time when you will be continually reminded by young innocents, like yourself, that cursing is wrong and is only the province of old curmudgeons and misanthropes like me. Then you will revel in it as if it is the one last bastion of personal freedom, anger, angst, and ennui."

"Huh?"

"Uncle Frank, stop it," Howie added.

Bill pushed the red door open, crossed the stoop and went into the studio. The comforting smells helped to settle Frank down. Howie remembered Jennie on the couch and on the beach, a large painting stood on an easel off to one side; Jennie on the red blanket. A surge went through Howie like a mild electrical shock, *"Stop that,"* he said to himself; *"for God's sake, you were just in church."*

"What are you thinking of?" Frank asked, looking at Howie, then at Jennie's picture, then back to Howie. "Just finished that, painted down below in the sand dunes, fact there is probably a bit of grit in the oils. Gorgeous day and gorgeous model, she's very beautiful, isn't she? Don't touch that, Bill, it's still wet, in this dampness it takes forever to dry. It's my homage to Goya's *La Maja Desnuda*; he also painted one called *La Maja Vestida*. The same model is in both paintings in somewhat the same pose I have Jennie in. She is clothed in one, nude in the other. Very provocative and those bastards during the Inquisition called them obscene, at least they didn't burn them like many other paintings."

"Don't get too close, Bill, she can bite," Rex said.

For the next few hours, Frank worked with the boys on their sketching, drawing and colors. Howie worked on some studies of a muskrat from a wildlife book in the stacks. Bill tried to draw a cup even while being continually distracted by the paintings lying about the studio.

"What are you working on, Uncle Frank?" Howie asked looking toward his uncle hidden behind a large canvas.

"A crucifixion; I have spent years trying to get the idea straight in my mind, and I think I have it. Strange but the pain is making it more understandable."

"May I look?"

"Yes, my boy, I think I have the concept."

It wasn't in oil but terra cotta conté pencil. The rough sketch had Jesus looking up at the viewer, hard thorns pointing in all directions, arms extended diagonally from lower left to upper right. The view, down the torso to the bowed heads of those gathered under the cross, to only one face that looked up, not at Jesus, but at the viewer. Howie could feel the painting's strength even if its color was only red orange.

"I think that changing the traditional view from below and upward gives a different perspective about how Jesus should be viewed. Are you God looking down on his Son or are you someone Jesus is looking to for help? And why is Mary also looking at you? That's her with her face turned up to the viewer." Rex walked behind Howie. "Structure, my boy, structure. To be a strong painting, it has to define a piece of space and time, tell you a story and place you in the scene in an instant. If you can accomplish this, the painting is on its way to being a success. Execution is critical, but structure is even more important. If not, well, it is just a lot of color spread about the canvas. Pretty maybe, would look good on a wall, goes well with the furniture, and won't scare the dog. I want to create a painting that requires you to take the furniture out of the room, and force the dog to howl and run down the street. There is no place for anything in a room with a great painting."

"Can I learn to paint like this?" Howie asked, turning to his uncle.

"Maybe, but to paint is to build, to build an image of time and space in two dimensions. A sculptor has the same problem only his is in three dimensions; one more complication, one more advantage. Yes, Howie, you can learn the techniques, how to handle and use the tools, become a colorist and then how to master pushing oil or color around a canvas, but it will be how you construct your world on that canvas that will make you a great painter. It's tough, success seldom comes; from the brain to execution, many problems and distractions make it difficult but . . . sometime it happens. Then you are in awe of yourself because it's like you are outside looking in at the artist, yourself. Then you want to live forever. But I won't," Frank Rex paused and looked over at Bill, "and I *will* get this painting done before I go to Spain."

They worked for another hour and the phone rang. Rex still had one of those two part phones with the base like a small tower with a cone off at an angle and a separate tiny megaphone you push up against your ear.

"Frank Rex."

He listened for a moment, then said, "Absolutely, will be great to get a little sun. See you in fifteen minutes."

Rex hung the earpiece in its cradle, "Boys, get your things together, that was your mom and we're all going to the lake, fifteen minutes; so let's get cleaned up and put your drawings away."

"What do you think, Uncle Frank?" Bill said holding up a drawing of a cup.

"Excellent, but I think you may have trouble holding water in that cup. Doesn't it bend a bit to the right?"

Bill turned the drawing around and squinted at it, "I know. I was trying to put a spout on its side, make it more useful."

"A cup is always useful, spout or not," Rex answered. "But the task was to draw a cup, not make an excuse for its execution. We'll work on it next time. Ok?"

Bill seemed disappointed but shook his head, "Next time."

Rex pushed his way through the canvases to Howie.

"What is this?" he said, holding up Howie's sketchbook. "It's well executed and I see the idea of the muskrat and its entrapment; I can almost see its pain. But it doesn't have any eyes, they're gone."

"Yes sir," Howie answered. "They're gone because they were plucked out by the ravens."

"You saw this animal, didn't you?"

"Yes a few weeks back, very sad and wrong; buried the thing deep so he wouldn't ever be disturbed. Threw the trap into the swamp and if I could have, I'd have thrown a rock at those damn ravens."

"The ravens do what God made them to do," Rex said. "They clean up the messiness of life, the dead and their leftovers. Can't blame them, it's the trapper who needs to be blamed, to be held accountable. No need to kill that animal for a buck a skin, no need at all. But the drawing is well done; keep at it. To be a good artist is to be a skilled draftsman, remember that."

"Too much to remember," Howie said with a laugh. "Way too much."

"That's okay, by the time you're my age you'll realize there is always too much more to learn, so you focus; you focus on those things that are important to you and that will always be enough."

A rap on the door and a hello from outside brought the three to their feet. The door was pushed open and Liz stuck her head around the frame.

"You fellows coming, we're hungry and there's chicken, potato salad, pickles, cider and lemonade. And we have a ways to walk so move along; you're holding up the train."

As they strolled through the woods, Doug asked Howie about the trees, the types of bracken and plants. Every year the path to the lake would fill back in, and every year it had to be recut. Charlie carried his rifle strapped over his shoulder; no one said anything about it, it was just there.

"When I was a boy," Doug said to Bill. "I was down here so often the path never had a chance to get overgrown; now it takes just a year to make it disappear. The pickers seem to help keep it open but only

for about a month, and then it seems to want to disappear."

Howie looked at the tops of the cattails by the pond as they passed, no one said anything.

A soft breeze blew off the clear water of the lake. A slight riffling of the surface changed the lake from a mirror to a shimmering reflection of the sky, almost a turquoise blue. They settled at the base of a dune, Liz and Anne spread out blankets, one was Frank's. Howie blushed; it was the red blanket Jennie had posed on. He wanted to stretch out on that blanket, to relive the moment.

"You okay boy?" Charlie's voice cut through his revelry.

"Yes, yes I'm okay, in fact this afternoon I feel perfect. Bill, let's go look for muskies and pike."

The two skirted the edge of the lake until they found the right spot and waded in up to their knees and studied the water.

"There's one, and another, a whole bunch of them."

Howie looked over his brother's shoulder. There, in amongst the sunken planks and debris, were four and five inch-long fish. They could be mistaken for minnows but their shape, sleeker and more sinister, set them apart.

"Think they are pike or muskies?" Bill asked.

"Muskies, I'm sure. See their eyes and the way they watch all around them and each other, they don't have fear, and even at this size they know they are the masters in their world."

"Hard to believe these little guys will grow up to be as big as that one at the powerplant."

"Yeah, hard to believe. There, look, that one just grabbed that small minnow, gone just like that."

"Neat-o."

"Lunch," Anne yelled.

The late afternoon became lazy and, except for a time when Charlie and Doug walked down the beach, they stayed together. Frank Rex talked about his trip to Spain; it seemed like his way of saying goodbye, but without all the tears and the clutching. He told another story about Hemingway and some of the people in Paris that he knew before the war, one was terribly funny, Howie almost spit his lemonade out; the other was sad, but also funny.

"This thing concerning the Suez Canal is something, don't you think, Liz?" Frank said. "Remember when we went through the canal, all that sand piled as high as the dunes, a godforsaken place, but it cuts a month of travel time instead of going around Africa. Now they'll probably go to war over the damn thing, senseless."

"There won't be a war, Eisenhower won't let us," Liz said.

"Don't know, too many fingers in the pie, too much regional power to be lost now that Nasser has control of Egypt, nothing would shock me."

"We can only hope. We only have cherries to pick, they control our lives," Liz said closing the conversation.

Late in the afternoon, a raucous noise rose up the beach and people and kids broke through the trees, ran to the beach and into the lake.

"The Martinez's have arrived," Charlie said with a laugh. "Guess the picking is done for the day. Roger will have gone home."

Ernesto Martinez noticed the Smith family, you could hear him admonishing the group in Spanish; they quieted down.

"I'll put an end to this," Liz said as she trudged through the sand toward the pickers. She turned to Anne and gave a wink.

Barbara Martinez walked toward Liz. There was a brief conversation, Barbara gave Liz a kiss on the cheek and then Liz returned to the family.

"Did you yell at them Grams?" Bill asked.

"No, my boy, they're always welcome here. No, I told Señora Martinez to be careful because of the drop off in that area and to have a wonderful time. I also said we had some leftover chicken, but she said they had plenty of food, in fact, she offered us tortillas and carnitas. I also told her they're doing a great job. She said it's great to swim in the sweet water, it wasn't like the salty ocean off the Texas coast; here they don't have to take a shower after swimming."

"Nothing but storms this summer, one after another," Charlie said looking to the west over the hills towards Old Mission. Huge clouds were beginning to build over the top of the ridge. "More rain in a few hours, just what we need."

"On the way back, you boys want to have some target practice?"

Doug asked. "We can use Gramp's twenty-two, I brought a couple of targets; what do you think?"

"That would be great Dad," Howie answered.

"Cool," was all Bill could muster.

Pulling everything together, the group started back through the woods to the farm. Near the pond, in the middle of the clearing, Charlie sat his pack down.

"This'll do, what do you think, Bill?"

"Yes; we can put the targets on the big pine tree and shoot from here," Bill said.

"You fellows be careful. We'll see you in an hour or so, but the way that storm is building, we may even see you sooner," Liz said.

Liz and Anne continued back up the hill toward the farm. Frank followed closely behind, said he needed to get back to work. The four men settled under the large pine in the clearing.

While Doug walked off fifty paces to the tree to tack one of the targets up, Charlie went over the rules of the rifle's use and operation.

"Never take the safety off until you're ready to shoot; this rifle is a bit different and I'll show you why," Charlie directed. "Always point the rifle away from yourself and never at anyone, even with the safety on. Always carry the gun pointed to the sky, never toward the ground; too easy to get dirt in the barrel. Never put your finger on the trigger until you're ready to shoot."

"Let's shoot," Bill said impatiently.

"You calm down," Doug said to his youngest. "When Gramps is done, you will shoot."

"Now, this is a Winchester Model 67, single shot 22 rifle. It's a bolt action, see when I pull the bolt back there is a slot to put a bullet in, then you push the bolt in and lock it. Then you pull the striker, it's this rifle's safety, like this, then settle it against your shoulder, aim, then gently pull the trigger. Simple. After shooting, open the bolt, the empty shell will pop out, and you're ready to reload and shoot again. Questions?"

Bill had heard this lecture before but Charlie wanted to make sure he remembered; Howie had heard the lecture many times, but it always stuck; he knew that you had to be responsible to shoot a rifle.

"For your impatience, Bill, you will wait until Howie fires five times."

"Dad," Bill said drawing out the 'a' till it sounded like a whine.

"Any more of that and you'll not shoot at all, young man," Doug added.

"Yes sir."

Howie settled to one knee, placed the cartridge box on ground next to his shoe, pulled a bullet out, loaded, set the rifle, aimed and fired. He did this four more times with practiced movements and, judging by the target, good accuracy.

"Good shooting my boy, good shooting," Charlie complimented. "Bill, I want you to go into the professional soldier prone position, you understand?"

"Yes sir," Bill answered. "On the ground, arm and hand used as a rest for the rifle, it is a steadier position to shoot from, more accurate."

"Excellent. Ready?"

Bill stretched out, put his arm in the correct pose, Charlie handed him the rifle. Bill cleared the last casing, inserted a bullet, pulled the striker, took careful aim, a deep breath, and on the exhale, pulled the trigger. A crisp crack was heard, Bill shot four more times.

"Very good, Bill, very good, I think you hit the target three times. Howie go get the target, please," Doug asked.

"Yes sir," Howie said, already on his way.

Howie stopped at the first sound of the bell; it was loud and impatient. He turned to the other three; Charlie was already running toward the path to the top of the hill. Doug looked at Howie, "Move. Something's up, move, now!"

Howie sprinted back to his father; the three took off after Charlie. They caught him at the top of the hill. Looking down the alley of apples, black smoke billowed above the trees.

"Shit," Charlie said and redoubled his speed.

They reached the clearing in front of the picker's quarters, the first two rooms in the old coop were burning, fire roared out of the last window, the curtains were on fire, and dark smoke billowed in surges. Liz held a garden hose and sprayed water through the window, but it was like trying to piss on a forest fire. Anne held a bucket under the hose bib on the barn. Albert Beck ran out of the last room, not yet on fire.

"They're all clear, Mrs. Smith, all clear," Beck yelled.

"Dad, does that sprayer have water or chemicals in it?" Doug asked.

"Huh," Charlie paused, then the same idea hit. "Water, just cleaned it, easier to leave filled for later."

Doug pushed the great doors of the barn open, climbed on the John Deere, and backed it up to the sprayer. Howie dropped the pin in place and ran out the door as the tractor pulled the sprayer into the center of the yard. Howie pulled the cord on the motor to the compressor; it kicked over on the first pull as if, today, it wanted to help. Charlie followed them out of the barn with a large hose. He threaded it on to the tank, pulled the valve open and water immediately gushed out of the nozzle. Doug held the hose and aimed toward the roof areas not burning then worked his way toward the fire.

"Back the sprayer closer," Doug said to his son.

"Can I help," Bill asked excitedly.

"Please get out of the way, son. Please. Howie another ten feet."

"Dad, I can help," Bill asked again.

"Bill, go over to mom and stay out of the way ... now!" Doug yelled.

"Now Bill, we've got to put out that fire," Howie added.

Howie, already on board, put the tractor in reverse and backed the sprayer slowly toward the quarters. Doug stood to one side and continued to pour water onto the fire. "Stop, that's good."

Liz still sprayed water from the small hose. The sound of a fire truck could be heard over the tractor and the noise of the compressor. It pulled around the barn and three men jumped off immediately, quickly assessed the situation, pulled hoses out, and added their water to the fire. Beck grabbed one of the hoses and held it while one of the volunteers steered water across the fire and parts of the building not burning. Within minutes, they had the upper hand.

Ernesto and Juan ran into the yard, breathing hard, Gonzalo followed on their heels.

"Señor Smith, what can we do?" Ernesto asked Charlie who was standing to one side.

"Go behind the building, see what's happening and let me know."

"Si, Señor." The two ran around the end of the coop and then quickly returned. "Fire is still on this side. The water is running over the roof and it is not spreading."

"Bueno, Ernesto. Bueno," Charlie answered.

Frank Rex walked into the chaos from the orchard, and stood toward the back of the mess. Three other cars pulled up the drive and five men piled out.

They had the fire under control in another five minutes. It did not spread to the rest of the cabins, and especially not to the barn. They ran out of water in the sprayer just as the fire was almost out, the fire truck finished the job. Charlie had Howie moved the tractor to the well to refill the sprayer, just in case.

"Good thinking, brilliant," Charlie said to his son.

"Remembered using that pressurized valve maybe a few years ago to spray up into the apples," Doug said looking back his father, "Thought if it could reach the top of the trees, it certainly could work here."

"Sure did," Charlie turned to the three on the fire truck. "Thanks Jimmy, and you too, Bill, Amos. Would've run out before we could've finished and then I wouldn't know where we would be right now. Thanks fellas; thanks to all of you."

Barbara Martinez and the rest of the family came up the path. "Madre Dios, my home," she said looking at the damage. "Señora Smith, are you okay?"

"Yes, Mrs. Martinez, I'm fine and so are the rest of us, lucky it didn't spread, but I'm sorry about your cabin," Liz answered.

"We can fix it, we have a few tents, and, if I need more, I can get more from the Miller's," Barbra turned to one of the young men, "Si?"

"Si, they have more stacked in their barn," one of the young pickers said. He was one of the boys staying at the Millers.

"I'll call the Miller's after this is cleaned up," Liz said. "We'll get you squared away for the night."

"Señor Smith, we saw the smoke and knew something was not right, so Juan and me ran up here," Ernesto said to Charlie. "Sorry we're late."

"No, it's okay, two more would not have made a difference until the fire department arrived. Again thanks, Jimmy, really owe you now."

Jimmy Dugan laughed, "No, Charlie, that's why they pay us the really big bucks for this part-time job. So we don't have to go begging." The rest of the volunteers laughed and added their two cents. Anne walked through the barn carrying a case of beer.

"Guess this is what we all need now, right boys?" Anne asked, setting down the beer, two cans of Coca-cola sat on top.

The firemen and family members each grabbed a beer and settled around the equipment; steam still rose from the end of the picker's quarters. Liz and Barbara looked through the door to survey conditions.

The clouds had moved over the farm during the time it took to put out the fire, a few drops left spots on the fenders of the tractor where Howie sat. He looked at his family, friends, and workers. He paused and looked about more closely.

"Mom, you seen Bill?"

Anne turned and looked up at her oldest, then around the area.

"Doug, where's Bill?" she asked.

Doug and everyone else quickly looked around for the young man. He was not there or anywhere in the yard, the barn or the other buildings.

"He ran away," a childish voice said with hesitation.

Barbra turned to Gonzalo, "You saw him leave? Quando, Gonzalo, quando?"

"Si, Señor Bill was standing there." Gonzalo pointed at the last apple tree. "He was yelling, but I could not hear him, he looked mad, then he ran into the cherries, then he disappeared. All the noise from the fire trucks and that thing," Gonzalo said, pointing at the sprayer.

"I could not hear anything."

Anne fell to her knees; Doug rushed to her, the rain began to fall harder.

Charlie ran to the spot where Gonzalo had pointed, Jimmy Dugan at his side.

"There," Charlie said, pointing. "Footprints."

Charlie looked back at the yard; everyone gathered around Anne still on the ground, Doug next to her. All were staring at Anne, only Howie looked at Charlie. Charlie looked into Howie's eyes, "We'll find him."

Bigger raindrops kicked up geysers of dust and muddy sand. The water ran off the roof of the blackened picker's quarters in sooty rivers.

"He couldn't have gotten far," Doug yelled.

A deep gut-wrenching boom rumbled up from the woods; another flash and a crack of thunder lit the yard.

"We need to move, now; I don't want that boy out in the storm."

"Where do you want me, Doug?" Frank asked.

"Your studio please; I don't want you out in this storm and besides he may go there if he gets some sense," Doug said. "I know you want to help but there are more than enough men here with the volunteers and ourselves."

The yard, as quickly as it filled to fight the fire, emptied to look for Bill.

CHAPTER SEVENTEEN

Howie stared into the black hole of the orchard where his brother had stood; rain slashed the trees; people yelled and rushed about; all was chaos. His mother, still on her knees, heaved uncontrollably, Liz held her shoulders. Doug and Charlie stood directly behind; Uncle Frank and Officer Dugan were talking.

"It's all my fault," Howie said to himself as he turned back to the orchard. "All my fault, I shouldn't have yelled at him, shouldn't have made fun."

"Howard Smith."

His grandmother's voice jerked him back, "Boy, you come over here and help your mother now!"

Howie slid off the wet tractor and ran to his mother's side.

"Help her to the house; I have a few things to do here. I'll be there directly." Liz turned to her husband, "Find him, Charlie, find him!"

Howie supported his mother as the two slowly walked to the house.

"Why would he run away like that?" Anne asked.

"Don't know Mom, don't know."

Howie grabbed a towel hanging in the entry and handed it to his mother; after she finished, Howie ran the towel over his head and arms. They went into the living room, the reconstruction almost done, the new roof kept the rain out. Anne sat in the large wingback; Howie took her hand and held it until Doug came into the room.

"You stay with your mother; we're going down below to see if we can find his tracks before it gets too dark. Two of the Martinez's have already left with Charlie; I am going with Jimmy to work from north to south."

"Find him," Anne said looking at her husband. "Please."

"Señora, may I sit with you?" Barbara Martinez said. She was standing in the frame of the door, Bonita at her side, Liz directly behind.

"Howie, come with me," Liz said. Howie followed her into the kitchen.

Barbara pulled the old rocker across the floor to be next to the wingback. Bonita sat on the floor.

"Momma, there are blackbirds with the boy," Bonita said.

"Yes my sweet, I'm sure there are," Barbara said. She held Anne's hand.

"Do you know why he ran away?" Liz asked after she had Howie sitting at the table.

"It is my fault he ran away, I treated him like a kid, wouldn't let him do what he wanted, he wanted to help, told him to get away. Told him there was a man at the powerhouse, still wouldn't believe that the fish didn't talk to us. Been upset about it, then I yelled at him to stay away from the fire," Howie answered, exasperated. Liz took his chin in her hand and pushed back his wet hair.

"There's something I've wanted to give you for a long time; had it all my life, almost since the first day my dad brought us to Elk River." Liz crossed the kitchen and pulled open a small drawer hung under the glass doors of the cabinets. She took out a red bag that fit into the palm of her hand. Pulling the draw strings open, she took out a flat grey stone. "This has been my good luck stone for over fifty years; give me your small hand."

Howie lifted his bad arm toward his grandmother and slowly

opened his hand. Liz gently placed the stone in his palm.

"This is the oldest thing you have ever touched. It was alive a billion years ago when all of this land sat at the bottom of a shallow sea. That ocean was similar to the coral seas you see today in National Geographic Magazines, but also very different. Long before dinosaurs walked on solid ground, everything lived in the sea; this stone was a piece of that world. See the patterns; they are the edges between living animals that clustered together for safety and security. They provided structure and support for each other and eventually, like everything, they died and provided the base for the next generation, billions of generations evolved and built on each other until they became us, standing here."

Howie pushed his thumb across the honeycombed pattern and he felt the weight of the stone, as if he could feel the weight of a billion years. "Thank you, Grandmother."

"I will not tell you to never lose it! That may or may not happen, who knows. But I will tell you, keep it in a safe place, then you can visit it in your imagination. Memorize the patterns and the feel, imagine what it was like a billion years ago in a warm shallow sea with strange fish and animals swimming and crawling around. You'll be living back then and now."

A small hand reached up behind Howie. Bonita's small fingers touched the stone and she traced the pattern with her fingertips. Howie looked down on the small face, her black eyes sparkled.

"Señor Howie, this is a good stone; it will give you strength and peace forever. It will quiet the blackbirds and will also quiet your soul."

Liz stroked the child's head, "You are very old for someone so young, child."

"When that stone was alive so was I, Grandmother," Bonita said.

Outside, a banging rattled the door, all three looked when it opened; Frank Rex shook the rain off his slicker and came into the room.

"Liz, is Anne okay?" Frank asked. "Everybody's out looking, so I'm going back to the studio. Just wanted to check."

"She'll be fine, Barbara's with her."

Howie rubbed the stone twice with his twisted thumb and then slipped the stone into the red bag into then into his pocket. Bonita smiled.

Anna walked into the room, Barbara followed.

"Any word, Frank?" Anne asked.

"Nothing yet, but it is getting so dark they could walk into each other before they see each other," Frank answered and left for the studio.

"Howie, you okay?"

"I'm fine Mom," Howie answered. "Do you want me to find Dad?"

"No, one son out in the woods is enough, I don't need two out there. Barbara has been a comfort; I am much better now; sorry I broke down, Liz."

"Phooey, don't worry about that. We'll find Bill; Charlie will find him," Liz said, comforting Anne.

For the next two hours the women and Howie waited in the kitchen for the men to come back. When the door finally opened, Charlie, drenched and cold, stumbled into the room.

"Sorry Anne, nothing. Searched the whole orchard and along the ridge, then down into the woods, flashlights gave out half an hour ago. Barbara," Charlie said addressing the Señora, "Ernesto and Beck are drying off in the barn. Says they'll stay there until it's light, then try again. I need to warm up, I'm freezing."

Barbara and Bonita left to join her husband. Liz poured him a cup of coffee, and pulled the wet jacket and soaked shirt off her husband. Howie saw what age and farming did to a body, it was strong and wiry, yet he could see the sagging of a long and difficult life in his grandfather's chest. Liz wrapped a soft yellow quilt around his shoulders, "To bed old man, too much to do in the morning. This storm does not stop the picking and we'll find the boy, and out of those wet clothes. I'll bring your coffee into the bedroom."

Another hour passed and Doug and Jimmy Dugan dragged themselves into the room; Frank Rex followed in their wake.

"Nothing, Anne. I'm sorry, going to get of these clothes and grab my raingear and new batteries and head back out. Jimmy needs to get into town to put out an 'all points' about the boy in case he took to the highway. Jimmy says he'll get a few more fellows from town and be back in the morning."

Anne lit a cigarette and placed it gently between her husband's lips; Doug took a long drag and exhaled. "You okay?" Doug said, looking at his oldest.

"I'm fine Dad. I want to go with you when you go. I have to go." Howie pushed his hand into his pocket and felt for the stone. "Please."

Doug looked at Anne, fear still in her eyes, but she understood. "Okay, you can come, but you'll stay near me," Doug said. "I thought we would work down toward the lake and along the beach, near the cabins. Maybe someone saw him down on the beach."

As Howie turned to get his slicker, they heard a crashing outside the kitchen door; everyone froze. Howie, the first to move, ran to the door and pushed the screen door outward into the wet night.

"I need your help young man, please help!" A huge man stood in the rain, his face washed with the light from the porch, dripped with a mixture of rain and dirt; Bill's body was draped in his arms.

"Mom," Howie yelled, but before Howie said another word, Doug had already pushed his way past Howie and was standing next to Bill.

"This way," Doug shouted. "Anne, clear the table."

The giant pushed his way into the room, gently insuring that Bill didn't clip the door's frame or anything else. He laid Bill on the kitchen table gently: Bill moaned a bit but otherwise lay very still, too still.

"What the hell?" Liz said as she rushed back into the kitchen, Charlie followed in her wake. She and Anne quickly looked over the boy. A small cut on Bill's forehead still bled, the rainwater from his hair washed blood down his cheek. Liz looked at the man.

"I think his leg is broken and his shoulder might be dislocated."

"What happened?"

"Get the boy taken care of first; what happened is irrelevant at the moment," the man answered, and then scanned the room, his eyes stopped at Frank for a brief moment then moved on to Jimmy

Dugan. Dugan stood with his back against the stove, pointing a gun directly at big man's heart. He raised his hands and looked at Charlie.

"Put that damn thing away, Jimmy Dugan, I don't think we will have any trouble with Mr. Walker. I assume you're Gideon Walker. Well, will we?"

Hands still up, "No sir, none at all," Walker replied.

"Please Jimmy, call the doctor. Get him on your radio," Liz said, putting her hand on Dugan's arm, helping him lower the gun. "We'll be fine."

Dugan put away his pistol and, excusing himself, ran out into the storm. Two minutes later he returned, "The doc will be here in ten minutes, said to keep the boy warm and keep his leg and his shoulder still."

Anne started to strip the clothes from Bill's soaked frame; he moaned when she tried to move his leg. She took the big kitchen shears and cut away his pants; Doug took a deep breath when he saw his son's twisted left leg and all that held it together was his young muscle; the shoe was missing from his left foot.

Anne patted Bill dry with a towel and washed the cut on his cheek, the bleeding had stopped. Bill's shoulder was already turning black and blue from the dislocation; it felt okay to Anne's touch.

"I popped it back in when I found him, his young body will weather that just fine," the man said, a large puddle spread at his feet and mixed with the rain left by the other men.

"You're Gideon Walker?" Charlie said.

"Yes sir, I'm summering down by the lake in the Gardner cabin, rented it until, well, until I leave."

Headlights slashed through the blackness and off the kitchen window, Dugan went out to lead the doctor to the house.

For the next half hour, Doc Abrams checked Bill out and managed to get some painkillers into him. Bill gained consciousness for a few minutes and smiled at his mother, then faded out.

"I'll take him to the hospital at Traverse; I'll call and let them know we are coming," Doc Abrams said. "It's late and they'll have to have an orthopedic doc there when we arrive. I know a good man.

Liz, phone?"

"This way," Liz said.

Anne ran her hand slowly across Bill's face. She turned to Walker, for the last half hour no one had said anything to him. "What happened?"

"I found the boy at the base of the big pine in the clearing. You know the one young man," Walker said looking at Howie. "He was all crumpled up and unconscious, from the looks of things, I think he was climbing that pine, and fell; probably bounced off a limb or two, before he hit the ground. Must be a foot of needles under that thing, saved the lad's life, I'm sure. There was a flash of lightening just before I found him, maybe the tree was hit and it bounced him out, not sure."

"They'll have someone there when we get to the hospital. You ready?" Doc Abrams asked.

Anne nodded her head.

"I'll follow," Doug added. "We'll need a car."

"I'm certain they will want him to stay, Douglas. That leg is bad and will need surgery. Yes, please follow. Mrs. Smith?" the doctor asked.

"Yes Doctor," both Liz and Anne answered at the same time and then smiled at each other.

"Anne Smith," the doctor clarified, "I want you in the back seat to hold him still, okay?"

Anne put a few of Bill's personal things and some clothes in a small suitcase. Doug and Dugan gently carried Bill to the doctor's car and slid him into place, his head on Anne's lap, he was still unconscious. Martinez's, Beck and the cousins came out of the barn as the rain stopped; they watched the Doctor and Doug leave.

Barbara walked over to Liz, "The boy, he'll be okay?"

"The Doctor thinks so, broken leg, hope to God that's all. He was pretty well banged up, but he's tough."

"Yes Señora," Barbara said with a smile. "He'll be fine, I'm sure."

"Yes Mamma," said a small voice from inside the folds of her skirt. "He will be well."

"Lordy, I forgot all about the fire, Barbara, I'm sorry. We need to get you resettled and..."

"No problem, Señora Smith. We have already set up an area for the cousins to sleep in the barn; they will be fine, as long as Mr. Beck does not snore too loud." Barbara looked at Albert Beck; he smiled and pointed at himself. "Tomorrow we'll set up the tents and get back to work. We will have carnitas and frijoles for a late dinner and very good beer. You wish to join us?"

"No Barbara, thank you. Your pork is out-of-this-world but tonight there is too much to do in the house, but thank you again," Liz answered with sincerity.

"Too bad, it is very, very good," Barbara said with a big smile.

"Si, it is very, very, very good," Bonita added.

Liz and Charlie slowly wound their way back through the cars to the porch, Howie stood next to Walker and his uncle, Dugan off to one side. Walker had one of Charlie's shirts on; it looked silly on the big man. Dugan watched Walker closely; he was not going to get out of his sight.

"Two shirts wouldn't have covered me," Walker said with a smile. "But it's warm."

"Come back in the house, Mr. Walker. I have a few questions," Charlie said.

The group stopped in the kitchen for coffee and carried their cups into the living room. Walker prowled about the room and peered into every shelf and scanned every book title.

"What a wonderful library, simply marvelous, and seems to be back in shape after the tornado. Did you lose many from the storm?" he turned to Charlie.

Charlie turned to Liz, his eyes asked "How does he know about the storm?".

"Just a few but they will be replaced," Liz answered for Charlie. "Well, Mr. Walker?"

"I'll try to start at the beginning. This afternoon, I was working at my desk; I'm writing a book about the years after the war in Germany, a family's story. My office is on the second floor, better ventilation and good view of the lake. I saw you and your family up at the beach; I continued to work through the afternoon. I could see clouds forming over Old Mission in the west and then watched you leave. A little while after that, I saw the pickers leave, they seemed in a hurry. Well, never mind I thought, and decided to take a walk, slipped my torch in my back pocket, lit a big cigar, love those damn things, and walked a circuit that went up to the base of the hill."

"Never see you about," Liz queried.

"Mrs. Smith, I always stay to myself; I live an almost monastic life." Walker looked at Frank. "It's the way I am and the way I like it. I don't get involved in other's lives, and I hope they stay out of mine. Just the way I am. Anyway, I love the rain and the weather, so primal, helps me write. So, after an hour or two, not sure how much time, don't wear a watch, I was at the base of the slope, was raining, and could see flashlights flicking about the orchard. Peculiar, they would be picking in the middle of the night, then I heard someone yell out, 'Bill.' Knew immediately what was up."

"You knew he'd run away?" Dugan asked.

Walker stopped and paused for a moment, "No, I didn't. That explains the gun, I guess. Right Mr. Dugan? That puts a different light on it, a very different light. So I headed back to the lake; maybe the kid was along the shore and I was closer than they were. I cut through the clearing and of could see the big pine in the flashes of lightening. Damn near tripped over the young fellow as I passed under that tree; so small and crumpled he was, almost like a pile of linen ready for the wash. Waved my torch over his face and could see he was alive, but hurt real bad. Felt about, could feel the shoulder was out and gently pushed it back into place. Nothing I could do for the leg, though."

"How did you know about the shoulder?" Charlie asked.

"Medic in the war, four years, from 1942 to 1946, worked my way across France to Germany and then spent a few years in Germany after the war. Us conchie's, after the war, had a lot of freedom, almost like the army couldn't wait to get us off their books."

"Conchies?" Howie asked.

"Conscientious objectors, young man, I refused to fight in the war if I had to kill. So I opted for a different involvement, became a medic. Tell you more about it later if you're interested. Didn't know what I was getting into when I made that call though. How are you

Howard? It's good to see you again," Walker said, looking at Howie.

"Mr. Walker," Howie asked, "were you involved with my brother's disappearance?"

"No, I was not, like I said, I found him at the base of the tree; how he got there, I don't know. I picked the boy up, light as a feather, and started up to the farmhouse here. Batteries went out, hard to carry the torch and the boy, so I dropped the light and, in-between flashes, managed to work my way to the trail and up the hill. Think I got lost a couple of times, or at least wandered a bit. Finally could see the lights from the studio, almost thought about going there but I knew there would be people here, so this is where I ended up. Lovely collection of books, just lovely, Mrs. Smith."

"Never mind that Walker, it's good the boy's alive even though I'm still not sure what happened out there. Said you were staying at the Gardener cabin?" Dugan asked.

"Yes sir, since early June. Will be here a few more months, then back to Detroit, Grosse Point actually, then back to Germany where I live now. Seeing an old friend in the area."

"Who?"

"A private matter officer, if you don't mind."

"I do mind," Dugan answered. "The boy was reported as a runaway when the picker's quarter were on fire, then you show up six hours later, the kid busted up, can't talk, that's where it stands. Too many unanswered questions."

"Never mind that, Jimmy, I am sure Mr. Walker isn't going anywhere. We've all had a difficult day, thank you for finding the boy and for your help. Can we give you a lift down to the beach?" Charlie asked.

"No, I can walk, but may I borrow a flashlight. Mine is somewhere down in the woods, had that thing since the war, great torch. Got it from a Tommy, an English soldier, Howard; they make good flashlights. That's all I need, but I'll try to find the thing tomorrow. I've overstayed my welcome, Mrs. Smith. I'll be going; I'm sure the boy will be fine."

"Again, thank you Mr. Walker, I hope to see you during the next few days," Liz said. "I'm not sure if we can repay you for your efforts."

"I am sure you will, good night Mr. Smith and you too, Howard."

"I'll walk with you to the top of the hill," Frank said. "I'm heading back."

Howie and Jimmy Dugan walked to the door with Gideon Walker and watched the two men disappear into the night. Howie wanted to know more about the big man. Jimmy Dugan wanted to put him in jail, at least until this was all sorted out.

CHAPTER EIGHTEEN

Charlie returned early the next morning, exhausted, but well caffeinated. He went to the hospital after Frank and Gideon left.

"Doug and Anne are staying with the Bill," Charlie said to Liz. "He was pretty banged up and his left leg is broken in three places. Doc thinks it happened when he fell, leg slammed against a branch or something like that. Shoulder was dislocated as Walker said; he taped it up. The boy's young body will heal well. Thinks he may have hit his head, but only a slight concussion. It's the leg that concerns him. They'll have to operate and reset the bone, poor kid."

"He'll be all right," Liz said, putting her palm against the man's cheek. "Walker saved the boy's life. If he hadn't found him, I don't know what would have happened."

Charlie poured another cup of coffee, pulled a chair out from the table, and lit a cigarette. "Doug's worried about his job. He needed to be back today to get that article out that he has been working on. In fact, his boss said some things on the phone that would have caused me to drive down to Chicago just to punch the man in the face. He may have to get out of here by noon, but doesn't want to leave until after the surgery, insists he will stay till then."

"It's hard to live these days most anywhere," Liz said. "Costs are starting to go up; you need money to live and raise your family, mortgages and everything high. Tough, real tough."

"Liz, you make it sound like the Depression. It's hardly that. Not even close, we are doing okay. We didn't have any money, none. Remember?"

"Yes, I remember, I hate to say it but it seemed more manageable then. Oh we're fine, us old folks hidden away up here, but for the kids, it's tough. Running just to keep up, never getting ahead or staying even."

"Is Bill okay?" Howie said standing in the door. "Couldn't sleep much, just stared at the ceiling. At least I didn't get kicked every hour."

"He'll be fine. Doctor has it under control but his leg will need an operation."

"Great, one more thing I'll have to deal with," Howie said with a smile. "He'll use the operation and surgery as his, 'What I did during summer vacation,' story. Great, just great."

"Well, since we are all up, we might as well have breakfast," Liz said.

Halfway through breakfast, a knock on the door and Charlie found most of the Martinez clan and Beck standing in a crowd just outside.

"Is Senior Bill okay?" Gonzalo asked.

"Yes, he'll be fine, broke his leg, they're fixing it. Probably will be in the hospital a few weeks," Charlie said to everyone, but only looked at Gonzalo. "Thank you for seeing him leave, Gonzalo. It was a big help."

Gonzalo smiled and took his sister's hand.

"We have work to do, Señor Smith," Ernesto said. "The cherries will not wait. We will be in the sours and heading toward the road. Roger should be here soon, so we will get started."

As if on cue, Roger pulled up the gravel and parked next to Charlie. He almost ran to the door. Liz told him everything they knew.

"That's good, glad you called last night when you found him, and sorry I wasn't here when the pickers' quarters caught fire, damn, should have been here, maybe could have stopped it. Was on my way over, but Lisa was having a rough night with the baby so I had to stay with her."

"Is she okay?" Liz asked.

"She's fine this morning; some days are like that. Carrying a baby, I guess, is just uncomfortable."

Howie walked out to the barn with Roger. The damage to the quarters was not extensive, just inconvenient for the Martinez's. Some were living in the barn now, others doubled up in the remaining rooms. The smell of burned wood, kerosene, and cooking fat hung in the still morning air. Howie poked his head into the damaged end of the coup. The small burner looked to be the most damaged and most burned. A piece of unburned curtain lay under the charred table.

"Maybe someone left the burner going when they went to the beach. When the wind started to pick up, the curtain may have caught fire when it blew near. From there the rest caught fire," Howie surmised.

"Very possible, in a hurry to leave, to get to the beach, forgot to turn it off."

"Looks like that's what happened."

"See, the valve is still open, lucky the canister didn't explode, just an accident, but a damn stupid one, a real stupid one," Albert Beck said, sticking his head through the door. "What a mess, what a mess."

Howie and Beck helped Roger get the trailer reattached to the tractor. The sprayer and tractor were still sitting in the yard from the previous afternoon, none the worst for their part in the fire. By the time they found the Martinez family, they had already filled twenty lugs. They loaded the lugs that had spent the night in the orchard; Ernesto had covered the stacks before they went to the beach. By midmorning, Howie and Roger had a full trailer and headed to the garage.

"With Saturday and Sunday's pickings, as well as today's, I'll take a load to the cannery at 2:00," Charlie said to Roger as they stacked the new lugs. "Should be a couple of hundred lugs. Still look clean but we will have to watch and see if yesterday's rain gets to the fruit.

Have to watch 'em real close."

Doug pulled into the drive just as Howie returned with the second load of the morning. Howie hugged his father; he could feel his exhaustion.

"Time for bite of breakfast, get an hour of sleep, then I have to go back to Chicago," Doug said to Liz, he saw the worry on her face. "Mom, I don't have an option."

"Of course you do, there're always options. And this is one of those times; your family needs you here, you know that! Here!"

"They also need money to live on, and the money's there," Doug said. "Bill's in great hands and he has everyone here. I can't do anything for a few weeks until he gets out. The farm is working smoothly and Howie can take over for me when I am not here. I have to go, it really pisses me off, but I have to go, Mom, there's no option. I'll call Anne when I hit Grand Rapids."

Liz watched Gideon Walker stroll across the drive to the house. "Good morning, Mr. Walker, breakfast?"

"Good morning, Mrs. Smith . . . Mr. Smith." Doug nodded. "I've spent the better part of the summer here and this is the second time I have been to this farm in less than a day. It's a strange life we live. Yes, I would love some breakfast; the boy, how is he doing?"

"He'll be fine, out of surgery this morning, but nothing else seems too damaged. Again, thank you for finding him and for all your help," Liz said.

"A very strange evening, here's your flashlight, and thanks for that. Yes, very strange, but I am glad the boy is okay."

Doug put his hand out, Walker took it. "Thanks Gideon, thank you from my heart and Anne's too. She said to give you hug, but I'll let her do that later," Doug said with a smile.

"Will gladly take it, when offered."

Liz made her second breakfast of the morning for the two men.

"When Bill woke up this morning, after the surgery, he told an interesting story," Doug said. "He remembered the fire and being mad that we would not let him help, said he was going to run away just to show us. Said he ran to edge of the hill and started down the slope when the rain started, fell twice, finally reached the huge pine, the one in the clearing and tried to climb it. Says when he was halfway up, birds began hitting him, then there was an explosion, then he woke up in the hospital. Quite a story."

Walker took a sip of coffee, "Makes sense, at least at the end of it. Mr. Smith, I found him at the base of that tree, busted up, lucky even to be alive. There was lightning just before I found him, in fact the flashes helped to light the way, glad I could help."

"Douglas, Roger thinks the fire was an unfortunate accident, somebody left the burner on, the curtain caught fire. I have a call into Jimmy; he will be out here later with someone from the county fire marshal's office to take a look," Liz said.

"You don't look like you're going to pick this morning," Gideon said.

"Going back to Chicago right after breakfast, have to get back to the *Trib*."

"You work at the *Tribune*? Great paper."

"Yes, I work in the feature section, working on an article about the Andrea Doria with a local Chicago angle. A couple from Evanston survived; so their story is good for a feature and a photo. The story is already a day late. My boss is all over me, regardless of how things are here. I'll go right to the office and finish it tonight, maybe get some sleep tomorrow morning."

"Believe it or not, I worked on a small paper in Germany," Walker said. "There were enough Americans all over Germany after the war so they needed news as much as anyone and in English. My German was okay but they wanted an American's perspective. I think the German editor really wanted an angle to get close to the goods flowing into the country, food and other things, especially tobacco. He loved cigars so we came to an arrangement. I was his front man, wrote some cover stories and other things that featured Americans helping the Germans, was able to help him and his family a little. Made a few dollars, split my time with a small hospital in the same town; I liked both jobs but then moved on. In fact, came back to Grosse Point for a couple of years, my father was ill and I needed to be here. After he died, I went back to Germany and my friends I have there. It's home to me now."

"Even ten years later, it is amazing how that war still affects things, ten years," Doug said. "I lost my brother there, in France." Liz quickly turned toward the two men. "Died in a small town, a small town like this one. I still miss him and so does this farm." Doug looked up at his mother and blessed her with a smile.

"It changed us all; I was full of myself and my ideals before the war," Gideon said. "I believed the fascists should be stopped but I also believed I was above killing. That's why I became a CO, thought I could moralize myself out of my predicament. The war showed me that evil must be confronted sometimes, and that killing is the only way to stop it sometimes."

"Is that why you're spending time down on the beach, alone?" Liz asked. "Hard to face the real world?"

Gideon looked at Liz for a puzzled moment. "Maybe, but mostly because I feel more comfortable without the complications of living with others; I'm set in my ways with my schedules, even living as simply as I do. I write for at least six hours a day, short stories and novellas at the moment. Working toward a novel buried somewhere in my head. I keep trying to pry it out but the task is terrifying." Gideon still looked at Liz. "If I may be so bold, is it possible to use your book collection as a library, would make things a little easier?"

"Of course," Liz answered. "We'll be in your debt for a long time. Besides, books are like early mornings, Gideon. You never know how the day will turn out until you put light on its pages."

"I have to get going, Mom," Doug said.

"I put a few things back in your bag after what Dad said when he came in this morning, it's in your room."

"Thanks," Doug said and then turned to Walker. "Gideon, my family and I owe you more than can ever be repaid. Thank you very much."

"You're welcome, and like most things, some debts get worked out in mysterious and unintended ways. Drive safe."

Doug retrieved his travel bag and briefcase, kissed Liz on his way through the kitchen, and, nearing the barn, he stopped and talked with his father. Charlie wiped his cherry stained hands with a rag, hugged him and watched as his youngest drove out onto the highway and Gideon Walker walked down the trail to the woods.

As Charlie turned back toward the garage, the nose of the tractor, followed by Howie high in the seat, split the orchard. Lugs of cherries followed.

"Was that Dad, Gramps?" Howie asked.

"Yes, boy. Had to get back to Chicago, he'll be back at the end of the week."

"Sure wish he could stay; seems so much happier when he's up here."

"Yes, I believe you're right, but as you're finding out, money speaks loudly and there is little of that up here. You have to go where it can be made. And Chicago is the place for your dad and for you and Bill and your mother. We would love to have you up here, but I will not operate a home for the unemployed. And besides, I can't afford you if you keep sitting up there; get down and help me unload these damn boxes," Charlie said with his best foreman-like voice.

Charlie and Howie left for the hospital after lunch and they returned with Anne in the late afternoon. Frank and Liz sat under the pear, drinks and a half full ashtray sitting on the small side table.

"How's he doing?" Liz asked Anne.

"Much better. They said the breaks were clean and the bone was not shattered. He will be in a cast for at least a couple of months; which means he may miss some school. I'll keep him up on his studies but, for someone as busy as that boy has to be, he'll be a basket case."

"Miss school? Maybe I should break a leg or something," Howie chimed in with a laugh.

"If you do, you'll miss a lot more than school young man," Anne said to her oldest with a smile. "There are many ways to inflict pain and I know most of them, so you be careful and there'll be no tree climbing for the rest of the summer."

"Mr. Walker stopped by this morning and asked about Bill; we heard Bill's story about running away. I am glad he was there to find him," Liz said.

"A loner and I understand where he's coming from," Frank said, turning a bit to get comfortable. "Some people carry their demons with them wherever they go, kind of like luggage. Every once in a while, you open the case and there they sit, nicely folded. You put them on, and, as they say, the clothes make the man, or the demons change the man." Frank grabbed the arm of the chair. Howie could see the intense pain in his uncle's eyes, tears came; his grip turned the back of his paint flecked hand white.

"You okay?" Liz asked.

"No sister, I am not. The pain is impressively sharp this fine evening," Frank said and took another swallow of bourbon. "But I will sit and wallow in all of your pity and enjoy the evening."

"Spaniard, you're incorrigible," Anne said. "There's an impressionable young man here."

"Anne, my dear, how will that young man learn to live well if he does not have good examples of how to live poorly? I am here to show him that life does not have to be sweetness and light all the time, sometimes it is like a bullfight where you and life move about in circles, one with a *muleta* that tries to confuse the other with trickery and distraction. And then, when you think you have it all together and the sword is ready, life gores you in the gut and rips you in two." Frank grimaced, and pushed his hand against his side.

"Let's get you home," Liz said, concerned.

"I'll help him Grams," Howie offered. "Uncle Frank." Howie extended his weak arm for his uncle to hold as he stood.

"Good night all," Frank offered. "Let's go, my Sancho Panza, adios all. To my Spanish castle, Sancho."

After Howie put his uncle into bed, he walked around the studio and studied the paintings and sketches strewn about the room. The human figure was the dominant theme in all of them, there were a few landscapes and still lifes but even these had a human sense to them with their shapes and curves. In a far corner, a stack of paintings seemed lost from the rest, a paint stained drop cloth covered them, only edges of the canvases showed. He tilted the paintings apart, one after the other; sketches and paintings were of lovely men posing, stretching, and even coyly looking at the artist, each displayed themselves. He knew he should not be looking at these, men never looked this way. These men were soft and sensuous, not tough and manly. There was an intimate seriousness to these pieces, more than those of women and religious figures and, except for the Christ scenes, these were personal. The last two shocked him more than the others; these were of Gideon Walker, nude and in a pose similar to the painting of Jennie on the beach. He did not have a beard.

Howie tilted the last of the paintings back and replaced the sheet. His eyes passed across the room and caught Jennie lounging on the blanket in the dune. Frank had completed the painting and she was beautiful, but the paintings of Walker were emotional and connected; they were very personal.

The crucifixion controlled the studio. Its evident strength expressed the same emotion shown in the male nudes. The color of Christ's face glowed, as if lit from inside, with an illumination that pushed through the skin, radiating a sensual passion. It was a great painting, maybe his uncle's best; the face of Christ was Gideon's.

His uncle knew Gideon Walker. But why the nude paintings and why did he paint Christ with Gideon's face? Why did Uncle Frank act as if he never knew who lived down on the beach and why didn't his family know Walker? Howie, lost in these juggling thoughts, slowly closed the red door and walked back to the farmhouse, the quarter moon dimly lit the path. He pushed his thumb across the billion years in his pocket.

Howie, Roger and Charlie worked through the rest of the week hauling, stacking and then restacking cherry lugs; they moved ladders down the sandy slope of the orchard toward the last of the picking along the highway. The Martinez family had settled into their new quarters, three tents stood off to one side of the courtyard, at the rear of the barn.

"Should be done by next Friday, Señor Smith," Ernesto said. "That is if God will allow this weather to hold."

"Yes, six more days and that should do it," Charlie answered.

"Si, then we're off to Indiana to pick tomatoes. I really hate that work, Señor Smith, I really do. Here we work in the shade and have the beach, like a vacation," Ernesto said with a grin.

"I know you're making a joke, Ernesto. I know. But work is work, sometimes it's hard, sometimes less so."

"But the tomatoes are cruel, no shade, it's backbreaking, for less than we make here, then further on south and then maybe home by early November, in time for Thanksgiving so we can be thankful for all we have. Señor, sometimes I wonder."

Gideon Walker stopped by twice during the next few weeks; Howie tried to find things to do when the big man came to the farm, things that wouldn't put them together.

The cherries were starting to show the effects of the rain and the heat, some were split and mold began to show on others. The pickers tried to cull out the bad cherries before they got into the lugs but some made it into them. Gonzalo put handfuls of cherries on one end of the conveyor belt while Barbara, Liz and Anne sorted out the bad and rotten cherries; sometimes it took two lugs to fill one clean lug. These would be hauled to the cannery quickly; if left overnight, they would have to be resorted. They worked into the night under lights hung from the rafters; Roger delivered the lugs to the cannery after midnight. All the orchards had the same problem. They all knew it was now or never.

By Sunday afternoon, everyone was exhausted. Anne spent every available hour with her son at the hospital and spent evenings with the cherries. Howie saw his brother twice, and Bill lauded over the personal service and treatment he was receiving. Doug arrived late Friday as tired as the rest. He stopped to see his son and Anne followed him home in Charlie's car. Liz announced late Saturday night that there would be no church on Sunday; the cherries did not have the day off and neither would they. But by mid-afternoon, there was a lull in the chaos and Liz declared a moratorium on work at 4:00.

"The beach," she announced.

No one had to be told twice. The Martinez's, headed down the hill en masse. Anne and Doug begged off and left to see Bill. Liz, Charlie and Howie walked through the woods to the dunes. Howie washed himself off in the lake and it surprised him to see his grandmother and grandfather walk hand in hand into the warm water. They both showed signs of age but were regal in bearing; straight backs and shoulders; they laughed and splashed each other. He never understood, until then, why they were so dear to him.

CHAPTER NINETEEN

Howie saw Gideon Walker on the crest of the dune watching the families. He saw the man differently, the savior of his brother on one hand, the unknown friend of his uncle on the other. *Who is this man?*

Walker waved and then turned toward his cabin. Howie went back to his grandparents lounging on the sand.

"I am going over to Mr. Walker's, I'll follow you up to the farm a little later," Howie said.

"Don't be too late, supper is at seven," Liz said. "Your folks will be back by then."

"Yes, ma'am."

A small porch extended along one side of the cabin open toward the lake, Gideon sat on a wicker chair smoking a cigar; the heavy aroma filled the small hollow in the dunes and hung about the porch like a light fog.

"Good afternoon young man, please join me." Gideon pointed to another chair on the deck. "I have some coke in the refrigerator, care for a bottle?"

Howie nodded and sat. Gideon retrieved the bottle, two in fact, and sat next to Howie.

"How's your brother?"

"Good, real good. They're bringing him back to the farm on Tuesday. Doctor says he's doing well and is strong enough to stay at home, told me he misses the aquarium and wants to know how everyone is doing."

"Aquarium?"

"We were collecting bugs and tadpoles for our aquarium on the day the stag was killed, we watch them grow, then we release them back into the pond. Too bad Bill is missing out right now, the tadpoles are frogs, and are getting their spots. He would love to see that," Howie paused and looked directly at Gideon. "I've seen the paintings, how do you know my uncle?"

"Frogs to your uncle, interesting transition, boy."

"Don't you call me boy, only family can call me boy," Howie said defiantly.

"Touchy. Well Frank calls you boy in our conversations, so where do I start and am I family?" Gideon said taking a long draw on his cigar. "Drink up," he said, pointing at Howie's coke with his cigar. "Franklin Rex and I go back almost twenty years, before the war; we met at a beach somewhat like this one, but in France, and have been close friends all this time. We have kept it as quiet and as hidden as possible. We both have family, or at least I did back then, and it was necessary not to be seen together. During the war he remained here painting; we sent letters back and forth and I offered my services for the war effort, doing the best I could do. As I said, I stayed in Germany after the war for four years working in a small hospital and a newspaper, but every November I would visit Frank in Barcelona where we could live together quietly through the winter."

"Live together? What do you mean? You can't do that."

"Howard my boy, yes we can and yes we did. And as far as I know, no one here knows about our relationship except you, and only because you asked about it. And now Frank is dying and I'm trying to help him as much as I can. He told me not to come but I had to. He means that much to me. Behind that crusty surface of his is a dear soul and a man I admire and care for. Care for very much."

"But that is not permitted," Howie said, more confused than ever. "You can't be together, it's not, it's not..."

"Right, moral? Howard, who knows what's right or wrong about these things? The Church, your parents, your grandparents, I don't know, that's for damn sure. Sometimes there're things about people you'll never understand, but understand this, your uncle and I care deeply for each other."

Howie looked at Walker and tried to grasp what Walker was saying. It was too much, yet it was also something he couldn't go and ask anyone about.

"When Franklin got sick, he told me to stay in Spain. I couldn't, besides, my family is gone, so I told him that I was coming to see him. He gave in and asked me to spend the summer nearby. He suggested the Gardner place, and here I am. We kept it from all of you, it was just easier. Now I'm just trying to help him through his tough days, help him to get his work done, finish what he started, something we all try to do in our own lives, to finish this life—completed. Most don't."

Howie's coke fell to the porch from his deformed hand; he tried to understand. His head spun; he thought he would have to hold it to stop it from falling off his shoulders.

"I have to go," Howie said, and quickly stood up. "I need to leave."

"Yes Howard, I appreciate what you're going through. I suggest you talk to your uncle. He said it might come to this at some point. Please talk to him."

Howie stumbled as he climbed down the steps, his bare feet caught in the sand.

"You okay?"

"I am fine, just fine," Howie answered and sat on the edge of the porch, putting on his shoes. He didn't say a word to Walker and dashed into the woods.

Howie cut through the clearing and stopped at the base of the large pine. He found Bill's missing left shoe mixed in with the pine needles. His eyes followed the trunk up into the tangle of limbs that formed a ladder that begged to be climbed. The target, shrunk from the rain, was still pinned to the tree. He saw his grandparents walking up the hill toward the farm.

"Not today," Howie said. "Not today."

The caws and complaining of the ravens high in the pine irritated the quiet of the late afternoon. One, two, then three flew out from the tree and spun circles about its crown. Their incessant calling ruined Howie's daze; he remembered Bonita's comment "Momma, there are blackbirds with the boy."

"I bet you had some part in all this!" Howie yelled at the birds. "If I didn't know better, I'd think you pushed him out of this tree and watched him fall."

Howie left the clearing and headed toward the hillside; he could just make out, in the early evening, the roof of his uncle's studio along the ridge. The ravens' calls slowly disappeared into the hum and chitter of the woods.

Frank Rex opened the red door after Howie's three knocks.

"Greetings boy, how are you this wonderful evening?"

"Well, very well, Uncle Frank. You?"

"Not bad, not bad at all."

The oily aromas of the studio washed over Howie as he stepped inside. Symphony music played in the background.

"Like that? It's a new recording of Rachmaninoff's *Rhapsody on a Theme of Paganini*. Rubinstein with the Chicago Symphony, just this year I think," Frank said as they crossed the room. "I have something to show you."

The large canvas stood facing away from the late afternoon light. Frank's view, and as he painted, was first to the canvas and then past it toward the lone pine, its jagged top etched against the blue sky.

"I'm almost finished."

Howie walked around the easel and stood transfixed by the painting he had watched evolve from red clay to paint to passion. He took a deep breath and slowly exhaled.

"I think that if you did not believe in God before you saw this painting, you would now," Howie said slowly. "Uncle Frank, it's wonderful. Christ's face is so real; I feel as though I have to try to wipe away the blood so He can see me through His agony and sorrow. Yet there is more, His love is also there. Yes?"

"Yes boy, it's there," Frank answered.

"It's a miracle," Howie said turning to his uncle. "I'm happy you finished."

"It's difficult, the pain these days is worse than ever. Today, for some reason, less; more like a nagging headache than the searing pain in the gut."

Howie stood in front of the painting and then looked about the room, his eyes resting on the stack of canvas covered paintings in the corner. "Why didn't you tell us about Gideon Walker?"

"I wondered how long we could keep it a secret," Frank answered with a smile. "Gideon was always surprised that I, of all people, could keep such a secret, since well before the war, I think, since that summer morning in Cannes. Only my sister would have understood, the rest probably would have only shunned me and said things that would have hurt the family. Me, I could've cared less. It's my life and I live it as I see fit. But the family did not need the burden my personal proclivities would have visited on them, so it was simpler this way."

"But I don't understand," Howie interrupted.

"Someday you will, it may be a few years but you will. People love for many reasons, and, for some, they also use it as an excuse. They paint their lives like I paint a canvas, sometime with broad bold strokes and sometimes with the tiniest brushes, huge cumulus clouds and tiny eyelashes. My life was comfortable, like tiny brush marks; then I met Gideon, since that summer my strokes are bolder and more colorful, even Liz noticed it. Told her it was a phase, she said I was getting better, especially at my work structurally. She always understood where my painting was going, probably better than I did. Gideon grounded me and he also allowed me to think of the future, to plan, something I seldom did. Our time in Spain and France was always special but we also understood we could not always be together; it was something we both understood."

The piano's notes held in the air, mixed with the linseed aroma and washed out into the pines.

"Let me turn the record," Frank said, as he crossed the room to the phonograph.

Howie followed his uncle and then turned to the couch, the couch where Jennie had posed. He slowly ran his fingers over the cushion where she had lain. His uncle stood at the table with the phonograph, and, as he picked up the record, began to shake, the record fell back on the turntable as Frank Rex fell to the floor. His eyes fixated on Howie, almost pleading for him to help.

"Uncle!" Howie yelled as he pushed himself away for the couch and fell to the floor, grasping Frank's head in his arms.

"Pills, the blue ones, two," Frank gasped.

Howie gently placed his uncle's head on a small pillow and ran into the bathroom. Pills littered the counters in various small dishes, the blue ones stood out from the rest.

Cradling his uncle's head, Howie placed two pills in his mouth and then the glass of water on his lips. Frank's pain pushed sweat out of his forehead, his whole body, rigid. Howie held him for five minutes and slowly Frank relaxed, his breathing became more regular, softness returned to his eyes.

"That was a bitch," he finally said. "Maybe the worst; help me to the couch, this floor is too fucking hard on this boney ass of mine."

With some effort, Howie pulled Frank to his feet and then to the couch, where he collapsed.

"Would you please give Liz a call and have her come down," Frank asked. "I need her here."

Howie looked toward the phone standing on the table in the corner. "You okay for the moment."

"Yes, but please call her."

"Hello," Liz answered.

"Grams, Howie. I am at the studio and Uncle Frank had a seizure or something. He needs you here."

"Two minutes."

In less than that, Liz pushed open the Andalusian door and took her brother in her arms.

"How bad, Franklin?"

"Very bad, Elizabeth, very bad; this one cut a part of my soul away, it's lying about over near the phonograph. Howie, be good and put the other side on, the one that has the piano concerto on it, and look for that fucking piece of my soul, it's yellow or something. If I'm going to die there must be music!"

Howie gently set the needle on the black surface: soft cords, singly struck, filled the air and then a wave of strings followed that felt like the sea as it flowed in then out. Howie turned toward the window, his uncle lay in the arms of his sister, and she caressed his cheek and beard, a Madonna and Child. Waves of pain passed over the man, Howie watched as he relaxed, and then went rigid, then soft as the pain sat on the sidelines for a while. The sharp light of the evening made Howie notice for the first time how gaunt his uncle had become. His cheeks, no longer full, like he had sucked a lemon, were pulled tight against the bones in his face.

Charlie gently tapped on the door and stepped into the room; Howie took his hand.

"It's real bad Grandfather," Howie said.

"He's a hardheaded son-of-a-bitch, the doc says he's toughed this out longer than most."

"Told me he had to finish this painting, his final one," Liz said and looked at the Christ and smiled.

"Sister, I hope, after all my years of decadence, that that painting will be my ticket into heaven," Frank said, with a short laugh punctuated with a cough. "Maybe God will have a touch of sympathy for an old shit like me."

"Howie, would you go down to the Gardner cabin and ask that Walker fellow to come up here; Frank needs his help."

"You know about Walker and Uncle Frank?"

Liz straightened a few stray hairs on her brother's head, "Howard there is little about this farm and my family I don't know. I have known for years, and I have accepted it even longer. Now, please get him."

Howie stepped out of the studio and started toward the path. His parents and Gideon Walker stood talking, in its center, the strip of rough grass between them. They turned and walked toward Howie.

"How is he?" Gideon asked.

"Not good, Mr. Walker. Had a seizure I think, seems hard for him to move."

"We found the note from Dad," Doug said. "We headed out here and ran into Gideon. He was coming from down below."

"Mr. Walker said he talked to you earlier today and may have confused you," Anne added. "He decided to come up and talk to all of us about Frank and why he's here. Your dad and I told him it was not necessary, we all understood. Now he's the one who seems a bit confused."

Anne looked over to Gideon and smiled.

"How's Bill?" Howie asked.

"Doing well, but I need to get him out of that hospital before he thinks this is how his life will be from now on. He watches TV all day, has someone to take care of him and get him food. That young man is in for a rude awakening," Anne said.

"Great, just what I need, a brother more spoiled than he already is!"

Seven people in the studio, in amongst the canvases and easels, just about filled it. When Charlie had to have a smoke, the place seemed suddenly roomier. Frank Rex recovered enough to sit up.

"We need to get you to the hospital," Liz said. "The doc will be here shortly and then he can take you there; we'll follow."

"Excuse me sister, no fucking way," Frank said. "I know I am dying, probably soon. If not, I'll probably shoot myself because of the pain, just joking young man. No, dearest, I am staying in this rat hole of unfinished canvases, paint and turpentine. This is my life and I want it around me when I leave it. Besides, the smells in the hospital will probably hasten my death by days. God, how can anyone work in a place like that?"

"Depends on your point of view, Uncle," Howie said. "Seems Bill likes it."

"He is too young to know better," Frank answered with a forced smile. "And besides, Gideon can help if I need anything, he's just a big lay-about anyway," he said smiling at his friend.

The spent the rest of the evening talking and getting Frank to relax. The doctor arrived and gave Liz some additional pills, said they were the strongest painkillers he could give Frank. He also gave Frank a shot in his upper hip that seemed to help him be more comfortable.

"I'll stay with him tonight, Mrs. Smith," Gideon said. "If there's a change, I'll call you."

"Thank you, Mr. Walker, and you can call me Liz; seems you're a part of the family now, and probably have been for a long time. Kind of like a younger brother I never knew."

"Thank you."

The five walked to the farm in the dark. Music, full of exotic horns and guitars, carried across the orchard from the Martinez's quarters. The rich smells of corn and cilantro mixed coyly with the dusty sweetness of the orchard. Howie remembered the final cords of the *Rhapsody* and how the two sounds seemed to mingle and twist about in the air above all of this.

"The picking is almost done, another year finished," Charlie said, to no one in particular. The sound of a sad guitar followed them into the house.

CHAPTER TWENTY

The next few days were as busy as the farm had been in years. The house was prepared for Bill's return from the hospital. Ernesto and the Martinez family, along with Charlie, Roger, and Howie, picked, hauled and sorted with the hope of finishing by the end of the week. The contractor completed the interior painting of the repaired living room, and, when done, did remedial repairs to the picker's quarters. And, in the studio, Gideon helped make Frank as comfortable as possible.

Liz decided that the small storage room just off the kitchen, in reality not more than a large pantry, could serve as Bill's bedroom until the family returned to Chicago. The few things it held were moved to the basement and a cupboard. A small bed frame, found in the barn, and a fresh mattress were jammed into the small closet. She added a small side table and it was ready.

"At least he won't have to climb the stairs," Howie said with all seriousness.

"And you'll continue to have that big bed upstairs all to yourself," Anne said with a smile.

"Well, okay. But he can't make it up and down the stairs and that leg of his sticks straight out when he sits; besides, he can even see into the kitchen when we eat. It'll work out fine."

"I agree," Anne said. "Too bad there isn't a window, but it'll only be for a few weeks until we head south."

Howie watched the painter brush out paint over the replastered living room panels. The low wooden crossbeams were left in their natural color; the shallow pitch of the ceiling above the beams gave the room height even though it was still low. Boxes of books stood off to one corner.

"I want those books away from the work," Liz said. "No dust, paint or rain. Besides, it'll give me a chance to brighten up the shelves with some varnish. And you, old man, promised me those new cherry shelves," Liz said to her husband.

"I'll start after the apples are picked," Charlie replied.

"I think there's some time between then and now to get started," she added, trying to give him a little push.

"We'll see how things go. After the pickers leave and the dust literally settles; still a lot to get done."

The apples were only about a week's work at best. Albert Beck volunteered to come back from his travels north to help with the picking; he was heading up to the Straits of Mackinac to see a friend that worked summers at one of the small hotels on Mackinac Island.

"I grew up with the fellow," Beck told Howie. "He and I had great plans, great plans, when we were kids. He was going up to Detroit to get a job building cars and send half the money home to his mother. The half became a quarter and then for a while almost nothing. He came home when she passed away, changed, very changed."

"What had changed?" Howie asked.

"Said he had never seen such hatred for black folks; was told he was taking jobs from good white kids and should go home to Mississippi, get the hell out of Michigan. They say the south is racist; he said it's not like the north, here it's more quiet like. But that changed when they needed our backs to build tanks and airplanes. The war changed a lot of things, a lot of things. He moved up to Mackinac after an injury forced him off the line; works as a handyman and a bellboy. Makes a good living and I see him some winters when I pass through Jackson. He still lives in the house his granddaddy built just after the war. He goes back when they shut the hotel down for the winter."

"The war?" Howie questioned.

"The war between the states, the war of emancipation, the Civil War, the Civil War," Beck added. "Hard to believe it was almost a hundred years ago; to some folk it's still being fought."

"What is on your list, Mr. Beck?" Howie asked. "Where're you going this winter, and what stories will you have next year?"

"Thinking about heading south to New Orleans, then jump a steamer to Rio de Janeiro, always wanted to see that town with its mountains and beaches, ah, the beaches. Did you know there is a sculpture of Christ standing on one of the mountaintops that is over one hundred and twenty feet tall? They say you can see it from everywhere, stands there like the Statue of Liberty in New York, and with its arms open like a cross, welcoming everyone, everyone. The music is wonderful and the food, spectacular. They also have a festival in the late winter called Mardi Gras; it's the day before Ash Wednesday, where the party goes on and on and on, and the women are, excuse me I forgot myself."

"Are what?" Howie said with expectation.

"Are very helpful to travelers," Beck added with a smile. "Very helpful, if you get my meaning, to travelers."

Howie smiled at Beck. Yes, he understood, after this summer he was beginning to understand a lot more than when he left school.

"So I'll be back in a few weeks to help your grandfather pick apples, make a few more dollars, and then south to New Orleans," Beck said. "I'm sorry but I'll miss you when I pass through, it's been an exciting few weeks here, very exciting."

"Could use a little less excitement, if you ask me," Howie added, as Beck walked back toward the barn.

The tractor and trailer pulled away from the garage and toward the orchard.

"You going to help or just stand there?" Roger yelled.

"Coming."

Howie ran and jumped on the back of the trailer just as it dove into the dark grove of trees. He held his hand up as they plowed through the lush dark green leaves; he could feel each leaf as it touched his palm, with his right withered hand he steadied himself on the trailer. The sun flickered through the crowns of the trees, the noise of the tractor all but drowned out the other sounds.

"Buenos dias, Barbara. How are you this morning?" Roger asked Mrs. Martinez as they pulled up to the temporary camp she had set up under the trees. Gonzalo and Bonita were sitting with her.

"Good, Señor Roger. Good. We're almost finished. Just a few more rows, then *terminado*, finished, done. Been a good year, made good money."

"Not bad, Barbara, not bad."

"Your brother is coming home this week, si?" Barbara said to Howie. "I understand his leg is in a big cast."

"Yes, Mrs. Martinez. It's very large and white; some of the nurses have signed their names on it. I wrote my name on it the last time I was there. He's coming home tonight."

"That's good; he needs to be here with his family."

Gonzalo and Bonita both shook their heads in agreement.

"Ask Señor Bill about the black birds, Señor Howie. They helped to make him fall, I think."

As if on cue Gonzalo jumped up and ran toward a small collection of bags and boxes to shoo away three of the birds as they stalked about looking for food.

"Go, *marcharse, vete!*" Gonzalo yelled as the three birds bounced twice off the ground and then flew into the treetops.

"See, they are nothing but thieves and I think they had something to do with your brother," Bonita said.

Barbara sat and continued to look through the punched cards making sure they were correct, a punch for each lug, looking through cards there were thousands of holes. She glanced at her daughter and smiled. "That's enough child; you have said more than enough, sorry, Señor Howie."

"That's okay; I know she says things that are not what they seem to be. But I will ask Bill anyway."

Roger and Howie made three trips from the orchard to the garage. Everyone could sense that picking was coming to an end. The sorting line doubled to help finish out the year, even the cousin, with his broken arm, helped with the sorting. He couldn't lift the lugs but he could pick out the bad fruit as well as Anne.

Anne and Charlie left for the hospital late in the afternoon to get Bill. Howie watched the car's rooftop disappear as it went down the hill; he turned and headed out to the studio. He could hear the singing from deep in the orchard, the songs had changed; they were more up-tempo, lighter, with a bounce to the melodies.

"Good afternoon, Howard, how are you this wonderful day?" Gideon asked after he opened the door. "Everything okay?"

The familiar smells tumbled out of the studio and into the garden; they seemed to pool around Howie as looked about at the roses and the tall hollyhocks.

"How is Uncle Frank, Mr. Walker?" Howie asked.

"Ask him yourself; he is over in the corner doing a bit of work on the crucifixion."

"Howie, is that you?" Frank's voice was soft, softer than Howie had ever heard it. "Come on over here and sit, so much to talk about. Grab your sketchbook."

Howie searched through the stack of sketchbooks and found the last one he had worked in. After Frank's seizure, the studio was more of a jumble.

"This painting is almost done. It's my best work. Father O'Brien was here yesterday to hear my confession and to give me communion. I think the real reason was to see the painting. It struck him dumb. He sat in that chair for an hour just looking; he kept wiping tears away from his eyes. Then he stood at the window, all he said was 'Thank you.' Gideon, not being Catholic and one of the few faults I am glad to say he's not afflicted with, talked with the priest about the arrangements needed for this painting. They also talked about the arrangements for my funeral."

"What are you talking about; you're not going to die."

"Of course I am; we all will die. It's our fate, our only answer to life. No escape, no alternative. There's no bargaining, there's no cheating.

We get the wonderful opportunity to live but it's our gift for only a short time, then it's gone. You must always treat the gift with respect; you must honor it. You must make the most of it."

Howie looked at Gideon.

"Howard, your uncle is dying. You're losing a wonderful man and I am losing the man I care more for than anything in the world. He and I have gone through his will and his estate such as it is." Gideon looked at Frank. "He's told me that everything must be finished before he dies."

"Then my life, as I have lived it, will come to an end and I'll be happy," Frank added. "I'm leaving this studio to you. All the paintings that are here will be left in your care. Do with them as you see fit. Looking about, some of them should be burned but I leave the decisions to you. Elizabeth has a few favorites, please give her what she wants, but I want you to have the rest. I think you understand them as well as anyone, and can certainly take care of them, especially the one of Jennie on the beach. I have seen you looking at that one; you should be ashamed." Frank smiled. "She's a wonderful lady and that painting captures everything about her. She wanted you to have it. She took the studio painting we did early this summer, the one I did when you first met her. That's all she wanted, but she insisted that you have the beach painting. Why, I don't know?"

Howie looked over Frank's shoulder at the painting; he could smell the warm sand of the beach.

"You can't give me the studio," Howie said. "What will I do with the studio?"

"I am sure you will find something useful, besides you can't have it until your eighteenth birthday; your parents will hold it in trust. It's yours though and they cannot sell it or give it away, so make the best of it. I am giving the house in Spain to Gideon; he has made it his own for so long that I almost feel like a visitor sometimes. I'll miss that house and, most of all, the people in town. That's one of the saddest things about all this dying bullshit, you never have enough time to say goodbye to everyone; there's always someone that gets missed or forgotten. If I miss someone, say goodbye for me, will you boy?"

"Yes, Uncle Frank, I certainly will. And to those that were false friends; I'll say that you had a special message for them: Fuck you."

Both Gideon and Frank laughed, until Frank took a deep breath and pressed his hand against his side. "I'm okay boy; the pain's just passing through. Those last pills the doc gave me have been helpful. I wonder where he kept them until now; I could have used them all along. Anyway, the paintings are yours, as well as all the crap lying about. I suggest that one of the first things you do will be to clean house, something I never got around to. There may even be some room if that happens."

"Yes sir," Howie answered while looking about the clutter. "Bill's due back anytime so I'll head up to the house; he would like to see you, I am sure. Feel up to it?"

"I'll see what I can do; I know he thinks that I'm an eccentric old coot. I don't expect you to tell him about Gideon other than he's the one that saved his life. Why don't we just leave it at that for now, okay?"

"Okay, can't figure out how I would tell him anyway. He had enough trouble with the pickers from Texas speaking Mexican; so someday, when it's right, I'll tell him."

Liz and Howie were sitting in the kitchen when the car pulled in. Howie quickly crossed the lawn and opened the door. Bill sat stretched out in the back seat, plaster cast and all. Crutches lay across the foot wells.

"Welcome your highness, your castle awaits," Howie said.

"Oh cut it out, just give me some help sliding out, then give me my crutches, been practicing with them."

"Yes, your highness."

"Stop it, and just help."

Howie held Bill as he slid out of the car, stood, steadied himself, and put a crutch under each arm. Anne stood to one side and smiled.

"Well, at least you got vertical," she said. "Let's see how you do crossing the lawn."

Bill managed to get to the screen door with little difficulty. He headed into his new room after Howie pointed out that he would not have to go up and down the stairs.

"I have gotten used to having my own bed, so this is cool. I even have my own room, first one ever. Neato," Bill said as he looked around the small pantry. "All mine. Let's go see the aquarium."

After the tour of the house and the frogs in the aquarium, Liz, Charlie and Anne had drinks on the porch, while Howie entertained his brother with stories about the picking, the Martinez's and the farm. Bill hobbled his way to the porch and saw that his Uncle Frank and Gideon had joined his family.

"Bill, I want to introduce you to Mr. Gideon Walker," Anne said. "Mr. Walker is the one who found you when you had your fall. He brought you to the house."

Bill looked for a long time at Gideon, "Are you Howie's good giant or bad giant?"

Walker looked at Howie, then back to Bill, "Yes, I believe I'm his good giant."

"Mom, couldn't talk about it much till I saw Mr. Walker here; wasn't sure if he was real or not, so I never said much, even when Officer Dugan asked all those questions at the hospital, oops, he said not to tell." Anne looked at Doug with a questioning glance. "I was pretty mad when the fire was burning, nobody would let me help. Dad kept telling me to get out of the way and all the noise and smoke, so I said to heck with you all; I wanted to go get the target stuck to the big pine."

"Officer Dugan came to see you?" Doug asked.

"Yeah, stopped by a few days after they put the cast on, talked a little, then asked me questions about Mr. Walker. I didn't know who he was taking about, said so. He didn't ask any more questions, signed my cast, right there," Bill said

"Do you know why he asked the questions?" Anne asked.

"No. Anyway I saw the big tree; the target was still stuck to the trunk. I hit it three times, pretty good. Right Grams, pretty good?"

"You're a dead-eye, William Smith," Liz said.

"Well, I decided to climb the tree, there're two lower branches and even in the rain I could get hold of them and work my way up, was getting real dark. Got maybe half way, at this point I knew I was in trouble. Too dark to see, and lightning flashing all around. Got pretty scared, Mom."

"I imagine," Anne said.

"So I tried to climb down and all of a sudden these birds started to flap and bang at me, all squawking and pecking. One bit my hand I think, I lost my balance and the next thing I 'member was you looking at me and it was real bright. And I hurt all over."

"We're just glad that you're okay, get yourself settled in, dinner is in half an hour," Anne said.

Bill looked at Walker again, "I thought Howie was crazy or something, always talking about this giant and nobody would believe him. Howie, I always believed you, even though I was sure you was crazy. Mr. Walker, are you the good giant?"

"I guess so. You think there's a bad giant?" Gideon asked.

"Don't know, but there's always a good and bad giant. Kind of like angels and devils, always a balance," Bill said.

"Smart thing for someone your age," Gideon said.

"Howie, we need to watch out for the bad giant, you never know when he'll show up. But Mr. Walker will defend us, won't you?"

"Yes, Bill, I am very sure he will," Howie said.

"Liz, does this boy deserve a reward?" Walker asked.

"Well, with all the chaos of the past few weeks, I had a few minutes to make the first cherry pie, care for a ..."

Before Liz could finish, both Howie and Bill answered simultaneously, "Cherry pie, yes, yes, yes. And ice cream?"

"And ice cream, but for desert, not before diner," Anne added.

"You staying near here Mr. Walker, never seen you before?" Bill asked.

"Mr. Walker is a friend of Uncle Frank's; he's staying down by the lake in a cabin," Anne said.

Changing the subject a bit, Charlie added, "Bet those ravens are nesting up there or maybe it's their rookery, the place they gather for the night, but who knows?"

Howie remembered what Bonita said earlier in the day about the birds and about his brother. "That child can be scary," he thought.

"A little later in the week we need to let the frogs and bugs go, put them back in the pond. Sorry you can't go with your leg and all,"

Howie said.

"Can't go," Charlie said with a laugh. "Of course he can and then we'll all go to the beach. We've just a few days left of picking then we are done, so we need a big celebration and the beach would be the best place for it; let's have everybody join us, even the Martinez's, it'll be grand."

"Dad, he can't do that. Those crutches would never work in that sand."

"We'll put the boy in the trailer and we can all tractor down the hill to the pond and then to the beach. The boy will not be allowed in the water but we can make a day of it anyway."

"Cool," Bill said. Frank managed a weak but broad smile.

After a noisy dinner and ice cream and pie, Anne and Doug sat alone on the porch. "This may be the first time all summer we've had a minute to ourselves," Doug said. "Quite a summer, are you doing okay?"

"Been rough, never thought I would think that it would be quieter at home than here, been through a lot. I wonder what's gotten into Jimmy?" Anne said.

"Yes, strange. He seems very concerned about Walker, maybe more than he needs to be. But he does, for some reason. Shouldn't know more than what's obvious, but if that's his thinking he could make it tough for Gideon."

"Yes, he could and he's got the law behind him," Doug said lighting a cigarette.

"I'm going into Elk River tomorrow afternoon to get a few things, Barbara said she needed to buy some clothes and I said I would help. You know how a few of those town folks can be, so I just offered to help her a little."

"That's good, they're a good family."

"Summer is almost over, then home, and maybe to some peace and quiet."

"We can only hope."

CHAPTER TWENTY-ONE

Anne and Barbara loaded up the station wagon with Gonzalo and Bonita; Howie wanted to walk through town one last time, so he tagged along. Bill stayed with Liz, occupied with the aquarium.

"I need a few personal items, Señora Smith. The kind that Ernesto likes, but is too shy to buy," Barbara said.

"I know exactly what you mean, men!"

"Si, he likes black with a touch of lace, last time I bought some Bonita arrived nine months later. My man does love my personal things," Barbara Martinez said with a smile.

Anne returned the smile, "Yes, men."

"Ernesto is coming into town later so you do not have to give me a ride home."

"Liz gave me a list of things that Howie can help with, we'll get home about the same time. Howie, can you meet me by the store in an hour?"

"Yes, ma'am, one hour," Howie answered.

Anne pulled the car to the curb; the group unloaded and went their separate ways. Howie headed to the power plant. Two fishermen stood along the catwalk, stringers hung in the foamy water, and each clipped to the railing. Empty beer bottles were lined up along the wall of the plant.

"Good catch," Howie said to the first.

"Smallies, must have been a school. Me and Stu here caught ten in just five minutes, then zip. But good sizes," the man held up one of the stringers, five nice plump smallmouth bass flicked their tails. "Good fish."

"Real good," Howie said as he passed behind the men and headed to the beach on the far side of the river. The late afternoon sun hung high over the Old Mission Point almost directly to the west. A soft breeze blew across the water, children played along the beach, a couple of blankets and umbrellas dotted the sand. After an hour walking the beach, Howie headed back to River Street. The two fishermen had left the catwalk and were loading their car, an old beat up pre-war Ford. Barbara, Ernesto and the kids were walking toward them, Howie waved.

"Hey kid, you know those spics?" the older man yelled out.

"What?" Howie answered.

"I said boy, you know those spics, those goddamn pickers, you know 'em?"

Howie looked at Ernesto; he could see that he had heard the remark. "Yes, I know them, they work for my grandfather."

"Well, the sooner they're out of here the better, don't need their kind around here," the younger man said.

"We sir, I don't think we need your kind around here," Howie said, shocked by his own adamancy. "Why don't you two just load up and leave."

"Kid, you telling me what to do or say, you little shit. Homer, did you hear what this little bastard just told us, told us to get out of town."

"We live here our whole lives and this little fucker tells us to leave. He's one bold son-of-a-bitch, for a cripple."

"Señor Smith, are you okay?" Ernesto said.

"Yes, sir, I'm okay. Just asking nicely that these fellows leave," Howie said.

"That's okay, Howie, we're leaving, Barbara bought what she needs and the kids are hungry."

"You spics shouldn't be here, go back where you come from," Homer said puffing himself up. "And take the bitch and your spawn with you."

Ernesto Martinez had fought for his country until he was wounded early in the war; he spent the rest of the time in Texas fighting the same types of bigots that now blocked the sidewalk in Elk River.

"What did you say?"

"I said take your bitch and get out of town."

"Come, Ernesto, let's leave, children to the truck."

"You having a woman talk for you, spic?"

"Why the hell don't you shut up and get in your car and leave," Howie said. "Better for everyone."

"Jesus H. Christ, now you have the kid speaking for you, what a coward."

Ernesto leaned toward the men, Barbara and the children held back, Howie felt himself being drawn to the men also, just like Ernesto. *"What the hell am I doing,"* Howie thought.

The older man smiled, and drew out a knife from its sheath cinched to his belt, a six-inch skinning knife. *"Oh shit,"* was all that Howie could think of.

"You call that dinky piece of metal a knife, please gentlemen, please gentlemen. What you need to carry is a real knife, a blade of fine Toledo steel, like this one," Albert Beck said as walked toward the group, flipping the blade open, the steel flashed the sun into the eyes of the younger man.

"Now you got a blackie doing your work for you, well I never. Homer, you ever seen anything like this, a spic defended by a kid and a darkie. I never."

"Look, you ignorant shit, and I mean that in the most liberal and civil of terms. Why should this gentleman get into some ruckus with the likes of you two assholes? You've embarrassed him, his wonderful wife, and his children, and you called him a coward. I've seen cowards and they're the type that stand and wet their pants when things get rough. Can I ask which of you two will be the first to pee in your britches?" Beck said, still flashing the knife in the eyes of the men, first one, then the other.

"You better listen to him, Mr. Beck knows things, things you should be afraid of," Bonita said from within the folds of Barbara's dress.

"And now babies, good God, Homer, I can't believe it! The whole Mexican circus is in town, God damn."

"Señor, you better believe it," the tone in Bonita's small voice shook everyone. Even the two men stopped and looked at the small child. "You don't want to die today, do you?"

The younger man looked at his partner, "Ah shit, Stu, let's get the fuck out of here, we're wasting time on this trash."

"Homer, no one calls me a coward," Stu said, and quickly lunged at Beck, his knife swung quickly through the air trying to slash Beck's face. Surprisingly, Albert stepped into the arc of the man's arm, blocked the arm so forcefully that the man dropped the knife; it flew harmlessly to the street. The man stood staring into the face of Beck, his nose not more than an inch from the man's face. Stu could feel the tip of the knife under his chin; Howie saw a sliver of blood trail down the engraved blade. Beck's other hand held the man's privates.

"Now sir," Beck said softly in the man's ear. "If you move, one of two things will happen, I will crush your nuts, which I would gladly do, gladly. Or the last thing you will see is the tip of my knife in your left eye ball. Your choice, sir, your choice."

"Stu, I said let's get the fuck out of here."

"Stu, I suggest you listen to Homer, he's trying real hard to save your life; me, I don't care one way or another. You're a worthless piece of shit, but somebody probably loves you. Well Stu, what's it going to be?" Beck asked.

Stu slowly raised his hands and nodded to Beck, then took one, then two steps back. Beck lowered the knife, but his eyes never left the man. On step three, the man rushed forward. Beck, anticipating the move, feigned to the left and threw his right fist at the man's nose. Between the momentum of the man and the speed of Beck's arm, the man was out cold before he hit the sidewalk. Beck's punch was faster than a snake's strike.

"Señor, I told you," Bonita said.

Homer knelt next to Stu, blood pumped from his busted nose. He looked at Beck, "Thanks for not sticking him with that knife, he's been drinking all morning and turns into an asshole, thanks."

"Apologize to the family sir, with meaning," Albert Beck said.

Homer pulled his baseball cap off, "Me and Stu there, are sorry ma'am, and to you, sir. I apologize. We're a bit drunk."

Stu started to move and slowly sat up, "Stu, you asshole, stand up and say you're sorry to these people, now," Beck demanded.

Homer helped Stu to his feet, blood covered his tee shirt, he looked at Homer, then at the family. "I'm sorry," said softly.

"Louder," Beck ordered.

"I'm sorry," Stu said, loud enough to meet Beck's needs.

"Get out of here," Beck said dismissing the two men.

Howie watched Homer open the trunk of the sedan and begin to put their gear away. Stu held a rag to his face, the bleeding had stopped. Ernesto and his family headed toward their truck, Gonzalo carried a large paper bag, Bonita's small feet flashed under the hem of Barbara's large skirt. He saw Officer Dugan's police car heading toward them, and, walking toward them on the sidewalk, was his mother.

The explosion came as Beck turned toward Howie. The shock on Beck's face stunned Howie. The force of the slug spun him around; he faced Stu, who stood grinning, a pistol in his hand.

"You think I'm gonna let a little fucker like you get away after what you did to my face, you black son-of-a-bitch. No one does that and gets away with it; what that little nit of a spic kid said was the fucking truth, but it's you who's gonna die, not me." Stu pushed Homer away as he tried to wrestle the gun from him. "It's you that's gonna die."

Howie watched Beck put his hand over the tear in the shoulder of his shirt, blood started to darken his upper left arm and his shirt. Howie moved to help Beck.

"Stay there Howard, don't move," Beck hissed.

"Yes, tell the tough kid to stay away, this is between us. You're tough with a knife; how you do with a gun?"

Howie watched the man as he raised the pistol and aimed at Albert again; to his surprise, Albert Beck just smiled.

"What you grinning at darky, what's so funny?"

Beck turned his head very slowly and looked over Howie's shoulder. Officer Jimmy Dugan stood facing the three, his own service revolver at arm's length, two hands on the grip.

"You really don't want to do that Stuart; you don't want to have me make Dotty a widow and your kids orphans. I really don't want to shoot you, but as there's a God in heaven, I will kill you where you stand if you don't lower that pistol. Now!" Dugan ordered.

"Listen to him, Stu, for God's sake, listen to him," Homer said.

Stu's nose started bleeding again, great globs dropped on his already bloody shirt, he slowly lowered the pistol; it dropped to the sidewalk near the skinning knife. Dugan walked into the mix and kicked the pistol away.

"Homer, get another towel for Stu, the idiot's nose is bleeding so much he could die from blood loss. Howie get Beck to Doc Abrams, looks bad but from what I see, he'll live."

"Are you okay?" Anne said, running to the scene after she heard the gunshot, "Howie, look at me, are you okay?"

Howie turned to his mother, "It's Mr. Beck, he's shot, need to get him to the doctor."

"It's you I'm asking about."

"I'm fine, it's Mr. Beck."

Albert Beck smiled, "Been shot worse Howard, this little thing's nothing." He winced when Barbara pushed a large towel over the wound in his shoulder. Bonita held another, just in case it was needed, Gonzalo held the shopping bag open.

"Not a new one Señora, please I'll be fine, just fine."

"Señor Beck, do not worry, I will charge you for it," she said with a grin. "And thank you."

"Ernesto, I suggest you get your family home," Dugan said. "I'll come out later and ask a few questions. But get them back to the farm. Mr. Beck needs a doctor, Anne can you make sure that he gets there."

"Yes, Jimmy,"

"Señor, you are very lucky today," Bonita said, standing directly in front of Stu, looking up at the bloody man. "Very, very lucky."

The rest of the week went quietly and quickly, almost too quickly, but by Friday at noon the last cherry worth picking was plucked, the last lug filled and the last card punched. The Martinez family, with Barbara in the lead, spent the morning organizing, stacking and folding all of the family's field blankets and baskets near the last row. Howie had just left with the last load of lugs, the sound of the tractor lost in the tangle of trees. Barbara walked over a few rows to look for a few of the buckets still left in the orchard; Gonzalo and Bonita continued busily chasing away the black birds from the tortillas and lunch baskets. It worked some of the time. They finished at 2:00.

Nervous cigarette smoke filled the air that evening, covered by the deep aroma of Walker's Cuban cigar. Scotch, bourbon, and shots of tequila were passed around. Howie snuck out the kitchen door after liberating a cigarette from his grandfather's pack. Albert Beck sat on a bench just outside the barn doors, smoking his pipe, his shoulder heavily bandaged. He grinned when he saw Howie.

"First damn fight I ever really lost, Howard. Only took my eyes off him for a second, but still don't know what I'd have done. I'm not Superman, not as fast as a speeding bullet. I'll be better prepared next time; yes, next time. Light?"

Howie, a bit chagrined, put the cigarette to his lips; Beck lit it with his golden lighter, the bright blue flame illuminating the young man's face.

"Thanks."

"Been an exciting summer, eh boy?"

"Too exciting, death, storms, cherries, it seems all mixed up."

"Howie, my boy, you're young and this'll only prepare you for what life will really be like. It's never easy, life will throw you curve balls and fastballs and you can live by swinging and occasionally striking out, or do nothing and hope to walk. Me, I always take a big swing, a big swing, sometimes for the fences and sometimes just a hard line drive; the idea is to get on base and maybe move a runner or two, just a runner or two. Understand?"

"I understand perfectly, if there's one thing I understand, it's baseball. Yeah, I get it. You have to go to bat and do your best; hopefully, I can do better than one out of three," Howie offered with a smile. "Yes, got to hit better than three hundred."

"Absolutely, I try to hit four-fifty, if I can, yes, four-fifty."

Anne came through the doorway, "And what are you doing young man?"

Howie tried to hide the cigarette quickly, with a sequestered mouthful of incriminating smoke, waiting for an opportunity for release, it pushed on his cheeks, he started to cough. Grey smoke danced in great huffs about his head, Beck and Anne laughed, something everyone needed after the last week. Bill, following his mother on his crutches, saw his brother and joined in, "I told him you'd catch him one day, and there'd be heck to pay. Are you gonna give him a *klip-she-klop-sha*?"

AUGUST

CHAPTER TWENTY-TWO

The days went quickly; Dugan interviewed the Martinez's, he told them that other than wanting to arrest the man for stupidity, which sadly is not illegal, he did charge the man with discharging a weapon inside the city limits, the punishment a hundred dollar fine.

"Wish I could do more but that's all I can do," Dugan said to Ernesto. "Beck wants to get away, so he asked that the attempted murder charge be dropped; with what the man had to drink and all, it would be hard to prove anyway. All I can prove is that he's a certified idiot; I know his wife, and his life will be hell for a while."

Tired, but glad to have the season end, Ernesto met Charlie on the porch to close out the cards. Ernesto offered Charlie and Liz his family's thanks. The picking ended three days after the fight.

"We thank you more than you can imagine," Charlie said. "It's been difficult, but the picking went well and we all made money. This is a little something extra for what you and your family did." Charlie handed Ernesto an envelope.

"Gracias Señora and Señor Smith. We're very thankful for this time here, and we will see you next summer, but please, can it be less exciting? Remember, we see this place as a vacation." The Smiths laughed and Ernesto placed the envelope in his rear pocket; he did not look at it. "We're almost packed and will be out of here early this afternoon, off to Saginaw again for a few weeks to help pull the beets, then south to Indiana for the tomatoes, then maybe north to Texas for the pecans; then home. We're never done."

"You need to settle somewhere, for the children," Liz offered. "It's not too bad here."

"Si, it's nice here, the beaches, yes, but the winters, they are too cold for these old bones, besides Señora Martinez has too many family in Texas, so that's where we'll be. But yes, it's soon time to settle. Besides, there're rumors we won't be needed in a few years to pick the cherries."

"You mean the shakers?" Charlie asked.

"Si, the shakers. I have seen them with the almonds in the south. They grab the tree around its truck with these huge steel arms and the tree begins to shake, like my cousin when he's trying to sober up. Knocks all the nuts off; could do the same with cherries."

"Maybe," Charlie said. "I've heard about them and one of the Millers has seen them at work. If they do come to this part of the world, yes, things will change. Maybe for the better, maybe not, just don't know."

"Yes, Señor Smith, we never know what change does to us, sometimes it helps and sometimes it hurts, we never know. I do know this; change will come like the spring follows winter. It will come and we will deal with it, si?"

"Yes, we will, Señor Martinez. Or, it will deal with us."

Howie stood on the grassy strip that ran through Liz's garden and watched the Martinez's pass with their parade of trucks and cars heading down the hill to the state road; Ernesto and Barbara in the lead with the big truck, followed by his brother and the cousins. Gonzalo waved from the back of the truck as they passed. Earlier Liz walked through the quarters with Barbara and they talked about the changes needed for next year. The state was now requiring many improvements to the temporary quarters for the pickers. Liz agreed that these were necessary but where the money would come from, she didn't know; they would have the winter to figure it out.

An hour after the Martinez's left, Albert Beck, bag over his shoulder, walked up to Liz and Howie. A loose shirt hung on his sharp shoulders, the bandages still visible under the neckline.

"Well, Mrs. Smith, I'm off for Mackinaw, Roger is waiting and going to give me lift as far as Eastport. I'll catch a ride the rest of the way. Howard, take care of yourself; you show great promise, great promise. I have my list as you well know, and this little nick won't set me back. So, no long farewells, if I can, I'll send you a note or a card delineating my progress, and God only knows, maybe I'll be back next year. No promises, no promises."

Beck stuck his hand out and gave Howie's left arm a good bell ringing, then to his surprise, Liz kissed him on the cheek.

"Thank you Albert, there were times this summer and then there were times, as you well know. But if it weren't for you, not sure it would have ended as happily. Thank you."

A bit embarrassed, Beck smiled and bowed as only a gentleman from a hundred years earlier would have bowed. Then, placing his narrow brimmed hat jauntily on top of his head, he tipped its brim and walked through the barn door to Roger's truck.

"Strange as it seems, I'm going to miss that scoundrel," Liz said.

"Me too, Grams, me too."

The next morning, Bill was perched on one of the chairs on the porch, his leg stuck straight out, the heel hung on the edge of another chair.

"This leg stills itches," Bill said to Howie. "It starts in the ankle and then moves up. Noth'en seems to help."

"Can't do anything about it, the doc says it means it's healing."

"Don't care, still itches bad, real bad. Anyway the frogs need to be put back in the pond and now that Dad's back, maybe we can do that later today. What do ya think?"

"Maybe, it's really Gramps' and Dad's schedule," Howie said. "They're finishing things around here now that picken's done. Saw

Roger early this morning with Gramps, then they headed into the orchard. After Dad arrived, he went straight in after them. I'm going see if I can help, maybe then we can go the pond and the beach like Gramps said last week. I'll try and find out."

"Cool."

Howie heard the tractor idling through the trees; occasional clangs could be heard.

"Good morning boy," Roger said when he saw Howie walk out of the trees. "Collecting buckets and stuff left about, start there, and, as we go down the rows, load them on the trailer."

"Got it, morning Dad, morning Gramps."

"Good morning son; your brother okay?"

"Ornery and complaining, yes, he's fine. Gramps, can we go to the pond and to the beach later?"

"Don't see why not, good way to wash off all this dust, besides, we can stop and see Frank. Bill would like that, and then I can get that fish tank out of Liz's living room."

"It wasn't that bad, was it?"

"No, but I had visions of one of those frogs in the sink when I shave in the morning, so it'll be a great relief to have them down in the woods where they belong."

For the next few hours, the group systematically searched the orchard collecting a few ladders, buckets, empty lugs, and bits of garbage left over from the organized chaos of the picking. They almost filled the trailer.

"How could we have missed all this stuff? Amazing," Roger said. "I tried to make sure we picked up as we went along this year. Obviously not. I'll take these lugs to the cannery; they can sort 'em out. The buckets can go to the barn along with the ladders; I'll burn the rest of the junk."

The group stood at the edge of the swath that the tornado cut six weeks earlier. Trees were twisted and knocked about, some uprooted, a few looked like they had been pulled apart by huge hands, and yet a few were bright green, as if nothing had happened. The only problem was they were lying on their sides, to stand never again. Most were shriveled or bare.

"Hard to believe we got almost eighty lugs out of this mess; they gave their best even after all this," Charlie said. "We'll start pulling these out of the orchard after the apples. We'll try to get as much done before the snows fall and the ground freezes, then it'll be impossible. And I was hoping to take Liz to Florida, but not this year again."

"You wouldn't like it Dad," Doug said. "Probably too hot for you."

Roger and Howie sorted through the debris and put the buckets and the ladders into the loft of the barn. They piled the garbage, broken lugs, cardboard and paper from the picker's quarters, as well as the burnt tables and mattresses from the two damaged units in the middle of the gravel staging area.

"Why here, Roger?" Howie asked.

"Lots of nails and metal in this junk; so after it cools, it's easier to rake it out. Burning it in the orchard will only cause mischief later."

The fire rose in a hot and smoky column, Howie thought of the other fires from the past few months, the fire with his vision of the antlerman, the fire in the birches and at the picker's quarters. Fire certainly put a stamp on this summer. Howie watched Gideon as he walked up the split path from the studio.

"Good morning Howie, Roger," Walker said, nodding.

"Gideon. How's Frank doing?" Roger asked.

"As well as can be expected; he gets around but cannot walk except to get to the bathroom. Can barely hold a brush, I have to lay out his paints. My God, is he particular."

Howie and Roger looked at each other and smiled.

"Yes, I know. Even after all these years, I have to admit he's still a pain in the ass. But that's one of things about him I've grown to like. He is a misanthrope and a curmudgeon but he channels that into his painting, wish to hell I could put that into my writing."

"Sometimes that works, sometimes it doesn't," Roger said. "Sometimes you just have to do what God intended. You have no choice in the matter, it is what it is."

Howie looked at the man like he had never heard him say anything before. *"Amazing, people are just amazing,"* he thought.

"Nice fire," Gideon said. "Saw the smoke and panicked, don't need more fire this summer; I've had enough." Gideon looked at Howie and smiled.

"We're going down to the beach, Bill wants to stop and see Uncle Frank," Howie said. "Do you think he would mind?"

"No, I think he would be happy to see all of you. Maybe I'll follow you down to the beach, need a few things from my cabin; haven't been there much these past few weeks."

The fire burned down to a pile of embers; Roger poked and prodded the pile to make sure everything was burned up. He pulled out some springs and cans; the rest would wait until it was cold. Walker headed back to the studio and Howie walked through the barn, heading toward the house.

"I need a smoke," Howie said to no one. He reached under the bench and found the cigarettes and matches and headed out into the orchard, lighting one of the sticks when he was out of sight. The shade from the picked trees cooled the heat of the late summer day. The smoke from his second cigarette filled the space under the trees. He followed the furrows cut into the sand from the tractor and was sure he found the spot where Uncle Frank found Eve; he spotted a bit of blue fabric stuck on a branch. He retrieved it carefully and gently wrapped the bit of cloth over the Petoskey stone; he rubbed the two together and slipped them back into the pouch and his pocket. He walked further and found the cherry with the big horizontal branch where he and Bill had sat and climbed onto the saddle, he lit his third cigarette.

Howie laid his head back against the trunk and gazed up into the branches, brilliant blue held the ragged saw-edged leaves apart, and, in amongst the dark green, a single cherry hung, perfect, glowing in the back-light of the sun, a jewel, a single ruby stone. Plucking the fruit with his misshapen hand, he rolled it about in his fingers, feeling its softness and ripeness and thought of Jennie and the red blanket. He put the berry in his mouth, closed his eyes and crushed the sweetly sour juice onto his tongue, separated the buff stone from the meat, swallowed the pulp and spit the stone out. Summer washed over him in less than a second. He headed back to the house via the **barn.**

"There you are. I've been wondering where you were," Anne said. "We're getting everything together to go to the beach. Bill has somehow managed to get most the bugs from the aquarium into the mason jars, one frog leaped out but I snagged him before he hit the floor. Nice catch if I do say so myself. Grams put a picnic lunch together; just waiting for you."

"I'll put my suit on," Howie said, smiling at his mother as he headed to his room. Would have been fun to watch her catch that frog, was probably heading to the bathroom, to wait for gramps.

Doug pulled the tractor and trailer closer to the house to make it easier for Bill to climb onboard. He laid his crutches out next to him. Anne and Liz hitched a ride along with the baskets of snacks, the frogs and bugs sat in a box next to Bill. He steadied them with his arm. Charlie and Howie followed the parade as it headed toward the studio.

"Frank's not doing well," Charlie said, away from the trailer. "Not sure how long he can make it, or even take it, for that matter. The doc says he could go on for months, he has a strong will to live and that makes a lot of difference. He's wrapping his life up and trying to finish everything he's started. But we always find something that still needs to be done. Eve didn't have that chance, there was little she wanted to finish, and there was little she did finish. Two souls, two different roads."

"I miss her, Gramps. The strange thing is we didn't get along and she was difficult, but I miss her."

"Thanks for that, I'll miss her forever."

The tractor pulled up to the picket fence surrounding the studio. Howie walked to the red door and knocked. Before the sound finished, Gideon opened the door.

"Good afternoon, Frank is excited to see all of you," Gideon said. "He's in the corner finishing a small landscape, I don't know why, but he is. You need help Bill?"

"No sir. I'll just slide off and get my crutches, getting real good with these things."

Howie waded through the canvases to where his uncle sat; a palette in one hand and a brush in the other, the palette shook. A small canvas held his muskrat, not trapped but on his back floating down the creek.

"That is exactly how I remembered him, Uncle Frank, exactly."

"Wonderful animals, no cares, no worries; just doing what God made them to do," Frank said. "This one's for you; something to help you remember this summer."

"There's much to remember."

Howie put his hand on his uncle's shoulder; it shuddered.

"Electricity boy, you gave me a shock, damn you are a bundle of energy. That'll get me through a few more days, I think, thanks."

Everyone found an empty place to stand; Gideon cleared a way through the jumble for Bill who managed not to knock over any paintings and chairs as he worked his way to his uncle.

"Good to see you up and about," Frank said. "Sit here for a moment, I want to talk with you, tell you some secrets. Then you can go to the beach."

Howie showed his parents his sketches and the crucifixion painting; Anne and Doug were proud of his work and stunned by Frank's painting. He tried to avoid the painting of Jennie but his mother pointed it out and smiled.

"You weren't here when he was working on this one, were you?" Anne asked. "From your blushing, I think you were, or maybe you wished you were. She's a very pretty woman, and Douglas, you stop looking at the painting right now."

The family laughed and they all noticed Howie's blush had migrated to his father. Bill stood up from his uncle's side, kissed him on the cheek and announced, "To the beach."

"I'll meet you down there a little later," Gideon said.

Liz and Charlie talked with Frank a moment and then they all managed to get out of the studio without tripping over each other. The loading was more efficient the second time. Doug turned the trailer around through the orchard and then headed down the trail into the woods. Howie turned to wave at Gideon and saw his uncle, through the window, dabbing a bit of paint on the small canvas. The cherries hid the studio as they followed the trailer down the hill.

In amongst the bracken, Doug suddenly stopped the tractor and turned off the engine. He stood, put his finger to his lips and pointed. A hundred yards away, a buck stood looking directly at the group, well antlered, not as regally as his sire, but just as assertive. He shook his withers and bounded into the bracken; two does jumped up behind him and followed him deeper into the woods.

"It didn't take long for the old man to be replaced, did it Howie?" Charlie said. "Nature abhors a vacuum and there's a good sign of it. He's already assembling his harem for the winter, bound to be a few more next spring. Did you see him, Bill?"

"Yes sir, neat-o."

Howie studied the path behind the trailer as the bracken was pushed aside as they moved deeper into the woods, in a narrow area a flash caught his eye. Reaching through the ferns he found Gideon's torch, the lost flashlight. He smiled.

"Good eye, Howie. Mr. Walker will be thrilled to have his flashlight back," Charlie said.

"Yes. He will," Howie answered.

The tractor pulled close to the pond, Bill chose to stay on the trailer and offered Howie the jars to put the captives back into the pond. Howie slid done the sandy slope to the edge of the water. Nothing had changed. He looked about for the snake but it was hiding. Dragonflies flitted about in their busy ways, left to right, up and down. He noticed two were connected; life always went on. He squatted by the water's edge and opened one of the jars. A small frog cleared the rim and flew into the pond in one leap.

"That's the one that tried to escape in the living room," Anne said.

"Thank goodness, I'm still sure he'll show up in my soap dish," Charlie offered.

Howie gently turned the jar into the pond and out swam the bugs and caddis, and all the other bits of life they had watched for the last two months. Bill watched with great interest.

"Make sure they all get back into the water,"

"They will," Howie answered. "Now for the second jar."

"Snake!" Bill yelled.

Howie jerked up and slid, bottom down, into the water with a great splash. He sat there soaking up pond water as he turned to his brother and his family, all were laughing at his expense.

"Very funny, very funny," was all he could muster. "At least I'm in my swim trunks this time." He released the other detainees while he sat in the green water.

The empty beach stretched as far as they could see, the Martinez's were gone and they had it all to themselves.

"It's like I remembered it as a little girl when my family stayed here," Liz said standing on the dune and looking up the shoreline. "There were times when we would come down here and not see anyone for a week. But there are more cottages now, like the Gardener's, and few others up a ways but still not many. Won't be like that a few years from now, it's too damn pretty to keep folks away for too long. Sad to see that happen, but today it is ours."

They picnicked near the water so Bill could get close. Charlie drove the tractor and trailer a few feet into Lake Michigan so Bill could wave his hand through the water.

"There Howie," Bill said pointing. "A muskie, a little bigger than a month ago."

Howie waded out and even though he couldn't see the fingerlings, he agreed they were getting bigger.

Gideon, smoking a large cigar, joined the group and sat next to Bill on the sand.

"I'm trying to make him as comfortable as possible, but it's difficult. He just loves to fight."

"Been doing that his whole life, Mr. Walker," Liz said. "Spain, Paris, Chicago, here. He's fought his whole life to stay alive, maybe even to stay sane. It gives him a good reason to keep going forward with his life. I thought he spent most of it alone when he was in Spain; I'm glad I know differently now. Thank you."

"Thank you for that, Mrs. Smith," Gideon said.

"I found this when we came down through the woods," Howie said. He held up a dark green flashlight. "Almost ran over it, the trailer broke through some of the bracken and there it was, sitting on the sand."

Gideon took the torch, as he called it, and sat it next to Bill on the sand. "Thanks, Howie, had it a long time, carried it with me wherever I went, would have missed it, thanks." He turned to Bill, "Young man, I want you to have this torch, never lose it. Remember, it was this light that helped me find you. Always keep it dry and clean and oil it occasionally to keep the rust out. Use good batteries too."

Bill took the flashlight. "Torch?"

"The British call it a torch. We call it a flashlight; I think their word makes more sense. An English soldier gave it to me just after the Battle of the Bulge. I was a bit shaken then and I needed to get back to my tent, it was bitterly cold and dark. He said 'Take this Yank and you'll never get lost.' So I did and now you have it. So I say to you Bill: Take it Yank and never get lost, again."

They wound their way back up to the farm as dusk settled in. It was all too quiet now without the Mexican music coming out of the quarters and the sound of Spanish lilting about. Doug pulled the tractor into the barn; he left the trailer attached. Everyone regrouped on the porch for cocktails and cokes.

Howie found some replacement batteries for Bill's torch and the spot of light danced through the evening on the ceiling of the porch, Charlie made shadow puppets with his hands. A large moth flew across the porch lamp and landed on the rough wall, near the light.

"A luna moth, Howie, very rare to see one," Liz said. "They live for only a week as a moth, never eat, and spend their short lives looking for a mate. They mate, she lays the eggs, then they die. Look there." Liz pointed to the dark shadows off the porch; another lime green moth flew from the darkness toward the light. Almost on cue the first flapped once and took after the second, they twisted together just below the ceiling, across the roof, back to the light and then, were gone.

It was quiet for a moment then Charlie said, "After that, I need a cigarette."

The family on the porch erupted into laughter.

"What's so funny?" Bill asked.

Howie sat back, wishing he could have a smoke, too.

CHAPTER TWENTY-THREE

Howie pulled the covers over his head. The first shafts of sunlight streamed through the window and danced with the tree leaves on the old wallpaper of his bedroom. Only a few more days and he would wake up in Chicago. High school and a whole new world was three weeks away; maybe he could make a little more money caddying. So far, it had been a good summer, a thick roll of money stashed in the upper drawer of the dresser proved it. A few more bucks and he would be a rich man at fourteen years old.

Howie thought about church later in the morning; then the afternoon he'd spend in Elk River, maybe fishing one last time. Bill asked him to catch one for him; he wanted to stay at the farm with Charlie. The smell of bacon forced him to push the covers down, get up and get dressed; Sunday's uniform would come later. He stood in the doorway of the kitchen and watched the familiar scene: Charlie sitting at the table, coffee in one hand, a cigarette in the other, grumbling over the newspaper and the strange disconnected world ten thousand miles away; Grams pushed potatoes back and forth in a huge black iron fry pan, bacon laid out on a towel, Dad reading yesterday's Record Eagle.

"Good morning son," Anne said, putting her hand on his blond head. "You okay this morning?"

"Great Mom, real good! Grams, I think I will have coffee this morning, need to get to like the stuff sometime and it might as well be now."

The people in the room looked at Howie like he had announced he was joining the priesthood.

"Say it's not so, boy," Charlie said with a laugh. "Doug, he's finally growing up. Thought it would never happen, come boy, sit by me, I'll educate you on the proper way to fix coffee."

"Was wondering the same thing, Dad," Doug added. "Next thing he'll be asking for is a cigarette," as he crushed his first one of the morning.

"Not a chance," Anne admonished. "It's bad enough around here; you don't have to encourage it."

"Amen," Liz said joining in.

"Weather should hold for a few weeks, if fall is normal," Charlie said changing the subject. "Could use the break, it's been a rough summer with the rain and the heat. But then again it's never easy."

Bill finally woke up and, after a short trip through the kitchen to the bathroom, settled into a corner chair, his leg out of the way not blocking any paths. Anne placed the dishes next to Liz; she began to ladle out scrambled eggs, potatoes and bacon and then transferred the plates to the table along with more coffee and juice.

Halfway through his second glass of orange juice, Howie saw Gideon crossing the lawn, coming toward the door. Howie stood, something was not right. Gideon paused at the door for a moment, before calling through the screen.

"Good morning all, Liz can I talk to you please?"

Liz stood wiping her hands on a towel, "Come in Mr. Walker."

"No ma'am, just a few words outside."

Liz crossed to the door and went outside and stood next to Gideon, she craned her neck upwards to look into his face. After a moment, she put the towel to her eyes and her other hand on his cheek, he leaned down and kissed her, smiled and walked back across the lawn; she returned to the kitchen.

After a moment to compose herself she said, "Frank died last night, seems it was in his sleep."

Howie quickly went through the screen door, passed Gideon and began to run toward the studio, tears started to form but were wiped away by his hand. He slowed, pulled the gate open and, with apprehension, stood in the half-opened red door. Music flowed through the opening; he pushed the door inward. The notes from the Rachmaninoff symphony carried through the small studio and filled it to overflowing, a slight haze of turpentine and cigar smoke hung in the room. Howie walked toward his uncle's bedroom, hesitantly.

Frank Rex lay on his bed; a well-worn white sheet covered him, only his face and hands visible. Howie knew Gideon must have arranged his uncle before he came to the house; Frank's face, no longer taut from pain, looked relaxed, almost soft. His beard, neat and crisp, hair combed. A large shadow cast itself over Howie and onto the bed.

"I found him this morning; he passed away during the night," Gideon offered, "I was asleep on the couch and went to see him early; he was gone. It was the best thing for him; he hated complex goodbyes and all the fuss. 'Today was a wonderful day,' he said last night, 'one of my best.' He was finished and complete."

"Did you..." Howie started to say.

"Prepare him? Yes I did, even clipped his beard a bit and combed that mop of hair. I'm sure he wouldn't have wanted Liz to see him the way I found him."

The studio began to fill with family. Liz sat on the side of the bed and placed her hand against her brother's face. Charlie stood immediately behind her; Doug put both his hands on Howie's shoulders.

"Where's Bill?" Howie asked.

"He's coming. Roger and Lisa pulled in for a moment on the way to early Mass. They're bringing him in their car." After Roger and Lisa arrived with Bill, the studio finally reached its bursting point.

"Mr. Walker, did you have breakfast?" Anne asked.

"No, Anne, I haven't."

"Let's move some of this crowd back to the house. I'll make you a good breakfast. This'll be a long day and we should all get something to eat."

"I'll stay here with Uncle Frank, be up to the house later," Howie said. "Bill, you want to stay too?"

"I'll stay, the couch is comfortable and I can put this leg up."

"Anne, I'll stay here with the boys," Doug said. "Dad, I think you need to get the doctor to make all of this official or whatever is needed. I think God will forgive us for not going to church this morning; I'll call Father O'Brien after the last service to begin the arrangements."

"He wanted nothing to do with the funeral home," Liz said. "Didn't want himself prepared or anything; wanted to be as natural as possible. We'll have the wake here tomorrow, funeral on Tuesday; if it can be arranged. Okay?"

"I'll talk to Father O'Brien after Mass today," Roger added. "I'll tell him you'll stop by later."

"Thanks Roger," Charlie said.

Half the group left and went back to the house, Roger and Lisa headed into Elk River.

"I'll miss him," Howie said to his father. "I'll miss him a lot. Next to you and gramps, he is the most important man I know. He'll leave a big hole in my life. He'll always be here, but just a bit out of my reach. I wish I knew him better, more to remember."

"I'll miss him also; he's been here my whole life. But I still never really understood him, James did, I think. They were very close; maybe it was the art they both had in their souls. I don't know, but that could have been part of it. Mom said, when James died, he was full of rage and hatred for what the war had done. He was almost inconsolable for weeks after the letter came, even worse than your grandmother."

Howie turned and watched his brother studiously working in one of his sketchbooks. Howie smiled.

"You doing okay?"

"Just working on this teacup, I need to make it hold water. That was one of the last things Uncle Frank said to me, so I need to make it perfect."

To Howie, the next few hours were a blur. The doctor arrived, as well as Jimmy Dugan. The doctor wrote up the death certificate. Jimmy made sure all the legal issues were dealt with, as few as there were, more out of respect for Frank Rex than anything official.

Father O'Brien came shortly after Dugan and the doctor left.

"Roger told me about Frank. I gave him his Last Rights when I was here a few days ago; he seemed to be a closer to the Church these past few months and his paintings certainly show it. We had some good conversations over the years, I'll miss him. Charlie, why don't you come up to the church later and we can make the arrangements."

Anne returned with fried egg sandwiches for Howie and Bill and a thermos of coffee for Doug; Howie also had a cup. Howie and his dad decided to collect the canvases and put them along the wall in the bedroom.

"Need to make as much room as possible," Doug said. "We can move Frank into the main room. It'll be better for the mourners when they come through. Liz and mom can set up food and drinks at the house. The weather is supposed to be good the next few days, so people can park at the house, walk out here and then head back for something to eat."

Howie made two trips with the canvases and set them near the stack in the corner; he peeked at the paintings of Gideon. He had grown to admire Gideon over the last few weeks; his attention to Uncle Frank impressed him the most. This man, his giant, was huge and intimidating and yet quiet and soft hearted; Howie knew that when Gideon Walker walked into a room, everything stopped, and only started again when he began to talk with people. The paintings showed that.

"Strange," Howie thought, *"how paintings of nude men are looked at differently than paintings of nude women; both can be strongly composed and executed, yet the reactions of people are very different."*

Charlie and Gideon sat two sawhorses in the middle of the room near the windows that overlooked the woods. Three planks bridged the gap, sheets were draped over the planks. The three men and Howie gently placed Frank on the sheet and then covered him with a beautiful quilt that had been his mother's. Howie was amazed at how light his uncle had become. Liz approved of the arrangement. She brought great armfuls of flowers from her garden and Frank's. Color, like it was pulled from his paintings, filled the room and scented the air of late summer.

They placed the Crucifixion painting on an easel off to one side, visible to everyone who entered.

Charlie returned from his meeting with Father O'Brien late in the afternoon.

"The service will be Tuesday morning at 10:00," Charlie said. "The funeral director understood why we wanted the wake at the studio; he will be here with the casket early Tuesday to prepare Frank for the service. He also contacted the cemetery and arranged for the excavation." Charlie turned to his wife, "I told him to bury Frank in the first plot near your father. That okay?"

"Yes, that'll be fine; it was the one he wanted."

After a quiet somber dinner, Liz talked about Frank and when they were young, traveling to Paris and Spain. She could never confirm the stories he told about fighting alongside Ernest Hemingway, but then again she could never find enough evidence to support that it didn't happen. She told Howie about the small art school on the Left Bank of the Seine that Frank attended twice, once before the war and once after.

"He was a stubborn proud man. He would paint the way he wanted to, not their way. That was probably why he was never popular with the art crowd. But his clients appreciated his work, they continued to come back and have him paint their families and then their friends. Even in these days of color photography, paintings give the subject more permanence and a sense of immortality. Something like sculpturing, the piece will go on forever; long after the subject is dead."

"Father O'Brien asked if the Crucifixion could be hung during the service," Charlie said. "He has a place for it in the church."

"Where?" Howie asked.

"He would like to replace one of the smaller paintings Frank did for the Stations of the Cross, the one where the crucifixion is, with this painting. I told him the family would be honored. I'll take the painting over tomorrow evening, after the wake. Four o'clock, Liz?"

"Yes, four to seven."

Howie remembered the start of the painting, the conté crayon in the early morning light. "*Structure*," Frank said, "*structure*." Howie smiled.

Howie spent a fitful night after the long day; his uncle was never far from his thoughts. The wind changed during the early morning and he heard it blowing through the pines behind the farm. Great swooshing sounds, almost like breathing. He would fall asleep, then wake, then sleep again.

The door in the hall opened slowly, a shape formed from the light at the top of the stairs.

"Howie, you awake?" his mother asked.

"Yes mother."

Anne crossed through the room and sat on the side of the bed after turning on the small lamp on the bureau.

"Are you okay?"

"Yes, actually I am. Been lying here thinking about Uncle Frank and this past summer; it's been something frightful and at the same time exciting. And now, with Uncle Frank dying, it all seems so unreal, like all this was going on around me and I'm just watching it. Like none of it's real and I've been making it up in my head."

"For a while this summer, we thought you were," Anne said. "Dad and I truly believed something was going on but couldn't figure it out. But in the end, it resolved itself and you weren't seeing things or imagining any of it. Yes, it was all unreal but very real."

"Yes, ma'am."

"Your father and I have been talking about the wake and the funeral, there's a point in the Mass where people can say things about the person; it's called a eulogy. It is a short but sincere recollection about the person. Liz is going to say some things about her brother but we were hoping you would be the one to give the eulogy."

Howie sat up in bed.

"Me, I can't do that. I don't know how to make a speech, what would I say? And what about Mr. Walker, he could say something, he knows him real well, better than most of us."

"I don't think people around here would understand Mr. Walker and Uncle Frank's relationship. There would be far more questions than answers. I'll help you get started and you say what's in your heart, what you remember and why you loved him. You think about it and we can talk a little later. Maybe Mr. Walker can help you; I think Uncle Frank would be honored to have you say something."

Anne left Howie and shut the door. In the early morning light, Howie's mind raced with thoughts of what to say. He truly loved and admired his uncle but how could he say something about a man and his entire life, how to shorten it into a sentence or even a paragraph, his uncle would need a book's worth.

After a somber breakfast, very different than when Gideon Walker walked to the door, Liz sat on the porch, a cup of coffee in her hand, Charlie next to her. Smoke hung about the ceiling, the air still after the front that quietly passed during the night. An overcast sky took all the shadows out of the landscape, Doug walked on to the porch, lit a cigarette and sat next to his mother.

"I think summer's over, Mom. I'll take the family back to Chicago on Wednesday. I need to get back and the kids need to get ready for school, I'll try to get back for the apples, just don't know."

"I understand," Liz said, putting her hand on her son's. "You need to do what needs to be done. We'll miss all of you."

"I am not sure where I am going with all of this? We love it up here but there's no way to make a living with two kids and all. Not a lot in Chicago either but at least there are opportunities."

"I know son," Charlie said. "Never was much of anything up here other than lumbering and farming. The lumbering died and farming is just hanging on. From time to time we've thought about following you down to Chicago but I could not, for the life of me, figure out what I could do there. All I know is this." Charlie waved his arm at the orchard. "This is all I have, all one man can say about his life."

"Don't get cynical on me old man; we've had a great life, and a great love. They may be all you think you're worth," Liz said, pointing at the cherries. "But they're nothing, they're just trees. They freeze, they burn, they live, and they die. They provide a few dollars a year in an attempt to convince and bribe us that they need us. Maybe they do, but we don't need them, we need each other. Douglas, I don't know what you need to do, that choice is yours and Anne's, but I do know that a lot of what's up here will be wanted by someone in the future: the lake, the beach, the woods, and the air. There's nothing like this in Chicago or any big city. Someday people will want to be here, even if for a short time, to get back to their roots. We'll be gone, but you and your boys will see it."

"What are all of you discussing so seriously?" Anne asked, coming through the door, surveying the three. "There's nothing more serious than what I have to tell you." A small smile formed.

Liz looked at Anne for a long moment and smiled, "When?"

"What are you talking about?" Doug said crooking his head.

"Men," Anne said looking at Liz with a big smile. "Maybe April, I think."

"What's in April," Doug continued and then, all of a sudden, he stood, took a step toward his wife, put his arms around her and gave her a soft kiss on her cheek. "April will be wonderful, you ready for this, one more time?"

"I'll let you know, but for the moment, considering the day ahead of us, I think a little good news is in order. I was going to say something yesterday but, as usual, Frank upstaged me by dying."

"He was that way, would always crash someone else's party or make sure his point of view was heard. But when I get the chance, I'll tell him this was going a little to the extreme. Don't you think, Liz?" **Charlie** said.

"Yes, Charles, he was always incorrigible, but that's why I loved him."

Anne and Doug stepped off the porch and slowly walked through the garden. Liz watched and wondered where they would be in ten years. "The little one will be Bill's age, Bill nineteen, and Howie twenty-four. How will they change, what will the world be like. Hell, will I even be alive? Will there even be a world to worry about?" She shook her head and cleared her thoughts.

The funeral director came out for a brief discussion with Liz and Charlie, before going out to the studio. They selected a simple casket, discussed the timing and the arrangements for tomorrow. Since Frank was not embalmed, the service would not be delayed or dragged out. Frank wanted it that way and he was getting his wish.

Anne helped Bill put on his Sunday outfit. She had laid open the pant seam to allow for the cast. Howie also put on a clean shirt and pants with a crease, socks and polished hard leather dress shoes. They all drove out to the studio, Bill's leg made Howie's seat a bit crowded and uncomfortable.

The visitors began arriving just before four. None had ever been to the studio and most were surprised it was even there. Some came because they knew Liz and Charlie; some knew Frank Rex, most came out of respect for the family. No one asked about Gideon and only one person asked how he knew Frank.

"Met him while traveling in Europe, you know he spent his winters in Spain," Gideon said to the visitor. "No, well he would spend his winters in Spain, actually near Barcelona. We became friends, and I would see him when he was there. Me? Actually I grew up in Grosse Point, loved it up here, but still live in Europe. Germany actually. But I was here for the summer, family matters, and I heard about Frank's death and thought I could help the Smith's, so that's why I'm here."

At times, the size of the studio required that people stand outside to talk and smoke. After they paid their respects to Frank, they all stopped at the house to see Liz and Charlie. Most did not stay long. The last few left before seven.

"Well, that's done," Liz said, exhausted. "About what I expected; Frank was always a bit outside the townsfolk. They thought he was that crazy painter out at the Smith's, only a few knew he grew up around here. I think some came to see if he was really dead. You doing okay?"

"I'm fine," Anne answered, knowing Liz had asked about the baby. "Been through this before, got a good idea what to expect."

"Have you told the boys?"

"Told me what?" Howie asked from the end of the kitchen table. "What?"

"Well, Howard Smith, and you too, William," Anne said turning her head toward the pantry. "It looks like you will be having another brother or sister in April. Can you handle that?"

Howie thought about what he heard. "That's great; just as soon as I help get one baby grown up, I have to help another."

"I heard that," a voice called out from the pantry.

"As I was saying, before being rudely interrupted, I have to start to raise another, all the baby sitting and all that other icky stuff with diapers and feeding. I really hope it will be a girl. I just couldn't deal with another boy."

"I heard that too," Bill said.

Howie ignored his brother's remarks. "That's wonderful, mom. Seems strange that Uncle Frank dies and another human being is going to be born, kind of like life in a small package."

"Well now Howard Smith that was profound," Liz said, "very profound indeed. How is your eulogy coming along?"

"Working on it, but not sure how it'll turn out, talked to Mr. Walker a bit, him being a writer and all, he suggested a few things. But I'm working on it."

Liz and Anne watched Howie leave and heard his footsteps on the stairs.

"Anne, he'll grow up to be a wonderful man."

"Who said he hasn't already grown up," Anne answered smiling at Liz.

CHAPTER TWENTY-FOUR

The morning broke fresh and inspiring. As promised, the funeral director met Charlie at the house and they went to the studio together. Howie and Doug walked out, following the hearse. This was men's work as Charlie put it, moving Frank's body and the coffin were not going to be easy. Gideon was sitting outside, smoking a cigar.

"I loved the man but after two days, things are beginning to get a bit strong in there," Gideon said with a smile.

The director looked at Gideon with a quizzical look. "Charlie, I told you it would be a good idea to embalm."

"And I said no, Mr. Connelly. Frank said no and that's the way it is, and the coffin was expensive enough to help us cover other expenses, so let's leave it there."

The three men and Howie pulled the coffin from the hearse and discovered that they each had to hold on to a corner to get it through the door. The door was not wide enough for a coffin and four bodies on each side, so getting the body out would be tricky.

"I think he knew all along this would happen, just one more laugh on us," Charlie said.

"Gramps I think he wanted to never leave his studio," Howie offered.

"I suggest we agree that that's the case. I'll get a sledge and pick and we will open a hole in the floor and leave him here, shouldn't take more than an hour or two," Charlie said.

"Fine idea Dad, much better here," Doug said.

"Sir, I don't think that's possible," the director interrupted. "No, not possible at all!"

"Doug, remember this, funeral directors do not have a sense of humor."

They set the coffin parallel to the bier; Gideon had placed a sheet over Frank's face. The four again took hold of the fabric and lifted Frank from the sawhorses and placed him in the coffin.

"He felt lighter than Sunday, Dad," Howie said.

"Yes a bit, maybe his soul had not left when we moved him the first time. When he saw all was well, he decided it was time and moved on."

Charlie looked over at the director. "Mr. Connelly, if you say one word about biology, we'll take care of everything, ourselves."

The director was obviously disappointed that he couldn't contribute to the conversation in a scientific way.

"There were a few biological functions that had to be dealt with, Mr. Smith, Doug you understand. I took care of them," Gideon added.

"Thank you, Mr. Walker, being an aide during the war did have some value."

Again the director looked at Gideon with curiosity. He looked over at Charlie and forgot the question he was going to ask.

"In days gone by, when a person died, they garnished his coffin with things of his life, to comfort him in his travels," Gideon said. "Gentlemen, what gifts do you have for Frank?"

Decisions had been made before they left the house; they were prepared. Charlie began the service.

"Franklin Rex, your sister offers these copies of Ernest Hemingway's *Death in the Afternoon* and the story *Big Two Hearted River*, to help you remember Spain and Michigan." He placed the books in the coffin. "Anne would like you to carry this candle as a light when you need it." He set the large white candle next to the books. "Gideon," Charlie asked looking at the man.

Gideon walked over to his friend and opened a small jar and

slowly poured sand over the corpse. "Sand from Spain, my dearest friend, may it mingle with your bones forever."

Howie placed a small painting of a teacup in the coffin. "This painting is from Bill, he says he will miss you very much and it now holds water," he turned and took three steps to the bookcase; there he slowly slid out a sketchbook. "Uncle, now that you are talking with Anna from the small village in Spain, please show her your sketches."

Doug retrieved an envelope and gently placed it on his uncle's chest, "I don't know whether you ever read this article, it was one of my first. It was about you and painting and your art; enjoy it."

Charlie turned from the group and walked to the red door and pulled a large folding knife from his pocket; reaching almost to the top of the door, he cut a long piece from its side; red paint chips fell to the floor. "Frank, almost everyone who has known you, loved you, tolerated you, and, in one or two cases wanted to kick your ass, has passed through that door. They all touched it. They'll be with you and your dust till the end of time." He placed the slice of the red door on the body.

The funeral director, a little put off by the ceremony, but, after being assured by Charlie it was over, closed and secured the lid. They found that the planks were longer than the coffin and after placing Frank and the coffin back on the sawhorses they used the extra purchase to easily navigate their way through the studio and into the back of the hearse.

"Everyone to the house to change clothes. Father O'Brien is expecting us at 9:30; we will not be late. Mr. Walker?"

"Not a problem, Charlie, I can easily get back to my cabin and to the car, completely forgot about the damn thing for the last few days. I'll see you there."

They followed the hearse to the farm; the girls came out and joined the men. They all stood together as Frank Rex made his last trip from the orchard, the studio, and the woods.

At 9:30, the family gathered in the community room behind the church. The Smiths', or at least the four adults, talked with Father O'Brien about the Mass and the graveside service at the cemetery.

Anne left the group and walked over to Howie and Bill.

"You two still okay?"

"Yes ma'am, Howie was telling me about putting Uncle Frank in the coffin; he said my painting was perfect."

"Yes, Bill. It was perfect and he'll hang it in his house in heaven," Anne said.

"Mother, even I know they don't have houses in heaven," Bill said.

"And how do you know that, young man?"

"Everyone has a mansion in heaven, houses are just not big enough," the grin on Bill's face made her smile.

"Howie, let's get your brother into the church and settled. Do you have your eulogy with you?"

"Yes Mother, inside my jacket," he padded his chest. "I practiced maybe fifty times, so I hope I can do it."

"You'll be fine."

Bill finally had mastered his crutches and with an open road and hard pavement he could not be stopped. He had a little trouble with the steps, but his cousin ran up to give him hand.

"Hello John," Bill said as they made the top step.

"Sorry we could not get over to see you, but I heard. I am glad you're okay. Cool cast. Can I sign it?" John Walsh asked.

"After we come back from the cemetery, we're all getting together in the hall," Howie added.

"Howard," a young voice called up from the bottom of the steps.

"Good morning, Margaret, how're you?"

"I'm very good. I'm very sorry about our Uncle Frank. I think, through my mom, a couple of steps removed, so I guess he was my uncle as well. He'll be missed. I know you liked him very much."

"Yes, Margaret, I did."

Howie moved Bill to the front row. Their parents sat in the center, then Bill, then Howie on the end; it would easier for him to stand at the appropriate time and not have to crawl over people. Liz and Charlie, and Roger and Lisa sat on the opposite side. Frank's coffin was placed in the center of the aisle in front of the altar and the communion rail. It was closed. The casket sat where Eve's casket had sat two months before.

A small bell rang, the congregation stood and Father O'Brien and two altar boys crossed the chancel and knelt before the altar. The priest stood between the boys in robes that Howie had never seen before, they were spectacular with color and designs woven into the fabric.

"Your uncle designed the vestments," Liz said before the service began. "Sadly, he never saw them in use."

"*Requiem aeternam dona eis, Domine,*'" Father O'Brien began.

The Mass proceeded and, after the Communion, Father O'Brien nodded to Howie. Taking a deep breath, and after a mother's gentle squeeze of his hand, he stood and walked toward the casket and placed his hand on the rich cloths the priest had laid over the remains, then proceeded though the gate in the Communion rail to the pulpit. Standing at the pulpit, he realized how much he had grown this summer, he could read his paper without standing on his toes. Howie looked out over the congregation and saw many faces he recognized and many he did not. Gideon sat in the last row, he smiled at Howie and it helped him relax.

"If my Uncle was a builder I would ask you how to measure the man. If he had been a writer I would ask for your words to describe him, and if he had been a farmer we would be talking about how well his farm looked and about the crops he grew. But my Uncle Frank was different, he was an artist and a painter, I will try to describe him with what he knew best, colors."

"To him red was life and it was death, he lived a life of lush deep vermillion and cherry red. Blue was Spain and the deep color of the Mediterranean, and the blue of Lake Michigan and the cerulean skies of both lands he loved. Green was the farm and the woods, the light celadon of spring cherries and the deep cobalt green of the pines and hemlocks. Yellow is in the buff colored sand of the dunes of Michigan that hid his secrets, and pink was the soft curve of a women's neck and the color in the face of the child in the Madonnas he painted." Howie looked at Gideon, he was smiling.

"But my Uncle also lived in black and white. His moods swung back and forth with the moods of these two opposite colors. Dark moody days were eclipsed by the brightness of sunny days; his love of the Church was continually challenged by his confusion over its public acts. He lived deep in the soul of the Church but many times the colors that the Church showed disappointed him."

"This morning, my uncle lies before you and God, in this church that, for many years, has become a gallery of his work. Not a gallery for his glory but for the glory of the Holy Family. For my uncle, the family was all there was. His parents, my grandparents, my parents and brother, cousins and close friends were his life; their memories and these paintings will keep him alive. I will never walk into this church without seeing my Uncle in the third row."

Howie slowly folded the paper and put it into his jacket's pocket. A hand sat on his shoulder and Father O'Brien extended his hand.

"Thank you, Howard, he would be happy to hear those words. Now it's my turn."

Father O'Brien stood to one side as Howie left the pulpit. Anne and Doug both smiled at their son, Bill gave him a nudge.

"The last time I met with Frank," Father O'Brien said, "he offered the Church one of his greatest paintings, in fact, the paint is still wet." He turned to an easel standing off to one side behind the pulpit; it was draped with a soft golden cloth. Father O'Brien slowly removed the drape and offered the painting of Christ to the congregation. Whispers rolled through the church and then one small pair of delicate hands began to clap, Margaret's. Soon the rest of congregation softly applauded the work and, through the painting, the man. Liz smiled through her tears. Father O'Brien gently raised the painting over his head and slowly carried it to the place, along one side of the church, where the older Crucifixion painting had been removed. He hung the painting. He smiled when he saw the red and deep blue oil paint on the tips of his thumbs.

The priest returned to the altar, Liz completed the eulogies with a few simple words and the Mass was finished. Father O'Brien announced the burial would be at the cemetery and would begin as soon as all were assembled. After the priest left the altar, the congregation rose and began to leave. Charlie, Doug, Howie and Roger stayed behind and helped the funeral director move the casket to the hearse.

"Certainly easier with wheels, don't you think Howie?" Charlie said with a smile.

Howie looked at his grandfather, "Mr. Walker?"

"He asked to stay off to the side, less questions that need answers. I tried to have him move forward but he's very comfortable with his place in all this."

The ride to the cemetery took just minutes. The sky was the blue Frank loved; not washed out, but sharp, edgy. The horizon was crisp; it had not started to grey. They sat the casket on the planks over the hole in the ground. Howie looked at another grave less than fifty feet away, Eve's marker had been placed and Charlie made sure there were fresh flowers from the garden there every week. People wandered through the cemetery looking at markers and old graves, many were family, most were curious.

There were few tears during the brief service, mourners placed red roses on the casket and Gideon placed one single white rose over the others.

"Liz, I'll meet you back at the house. It's important you meet with your family and friends; we'll have dinner later. My treat."

"That's not necessary, Mr. Walker."

"No arguments, I'm making dinner and it will be ready at 6:00. So take your time and I'll see you then."

"Thank you, Gideon."

Howie stood on the small hill that overlooked the family plots and watched the priest and the workers repeat the same rituals to lower the casket into the ground that they did with Eve. Father O'Brien stood stiffly over the grave and slowly poured the sandy dirt onto the casket, Howie thought of the sand from Spain, crossed himself and turned away; he did not want to see the grave being filled.

When the family returned to the church hall, they found it already crowded; food appeared from everywhere. The casseroles, hams, fried chicken, bean salads and coleslaws sat in large bowls arranged on the long tables. Liz and Anne were amazed. Bottles of coke and root beer were nestled in ice in large galvanized tubs. Bill asked his cousin to help him load a plate with food and then they retired to a corner table, he placed his leg on a folding chair and put a drumstick in his mouth. John took a pen and wrote on the white plaster. Howie smiled at his antics.

"That is a beautiful painting, Howard. Our uncle was very good. I could feel the pain in the face of Christ and the women at his feet. It will serve his memory for a very long time."

"Thank you, Margaret."

"Hungry? I haven't eaten since last night with communion and all; I'm starved."

Howie realized that with all the excitement he hadn't eaten since the evening before. But now, he was famished.

Both found an opening in the line and she helped hold his plate as he filled it. Howie pulled two cokes from the ice chest; Margaret pointed to a table in the corner.

"That was a wonderful remembrance this morning; I could see Uncle Frank in all the colors you talked about, especially the Spanish red. I was only at his studio once, a few years ago when my father had Mr. Rex paint my picture. I remember the deep red door to his studio. A wonderful red, almost like it was on fire. The studio was very mysterious and, if think about it, very crowded with paintings."

"It still is; paintings are everywhere."

"I sat for about two hours; Dad still says whenever he talks about the painting that I fidgeted the whole time. It's hanging in the living room. Mr. Rex almost gave up, but finally got most of what he needed; he finished it without me. I don't think it looks like me, but then again I was eleven when it was painted. I am much more mature now."

"She's becoming a woman," Howie thought, and admired what he saw. Her red hair fell to her shoulders, her face and most certainly her body had begun to fill out as only a woman's would and her eyes sparkled.

"We're going home later this week, maybe tomorrow," Howie said. "It's up to Dad. But between the funeral and everything else, Mom started packing up all our stuff, so I think we're leaving tomorrow. It's been a wonderfully strange summer, Margaret. One, I know, I'll never forget."

"I really enjoyed the Cherry Festival, really."

"So did I, finished?"

"Stuffed, let's go for a walk. It's so nice outside; a short walk would be great."

Howie scanned the crowd and caught his mother's eye. Anne waved and Howie pointed to Margaret and then to the outside. Anne smiled and turned back to the group of people and their conversation.

Howie held the door for his cousin and they both walked toward the far side of the church. The small hill the church sat on overlooked Elk Lake, and, through the trees, Lake Michigan. A small clearing contained a bench and the view. Margaret sat and patted the bench and offered a seat to Howie. Not knowing exactly why, Howie sat.

"I'll miss you a lot when you go home. I mean it, I'll miss you a whole lot."

"Margaret, I'll miss you too," Howie said, not exactly understanding the meaning of her comments.

Howie turned his face to hers and, without any warning, Margaret placed both her hands on each side of his face and kissed him. Not a quick peck on the lips, or a cousin saying goodbye type kiss, it was an exploding flashbulbs and ringing carnival bells engulfing kind of kiss. For Howard Smith, it was the most exciting thing he had ever done in his life. *"Don't stop,"* was all he could think of. Margaret stopped.

"Why?" Howie asked, as if Christmas had passed too quickly.

"Why, what?"

"Why did you stop?"

"A girl has to breathe, Howard."

"Well, you should learn to hold your breath," and, for the first time, Howard Franklin Smith kissed a girl, or in Margaret's case, a young woman. The lights and bells returned, and a not uncomfortable feeling began to grow. His breathing was short, yet deep; Margaret's breathing the same. He held her close and the light fragrance of her face and hair intoxicated him. He later remembered looking at the church through a gauzy view of auburn hair. He took deep breaths, and she kissed him back.

Finally, they sat back against the bench, she took his withered hand.

"I *will* miss you. Please write me a note or two, I'll write you. We should not be serious pen pals but a short letter or two to talk about music or art or school or even baseball would be nice. Maybe when you come up for Thanksgiving or Christmas we can see each other, I'd like that. I'll be away in Detroit, but I can come back here any time you're here."

Howie ran his tongue over his lips; he could still taste her kiss. "Yes, letters would be nice, but I am not sure what the folks have planned for this winter. I'll write you and let you know."

"We need to get back, people may talk," she said with a smile.

"I hope so," Howie said without thinking.

She leaned over again and kissed Howie, a long, and lasting through the deep snows of winter kiss.

The ride back to the farm was quiet except for Bill pointing out the new signatures all over his cast. Even Father O'Brien had signed it.

"This one was from Margaret; why she wanted to sign my cast I don't know. She said something about you Howie, and that you'll remember her each time you look at my leg. Girls are weird, just plain weird."

Howie smiled and looked at her name on Bill's cast. She was right.

"We're heading home tomorrow boys, get your suitcases packed this afternoon and any stuff you want to take home. You can probably leave your fishing gear at the farm for next summer. Okay?"

"That'll work, Mom," Howie answered. "I'm going out to the studio for one last look and tidy it up a bit. Grams said she'll lock it up later in the month for the winter."

"Do not stay out there too long. Mr. Walker said he would be making dinner; he's also leaving, going back to Germany."

"I'll miss my giant," Bill said. "He's such a nice man for someone so big and hairy."

Howie kicked the sandy dirt as he shuffled his way back down to the studio. He passed through the barn to grab his cigarettes before he headed out. The apples in the trees were just starting to take on color. *"Another month at least,"* he thought. He stopped at the door and ran his hand down the bright raw edge where his grandfather had cut away the wood. He pushed the door open and the fragrance of cigar smoke pushed its way past him and out the door.

"Wonderful service, Howie, it was absolutely wonderful. Frank, even in his foulest of moods, would have agreed." Gideon sat in the corner couch, a large cigar in his fingers. The window stood open and he looked over the woods, deep into the forest. "Go ahead, I won't tell."

"What?"

"Have a cigarette, it's not a secret and I really hate to smoke alone."

Howie had never been given permission to smoke, and it seemed strange. He pulled a butt from the pack and Gideon pitched his lighter to him. Howie caught it and felt the heft of it. He looked closely at the golden lighter and all of the intricate carving and relief on its face.

"It's beautiful isn't it? Your uncle gave that to me almost five years ago; it was crafted by a wonderful jeweler in Barcelona, a birthday present. Every time I light one of these Havanas, wherever I am, I think of Frank and wonder what he's doing. Now I'll remember the man and what he was. Ever smoke a cigar? No, well since we are alone and I'll tell no one, here, try one."

Gideon took out a case from his breast pocket and extracted a dark cigar about four inches long. He took his penknife and cut the tip off and pitched it to Howie.

"First you toast the end. Light the lighter and role the tip of the cigar in the fire, then after it is singed black, place it in your lips, and draw the fire in to the tip. Roll the cigar as you light it for an even start. Good, good job. No need to inhale; let the smoke sit softly in your mouth and then exhale, takes a bit of practice. I'm also sure your mother would kill me dead if she saw us together, for this and many reasons."

Howie felt the jolt of the nicotine, stronger than any cigarette he had ever had, yet also pleasant and strangely satisfying.

"I'll be taking the paintings your uncle made of me when I leave, if you don't mind. No reason for someone to come to conclusions later and put one and one together. I know all of these are yours now, but with your permission I would like to take them."

Howie took another draw on the cigar, his eyes started to water. "Yes Mr. Walker, please take them and any other's you like; Uncle Frank would surely want you to have them. This is pretty good."

Gideon smiled, "I was also young when I started to smoke, nasty habit, yet comforting."

"Gramps said you were a conscientious objector during the war. He didn't seem happy when he said it and even my Dad didn't like the idea."

"I can understand it, many of my views and beliefs were different before and during the war, different than they are now. It seemed fashionable among the crowd I hung around in college and before the war. Seemed very cool to be against killing people and having lofty ideals about peace and seeing the world as one big happy family; all we had to do was talk about our problems and they would be amicably resolved and there would be peace forever. We never faced unchallenged evil of the most hideous kind; it was beyond us to think it could even be out there, from our snug and cozy college rooms and halls. So we took on the mantle of pompous superiority and philosophy and sat back and allowed all the hatred and evil to grow. Let me tell you a story."

For the next hour, Gideon Walker told Howie about the Battle of the Bulge and the aid camp. He finished one cigar and lit another. Howie said one was more than enough, in fact, half of his cigar sat in the ashtray. Howie sat imaging all Gideon had gone through, and the killings.

"Only Frank knew what happened that night; he was the only one outside of the station that knew what happened. Still, to this day, I don't think even the men in the cots knew what really went on that night. Most lived through the rest of the war; but they would all be dead if I hadn't done what I did. I live with that thought even though I still have nightmares."

"I believe you did what you had to do. I don't know much, but this summer has been so eye-opening that I'll take much of this back to school to learn about: art and color, philosophy, the migrants, the storms, and even you and my uncle and your friendship. I think all of these things have pushed me to grow up."

"Howie, to even think about those abstract thoughts and ideas at your young age is more than most men ever think of in their whole lives. I know this for a fact: It's easy to wander through life reflecting, like a mirror, what you see about you, to fit in, to never challenge what you see or even what you believe. This I know very well. It's when you do challenge and learn and educate yourself that you become a man. We are in some tough times; changes that will turn the world on its ear. The world is in a tenuous spot, and sadly many who govern are thieves and villains, there will be a lot of trouble." Gideon took a long draw from his cigar. The smoke filled the room; small eddies stirred by the light breeze that blew through the window.

"I have to pack," Gideon said. "Like you, I'm leaving tomorrow. I'll see you tonight at dinner; I am cooking a wonderful paella, something I make in Spain, your grandmother loves it. The one thing I'll miss is spending time with your grandmother. She's a gracious elegant woman. It's amazing to say it, but she's probably the most beautiful woman and farmer I've ever met." Gideon smiled, stood, tapped the ash off his cigar, shook Howie's hand, and walked toward the Spanish door. He picked up a bundle of canvases wrapped in brown paper, and closed the door behind him.

Howie stood at the window and watched his giant stroll down the path into the woods. He lost sight of the black head of hair as it bobbed its way through the trees, but a white cloud puffed up from the bracken, like a smoke signal, giving away his location. The smoke sat amongst the maples and sumac until it drifted away.

Howie straightened up the room, cleaned the ashtray, and put away canvases and bottles of thinner and turpentine. He looked in the refrigerator and took out the perishables and old food and put these in a bag to take back to the farm. The bottles of wine and beer and cokes he left, he would tell his grandmother so they wouldn't freeze during the winter. He took one last look around, closed the Spaniard's red door behind him, and walked back to the farm.

CHAPTER TWENTY-FIVE

Howie woke very early before the sun had started to brighten the sky. He dressed quickly and silently went down the stairs to the kitchen. The door to Bill's room was closed. He slowly opened the screen door and just before he went outside his grandmother's voice stopped him cold.

"Where do you think you're going, young man?" Liz said. She sat at the far end of the kitchen table; in the dark and he did not see her.

"I thought I would take one more walk below the hill, I'll be back before breakfast Grams. Tell Mom, if she asks."

"Be careful, I understand."

"Dinner was wonderful Grams, just wonderful." He looked out at the long table that had been set up in the garden, still covered with bottles and dirty dishes. Two table settings sat undisturbed.

"I never leave such a mess, never. But Gideon's dinner was wonderful; it's been twenty years since I've had such a treat. How he found all those things to make it, I just don't know, but that's why I'm up so early. When it gets a little brighter, I'll start. But for now, it's pleasant just to think about it."

"Need some help?"

"No, you go on, it's not a big deal, but you can help me wash the dishes when you return."

"Absolutely, Grams. You miss him a lot, don't you?"

"Howie, Frank was a special man. Complicated and yet very simple in his approach to life; yes, I loved him a lot. We went through many trials and difficulties in our lives together. Yes, I will miss him forever, as much for what he was, as well as what he could have done. We all leave things undone when we die, no matter what we do to prepare for it. Go down to the woods and enjoy your stroll, see you in a few hours."

The dinner eaten the night before was as much a celebration of Frank Rex's life as it was a recollection of the Rex and Smith families. Howie wished he could write down the stories that bounced around the table, Frank in Spain as a boy, climbing the Eiffel Tower, rowing a boat in Hyde Park, painting school in Paris. Gideon told stories of bullfights and summer wine in the hills above Barcelona. Anne told the story of the first time she met Frank, and all Bill could say was how scary she made it sound.

Gideon told everyone he was also leaving the next day. Frank had given him his tickets on the *SS United States* headed back to France. He would catch a train in Traverse City then transfer in Detroit for the train to New York. The boat was leaving in a week, so he had a little time to relax after he arrived in New York.

Anne talked about the baby and how different next summer would be. Liz told Charlie to get the old baby stuff out of the barn and have it ready. Next summer would be a delight with the sound of a baby bouncing about the house and the orchard once more. Bill voiced concerns about diapers and babysitting, but no one paid him much mind.

The sun pushed its new rays through the pines and maples as Howie walked deep into the woods. Light and shadows played games with his mind. He shook off the visions and said out loud, "Stop. No more, stop. No more of these games in my head. No more."

His toes, once again, pushed deep into the cool dry sand when he reached the dunes above the lake. The sun, now about a hand high over the horizon, just brushed the treetops; the lake was like a mirror that reflected the far shore. Howie was sure that, if he stood on his head, he'd have trouble telling which side was real. He rubbed the Petoskey and thought of what this land looked like when the hard stone was alive. Would they have imagined him like he was imagining them? Probably not, "I wonder if my bones will be in someone's pocket a billions years from now," Howie said to the lake. "I wonder."

He passed the dune where Jennie posed for Frank's painting. It occurred to him that he hadn't seen her at the funeral or even the wake. He didn't understand why she wouldn't have come to say goodbye. He wandered through the dunes making sure to miss the Gardener cabin. He could see one light in the second story window.

"I wonder if I'll ever see that man again," Howie thought.

He waded along the shore of the lake for a couple of hundred yards. The warm water in the shallows washed the sand from his feet; a large fish jumped up and a spray of minnows flew across the water. Within seconds the water glazed back to a mirrored surface, like magic.

He turned back into the woods, taking the woodland trail this time, not the one through the clearing. The trilliums, now green, were beginning to droop from the summer heat; he remembered one spring when the forest floor was white with their nodding blooms. Green caps of leaves pushed through the debris, cluster of white flowers hung by the thousands. Now, in late summer, a more somber appearance held the forest, the ferns and bracken were the dominant plants. Deep shade cooled the sandy ground.

Howie remembered that somewhere in this part of the woods his father and Uncle Jim had built a small cabin, but time and weather had pushed it back into the ground. He looked about for the ruins but they had settled below the bracken, lost to sight but not to dreams. Maybe when the trilliums were in bloom, he would find it again.

Even in the deepest part of the woods, when a tree fell, a small clearing would form. Sometimes it would last a few years, sometimes longer. Howie always wondered why nothing filled this one particular clearing in this part of the forest. He could see it from a hun-

dred yards because the sun threw warm yellow shafts of light into the bright green of the ferns covering the ground. Howie walked into its center, the sun warmed his face and shoulders, a cicada buzzed in the background, and, drifting through the buzz, he heard the sharp tapping of a woodpecker. He pushed his arms out from his shoulders, and formed a deformed shadowy cross against the bracken and spun slowly on his bare heels, the sun washed over his whole body. He took deep breaths of musty and woody air; and thought he smelt morels. Stopping, he waited for his balance to return.

He almost stepped on it before he saw it. He dropped to one knee slowly to behold the most beautiful flower he had ever seen. Afraid, tentative, he extended his twisted fingers, but could not touch it. A Pink Lady's Slipper sat amongst some small ferns that provided a peasant's bed for it to rest on. Not more than a foot high, the soft pocket of pink, like a slipper, hung below two outstretched pink spotted wings connected below a hovering cap of white holding more spots; so sensuous, in some ways human, organic, sexual. Howie looked about and found four others pushing their faces toward the sun. He sat on the sand for a few minutes and then stood and slowly turned again and again, the center of a magical clearing. He remembered his grandmother saying these flowers were so rare she could go for years before she would see them again. They never survived being dug up and transplanted; they would just disappear, so she would always leave them where they were, hoping to see them next year.

Smiling, Howie pushed his way back into the woods and, within minutes, climbed the trail back up to the orchard. The house was still quiet when he pushed the screen door open, the long table, clear.

"Good morning, boy. Good hike?"

"Yes sir," Howie said to his grandfather. "It was good to take a walk through the woods. I will miss them. Grams," Howie said turning Liz, "I saw the clearing where the Lady's Slippers' bloom. There were five, it's a wonder."

Liz dried her hands with a towel, "Five, my goodness, never seen more than three at a time, after you leave I'll walk with Charlie and take a look for myself. They're such glorious plants, simple yet proud, difficult yet complicated in their need for special ground to grow.

Kind of like that old man sitting there," Liz said, pointing toward Charlie.

"Unkind woman, unkind; I can grow anywhere. Boy, after all these years, she still doesn't understand my needs, never has. I just don't understand; thought by now I would have trained her better."

"Old man, the trainer is always sure he's trained the tiger, but he has also learned never to turn his back."

Howie smiled at the loving banter between his grandparents, it had always been this way for as long as he could remember. Even his parents occasionally waded into the loving sarcasm of married people. Howie grabbed a towel and started to dry the dishes.

Doug and Anne, carrying the first of the boxes and suitcases, jostled their way through the kitchen and sat their loads just outside the door.

"When you're finished drying, get your things and set them outside. Dad says we need to be on the road no later than 10:00 if we expect to get home before dark," Anne said to Howie. "At least it won't be too hot."

"And no rain," Charlie added. "The weatherman said it would be dry for the next week. Been a stormy and wet summer, I am glad we did as well as we did."

"Everyone forget about me?" Bill yelled through the closed door of his improvised bedroom.

"No, we did not, it's just that we didn't need that white cast of yours clogging up the aisles here," Howie said.

"Great, now I'm considered a nuisance."

"You're always a nuisance," Howie said as he pushed open the door. Bill was dressed and resting on his crutches, his bags packed and ready to go. "Been busy have you? Good for you. I'll carry your stuff to the porch, then you can sit over in the corner next to Gramps where you'll be out of the way."

"I'm starved," Bill added, as he waddled his way to the corner chair.

"Breakfast in thirty minutes, Dad and I'll cook; you girls finish the packing and organizing," Doug said. "Mom made fresh bread yesterday, when I don't know, but she did. So eggs, bacon, toast and the usual, Howie can make up sandwiches for the drive. Coffee anyone?"

The route to the porch and the cars went through the kitchen so for the next half hour a complicated dance developed between the cooks and the packers. Bill sat in his corner and occasionally gave a play-by-play commentary.

"That's enough, you're not Jack Brickhouse, and besides, that was not an error, the box bottom opened and spilled, through no fault of the player," Anne added.

"I call them as I see them; that was a bobbled play, an error."

"Bill, you can never make the players happy, so go right ahead and call them as you see 'em," Charlie said with a laugh.

After breakfast, Doug and Howie spent almost an hour packing the back of the wagon.

"It wasn't this full when we came up here in June, what happened?" Doug asked.

"Not sure Dad, I am only taking a few paintings from Uncle Frank's studio and my sketch books. Not much else. I guess it's just the way of things; junk expands to fill the space available. Next year there will be more, with the baby. So either we get a bigger car or one of us needs to stay home."

"You?"

"No sir, I love it up here. So maybe we can leave Bill home. He's so much trouble and such high maintenance."

"I'll talk to your mother," Doug said with a laugh.

Howie watched as his grandmother walked through the garden with its bright oranges and rich yellows. She snipped a flower here and then pulled a weed there. Her white wavy hair and stately manner caused Howie to smile and shiver. Liz stopped at the tall hollyhocks and pulled a few of the seed packs off the stems. These tight little bundles held hundreds of seeds and were remarkable in their shape and design. She put them in an envelope and beckoned to Howie with a wave.

"These are for you. Let them dry out this winter and put them in the ground next spring, they're tough but make sure they go in the ground after it has warmed a bit. These are from France maybe forty or fifty years ago, and I've kept them alive and in this garden that long. Time to move them to new ground, so give them a try."

Howie took the envelope and put it in his back pocket. "Thanks, Grams." Howie gave his grandmother a kiss on the cheek; it was much softer and more delicate than her deep farmer's tan promised. He felt her take his withered hand and give it a squeeze.

Liz went into the house and returned a few minutes later carrying a few books. Bill had been relocated to a chair on the porch; she placed the books in his lap. "Young man, it's time you started to educate yourself about the world, what's possible and what the future might be like. When I was in Paris, I was about your age; my father took me to a bookstore that, while even in France, sold books in English. There, he bought me these two books and I'm giving them to you. Both were written by a wonderful French author, Jules Verne. The first is *Around the World in Eighty Days*, and the other is *Twenty Thousand Leagues Under the Sea*. They are both adventure stories but they will also whet your appetite for travel and knowledge."

Bill took the books and immediately opened the covers, a drawing of a submarine jumped out. "Neato, thanks Grams."

Anne and Howie made a pass through their rooms looking for errant socks and shoes, none were found. Liz walked down the stairs carrying a large white and yellow bundle and almost ran into Anne as she turned the corner of the door from the kitchen.

"Anne dear, this is a quilt I made almost thirty years ago, I think Doug was maybe four or five at the time. Pieces were from some of my mother's leftovers and other bits. I like it because it's light and summery, with no intruding dark colors. You take it and hold the little one in it so that she, and it will be a she, will be covered in years of family love."

"Thank you, Liz," Anne answered. "I have seen this for years and have always loved it. Thank you, and thank you from the little one. A girl you say, I'll see what I can do."

Howie spread peanut butter on slices of bread on the kitchen counter; four sandwiches already stacked and wrapped in wax paper.

"Those are ham and cheese, Mom. Bill wanted peanut butter, apple butter and butter on his sandwich. He said 'make me a butterfly sandwich', so there it is. And he can have it all to himself. There's a pint of sweet and sour pickles from the cellar, two jars of lemonade, and a tall thermos of coffee. I think we're ready."

"Good job," Charlie said. "Should hold you over until Benton Harbor, after that you're all on your own."

Bill, now quite proficient with the crutches, managed to get into the back seat by himself.

"You use the bathroom?" Anne asked.

"Yes ma'am, all set. Good 'til Manistee."

Howie turned to his grandfather and gave him a strong handshake and a hug.

"I'll miss you Gramps, but maybe see you this winter during vacation. It's up to Dad."

Howie gave his grandmother a hug and thought of the stone and the seeds in his pockets. "Love you, I'll write."

"You always do, I'll look forward to your letters," Liz answered.

Howie climbed into the backseat, next to his brother. They both watched as their parents exchanged hugs and kisses to Charlie and Liz. It surprised Howie as he watched his grandfather place both his hands on his father's shoulders and speak slowly and directly to him. Anne and Liz stood to one side and listened. Doug nodded and then wiped his eyes; Charlie smiled. Liz gave her youngest boy a peck on the cheek and then swatted him on his butt like he was a ten year old; then Anne did the same thing.

"Adults are weird," Bill said, "just plain weird."

Doug and Anne settled into the front seat. Liz and Charlie followed next to the car as it slowly crossed the gravel in front of the barn. Charlie patted his son's arm, and waved to the boys. Bill waved back.

Doug turned the car toward the top of the drive and slowly accelerated. Howie turned and watched his grandparents slowly disappear as the car went down the drive to the state highway. Rows of dark green cherry trees cherries passed to his right, row after row flowed deep into the orchard as far as he could see. Stopping just before the highway, Howie saw one lone red bucket sitting under the last cherry, on its side, empty. *"Tomorrow we'll be home or am I leaving home to go somewhere that really isn't home."* He wasn't sure.

On the highway, they passed the end of the orchard and Howie watched the tall pines and hemlocks along the top of the ridge that formed the first bulwark against the press of the peopled world he lived in. *"How long would they last,"* he thought? *"How long?"*

FINIS

ABOUT THE AUTHOR

Gregory C. Randall was born on a hot and muggy day in the summer of 1949 in Traverse City, Michigan. He spent many summers of his youth and college days on a farm near where he was born. The son of a journalist and entrepreneur, Greg has never forgotten his roots.

Mr. Randall is the author of fiction and non-fiction works available through the usual outlets and the Windsor Hill Publishing website.

Californian by choice, Mr. Randall makes his home in Walnut Creek, California with his wife and constant companion. In an effort to immortalize their springer spaniel, Darcy, he is also mentioned here.

For more information about *Elk River* and planned sequels, please visit:

        http://elkriver-thenovel.blogspot.com/